THROUGH A YELLOW WOOD

Carolyn J. Rose

THROUGH A YELLOW WOOD

Carolyn J. Rose

For Lorin Rose

And for the dogs that joined us on our journeys

Acknowledgements

Thanks to Harry Oakes, International K9 Search and Rescue Services Coordinator/Instructor, for a wealth of information about search and rescue dogs. Any errors in this story are all mine.

And thanks to my brother, Lorin Rose, for filling me in on the process of building a house, and for answering questions about everything from guns to lumber to building codes to leaf buds. Again, mistakes and errors are mine, all mine.

Finally, a hug and a kiss to my aunt, Muriel Rozzi. The family chart she spent years constructing inspired a plot thread for this story.

CHAPTER 1

Another April.

A year since I returned to Hemlock Lake in a vain attempt to disrupt the agenda of destruction and death set by a man once my friend.

Seven months since he shot me and torched my family home.

It seemed like years since that night of blood and fire.

It seemed like just a few days had passed.

The blaze left only two charred exterior walls, the porch pillars, and a mammoth stone fireplace. Like a battlefield monument, its chimney marked the spot where Ronny's rage converged with my long-delayed realization of its force. The towering smokeshaft cast a grim shadow of failure. I wanted it gone, but it was my great-grandfather's stonework and one of the few remaining artifacts of my past, so I felt obligated to preserve it as I rebuilt.

But last week a frowning building inspector told me the flue tiles were cracked and the mortar compromised. It had to come down.

Jamming the pry bar into the crumbling mortar between scorched fieldstones, I threw my full weight

1

against it. The top stone rocked a quarter of an inch, giving me a shade more purchase. I rammed the bar's prongs deeper, my left shoulder throbbing along the scars left by Ronny's bullet and the surgery that repaired blasted muscle and shattered bone.

From the corner of my eye, I saw Camille emerge from the garage, her cinnamon hair glowing even in the watery light of the spring sun. With a grunt, she dumped four cans of fossilized paint into the battered open trailer hitched to my SUV.

"Man versus fire-gutted chimney, a duel of mythic proportions." She swept her hands through the air and spoke with the cadence of a midway barker. "The likes of such a battle seldom seen in the Catskill Mountains. Who will triumph? Dan Stone? Or rocks left by the last glacier departing for Canada?"

I shot her a scowl. "When did you get a degree in geology?"

She batted that aside. "If you hired a guy with some heavy equipment, that chimney would be down by now."

I bounced against the pry bar. "And miss all this free physical therapy."

She rolled her eyes. "Must be a guy thing. A Stone thing."

"And muscling years' worth of my father's crap out of the garage is a woman thing? A Chancellor thing?"

"Some of it might be worth saving."

"For what?" I laughed and bounced against the bar again. "For that time after nuclear winter when dried-up varnish, broken tools, and bent nails will be used for trade and barter?"

2

She planted her fists on her hips. "There's a lot more in there besides—"

With a grating rip, the stone sprang from its mortar cradle and thudded to the ground six inches from my feet.

"One of those rocks will smash your toes."

"Steel-toed boots." I scraped out chunks of decaying mortar, breathing in the faint scent of smoke and lichen.

"Not the point. God forbid you should ask anyone for help. God forbid you should, just this once, not do it alone." Camille headed for the garage firing another volley over her shoulder. "It's not like you can't afford to hire someone. The place was insured to the hilt."

True. And then there was the legacy. Money from my mother. Money my father withheld in the first of two acts of vengeance because I wasn't agreeable clay for him to mold. The second act of retribution was changing his will after my mother died, leaving the lodge and family land to Nat and giving me just twenty acres in a crease between ridges above the Birchkill. The land was as steep as a cow's face and a hike from the nearest road or power line. If Nat hadn't killed himself . . . If my father hadn't had a stroke the next day . . .

But they had.

And this blighted inheritance was now mine.

When he went through the lockbox my father stored at his office and discovered my mother's handwritten bequest, the family lawyer, a spider of a man with fourscore years on this earth, was stunned. My father's duplicity hadn't surprised me, but his failure to destroy my mother's deathbed document had. Never before had he left a task undone. But never before, to my knowledge, had she crossed him.

To honor her spirit and thwart his, I put aside thoughts of leaving Hemlock Lake and made plans to rebuild the lodge in my own image. I would live in it with Camille whose strength and confidence would have both frightened and repulsed the man who raised me.

Squatting, I hoisted the fallen rock and walked spraddle-legged to the growing pile near the dock—the dock where three fresh boards replaced the ones stained by Ronny's blood last fall.

I dropped the rock on the heap. It hit, bounced, and hit again. The hollow cracks echoed across the lake like the shots that brought Ronny down and killed him. Jefferson's shot. Camille's shot.

A faint chirp punctuated the final echo.

"That's your phone." Camille tossed a quartet of gallon cans into the trailer and nodded toward the quilted flannel shirt I'd stripped off and flung across the hood of her car. Winter was in full retreat, but a skulking fog filtered through the woods, the sun was weak, and the glide of wind across the lake bit like a horsefly. I longed for the humid heat of summer, courted it in a T-shirt, wooed it with raw, prickling flesh.

Camille took a step toward the phone. "Want me to get it?"

"Let them leave a message." I arched my back, massaging the muscles at the base of my spine.

The phone chirped again and Camille laid a hand on the shirt. "It could be important."

I shook my head. Since the night she and Jefferson Longyear pulled me from the bloody lake, my definition of important had narrowed. The short list included watching the sun rise and later sink beyond the lake, reading books I hadn't had time for, walking the ridges I prowled as a boy, and waking in the night to draw Camille close against me, nuzzle the crook of her neck, and inhale the warm scent of her skin—a mix of sweat and soap and sleep and woman. That was my opiate, my secret addiction.

Or was it a secret?

Perhaps Camille only feigned sleep to feed my habit.

"It could be the architect," she said.

"Or someone selling aluminum siding for canoes or collecting money to buy contact lenses for cats."

Laughing, Camille headed for the garage. The phone went silent. With long loose strides, I worked the strain from my back, returned to the chimney, and hefted the pry bar. The phone chirped again.

Camille loped to the car. "They're calling back. I told you it could be important."

I leaned against the bar. In my experience, when someone around Hemlock Lake called back, it was more likely that person knew you were home and wondered why you weren't answering. Insulted, curious, or seeking entertainment, they dialed again to goad you.

"Someone could be hurt." Camille patted the shirt, searching for the pocket that held the phone. "In trouble."

The stone tumbled free, thudded to the ground. "Tell them to call 9-1-1."

She shot me a dark look and I turned my back, firm in my resolve not to step into the vacuum created by Ronny's death. Give the devil his due— he'd taken care of folks around here, lending a hand, giving advice, running the volunteer fire company. Most never saw that his actions were less about neighborliness than about control, about making himself indispensable, vital, the man everyone was indebted to.

"It's Mary Lou," Camille called.

I nodded, went after another stone.

"Working on that chimney," Camille said. "It's down to where he doesn't need a ladder." After a pause she chuckled, a sound as rich and satisfying as strong coffee. "You know he won't. He says it's physical therapy. Intends to do fifty rocks a day until it's leveled."

Her feet crunched on the gravel of the drive and she chuckled again. "As far as I know, except for his struggle with those stones, his schedule is wide open. But you'll need to ask him yourself."

I sighed, cursed the fickle folds of ravine and ridge that allowed cell phone reception in this particular spot, dropped the pry bar, and turned to take the phone.

"Be nice," Camille whispered.

I rolled my eyes. "Hi, Mary Lou."

"Dan. I know you're busy, but Lou Marie and I are worried about Clarence."

I ran a mental census of Hemlock Lake but didn't get a hit. "Clarence?"

"Clarence Wolven," she said with a hint of exasperation. "Your mother's second cousin. You must have met him when you were a kid. At those family picnics your grandmother put together."

Family picnics? I conjured vague memories of pies in wicker baskets, women in flowered dresses, hot dogs scorching on a grill. If Mary Louise Van Valkenberg said Clarence Wolven and I were related, it was true. Genealogy was her passion and she helped Hemlock Lake residents tend a forest of family trees. The past, she often said, was the seedbed where the future sprouted. The past had the power to shape us no matter how little we knew of it, where we were transplanted to, or whether we turned our backs on it.

"Never mind that now," she said. "Someone needs to check on him. He lives northeast a few miles as the crow flies."

"Ah." I gazed at rising ridges and slope-shouldered mountains in that direction. "And how far is that if the crow has to drop what he's doing and drive?"

Camille flicked my chin with her fingernails and strode to the garage.

Mary Lou sighed. "Well, it's a piece beyond that old summer camp that's gone to rack and ruin. And the road's pretty rough. Clarence isn't the sociable type. He doesn't come out unless he needs to. But he's always in here the first of the month to pick up his mail."

The first fell on Monday. Clarence was two days overdue.

"He trains dogs," Mary Lou added. "Search and rescue dogs."

Faint memory niggled at my brain. "Did you try calling him?"

"I was born at night, Dan Stone, but it wasn't *last* night. I did that first thing. Phone's dead."

"Ah."

"Phone company says the line must have gone down in that big wind we had a few days ago. He never reported it."

Camille staggered from the garage with a half-full sack of cement mix clutched to her chest. The sack was torn in several places and didn't yield in her embrace. The mix had set in the bag. "Maybe he's off on a search."

"I thought of that, too," she snapped. "He never takes all the dogs and he calls Mitch Shultis to feed the ones he leaves. Mitch never heard from him."

"Maybe he left in a hurry and forgot to call."

"Clarence wouldn't forget, not if there's a dog involved. I know it's silly to worry. He's as tough as an old boot. But the dogs—"

"One's just a pup. Clarence ordered special kibble for him." Lou Marie took over the conversation, probably snatching the phone from her sister's hand. "He's foxhound and who-knows-what. Nose as long as my arm. Stubborn, Clarence said, but smart as they come."

Enthusiastic exaggeration from a woman who, until last fall, cast a pall over anyone who patronized the general store attached to the post office presided over by her sweet-natured sister.

"Jefferson's waiting at the schoolhouse," she added.

I bristled at the presumption. "When did I say I would—?"

The dial tone provided the only answer.

8

core. Back from among the presumed dead, no longer a ghost haunting the hills, as substantial as those stone steps. "Howdy, Sergeant."

His voice was deep and rough, as if his vocal chords rusted over during years lived on the fringes of civilization.

"Dan," I said for the hundredth time. "Just Dan. I quit the sheriff's department, remember? I'm a civilian. Same as you."

"Dan," he said without conviction. He came around to the passenger side, climbed in, and drew a folded paper napkin from the pocket of a denim jacket still stiff despite a winter of wear. "Lou Marie drew us a map."

He smoothed it across the console between us. "Treats me like I'm six years old some of the time." His voice held a mixture of apology and pride, telling me he didn't mind all that much, no more than I objected to Camille fussing over me.

I glanced at the napkin. A yellow splotch marred one corner. Mustard. Lou Marie didn't toss out anything until it served its last useful purpose. "You can't complain about the meat on your bones."

He patted his gut. "Gained twenty pounds since Camille pulled us out of the lake. Fried chicken, meatloaf, potatoes cooked six ways from Sunday. Best eatin' I ever did." His face creased into a grin and lines webbed out from behind the steel-rimmed glasses that shielded eyes frosted and faded by years of hard living, eyes fathomless with the pain of events he couldn't forget or couldn't quite remember. "Doctors up at the VA say I'm a case study in rehabilitation and rejuvenation. 'And toss in reincarnation,' Mary Lou says."

11

I nodded. This was a regular topic—the forces that brought him back to Hemlock Lake to keep its dark waters from claiming me and the forces that drove Camille to the same place. Fate? Karma? His? Mine? Hers? Were the strands of our lives now entangled forever?

"Keep feeling there's something else I'm supposed to take a run at." Jefferson touched the mustard stain. "Wish I knew what it was."

"Maybe just life itself." I shifted into gear, not inclined to venture far into these philosophical waters. I spent my recovery intentionally not considering higher powers, destiny, and free will, filling my mind instead with fantasy and science fiction. Lately I paged through architectural magazines and seed catalogs. Practical. Of this earth. "Maybe all the rest belongs to you because you did what you were meant to."

He worried a metal button on his jacket. "Did a piss poor job of it."

Meaning his bullet took Ronny down, but not out.

"It was dark. You weren't familiar with the gun. You don't have 20/10 vision anymore." I pulled onto the road that crossed the dam. "I would have missed him completely."

"It won't happen again."

His voice was grim and certain. I felt a chill settle across my shoulders and tapped the gas pedal, making the engine roar, the tires burn pavement as the road scaled a ridge. Since he got his glasses, Jefferson took target practice at the sandpit beyond Freeman Keefe's place in Bluestone Hollow. Some days shots echoed from the mountains just after dawn, but often I heard them in the blue winter twilight, and twice long after sunset in the dark of the moon.

I asked Mary Lou if she thought he was paranoid or delusional. "Is he likely to hallucinate about that jungle war, set up a sniper's nest in the belfry of the church, pick us off as we get our mail?"

"He knows where he is, Dan. And he knows who he's among."

"But he has flashbacks." He told me about one. Left me feeling gut-shot for days.

She brushed that away. "He'd never hurt one of us."

Later I realized that her eyes hadn't quite met mine.

Jefferson put his hand over his heart. "Next time I won't let you down."

"You didn't let me down then. You kept me afloat." I tapped the map. "We're coming up on the road to that old camp soon. Where do we turn off?"

He bent and traced a line with a callused finger. "There's a long downhill and then we cross the Birchkill and just beyond we take a sharp left and head up over a ridge." He snorted out a laugh. "It's not much of a road and there's no sign. Lou Marie says we're bound to fly right past it. Claims you drive like a bat out of hell with its butt on fire."

I rolled my eyes. Lou Marie, whose top speed was rumored to have been 37 on a steep downgrade, hadn't been behind the wheel of a car for more than two decades—since the early months of the ill-conceived feud with her twin when she refused to pay half of the car insurance and demanded that Mary Lou buy her share of the vehicle. For reasons ranging from fear to pity, others had folded Lou Marie's errands in with their own ever since.

The rift between sisters was healed now—thanks to Jefferson's return and Mary Lou's placid and forgiving nature—but Lou Marie refused to try for a license. If I polled Hemlock Lake residents, I'd find most felt relieved by that decision. "Erratic," was how Jefferson described her driving in the days before he went off to war. "Likely to steer right at an on-coming car and then cut back and slide two wheels into the ditch. No more depth perception than a one-eyed cat."

Mary Lou put a kinder spin on her sister's driving. "She's the nervous type. Jumpy. Easily distracted. She compensated by holding the wheel so tight her elbows locked."

"Our male pride is on the line," I told Jefferson. "We either hit that turnoff or claim we did."

"We'll hit it." He braced a hand on the dash and leaned closer to the windshield.

We wound out of a turn and I saw the Birchkill sparkling like a silver ribbon threaded among patches of crusty snow dark with winter debris. The stream coursed through green-blue stands of spruce, around gray boulders mottled with lichen, and into clumps of chalky birches. Stark against the decay of last year's leaves and vines, their limbs and trunks shattered by January ice, those birches stood like marble columns from a temple long destroyed. Impaled on their shadows, two trout fishermen in down vests and hip boots cast their lines over frothing water. I shivered and turned my attention to the road again.

"Cold sport," Jefferson said. "But damn good eating at the end of it."

Last summer he consumed dozens of trout, all caught without rod and reel, designer flies, boots to

14

temper the chill, or a fishing license. "Going to get some legal ones this season?"

"Might. If I find time. Those two women keep me damn busy." He turned in the seat to get a better look at the stream. "But nothing beats fresh trout fried up with a little cornmeal or fancy bread crumbs. Toss some potatoes and onions in the pan and you're eating like a king."

My stomach rumbled, reminding me of the sack lunch. "It's not trout, but Camille packed a lunch and when we hit that road, I plan on eating it." I nodded toward the bag. "With your help."

"Happy to oblige." He jabbed a finger to the left. "Road's coming up after the bridge."

I feathered the brake and we rolled across the narrow span at a speed even Lou Marie would approve of, passed a glossy maroon truck I figured belonged to the fishermen, and coasted into a slow curve to the right.

Jefferson tapped the windshield. "See it?"

I shook my head, stared into the woods, feathered the brake again.

"Just before the angle of that stone wall." He aimed a blunt forefinger. "See the sun reflecting off the ice in those ruts?"

And then I did. Parallel lines of crystal, slow to melt in the shade of pines crowding either side of the twin ruts. "Got it. Hang on."

The SUV's front wheels dropped off the pavement, broke the glaze of ice, and shimmied into mud-slick furrows. I eased out of them and drove with my left wheels on the crown, the right ones churning through a welter of twigs and rotting leaves on the shoulder. We slid into a patch of sunlight and I braked to a stop and turned off the engine.

Jefferson dug into the sack, brought up a sandwich, and folded back the foil on one side. "Looks like turkey and Swiss on rye." He sniffed at it. "With red onion, mayonnaise, and a touch of horseradish."

"Meet with your approval?"

He grinned and bit off a chunk.

I lowered my window to a faint breeze and excavated the other sandwich and plastic sacks of potato chips and oatmeal cookies. "Do you know this guy? Clarence Wolven."

Jefferson shook his head and swallowed. "Lou Marie says I ought to—from before—but I can't recall." He shook his head again. "There's a shitload of stuff I can't recall. And what I do seems . . . not the way it should. Like the smell of her hair and skin."

I bit and chewed, feeling horseradish flame in my sinuses, onion sharp on my palate, cheese damping the fire, mayonnaise smoothing the edges. A masterpiece of bread and fillings.

"Can't tell if my memory's at fault or if my senses got dull or if things just *aren't* the same."

I worked on another bite. "Could be she changed her soap and shampoo or even her diet. It's a fact our senses diminish as we age, and I think I heard somewhere that the storage and retrieval system in our brains doesn't work like a computer. When we call up a memory to examine it, the mental image we file away is a shade different." I peeled back foil for another bite. "But maybe I heard that wrong."

"The mind's a hell of a jungle, isn't it? Filled with dark places and deep water and tiger traps we must

16

have dug ourselves. Who else could get in there?" Pain and confusion flared in his eyes. "But damned if I can recall digging."

I wondered again about Jefferson's stability. Would some deranging flash from that nightmare war overtake him? Did he have enough certainty about the present to turn aside and let horror roll by?

I hadn't.

Last summer the truth about the way things had been between my brother and my wife sent me careening down a dark tunnel toward suicide. If Camille—

I shook that off. "Maybe this old guy got busy with his dogs and lost track of the days and never noticed his phone was out. We'll get up there and be cussed at for disturbing his peace."

Jefferson grinned. "Lou Marie and Mary Lou won't live that down anytime soon. I'll make sure of it."

He stuffed the last of his sandwich between his lips and dug for a cookie. I followed suit, watching a chipmunk scurry along the stone wall parallel to the road. Another appeared from a crevice and they chased each other among rocks tumbled by frost and roots. Tossing the last bit of cookie for them to find, I started the engine.

The slope got steeper, the ruts deeper. My rig wallowed in sticky mud, on the verge of high centering. Then the wheels caught with a vengeance on a fill of rocks and brush, heaving us forward with a bone-rattling, teeth-snapping lurch. Jefferson braced a hand on the dash. "No wonder he doesn't come to town but once or twice a month."

I didn't respond, afraid I'd bite my tongue with the next jolt.

Jefferson lifted the napkin map and peered at it. "Doesn't look to be much farther. Not that this is to scale."

The road crested a ridge, ran along the spine, and plunged through a stand of oak. A few clusters of brown leaves swayed in a wisp of wind, their shadows grasping at us, falling short. Jefferson pointed and I spotted the ridgeline of a gray-shingled roof. We snaked past a spring welling between the roots of a mammoth maple, passed a rotting springhouse, and emerged onto open ground.

To our left, a huge meadow, brown and gray with winter-killed vegetation and bordered by spindly young birches, stretched to the forest. To our right, broken cornstalks hunched in a furrowed field. A long, low building jutted across the far edge of that field, screening the lower part of the house.

"Must be the dog pens," Jefferson said.

I grunted agreement.

The road angled into the graveled space between buildings where a once-black truck stood in front of an open garage door, roof splotched by years of weather, bed riddled with rust. As we passed the end of the pens, I spotted chain-link fencing and eight concrete runs. I glimpsed scruffs of pelt, legs, tails.

Not a muscle twitched.

Not a muzzle lifted.

Jefferson turned in his seat, rolled down the window. "What the—?"

My hand slid to my belt and the gun no longer there. I braked, turned off the engine, listening

18

hard, hearing only the low sigh of a rising wind and the raucous cry of a jay.

"They're dead." Jefferson's voice was hollow. "All dead."

I turned my gaze to the house and the figure sprawled on the stone steps. "So is he."

CHAPTER 3

Jefferson unbuckled his seatbelt and swung his door wide.

I gripped his shoulder. "There's nothing you can do for him."

"Yeah." Sagging, he removed his glasses and pressed his palms into his eye sockets. "He's long past mortal assistance."

I studied the thick crust of blood on the lower steps, the bloated torso, the ravaged face, a lazy fly circling. This was no fresh kill.

I drew the cell phone from my pocket and flipped it open. No signal.

"We're behind the ridge." Jefferson hooked a thumb in the direction we came. "Need to get higher." He slipped his glasses back on and aimed his chin at the body. "I'll stay. I had practice passing time with the dead and he deserves respect, even if it's late in coming. Whoever did this is long gone."

I felt that too. The skin on the nape of my neck didn't prickle with the feeling of being watched; the air didn't feel tight around me. My gaze slid to that ruined face. What had Clarence Wolven done to bring down this rain of death? "Probably shouldn't drive. In case there are tracks we didn't obliterate on the way in."

"Or the rain didn't wash out last night." Jefferson reclined his seat and stretched his legs.

I opened the door, eyed the ground, noted no recent tracks, slid out, and picked my way along the road. As I passed, I glanced at the dogs. Each one lay at the front of its pen. Each had been shot in the head.

Had the killer forced Clarence to call the dogs out of their kennels, perhaps even hold them for execution?

That image drove a serrated knife of pain into my gut. Turning my back on the pens, I walked faster, heedless of where I set my feet. This killer had been methodical, cruel beyond reason. He would have left little to help investigators give him a name.

Icy sweat slicked my skin by the time I reached the brow of the ridge and flipped open the phone. From memory I dialed the private number for the sheriff's office, got Clement North's secretary, gave my name and told her it was urgent. In ten seconds I heard his gruff, familiar voice.

"I was wondering if I'd ever hear from you again."

He said it not in a joking way, but as fact, as if he *had* often wondered, maybe even hoped to hear my voice. In my opinion—an opinion shaped by the failures of my final months on the force—I'd been more trouble than I was worth. But for all his bluster, North was a compassionate man.

"I thought things were all settled up there," he rumbled. "Quiet."

21

"They are. This is something else. An old man. Murdered. A search dog trainer. Clarence—"

"Wolven." He sucked in a sharp breath and his voice tightened. "How?"

"Shot. His dogs too."

"Damn it!" I heard a slap, guessed it was his palm hitting his desk, then the creak of his chair. "When?"

"Maybe a few days ago."

"I'll get a team on the way. You stay—" He cleared his throat. "You mind hanging on until they arrive?"

I noted the order backed off on. I hadn't worked for him since the recognition of Susanna's disloyalty and Nat's betrayal drove me to the rim of hell. But I owed him, would always owe him. "I'll stay."

The walk down off the ridge was both endless and fleeting. "Sheriff's got a team on the way." I leaned against the rear door of my rig, trying to look anywhere but at those dogs, trying to think about anything but how they came to Clarence despite the smell of blood, the acrid scent of fear, the anguish that must have filled the old man's voice when he called them.

"How come you didn't use his dogs when you were hunting me last summer?" Jefferson asked after a long silence. "You could have run me into the ground or out of the county."

A vague memory skittered across my brain. Had someone—Freeman, maybe?—suggested that we get Clarence to help? Had someone else—Stub?—asked and been told to go to hell. It came back to me, Stub saying Clarence refused to join "a pack of fools chasing someone who wasn't lost and didn't want to be found, who did nothing except make off with a

22

few cans of food and scraps of old clothing. "Clarence had rules. You didn't fit his criteria."

"Lucky me."

He had been lucky. If Clarence had brought his dogs, the search teams might have gotten close enough to glimpse Jefferson and—no matter my instructions to leave capture to officers of the law—shot him.

A hawk floated out of the sky and canted into a wide spiral above the field. Cawing, three crows rose from a stand of pines to harass it. The jay I'd heard earlier fluttered to the rooftop and added its cries to the mix.

Jefferson levered the seat upright and leaned out the window. "What do you suppose they're saying?"

"Probably the usual avian curses and derogatory remarks about parentage. In bird-speak."

Jefferson laughed. "Bird-speak. I like that. Bird-speak."

He frowned and cupped his hand around his ear. "Did you hear that?"

"The birds?"

"Something else." He opened the door. "A whimper."

We cocked our heads toward the kennels. "You think one of them is alive?"

I scanned the line of dogs. Not a trace of movement except the lofting of a few fat flies and the breeze combing their guard hairs.

He crimped his lips and squinted at the line of death. "Let's go over it again. The crows went after that hawk and I wondered what they were saying and you speculated they were cursing in . . ." He swung his feet to the door frame. "Speak," he commanded. "Speak."

And then I heard it. A faint mewling from the far end of the line. The eighth pen. The empty pen.

Clamping my arms to my sides, I contained a shudder of revulsion and helplessness. The wounded dog must have crawled into the kennel, was probably half an inch from death. "Go along the rear wall so we don't destroy any evidence."

"Right." Jefferson vaulted from the SUV and strode through the rain-slick dead grass between the cornfield and the rear of the kennel. I followed, trying to match his stride and place my feet in his prints. Each kennel had a hinged rear hatch secured with a hold-down clamp. Between kennels four and five was a narrow shed.

Jefferson halted beside the last kennel. "Speak," he ordered.

A faint yip came from behind the hatch door. He reached for the clamp.

"Hold on." I transferred the phone from my shirt pocket to my jeans, stripped off my shirt, and wrapped it around my hand. "Can't believe he opened that hatch or the dog would be dead, but . . ."

I nudged the clamp and pulled the hatch wide. We bent to peer inside.

Our bodies blocked the light, but sunlight slipping through half a dozen holes in the front of the kennel illuminated what looked like an old sofa cushion, a tangle of blankets, and a tight ball of black, white, and reddish brown hair. A pair of eyes glinted at us and the dog whined and scrabbled toward the rubber flap to the pen, dragging a left rear leg horribly swollen.

"It's okay, little guy," Jefferson said in a soft voice. "It's okay, pup." He pulled away from the opening. "Smell that infection?"

I sniffed, caught a warm and putrid odor that made my throat constrict.

"We got water left?" Jefferson asked. "Food?"

"Yeah, but . . ."

"If the crime scene guys get testy I opened the kennel while you were up the hill."

I brushed that aside. "We'll share their wrath."

I scavenged the remains of our lunch and returned to find Jefferson crooning "Old Blue." He took the bag of chips, crumbled them, and tossed them into the kennel. I opened the jug and filled the lid with water. He shoved that beside the battered cushion and we squatted in the grass, our faces turned to the clean breeze.

"Guess this one wouldn't come to Clarence," I said.

"Yeah, must be the pup. He told Lou Marie it was stubborn and willful but it had potential."

"It was smart enough to disobey a call to death. Did she mention its name?"

Jefferson shook his head. "No. Neither did Mary Lou. That means Clarence didn't say. At the end of the day, those two hash over everything that gets said where either of them can hear it."

I grinned. "Spoken like a man who likes silence now and then."

"Didn't say that. But sometimes I— Hey, he's gonna drink."

I peered into the gloom and saw the dog sniffing the water. "Good pup," I coaxed. "Drink. It's okay."

The dog jerked his head up, showing the whites of his eyes, then lowered his long muzzle again. I held my breath. His tongue curled into the water and he drank, watching us all the while, body trembling, blood-crusted tail held low.

"That's a good sign," Jefferson whispered. "He might make it if they get him to a vet soon."

"I'll phone the sheriff and let him know there's a survivor." I stood, eager to be doing something, and jogged to the top of the ridge.

North was on another line and I passed the time catching my breath and watching a pair of robins at their nest. One placed a length of grass. The other moved it. I smiled, thinking of my own situation. Camille was full of ideas for furnishing the new lodge and I was happy to let her plan. Towels, sheets, spreads, and drapes didn't interest me, fixtures and fittings weren't my domain, and the thought of agonizing over subtle shades of paint colors made me itch. But I'd go to the mat for good lighting and comfortable chairs. Not those puffy ones that embraced like an octopus and were reluctant to release, but chairs that allowed me to relax while remaining alert.

And that summed up my relationship with Camille and probably hers with me—comfortable and relaxed with what we had, but alert to the possibility that it might not last. Both of us had been betrayed. Both of us were wary.

On the day she said she wanted to stay with me, I dropped to one knee and proposed. She placed her fingers over my lips. "That can wait. We have the rest of our lives to define the way we want to be together."

That was enough for me.

"They should be there inside half an hour." North's voice rumbled in my ear.

26

"One dog's still alive. His leg's infected. It's pretty bad."

North groaned. "I'll call dog control and get them headed that way."

"What will they do with him?"

North groaned again. "Probably put him down."

Survive a hail of bullets, go days without food and water, then a needle stops your heart. "But—"

"County's short of funds. I'd be crucified for spending what little we got on a dog."

My head bought it; my heart wouldn't. "He deserves better."

"I agree. But a lot of taxpayers won't. And if he pulls through, then what?"

"I'll pay for the vet." My words surprised me. "I'll keep him."

CHAPTER 4

Stub Wilson lifted the first of two pitchers of beer Merle McDaniel set on the round table in the far corner of the Shovel It Inn and poured for his wife. The beer frothed and Marcella scowled, deep-set brown eyes retreating beneath brows I bet hadn't been tweezed since her wedding day. Too late, Stub tipped the glass to reduce the head, sloshing beer onto the table.

"Sorry," he muttered, setting the pitcher down and yanking a wad of napkins from a metal dispenser. Marcella snatched her glass from his hand, wiped the wet sides on the sleeve of his gray coverall, and moved her chair a few inches toward the empty place held for Priscilla Denton.

Shielded by the red checked plastic tablecloth, Camille nudged my knee with hers. I nudged back, signifying that the first part of the Friday night ritual had been fulfilled: Stub had attempted a patriarchal gesture, screwed it up, and been belittled.

Camille wove her fingers with mine and I knew—because we talked about it more than once—she felt

28

pity for Stub and empathy for me. Stub, who had been the number-two man in the volunteer fire department, yearned to be the go-to guy for the community. Stub longed to fill the vacuum created by Ronny's death, craved responsibility and respect. Unfortunately, he lacked Ronny's force of character and Renaissance-man abilities. Sadly, Stub was more suited to fill another vacuum—the one created when Ronny murdered Willie Dean Denton, the clumsy class clown of Hemlock Lake. The harder Stub tried to be like Ronny, the more he became a version of Willie Dean.

As Stub dropped off the respect radar, folks turned to me. Resisting obligation, I kept rooting for Stub while Camille counseled me to come to terms with what I couldn't change and set limits I could live with.

Stub finished filling his own glass and passed the pitcher to Freeman Keefe who splashed out a little and passed it on to Alda as if the handle burned his hand. Freeman was a cautious man who learned from his own mistakes and those of others and who preferred bourbon to beer. When he was under Alda's watchful blue eyes, he didn't drink enough of either to intoxicate a hummingbird. As the pitcher passed from Alda to Pattie Bonesteel and on to her husband Evan, Freeman gazed at the bottles behind the bar, then scratched his head and asked the question we'd all repeated for the past two days, "Why would anyone kill Clarence Wolven?"

"And his dogs." Evan parceled out the words as if he had only a few thousand left for his lifetime. Filling his glass halfway, he glanced at me and cocked his head. I poked my chin toward the second pitcher making its way from Lou Marie to Jefferson to Mary Lou to Camille. Evan nodded and poured himself the dregs from the first. Slight though he was, Evan put away beer like a camel with a long thirst. Since our informal Friday-night gatherings began at the turn of the year, he made sure not a drop went undrunk. Yet he never walked off in anything but a straight line, never left without paying his fair share.

"Clarence didn't leave that hollow much. It's hard to piss someone off if you hardly ever get out," Lou Marie observed.

A statement that revealed either Lou Marie's limited self-knowledge or limitless self-centeredness. Or both. Long before Jefferson returned from the land of the missing, she'd elevated pissing people off to an art form. Six days a week she irritated dozens without leaving her general store and without uttering more than a few words.

Lowering my head to sip beer, I glanced around the table and noted everyone doing about the same—beer going in prevented smart-ass comments from coming out. Lou Marie frowned at Jefferson who rubbed at his brush cut with the flat of his hand in a way he did when he was searching for the right thing to say, or was puzzled by the ways of the world he came back to after the long mental break with reality that followed his return from Vietnam.

Mary Lou plunged into the conversational gap widening around her fraternal twin. "Clarence didn't suffer fools gladly."

I leaned forward, wondering if she meant anyone in particular.

"Well, he saw all kinds of fools working on the state roads like he did," Stub observed. "Speeders, litterbugs, drunks."

"And the fools he worked with," Lou Marie added. "Break-takers and shovel-leaners."

"Clarence pulled his weight and then some." Merle set another pitcher at Evan's elbow. "He was no shovel-leaner."

"I never said he was. Did I?" Lou Marie smacked the table with her palm and, beneath the softening pounds she'd added to her spare frame, her neatly cut and combed hair, and the light touches of lipstick and mascara, I glimpsed the tormented, vitriolic woman of the past. "Did I?"

Merle shuffled back two steps. "Well . . . uh . . ."

Camille raised her hand like a schoolgirl. "Tell me about Clarence Wolven." Turning from Lou Marie's glare, she nodded toward the east, in the direction of Clarence's house. "Did he always live up there?"

Mopping his upper lip with a bar towel, Merle beat his retreat.

"Just for the last ten years," Mary Lou said.

"Twelve," Lou Marie corrected.

"Twelve," Mary Lou agreed with serene grace. Always the peacemaker, she long ago forgave her sister for accusing her of destroying letters Jefferson never sent. Lou Marie, on the other hand, didn't apologize for twenty-five years of recrimination. "Clarence used to live down across the river—close to his job. Then he retired and bought up here." She inclined her head toward me. "Your mother sold him a chunk of land."

"Gave him a sweet deal. And donated the rest to the state for the Forest Preserve." Lou Marie sniffed, making it clear she wouldn't have done the same.

I'd heard nothing of that sale or the gift to the state. In fact, I never knew my mother owned land in her own name.

"Made the deal when you were at college." Lou Marie said "college" the way some might say "prison." "Out there in Arizona."

That explained why I missed the sale and what I suspected must have been a vicious argument with my father about the donation. Knowing my mother had crossed him more than once increased my admiration for her.

There was silence for a few seconds, then Stub cleared his throat and picked up the story. "Clarence passed up a couple of places closer in. He wanted room to run his dogs."

"Likely too he wanted to be far enough from his neighbors so no one had the right to complain about their barking." Freeman motioned for Evan to fill his glass and pass the pitcher.

"Some folks," Lou Marie carped, "complain about the least—"

"Did he always train search dogs?" Camille overrode her, earning herself one scowl, half a dozen quick nods, and a slow wink.

"No," Evan said.

A few seconds crawled by, ticked off by the sputter of hot grease and the clatter of plates in the kitchen. Evan drained his glass, but contributed nothing more. Freeman shook his head in what I knew was mock disgust at his best friend and passed the pitcher his way. "He started after he retired. Because of that little boy. The one that wandered off from a campground south of here."

"That was the saddest thing. Makes me tear up every time I think of it." Alda dug a tissue from the pocket of her embroidered smock and held it to her nose. "His mother turned her back for a minute. That's all. One minute."

Freeman put his arm around her. "A bunch of us went down to help hunt for him. Clarence came over on his days off. We tramped the woods for most of a week. Didn't find a trace."

"Clarence always said they should have brought dogs in sooner," Marcella said. "The day that child went missing."

"The very hour," Pattie insisted.

"It preyed on his mind. And years later, when a hiker found that tiny skeleton with that green-and-white-striped T-shirt, Clarence . . ." Alda blew her nose and Pattie echoed the sound with a tissue of her own.

"After he got the house and kennels built, he went out to Ohio I think it was," Freeman said, "and learned how to train search and rescue dogs. Came back with two young ones."

Alda balled the tissue in her hand. "He said he'd never stand by and wait to be asked. Not if there was a child lost."

"And he didn't," Pattie sniffled.

"One time he drove all the way to the ass-end of Maine," Stub said. "Went deep in those woods. Gone all night."

"And he found that child. A little girl," Alda crowed. "He brought her out."

Camille glanced at me, her eyes glossy with tears, then bent to her purse and plucked out a tissue.

This was the stuff of legends, legends I'd never heard. But then, I'd been away, at the teaching job I got after college, then living in Flagstaff and carrying a badge. When my mother's cancer brought me back four years ago, I was married to Susanna, consumed by misguided love. After her death, I was oblivious to little beyond pain and rage.

"He never married, never had kids of his own, but he loved children. It tore him up when a child was lost." Mary Lou rolled her beer glass between her palms. "I just can't see why anyone would kill Clarence."

I couldn't either. The investigators must be gnashing their teeth in frustration. I felt the shameful relief that comes with being in a spot where I couldn't be held responsible for lack of progress.

A whiff of fried onion rings made my stomach rumble.

"You ready for these?" Shirley McDaniel leaned across the space between Stub and Marcella and set an enormous platter filled with golden rings in the center of the table.

"Oh, yeah." Camille tucked the tissue in the pocket of her jeans. "I could eat those every day of my life."

"Well, lord knows how many days we have *left* in our lives." Priscilla Denton pushed past Shirley, planted her broad hips in the vacant chair, and motioned to Evan to pass the pitcher. "With another killer on the loose."

As always, the arrival of Willie Dean's widow spawned a few seconds of uneasy silence. Camille, who had been reaching for an onion ring, clamped her free hand on my thigh as if to hold me in my seat and keep me from fleeing the soul-eroding guilt I couldn't run far enough to escape. I hadn't saved Willie Dean. Yes, eventually I bumbled my way to the truth and cleared his name, but that only underlined my failure. The others bore no blame for his death, but they felt contrite because they hadn't liked Willie Dean much, hadn't liked Priscilla much, either.

I don't know if Priscilla knew that, but as each month went by, she took more advantage of their discomfort. Now she reached for the platter and scraped a dozen rings onto a small plate. "Where's the sauce?" she asked in an imperious voice.

"Right here." Shirley set two bowls of her special mixture on the table. As Priscilla used the contents of one to smother her rings, Shirley exchanged an eye roll with Alda. "I'll bring another bowl in a minute."

Priscilla lifted a dripping ring to her lips. "Did you order yet?"

"We were waiting on you," Stub assured her.

She nodded like a monarch, stuffed the onion ring into her mouth, and seized a menu from the sheaf propped between the napkin dispenser and a pair of green glass salt and pepper shakers.

By tradition—begun the first night she joined us—we all chipped in to buy Priscilla's meal. Lou Marie contributed only that first time and then kept her wallet snapped, pointing out that, "Priscilla is worth more now than when Willie Dean was alive. And she's packing on pounds like a bear in late summer."

From their body language and the glances they exchanged, I suspected the others were fast reaching the limits of both charity and good nature. I'd heard Freeman tell Evan he was getting tired of bankrolling Priscilla's Friday feeding frenzies. If Priscilla continued to flaunt her entitlement, the slow shift toward Lou Marie's line of thought would become a stampede. As part of my self-imposed penance, I was willing to pay as long as Priscilla was willing to eat. Camille agreed that was my choice, but warned that before long Priscilla and I might be the only ones at the table.

Priscilla took a long drink of her beer and closed the menu. "I'll have the burger with blue cheese, extra fries, slaw, and apple pie with ice cream," she instructed Shirley. "French vanilla. Two scoops. And don't skimp on the blue cheese."

"Got it." With another eye roll, Shirley flipped open her order pad, scrawled a note with a runty pencil, and cocked her head at Marcella who ordered a chef's salad, light on the dressing.

"If a stranger killed Clarence for no reason, there's no telling who might be next." Priscilla lifted another onion ring and aimed it at Marcella, sending a spatter of special sauce across the tabletop.

Marcella cringed, moved her chair closer to Stub, then rallied. "The town is filling up with strangers, folks in that new development and their friends. And it seems like most of those strangers use *your* dock. You're the one who could be next."

"I'm taking precautions." Priscilla licked sauce from the onion ring. "I'm having Luke put new locks on all the doors tomorrow."

"Including your bedroom door?" Lou Marie asked in a syrupy voice.

Camille's mouth formed a tiny *O*, Shirley dropped her pencil, and Jefferson rubbed his brush cut, but Priscilla didn't blink. Either she didn't get the insinuation or had been anticipating it. "No need. Luke's a light sleeper. Nothing will get past him."

I noticed she made no mention of where Luke, the handyman she hired in early March, slept. None of my business. If Priscilla found comfort with the bowlegged, balding, taciturn man stranded in Hemlock Lake when his rusted pickup gave up the ghost in a cloud of radiator steam and scorching oil, then more power to her.

"And he's good with a gun."

Jefferson raised his eyebrows and his gaze met mine. I nodded. That recommendation needed context, background. I made a mental note to find out more about Luke, starting with his last name.

Priscilla munched down her last ring and beckoned for Freeman to pass the platter. "One thing I learned last summer. We got to take care of ourselves." She looked straight across the table, her gray eyes on me like a cold shadow. "We couldn't depend on the law to catch that last killer. We'd be fools to think we can depend on the law this time."

CHAPTER 5

"Let it go." Camille handed me a mug of coffee and leaned against the fender of the SUV. "Seriously, no one expects you to find the person who killed Clarence Wolven. You're a civilian now."

"Tell that to Priscilla," I mumbled into the steam rising from the scalding brew.

"Maybe I will." She thrust her chin at the lake. "Maybe I'll drive over there right now and tell her she better stop milking Hemlock Lake like a cash cow before it kicks over the bucket and plants a hoof in her bulging butt."

I snorted at the image, sputtering coffee down the front of my T-shirt. "Maybe I should give you the let-it-go lecture."

"Yeah." She squeezed the bridge of her nose. "I'm getting fed up with her queen-of-all-I-survey act. And I bet that if Lou Marie hadn't bailed out on chipping in, someone might have said something to Priscilla by now—Alda maybe. As it is, no one wants to be cast in the same miserly mold as Lou Marie." Camille tossed the dregs of her coffee onto a patch of weeds by the side of the garage. "I'll bet she has half a million dollars stuffed in her mattress."

"In pennies."

Camille chuckled. "Okay, I guess if we can laugh, we've let it go—at least enough to get back to work."

I sipped at my cooling coffee. "My mouth isn't lined with asbestos like yours. Give me a few minutes."

"I'm in no rush." She nodded toward the dog hobbling in a stripe of sunlight along the edge of the lake. "It's a shame the vet couldn't save his leg."

It was sliced off clean at the hip. Stitches and drains puckered shaved skin stained orange by disinfectant. A white plastic cone-shaped collar extended to the end of his nose and kept him from chewing at the stump. Despite my fears, he hadn't bared his teeth or growled when I scooped him up at the clinic and set him in the back seat. "The vet says he'll get used to it, that his body will twist so the leg is centered and gives him stability."

"Like an easel," she mused. "Or a milking stool."

The dog sniffed at a rock and attempted to lift the lone rear leg. He swayed, staggered, then fell over on his wounded left side with a yelp.

"You poor little thing." Camille took a step toward him.

"Don't," I cautioned. "He has to figure it out for himself."

Halting, she hugged herself. "You're right. But I feel so sorry for him—all of his dog companions shot, his owner murdered."

Wrapping my arms around her waist, I rested my chin on her shoulder, inhaling the warm vanilla scent of her shampoo.

"Do you think Priscilla's right, that someone killed Clarence for no reason?"

"No." There was always a reason—no matter how vague or sick or spontaneous.

The dog got his front feet under him, performed the canine version of a pushup, rocked forward until the lower edge of the cone collar dug into the ground, and planted the rear leg.

Camille punched a fist in the air. "Way to go!"

"Yeah. The vet said it won't take long for him to build up muscle in that leg and figure out how to balance."

The dog looked back at us, sniffed the rock once more, hopped a 180, canted the legless hip, and squirted. "See, he's getting the hang of it."

Camille blotted her eyes with the tail of her bleached denim work shirt.

I hugged her tighter and kissed the top of her head. "You're crying over a dog taking a leak?"

"Just a little." She sniffled and blotted again. "The triumph of hope always makes me teary."

Smiling, I spanned her waist with my hands, turned her, and lowered my mouth to hers. A single bark from the dog and the crunch of wheels on gravel brought us back to the world.

Camille broke the kiss, peered over my shoulder, and gasped. "That's Rachel's car." She turned to face the drive, crossing her arms over her chest, then uncrossing them and sliding her hands into her pockets.

My muscles tightened and I longed to slink away and let Camille deal with whatever this was about. I hadn't seen Rachel for eight months, since a few days before her son tried to kill me.

While I was in the hospital, she moved her orphaned grandchildren to the county seat. Everyone agreed it was better that way, and everyone knew it was worse. Justin and Julie escaped the knowing glances that accompanied endless small-town gossip about their father's crimes, but they were also deprived of small-town support. I knew first-hand there was something to be said for having secrets laid bare and dissected. That process allowed for healing, closure.

As far as I knew, Rachel hadn't been back—she rented out her house and got Stub to check on it and on Ronny's—but many times I wondered what I'd say if I ran into her somewhere. When I mentioned that to Camille, she said she'd worried at the same question and decided Rachel might be grappling with similar concerns.

Now we'd find out.

I eased Camille's right hand from her pocket. Her fingers were chilled. "I'm glad you're here. I'm not scared of much, but this . . ."

"Let her have her say," she said without turning to me. "It took a lot for her to come up here, so let her get it all out."

I nodded and we squared our shoulders and faced the car, an aging hulk with a muffler going south and a symphony of squeaks that told me the shock absorbers had signed up for the same trip. Rachel gripped the wheel with both hands, hunched forward, lips pursed in concentration. Julie squirmed in the passenger seat.

My throat constricted. Why bring Julie to this bloodied piece of ground?

41

Rachel stopped with a squeal that told me the brake pads were as thin as a political promise. Ronny always serviced the car. Without him . . .

Julie flung the door wide. "Uncle Dan! Camille!" Arms pumping, brown hair flying like a flag, she hurtled from the car. The dog barked and she skidded to a halt and stared at it. "You got a dog! He's hurt. What happened?"

Before either of us could answer, she raced to him, her slender blue-jeaned legs a blur. "What's his name? How did he lose his leg? Can I pet him?"

"If he lets you," I called. "Go slow. Don't startle him."

Julie skidded again, lost a yellow flip-flop, toed back into it, and approached the dog, arms held wide as if walking a balance beam.

"She seems manic," Camille whispered. "You see to her and I'll . . ." She nodded toward the car where Rachel fumbled with her seatbelt, then gave my hand a squeeze, and trotted off before I made even a pretense of arguing that I had the easier task.

I watched as she opened the driver's door and leaned down with a smile. By the count of ten the smile hadn't faded, Camille hadn't jerked away. With a sigh of relief, I slid my gaze back to Julie, on her knees with her arms wrapped around the dog's neck. His tail, washed and combed out during his stay at the vet's office, waved like a white pennant in the sunlight and he licked her chin and nose as if she was a long-lost friend returned with a bag of dog treats. If I was unaware of the past, I might think that loss and pain and horror had never touched the lives of either.

"He likes me," Julie called. "Where did you get him? What happened to him?"

"I, uh, got him from a man up across the mountains. He, uh, got hit."

To my relief, Julie didn't ask by what. "What's his name?"

"He doesn't have one yet." From the corner of my eye I saw Camille helping Rachel from the car. The older woman was gaunt, her skin translucent and the gray-yellow tint of newspaper left in the sun.

"Do you just call him Dog?"

"So far." I gave Julie my full attention. "But I'm open to suggestions."

"How about Tripod?"

No way.

I cocked my head, pretending to think that over. "Hmmm. Descriptive, but it doesn't say much about his character, his canine credentials."

Julie nodded as if that made perfect sense and went nose-to-nose with the dog, the cone pressing against her forehead and her meager chest. "Tell me about yourself. What's your favorite music? Do you like fries or chips with your hamburgers?"

The dog gave her a goofy grin and licked her nose. She giggled and wiped her face on the sleeve of her bright orange T-shirt. "Maybe I'll call you Mister Slobber Lips. Or Drool Baby."

The dog, seemingly unfazed by the indignity of those names, waved his tail in a wider arc.

"Nelson," I said. "Why don't we call him Nelson?"

Julie glanced over her shoulder and wrinkled her nose exactly the way her mother used to. My heart jolted at a memory of Lisa getting off the school bus at the start of our freshman year.

"Nelson?" Julie asked in a mocking voice. "That sounds pretty dumb."

43

"Dumb? Horatio Nelson was a famous British Admiral. He lost an arm in battle but lived to fight again."

Julie frowned, but turned to the dog and tried it out. "Nelson. Do you like that name?"

The dog looked at me and barked.

"I guess he does." Julie buried her face in the hair of his neck for a moment, then stood, brushed off her knees, and pointed to the dock. "Is that where . . . where my dad died?"

I swallowed, throat burning, wondering exactly what she'd been told and by whom. "Yes." The word was a rough whisper.

"Where the new boards are?"

"Yes."

A week ago Freeman and Evan had turned up and, without asking, ripped out the old planks and sawed fresh ones to fit. The lumber, they told me, came from Ronny's mill. He cut it last summer. Neither mentioned the irony and within an hour they were gone, taking the stained planks with them. "That's the place," I told Julie.

She turned to me, eyes dark with pain, confusion, and anger. "Justin says I shouldn't hate him, but I do. He killed our mother and Willie Dean and then he tried to kill you."

I swallowed again. "He was sick," I ventured.

"Then he should have gone to a doctor." She crossed her arms at her waist, bending a little as if her stomach ached. "Instead of burning and shooting and hating."

Feet dragging, I trudged to her side and gathered her into a hug. Over her shoulder I saw Camille and Rachel locked in a similar embrace, Camille smoothing the older woman's hair. Whatever Rachel said, it hadn't been confrontational.

"Your father was too sick to know he needed help. People get like that sometimes."

Her shoulder blades were sharp beneath my hands. She was taller and thinner than when I'd seen her last and when she wormed a hand up and wiped her eyes, I saw she'd drawn blood gnawing her nails to the quick. I wondered if she was getting the help she needed to process the horror Ronny bequeathed her. And Justin? He'd idolized his father, thought he could do no wrong. How could he reconcile that with the truth?

"I don't tell Justin what I think anymore." Julie dropped her voice to a whisper and directed the words at my shirt pocket. "He gets all mad and scary, especially since the coach took him out of the last football game because he punched out a guy on the other team. Last week he punched the wall right next to me and his fist went all the way in and came out bloody and I locked my door and I didn't come out until I heard him drive away."

So Ronny's rage lived on in his son. Chill foreboding coiled in my gut. I patted Julie's back and muttered that he'd work it out in time.

"He doesn't go to school and he won't go to the counselor anymore because he says it's a bunch of bull." She shrugged. "I still go, but the guy's pretty lame. He just asks me what's going on and how I feel and then sits there and waits for me to talk."

Having refused professional help when Susanna died and Nat killed himself, and having turned it down again after the events of last fall, I was in no position to argue for therapy, but I took a stab. "That's how counseling works. He wants you to talk

45

so he can see where you are emotionally. Then he can help you figure out what you need to do next."

"Justin says we pay him a lot of money for nothing."

Was Rachel short on funds? Or was Justin rationalizing his decision?

"If that counselor's such a big fat expert, why doesn't he just tell me what to do?"

"You're a teenager. He's an adult. Chances are you wouldn't listen."

"I would so." She backed out of my embrace.

I arched my brows. "Like you always do what your teachers tell you? What your grandmother tells you?"

"That's different."

"Maybe a little. But counseling takes time." I winced. Talk about lame.

"I've been going since before Halloween. Every other Wednesday."

I sighed. Time to a teenager wasn't the same as time to someone my age, someone Rachel's age. It was measured in the same way, but the seconds, minutes, and hours accumulated at different rates on different days.

"And I hate where we live," Julie said. "It's not even a real house, it's just an apartment. And I hardly know anyone around there or at school. And the bathrooms are ugly. I want to come back to Hemlock Lake."

"Uh . . ." I glanced around, saw no sign of Camille and Rachel, and guessed they'd gone into the garage where Camille had rigged up a makeshift kitchen. Lawn chairs flanked a table from a thrift store and the old workbench served as a counter with a coffeepot, a microwave, and a mini

46

refrigerator to hold sandwich meat and cold drinks. Even Nelson had deserted me. I spotted him hopping along the margin of the lake, cone to the ground. "What does your grandmother think about coming back?"

"I don't know." Julie kicked at tufts of winter-blasted grass that had taken tentative hold between the stones in the path, then walked to the edge of the lake. "It's hard to talk with her about anything because she cries a whole lot. I know she misses her house and her friends, and she doesn't like the ugly bathrooms either, but she says she made her bed and now she has to lie in it."

Meaning Rachel had to stick to the decision to move? Or meaning she was shouldering blame for the monster Ronny became?

That chill fear coiled in my gut again and I wondered if she saw the same qualities in Justin.

Her back to me, Julie stood on one foot and dangled a flip-flop over the water. "I wish I could live with you and Camille."

I shook my head, then caught myself, feeling guilty about my gut reaction, glad she hadn't seen. I should have realized that request was coming. "We, uh, don't exactly have a house, kid."

"You do too." She pointed across the lake at the Brocktons' home where Camille and I had been staying since I was released from the hospital. "Right over there."

"But we're moving out in a few days." I tried to infuse my words with patience without sounding as if I was talking down to her. "The Brocktons are coming back from the south and we're going to camp in the garage here while the new house goes up."

She turned and pressed her hands together as if she was praying. "I could camp with you. I have a sleeping bag and a lantern and everything."

How could I make this seem more an ordeal than an adventure? What could make a teenage girl lose interest? "We'll be pretty cramped. And we won't have cable TV or the Internet. No hot water, either. No water at all except from a hose out back."

She pulled her cell phone from her pocket and flicked it on. "My cell phone works here. And I can get clean swimming in the lake."

"No soap allowed in the lake." I pointed to a portable toilet beside the garage and ramped up my argument. "And that's our bathroom. It could get pretty smelly on a hot day."

Julie made the "gag me" sign but didn't give up. "I'll hold my nose. Please, Uncle Dan. I'll help you all I can. And I don't eat much." She crossed her fingers the way little kids do when they fib. "Well, not too much."

"I bet you eat like a young horse. The only way I'll get anything for myself is if we serve nothing but beans."

She repeated the "gag me" motion. "Yuck. I hate beans."

"I remember," I said with a smile. "But the truth is we'll be too busy working on the house to cook much."

"That's good 'cause I can't cook anyway and I hate doing dishes." She pushed that idea away with both hands. "But I'll play with Nelson and feed him and teach him tricks."

I glanced at the dog, his wound so apparent. Three days ago I'd seen him for the first time and, within minutes, pledged myself to him.

"Please. Please, please, please. Please, Uncle Dan."

Uncle Dan. She started calling me that when she was too young to understand that friends were different from family. I closed my eyes for a moment. Julie was wounded too. What kind of a man rescues a dog and turns away from a child?

"We'll have to wait until school is out," I temporized. "Then maybe—but only if it's okay with your grandmother and Camille—you could hang out here for a couple of weeks."

She flung herself at me, wrapping her arms around my neck and kissing my cheek. "Thank you, thank you, thank you."

"Don't thank me yet." What would Camille have to say—both about Julie's summer visit and about not discussing it with her before I made the offer? "It's not a done deal until everyone agrees."

"They will. I know they will." Julie released me and trotted toward the garage. "Maybe I can even hang out here *all* summer," she called over her shoulder.

Bargaining already.

I followed, taking my time. What was I letting us in for?

CHAPTER 6

When I reached the garage, Julie was on her knees on the concrete floor, pleading. She repeated all the arguments she used on me, then crafted new ones, insisting her grandmother would have more peace and quiet and wouldn't need to tell her to pick up her dirty clothes, wouldn't have to drive her places, could cook only what she liked, and wouldn't find dirty dishes in the bedroom.

Rachel, head bowed, spun a mug of tea with quivering fingers and seemed almost unaware of Julie or her pleas and promises. Camille wore the smile she used when she felt laughter wasn't appropriate, but when she looked at me, I saw that smile was only on her lips—her eyes were bright with tears.

Thrusting my palms out, I spread my fingers, and mouthed, "Sorry."

Camille blinked, pushed her chair back, and fished a can of cola from the refrigerator. "Why don't we go for a walk?" She offered the can to Julie. "I'll show you the outside sink where we'll wash up and we'll kick the idea around."

Julie bounced to her feet, snatched the can, scooped three cookies from a paper plate on the wobbly table, and dashed out the door calling for Nelson.

"Nelson?" Camille rolled her eyes, bumped me with her hip as she passed, kissed the point of my chin, and whispered, "Rachel needs to speak with you. I'm all for it. But it's your call."

With a wince, I took Camille's rickety aluminum lawn chair and braced my fingers on the edge of the table. "How are you doing, Rachel?"

"I'm getting by." She raised her head, revealing the strain of the past seven months etched in lines spreading from pinched lips across sunken cheeks. The eyes behind her rimless glasses were empty of everything except anguish. "Thank you."

Those words hadn't been among the ones I imagined she might speak when we met again. "For what?"

"For making that offer to Julie." She lowered her gaze to the table. "For not running me off when I came down your driveway."

"Why would I do that?"

"Because I failed you and Lisa and Willie Dean last summer. I should have said something, done something. But he was my son; I just couldn't believe he . . ." Her hands tightened around the mug, fingertips white with pressure. "And I failed Justin and Julie—I'm *still* failing them."

I reached out and covered her hands with mine, feeling fragile bones and knotted knuckles, fingers cool despite the warm tea in the mug. "You're doing the best you can."

51

"I'm not." She shook her head. "I try, but it's a young world and I don't have the knowledge of it or the heart for it and . . . and I'm dying."

Those also hadn't been words I anticipated.

"Ovarian cancer." She raised her chin, eyes flinty with pain and the determination to bear it. "There's nothing the doctors can do."

That explained Camille's tears. I pressed my hands against Rachel's.

"It's gone too far. Anything they try will make me weaker, sicker, worse than I am now. I have a few months, maybe more, maybe less."

A high-pitched whistle floated up from the lake. Julie called Nelson's name and ordered him to fetch a stick.

"The kids don't know," Rachel said. "And they don't need more misery." She clutched my hands, her nails pressing into my skin. "I came because I need your help."

"Anything," I said, meaning that, yet dreading the terms to be set, the means of payment.

"Julie loves you. And I know that you love her. Lisa's family would take her, but their lives are hard compared to what she's known." Rachel worried her lower lip. "It would mean the world if you would be her guardian, give her a home."

I closed my eyes for a second, saw Julie hugging Nelson. "Of course."

"Thank you, Dan, thank you." Her eyes glistened with tears. "There's money for her keep. There will be more when my house sells."

I waved that aside. "Let's worry about that later."

"There might not be much later," she said, her voice cool and practical. "But we'll put it aside for now."

I nodded, then considered the other part of the equation: Justin. "What about—"

"Justin wants to go into the military. I'm going to meet with his recruiter on Monday." She released my hands, removed her glasses, and rubbed her eyes. "I don't know if it's the right thing, but he's close enough to eighteen, he won't go to counseling or school, and he gets angrier every day. For a time I thought he'd find his way with his friends and his football games, but he got into one fight too many. And the girl he was sweet on broke it off."

Rachel slipped her glasses back on; her eyes bloomed behind the thick lenses. "He transferred to the school where Julie goes, but things didn't get better. I'm afraid he'll turn out like . . . I don't know what else to do to save him."

"The military might channel his anger."

But he'd buck the chain of command, perhaps to a bitter conclusion. Like his father, Justin prided himself on his strength and abilities and, like Ronny, he was arrogant and short-tempered. His definition of being part of a team meant leading that team, bossing that team. When he came up against a veteran drill instructor, would he develop more self-awareness and bend, or would he hold fast to his beliefs and break?

Rachel pursed her lips and shook her head as if she had the same thoughts.

"When he gets out, he'll have a home with us if that's what he—"

"Grandma." Julie dashed into the garage, shot me a smug smile, and wrapped her arms around Rachel. "Guess what? Camille says they'll make a bedroom for me in the corner of the garage and I can come for the whole summer! As soon as school is out."

Rachel smoothed Julie's fly-away hair. "I hope you thanked her."

"Eek." Julie sucked in a breath. "I forgot."

"Well, thank her now," Rachel said in a kind but no-nonsense voice. "And thank Dan too. Then we've got to get going if you want to stop at the mall."

Julie bolted around the table and crushed me in a hug. "Thank you, Uncle Dan. Thank you so much."

Before I could reply, she shot out the door, calling, "Camille. Thank you. Thank you."

Rachel blotted her eyes with a napkin and placed her hands on the edge of the table. "You're a good man, Dan."

"I'm just . . . doing what needs to be done. Anyone else would do ex—"

"Anyone else would think about it first," she said with the barest trace of a smile. "You always had a powerful moral compass, Dan. You held to true north even when others lost their way."

Lost their way. A euphemism for adultery, betrayal, arson, and murder.

Rachel scraped her chair on the paint-mottled concrete floor and struggled to stand on trembling legs.

I leaped to her side, but she refused the arm I offered. "I have to do it myself as long as I can."

"You're right." I would do the same. "When will you tell Julie?"

"She's had enough grief without worrying about me every day until I go into the ground." Rachel shuffled toward the door and I kept pace, the hand she refused a few inches from her elbow. "If I can hang on until school is out, until she comes to you, then I . . ."

Turning, she clutched my arm. "I'm saving up my pills, gritting my teeth a few extra hours every day until I have enough. I know some folks frown on that, and I know they might cut me open after I'm dead because of it, but I made my decision. When the kids are settled, and when it gets to where there isn't any pleasure to make up for the pain, then I'll find my way to Buck and Lisa . . . and Ronny."

My throat constricted. I swallowed hard and bent to kiss her cheek. "My moral compass is fine with that, Rachel."

"It will be better that way. Over quicker."

I didn't know if she meant her own pain, or that of her grandchildren. "And it will be on your own terms."

She squeezed my arm. "Yes. I knew you'd see that."

When the last squeal and rattle of Rachel's car faded, Camille clung to me and railed against fate. "What a horrible thing. For her and for those children. It's like a slow-motion train wreck."

I twined my fingers in her hair and nuzzled her ear. "Maybe this will be the end of it, the last wreckage on these tracks."

"It would be nice to believe that." Planting her hands against my chest, she shoved us apart. "I know I said I was all for this, but what do we know about raising a teenage girl?"

I shrugged. "At least you *were* one."

She snorted. "I bet you'll use that biological excuse every day."

"If I can get away with it, sure."

She mock-punched my shoulder. "Well, the only thing I know is that we have to be on the same page. Back each other up." She glanced toward the ruins of the lodge. "We'd better get to work. Those stones won't jump out and roll to the pile on their own."

"That's a sad fact." Squaring my shoulders, I headed for the charred chimney, Nelson hopping at my side. "Don't you get in the way," I warned him. "It would be the height of irony if a stone broke your back and killed you now."

He looked up at me, tongue lolling from the corner of his mouth, panting hard from his workout with Julie. As if he understood, he canted his head toward the chimney and then trundled to a puddle of sunlight twenty feet away and flopped down. I remembered something my grandfather said about a woman who married well and would have a comfortable life: "She set her ass in a butter tub." Nelson, it appeared, had found a tub of his own right here.

"Your phone's ringing," Camille called from the depths of the garage. "Want me to get it?"

"Not if it's Priscilla. Or Lou Marie."

I bent and grasped the pry bar. "Don't ever grow opposable thumbs," I warned Nelson. "It will be one chore after another from that day on."

He yawned and closed his eyes.

"I don't recognize the number," Camille called. "Maybe it's the architect."

"Better get it. Tell him we have to change the plans to make room for Julie." That would make him smile like a crocodile and reach for his calculator.

56

Jamming the bar into the crumbling mortar between a pair of stones, I threw my weight against it, heard grating, felt a half-inch of give. The effort tweaked a muscle in my back and I sucked in a breath. A smart man would put aside his pride right now and call in some heavy equipment.

"It's the sheriff." Camille stepped from the shadow of the garage. "He says you can call back if you're too busy to talk."

Groaning, I dropped the pry bar and met her halfway, doing the math. Saturday afternoon plus Sheriff North calling equaled . . . well, I wasn't sure, but I doubted he was soliciting for charity. I took the phone from Camille's hand. "What's up?"

"Too damn little on the Wolven case."

I stiffened, feeling both cold dread and something I was embarrassed to admit felt like a sizzle of excitement. I hungered for a taste of this investigation the way a smoker hungers for that first cigarette in the morning. "So you're calling *me*?"

He sucked in a breath—wrestling with that recalcitrant pipe I imagined—and muttered a response. "You're dialed in up that way. Thought maybe you'd heard something."

"Just a lot of talk about locking doors and watching out for strangers." I waited out a few beats of silence, then added, "No speculation about motive. The man was a local hero."

Camille nodded as if satisfied about the nature of the call and returned to the depths of the garage.

"Hmmm."

I heard a tapping, then the rasp of a match. I smiled. The county building had gone smoke-free over the winter, but the deputy who patrolled the roads around Hemlock Lake told me with a laugh that no one would be stupid enough to cite the sheriff for violating that rule. Clement North had been in office a long time. He knew secrets.

And so it came to pass that a county maintenance crew turned up the day the ban took effect and installed an exhaust fan in the wall behind his desk. They also installed dual switches— one beside the fan and the other in the outer office. When she heard him fire up, his secretary hit that switch and closed the door to his office.

"You mind taking a drive up there tomorrow?" North asked.

A Sunday drive to a killing field, the perfect capper to the weekend. "For what?"

"Thought maybe you could look around. See if you can spot what we're missing, what's not right."

"We" meaning investigators, not North himself. His job was largely political and administrative, paper-pushing and budget-building. But he'd gone to his share of crime scenes through the years. "I've never been up there before the other day. I have no idea what's right or not right."

"Fresh eyes might spot something we didn't."

I glanced at the chimney and the trailer loaded with scrap bound for the dump, thought about all that needed doing, tried to put aside my growing curiosity. "I doubt it."

"Won't know until you take a look, will you?"

I glanced over my shoulder, saw Camille with her arms full of old mayonnaise jars, listening, brow furrowed. She'd never say I shouldn't do it, but she might bring up my own arguments about wanting to be uninvolved. I couldn't have it both ways, couldn't make arbitrary exceptions to my rules.

But why the hell not?

Being unpredictable and erratic might, in a strange way, give me more control. Besides, in the past few days I hadn't run from responsibility, hadn't even walked away or stood still and let it pass me by. I was about to become a surrogate father. And I had a dog.

I turned my gaze to Nelson, sunning the stump of his missing leg. What had he seen? Did dogs actively recall events they witnessed? I turned to Camille, saw her nod as if she heard my words before I spoke them. "All right. I'll go up there."

"Thank you, son. I knew I could count on you. I'll have a deputy drop off the key first thing in the morning." Another match struck and he sucked at his pipe. "Now there's one more thing."

"What's that?"

He cleared his throat. "It's odd. Like one of those weird coincidences in those newspapers you see at check-out stands."

"Coincidence?"

Camille raised her eyebrows, set the mayonnaise jars on the ground, and moved closer. I tilted the phone so she could hear. "What kind of a coincidence?"

"Clarence Wolven was an only child and a life-long bachelor. No children. We've been hunting for his next of kin and it seems like . . . well, it seems like the next of kin is you."

CHAPTER 7

Next of kin.

The words rang in my head like the peal of a slab-sided bell. Next of kin to a dead man. Next of kin. Last of kin.

"Dan? You there?"

Camille shucked her leather work gloves, unfolded my fingers from the phone, and put it to her ear. "He's here, Sheriff. Just rattled."

She listened for a moment. "No, we'll take care of it. He was a fine man. He deserves a proper funeral."

She listened again and then said, "Just let us know."

She clicked the phone closed and tucked it into the front pocket of her jeans. "He'll call us when they're ready to—"

"Release the body," I said, seeing Clarence sprawled on the steps, thinking about that word, "release," its definitions and shades of meaning, especially the ones that no longer applied to the mortal remains of Clarence Wolven. He couldn't let go of anything, take the tension off a mechanism, or make something available to the public. He could no longer be fired from a job or set free from a duty. Unless life was considered a duty.

"Are you all right?" Camille peered into my eyes.

"I'm great. Fine. Terrific. Won—"

"Okay. Stupid question. Did you know you were related to him?"

"Not until Mary Lou mentioned it the day I went up there. He was second cousin to my mother."

Camille counted on her fingers. "So one of your great-grandparents and one of his grandparents were siblings?"

I shrugged. "If you say so."

"But you didn't know him?"

"Mary Lou says I met him at family picnics when I was a kid. But I can't conjure a memory."

"Seems strange that you didn't run into him after you came back from Arizona and worked for the sheriff."

"He only came out of that hollow for supplies and searches and the only search I had anything to do with was the hunt for Jefferson last summer. Clarence passed along word that we were a pack of fools and he wouldn't bring his dogs out to encourage us."

Camille chuckled, a sound that made me think of warm syrup. "I think I would have liked him." She poked her chin toward the south end of the lake and the ridge where my ancestors lay. "Is there a place for him in the cemetery? Do you think he arranged for a spot when he moved up here?"

"I don't know. Call Pattie. The Bonesteels donated the land for the cemetery and laid out the plots. She'll know if he has space reserved or where she can make room."

Camille slid the phone from her pocket. "Should I call Reverend Balforth?"

I groaned. Funerals—as Mary Lou told me last summer when my father climbed aboard death's dark coach—were for those whose tickets for that last ride weren't punched yet. Clarence had earned a place in the heart of this community and folks would want to mourn and honor his commitment to the lost. But Balforth's graveside sermons made me think of a dull dental drill whining through the haze of a numbing injection. I'd suffered through three of his recitations last summer and hoped it would be years—or never—before I was obligated to listen to another.

And then there was the question of whether Clarence Wolven had been a religious man and whether he'd subscribed to Balforth's particular brand of belief.

But what it came down to was that Balforth was the only game in town—the only game in several towns. He preached at three tiny churches each Sunday and presided over christenings, weddings, and funerals.

Camille seemed to read my thoughts. "He reminds me of a turkey vulture and he reads his sermons like he's reciting one of those old rhyming poems from grade school, but . . ."

"I know. He's it. Unless we bring someone in from outside."

We let that last word settle between us for a moment and then she tapped the phone. "I'll call him. And I'll see about getting an obituary written. And talk with Mary Lou about who ought to be notified." She nodded toward Nelson. "Maybe other dog trainers would want to come. Or some of the lost people he found."

"You sure you don't mind?" I hoped the relief in my voice wasn't too obvious. "It's a lot of work."

She shrugged. "It is, but I have time."

"Just so you know that Lou Marie will find fault with whatever you do." I tried to keep my voice light, but dark anger weighted the words.

Camille flipped her hand. "I can deal with her."

"But you shouldn't have to. She shouldn't treat you like hired help."

"Get over it, Dan." Camille gripped my forearms. "On her scorecard I've got three strikes against me: I'm an outsider, I'm not pure white, and you and I are living in sin."

I slid my hands to her hips and pulled her to me. "We could change that part. Just say the word."

"One of these days I will. But it won't be for the sake of pleasing Lou Marie." She kissed the point of my chin. "Besides, I don't give a damn that she doesn't like me. I'd be more worried if she did."

I laughed. "As long as you mean that. All of it."

"I do."

"I like the sound of those two words."

She wiggled from my embrace. "So you're going back up there? To Clarence Wolven's?"

I deflected the intent of the question. "I'm the next of kin."

"I'm not talking about that and you know it." Her eyes flashed cold fire. "You don't have to do this."

"I want to."

She sighed and handed me the phone. "All right. Just don't go alone."

I spun off the highway a shade too fast and Jefferson braced himself with a hand on the dash and leaned into the turn. The ruts were deeper and wider than before, dug out by the tires of patrol cars and the vehicles that took away Clarence and his dogs. "What is it we're looking for?"

"I have no idea. There's nothing in those papers that jumped out at me."

I fought the wheel while he shuffled through the documents in the manila envelope the sheriff sent along with the deputy who delivered a duplicate of the house key. One page listed articles of clothing and items taken from Clarence's pockets: three keys on a metal ring, jackknife, handkerchief, short pencil, compass, and broken bits of dog biscuits. The next page noted that the house had been unlocked when investigators arrived and listed the items they'd taken: answering machine, bank statements, monthly bills and phone records, letters from other dog trainers, a photograph album, a log book with sections tracking the routine and performance of each dog, and a lockbox containing Clarence's birth certificate, birth and death certificates for his parents and grandparents, social security number, papers relating to his property, and his will.

The sheriff had copied the entire document so I could see it didn't offer a motive. Clarence's executor, an attorney with an office in the county seat, was directed to pay for his cremation, find homes for his dogs, and sell his property to benefit specific search and rescue organizations.

I'd felt a jolt of relief when I read that last part. I wouldn't have the burden of an inheritance passed down from a man I couldn't remember, the guilt of profiting from a gruesome death.

Jefferson grunted. "Can't see that this was about money. What does that leave?"

"Love. Jealousy."

"The man loved his dogs. You think one of them wanted a little more attention and an extra scoop of kibble?" He stashed the envelope beside the seat. "Maybe a neighbor got pissed off about the dogs barking or running loose."

I thought that over. "Except he doesn't have any neighbors within a mile and disputes generally build over time. Neighbors complain to other neighbors, complain to the law. Someone would have heard about it."

He chuckled. "Someone meaning Lou Marie and Mary Lou?"

"They'd be my first two choices."

We rode in silence for a bit before he said, "Okay, how about blackmail?"

"Money has a way of leaving a trail, so that theory holds only if he took payment in cash and stashed it in a coffee can." I pointed to the manila envelope. "There's a notation in there that bank statements show just his pension and social security checks going in."

"Come to think of it, I heard Lou Marie say the dogs ate better than he did. Except for what he grew in his garden, he lived on bacon, eggs, potatoes, applesauce, chocolate pudding, frozen green beans, and canned ravioli."

"Nothing wrong with canned ravioli. If you've got a taste for it."

"I sure did when I was a kid." He rubbed his stomach. "Used to eat it cold. Right out of the can."

We rode in silence for a minute before Jefferson ventured, "Maybe it was revenge."

"That would explain making Clarence call the dogs to their deaths."

"But revenge for what? Like Lou Marie said, it's hard to piss someone off if you don't get out much."

I didn't bring up Lou Marie's ability to do just that. Jefferson seemed oblivious to the increasing glimpses of her dark side, but perhaps he was in denial. If so, how long could he sustain that?

"Maybe it was revenge for something that happened long ago." I made a mental note to ask Mary Lou if she recalled any gossip about disputes. "They say it's a dish best served cold."

"How cold? Could the killer be as old as Clarence?" Jefferson rubbed his brush cut again. "Seems like you'd grow weary of carrying a grudge when your parts start giving out."

"Or that grudge is all that keeps you going."

My rig tobogganed down the ridge, and I stopped where I had four days earlier and cut the engine. For a few seconds we listened to the ping of cooling metal, the thud of mud dropping from the undercarriage, and the cries of that jay, then Jefferson released an explosion of air through his lips and swung his door wide. "Let's get it done."

By unspoken mutual consent, we turned our backs on the dog pens and walked up opposite edges of the steps, skirting the dark stain in the center. Except for faint tracks leading to a boot scraper and the coco fiber mat laid before the door, and except for a few pine needles here and there and an old broom leaning against the wall at the corner of the house, the narrow porch was clean and the windows on either side of the door sparkled.

66

I wiped my feet on the mat and got out the key. Despite its sharp edges, it slid into the lock as if the channel had been recently oiled, the bolt clicked back smoothly, and the hinges worked without a hint of a squeak. Clarence had taken good care of this place.

The door swung in on a wide living area with an oak floor, a towering stone fireplace, and a kitchen strung out against the far wall. Furnishings were sparse: an oval braided rug, a green plaid sofa with a brown blanket folded in one corner, a yellow-brown puffy chair beneath a three-globed lamp, a square table holding an aging boombox and a scatter of compact disks, and a rack filled with magazines. Built-in bookshelves lined the perimeter of the room, crouching beneath the windows and scaling the walls between them. Here and there, short stacks of books leaned against the shelves as if waiting for space to become available. At the edge of the kitchen, a round oak table no more than two feet across hunkered between two ladder-back chairs.

"Nice place," Jefferson said. "Small, but it feels complete."

I nodded. I had the same feeling. Complete and clean—except for smudges left by crime-scene techs and few indistinct footprints just inside the door.

I stood on the threshold for a long moment the way you do when you're waiting for a sign of welcome or warning. I glanced at the boot scraper and remembered the scabs of mud on the elbows of Clarence's flannel shirt and the knees of his overalls, the thick clumps of it on his boots. He'd been somewhere beyond his yard and kennels. He'd fallen at least once. And he hadn't cleaned his boots and come into the house when he returned.

Because he had no time.

That thought acted like a trigger. Fear, rage, and confusion exploded in my mind. I felt grief without comprehension, without boundary, without end. I gripped the doorjamb.

"You feel him?" Jefferson steadied me with a hand on my shoulder.

The air hummed like a high-voltage wire. "I feel something. Something angry. And sad."

"A spirit takes time to settle and move on after death comes out of nowhere. I felt that too many times. Over there." His grip tightened for a second, then relaxed. "Sometimes I talked to them. Don't know if that helped them any, but it did me. Seemed less spooky when I was talking."

Spooky. I held back a shiver, wishing he hadn't used that particular word. If you'd asked me an hour ago, I would have said I didn't believe in ghosts. Yes, Susanna and Nat had haunted my dreams, but I never felt they were with me in daylight the way I felt Clarence now.

Like him, they died suddenly, Susanna strangled by a tow rope on the lake, Nat an hour later by his own hand. Surely there was enough horror and grief and remorse to keep their spirits unsettled. But perhaps my own grief and horror put up a wall to turn them aside during my waking hours. Or perhaps they reunited after they crossed over and poured their emotions into each other as they had on this side of . . . Of what?

I turned my head to look at Jefferson. His eyes were closed and his lips were set in a grim line. "What did you talk about?"

He stayed still and silent for a few beats, then shook himself like a dog coming in out of the rain. "Nothing much. Just talked, you know, talked to convince myself I was alive, talked loud because I was scared shitless I'd hear them talking back."

I cleared my throat and started in a whisper, feeling like a kid whistling his way past a graveyard on a moonless night. "We're here to help the sheriff, Clarence. We're going to take a look around, but we'll put everything back the way we found it. We're looking for the reason you . . ." My throat tightened and I swallowed hard. "If you can, maybe you could lend a hand."

The humming faded, then ceased. Had I imagined it? Had that imagining resurrected Jefferson's memories? With soft steps, I entered the room, Jefferson close behind, and crossed to an archway that gave on a narrow hall broken by three doors. The one to my left opened on Clarence's bedroom, a square space with a tall double bed with stubby bedposts, a nightstand stuffed with magazines, another powerful lamp, a cedar chest, more bookshelves, and a window that looked out over the porch. The bathroom had blue tile and bright green towels, and the office along the hall to the right was just large enough for a desk, a chair, and another bookcase, this one packed with works on dogs and dog training.

"The books?" Jefferson asked.

I thought my way through that. Clarence had a pack of dogs, but only a simple deadbolt on the door and wide windows anyone could punch right through. He hadn't lived like a man who had valuables he feared might be stolen. And if there was something he wanted to protect, there were

69

better choices than sliding it into a book, choices like burying it in the woods or building a fireproof cubbyhole in a wall or floor.

The door was unlocked when investigators arrived. Either Clarence, like many folks living this far off the beaten track, didn't lock his doors much, or the killer unlocked the door and left it that way. And if the killer searched the house, either he knew exactly where to find what he was looking for, or his was the neatest search on record. Except for the mug, plate, and cutlery in the sink, a frying pan on the stove, and stacks of books here and there, everything seemed to have a place and be in it.

If I slaughtered a man on his front steps, I wouldn't hesitate to trash his house. Unless I got scared off.

But this murder didn't feel like the work of someone who scared easily. And there was just one road in. By the time he heard a car coming, it would be too late for the executioner to do anything but stand his ground and kill again.

I shook my head. "I don't think there's anything hidden in the books."

"Maybe it wasn't hidden. We should look for a spot without dust, or a gap on a bookcase."

"Except I don't see any dust." I pointed to the books stacked on the floor. "And there are plenty of spares the killer could have used to plug a vacant slot."

"Well, those were my best ideas." Jefferson rubbed his brush cut. "Maybe I'll poke around in the pantry and closets, comb through the garage, check the mattress, look under the rug."

"Might as well give it a shot while we're here. I'll go through the office."

70

For two hours we sifted and searched. Jefferson moved every tool, box, and can in the garage, checked every item in the pantry, and pulled up the folded newspapers lining closet shelves. Calling out every now and then to update me on his progress, he removed drawers to look behind and beneath them, tapped walls and baseboards, and peered into the base of the lamp.

Investigators had taken Clarence's files from the desk, but I went through what remained: pens and pencils, a broken plastic ruler with the name of a political candidate who likened himself to a loose cannon, rubber bands, paper clips, a couple of pamphlets about good nutrition, a magnifying glass, and a book of blank checks. I looked beneath the phone which was working again, took out drawers and searched for a hidden compartment or something taped behind them, turned the chair upside down, moved the bookcase out from the wall, and sorted through its contents. The closet held spare clothing and shoes and not a damn thing more.

Together we scanned each blank wall for a nail without a picture, a hole without a nail, or a darker or lighter spot where something might have hung. We pressed against each rock in the chimney and trod each floorboard listening for a squeak or a hollow sound.

"We've still got the books." Jefferson massaged the back of his neck. "Could be he cut the center of the pages out of one to make a hiding place."

"I didn't think of that."

He smiled. "I tried not to."

We sighed in unison, then attacked the task, pulling each book from its shelf, thumbing through

71

it, shaking it, checking behind it, putting it back. Clarence had an eclectic collection, and I handled at least a hundred I'd like to own—classics like *Moby Dick* and *The Last of the Mohicans*, military history, science fiction, and westerns. Did being next of kin carry the privilege of being allowed to cull ahead of book scouts and dealers if I paid a good price?

When we finished, the sun was low in the sky. Fine dust hung in the rays fanning through the windows. My eyes were gummy, my nose clogged, my throat raw.

Jefferson sneezed and blew his nose into a red bandanna. "I'm with you to the end, Dan, you know that. But if Clarence was keeping a secret, he wasn't keeping it in here. Or else the killer got to it."

I nodded, fished the key from my pocket and turned it in the lock. As I pulled it out, a spark arced from lock to key. I jumped, shaking my fingers. The key fell to the porch, chiming against the boards.

Jefferson stooped and picked it up. "We're doing the best we can, Clarence. Sorry we disturbed you."

"Thanks for your hospitality." I pocketed the key. "I'll help your lawyer take care of the property."

Neither of us turned our heads toward the dog pens as we trudged to the SUV. And neither of us spoke. In a few minutes we were wobbling in the muddy ruts on the final downgrade before the county road.

"Looks like we'll be doing some pushing." Jefferson pointed to a rusty green truck hub-deep in the furrows. Rooster tails of watery mud sprayed behind its spinning wheels, the transmission whined like a saw hitting a knot, and a fog of blue smoke swirled up the slope.

I tapped the brakes and slithered to a stop twenty feet away. "Any idea who that is?"

"No, but he can't drive worth a shit." Jefferson opened his door, swung out, and strode toward the truck, making a "time out" sign with his hands and yelling, "Shut it down before you make things worse."

The whining ceased and I climbed out into silence and the acrid odor of scorched rubber and hot oil. As Jefferson approached, the truck door scraped open across the top edge of the rut and a man clambered out. He looked to be in his early twenties, shorter than Jefferson by half a foot, with sandy brown hair, a spotty beard and a wispy and uneven mustache. He chewed at it with his lower teeth and bobbed his head.

"Sorry to block your way," he said, his voice higher and breathier than his barrel chest led me to expect. "I thought if I gunned it I'd get loose."

Jefferson turned to me and rolled his eyes, then walked to the rear of the truck and bent to get a closer look at the wheels.

"Speed's not what you want," I said. "When you get dug in, the trick is to rock it."

"He plowed it in too deep for that." Jefferson held his hands apart to show me the depth of the rut. "This won't be pretty." He advanced on the driver. "You got a shovel? A hatchet?"

The man's eyes widened, his face blanched, and his chin retreated into his black turtleneck sweater. "Why?" he squeaked, raising pale and pudgy hands as if to defend himself. "What are you going to do?"

Stifling a laugh, Jefferson turned aside.

"We're going to cut brush to put under the wheels and fill in the ruts so you can back out of there," I told the quivering man.

"Oh." He flushed, lowered his hands, and wedged them into the pockets of a pair of crisp jeans. Jefferson wiped at his eyes with his shirt cuffs.

"You've never been stuck before?" I asked.

He shook his head. "I've never been on a road this bad. It's not even on my map."

My cop sense tingled; I thought of the discussion about strangers we had a few nights ago. "Then why are you on it?"

Jefferson's eyes narrowed. He edged behind the man, closer to the truck. Stooping, he peered through the open door.

"I'm a reporter," the man bleated.

"He's got a camera in there," Jefferson said. "And a notebook. Don't know what's under the camper shell."

"My name is Colden Cornell," the man said, his voice infused with a few degrees of confidence. "I work for the *Mountain Missive*. It's a weekly that started up last year. I have some back issues if you're interested. I don't work there all the time. I'm a freelancer and—"

"You came to write about Clarence Wolven's murder." I finished his sentence. "And take pictures."

He flushed again and bobbed his chin into his sweater.

"Nothin' to see except an empty house," Jefferson said.

"And the dog pens." Colden's head bobbed again. "Those poor dogs. All dead."

Jefferson cocked his head at me and I made a slicing motion with the side of my hand. If this reporter learned about Nelson, he'd want to see the three-legged survivor, write a story. "Yeah," I said. "Every last one, dead."

"And there's no way you're getting this truck up there until the road dries out." Jefferson bent to lift a slab of stone and slide it behind a wheel.

The reporter frowned. "You got up there."

"I've got four-wheel drive."

He studied me. "Are you with the sheriff's department?"

"Neighbors," Jefferson said. "Keeping an eye on the place. Making sure no one breaks in."

"Oh. I'd never do something like that." Colden shaded his pale eyes and gazed up the hill, then at the hiking boots on his feet. "Maybe I'll walk. How far is it?"

"A long way," I exaggerated. "All as bad as this hill—or worse."

He frowned, chewed at his mustache, then shrugged. "Any chance you could give me a lift? I'll mention you in the story."

"Gotta get back." Jefferson broke a limb off a small pine and stuffed it behind the wheel. "Gotta get to church."

"Church?" I asked as we followed clumps of mud from Colden's truck along the road back to Hemlock Lake. "When was the last time you went to church?"

"1971," he said without hesitation. "32 years ago this summer. Prayed for a good number in the draft lottery." He was silent for a few seconds. "Lot of good that did."

75

I grunted agreement. "And where did you get the 'neighbors' story from?"

"Probably the same place you got the 'all the dogs died' story."

I nodded, navigating a tight turn. "I don't want that dog and his shaved stump used to sell papers."

"Damn straight."

"Besides, Clarence chose to live a private life. He deserves a private death."

CHAPTER 8

The next day I called a guy Stub knew who allowed as how he'd be glad for the work and could make it out my way in an hour or so. By the next afternoon the site was cleared and he went to work digging the foundation, including an area for the addition the architect agreed to get right on. Where we'd planned for one bedroom and a small bath upstairs, we'd now have a larger bath, two bedrooms and more closet space—something Camille assured me a teenage girl needed.

"For girl things," she elaborated. "Dresses and tops and jeans and shoes. Lots of shoes."

I nodded, remembering Susanna's collection of sandals and slip-ons and heels in all heights. An image of her bloomed in my mind. She wore a pale blue sundress and white sandals with heels that tapped the stone pathway as she walked; her hair drifted behind her, shimmering in the sunlight. I closed my eyes and pressed my hands against the sides of my head as if I could crush out all emotion and squeeze that memory down to a smudge of color.

As if she saw into my mind, Camille laid a hand on my shoulder.

I forced myself to remember that Susanna's shoes were gone, donated to a women's shelter. For a fleeting second I wondered about the women wearing them now and whether they'd been able to change their lives.

"I'm okay. Just a memory."

Camille must have invasive memories too. Flashbacks about the husband who killed her unborn baby and her mother.

And Jefferson. Images must explode like mines in his brain.

Camille tightened her grip for just a second, then traced a finger along the design we'd roughed out on a flattened brown paper bag. "It won't really cost that much more—and we get a lot of extra space downstairs too."

I smiled at the anticipation in her voice. She'd been so cautious when we started planning, tentative about making suggestions, as if she had no right or I might feel crowded. She coaxed me into working out a comprehensive budget and hewed the line right up until Monday when she added a mudroom, enlarged the pantry and library, ordered a jetted tub for the master bath big enough to float a small canoe, and increased closet space in our bedroom.

"Money isn't the issue. But if we have space, there's a tendency to fill it." I played devil's advocate. "Remember everything I hauled out of the attic last summer? And all the junk you carried out of the garage? I don't want to be a packrat."

"You won't. I'll see that you don't. And besides, most of the space is for me." She stood on tiptoe and brushed her lips against mine. "I need girl things too. Frilly things. Lacy things."

"Ummm." I nuzzled her neck, no longer thinking of Susanna, imagining the whisper of slick fabric on Camille's warm skin, the new sheets and pillowcases she put on our bed this morning. They should be christened. Why not this afternoon while the sun was bright and the breeze just an insinuation?

"What's Nelson doing?" She pointed toward the lake.

I kissed the tender skin behind her ear, making a promise to myself, and turned to see the dog casting left and right on the rocky beach at the margin of the water. "Looks like he's tracking something. Maybe a fox. Or a raccoon."

"We better hope it's not a coyote or that bear we saw up by the Silver Leaf Hollow Road last week. We probably should start locking the food away and securing the garbage. No point in inviting visits from wildlife."

Nelson cast farther to the left, paused, and swung right, only the tip of his nose protruding from his cone.

"Were there as many coyotes and bears around when you were a kid?"

"No. Never saw a coyote until I got to Arizona. As for bears, only in the lean and dry seasons." I chuckled. "Good thing, because we used to camp up in the mountains provisioned with a pound of bacon for breakfast and enough cookies to choke a horse."

"You might as well have coated yourselves in honey and rolled in sunflower seeds. Didn't your mother worry?"

I pondered that. She must have. But my father would have laughed at her fears, maybe said that a close encounter with a bear was a rite of passage that would make men out of us. I'd have run, for sure. But Ronny and my brother—

"I hope Nelson doesn't round up a skunk," Camille said. "He'll be sleeping outside if he does."

"You mean like he should be now?" I teased.

The first night he was with us I found him at the foot of our bed. She told me she'd put him there in self-defense—she couldn't sleep with him whimpering—and as soon as he healed he'd be on the floor. But I suspected Nelson's sleeping arrangement was permanent and part of the reason she decided we needed a king bed in the new house. "He's not likely to come across a skunk in the daytime."

"Unless it's rabid."

"Well, he's had his shots. And chances are he'll get sprayed sooner or later." There wasn't a dog owner in town without a super-size can of tomato juice on hand for just such an occasion.

She wrinkled her nose. "Can't we teach him to stay away from them?"

I didn't know much about dogs. We had only one when I was a kid, and that was a retriever my father trained to bring in the ducks he shot. I never liked the aroma or taste of duck, no matter how my mother cooked it. At dinner time I breathed through my mouth, cut the meat into pill-sized chunks, and swallowed them without chewing. As for the dog, he had no use for me and, since he usually smelled like a swamp, I made no effort to win him over.

"I think dogs learn by doing, by repetition and reinforcement. We can't show Nelson a picture of a skunk and tell him to steer clear."

She wrinkled her nose. "Maybe we could borrow that stuffed skunk from the Shovel It Inn."

"I don't know if it would smell much like a real skunk after all those years in the bar."

"Probably not." She shrugged and leaned against me. "I guess he'll learn the hard way. But I bet it takes only once. He's smart. He already knows how to bark to tell us he needs to go out."

I remembered the logbook listed in the inventory of items investigators removed from Clarence's house. Perhaps I'd ask the sheriff to copy the page for Nelson so I could see what training he'd had. Except there wouldn't be a page marked "Nelson."

I felt a stab of remorse. I hadn't thought to check what Clarence had named this dog.

Raising his muzzle into the faint breeze sifting down the ridge, Nelson hopped up the slope toward the far side of the garage. Camille pointed. "What's he doing now?"

"He's either got the scent of something new, or he's still tracking whatever he was interested in before."

"But he's not sniffing the ground."

"Scent hangs in the air." I kissed the nape of her neck. "Travels on the wind."

She tipped her face to the breeze and sniffed. "I don't smell a thing."

"You're not a dog. And you don't have a nose like his."

"That's something to consider on those days when I'm not happy with what nature gave me." She rubbed her nose with her forefinger. "Is that what makes a good search dog? A big nose?" Stretching, she threaded her fingers through my hair. "Or is this where you tell me it's not size, but what you do with it?"

"That's the script we learn at man school," I said with a chuckle. "But dogs with longer noses probably have an advantage when it comes to following a scent. I'll bet Nelson can smell a hundred times better than we can. Probably more."

"A hundred times." She sniffed the breeze again. "I've still got nothing. Except piney smell."

"If he gets sprayed by a skunk you'll be grateful for your comparatively diminished sensory capacity."

"Ooohhh." She tousled my hair and tipped her head to kiss the blade of my jaw. "I love it when you use those big words."

"Be nice to me and I'll brush up my vocabulary before we go to bed tonight."

"Tonight?" She thrust her chin toward the garage. "Why wait?"

With a crow of laughter, she pushed off against me and loped away, calling, "Race you," over her shoulder.

I didn't even try to beat her. Even if I lost, I'd win.

Later, lazing in a slant of sunlight on the dock, we watched Nelson tasting the wind once more.

"Do you think he's looking for something?" Camille asked. "The other dogs? Or Clarence?"

"I don't know." I knew that dogs remembered people, places, and commands. And I knew that dogs could miss someone. My father's retriever whined and moped when he was left at home. But I didn't know whether dogs thought about people they hadn't seen for a few months or years, the way I might wonder what became of my college roommate.

"How did Clarence train them to search?"

"I don't know that, either," I admitted. There must be books on the subject. Or perhaps Clarence kept notes.

Nelson turned in a slow circle, keeping his lone rear foot in place, like the point of a compass.

"You don't know much, do you?" Camille leaned down, dipped her fingers into the lake, and flicked water at my face. "Maybe Clarence took a smelly sock out in the woods and let the dogs loose to find it. Maybe he put the sock someplace different every day."

"Could be. He owned a lot of acres right up against state land."

Mitch Shultis, who fed the dogs when Clarence was away, owned another big chunk. As that proverbial crow flapped his wings, Mitch's place was about a mile from Clarence's. Farther if the crow followed established roads. I dredged up a fuzzy memory map of the area and—

A map!

A man as neat and organized as Clarence might have marked out search areas, rotated through them. Closing my eyes, I culled my recollections of his house and the inventory of what investigators had taken. I hadn't seen a map on his walls, hadn't noted any mention on the list.

Camille wiped her wet fingers on her shirt and gazed at Nelson who had belly flopped on the stepping-stone walk to the lake, but kept his nose pointed toward the top of the ridge. "I can think of a dozen reasons someone might kill a man, but the dogs . . . I just don't understand that. Those dogs were locked in their pens. They couldn't hurt the killer."

Ideas careened through my mind. Had Clarence come across something in the woods? Had the killer followed him home and killed the dogs so they wouldn't lead anyone back to it?

CHAPTER 8

The next morning, we drove to the county seat and I dropped Camille off outside a long block building covered with signs claiming rock-bottom prices on carpet and linoleum. "When will you be back?" she asked, leaning in the driver's window to straighten my collar.

I computed driving time to the sheriff's office, added thirty minutes, and factored in a running reconnaissance through the aisles of a nearby plumbing store—the only destination I discussed with her before we headed out. Then I cupped the back of her head and gave her a lingering kiss. "Two hours tops."

"Okay." She smiled, but then her eyes narrowed. "Was that an attempt to cloud my mind?"

I played dumb. "Huh?"

"I want to believe you're finally taking the choice of fixtures seriously, but I saw you riffling through those inventory pages from Clarence's house. What are you up to?"

"Nothing." Reflexively, I tried the same kind of lie that never worked with my mother or my teachers. "I'm going to look at sinks. And faucets."

85

Camille rolled her eyes. "You're going to the sheriff's office. You've got an idea about the case."

A flush of embarrassment scorched my ears. Why had I thought lying would be simpler than telling the truth?

With a shake of her head, Camille said, "Well, go ahead. But before you take off, tell me you're not doing this because of Priscilla Denton or because you feel obligated to the community. Tell me you came up with something you think everyone else missed."

"I'm not. I have," I blurted like a teenager promised a release from detention if he confesses. "At least I think I have."

"That's good enough for me." She slapped the side of the SUV. "Two hours. And you owe me lunch. *Not* at a drive-through burger place."

Buoyed by her confidence, I laid my theory out for Sheriff North, pacing in front of his desk. "Clarence's boots were crusted with mud. So were his knees and elbows. I think he was up in the woods, he came back in a hurry because he saw or heard something, and he fell along the way—at least once."

"He was an old guy." The sheriff scratched a bristling eyebrow with his thumbnail. "Been a lot of rain lately. Maybe he got into a patch of mud right there in his yard, took a spill carrying firewood or walking out to feed the dogs."

"I admit it's fragile, but my theory offers a reason for the killing."

"More like far-fetched than fragile." He stood, hitched up the jeans that were part of his Saturday uniform, walked to the map of Ashokan County that covered an entire wall of his office, and tapped a spot north and east of Hemlock Lake. "Besides, what's out there he could have stumbled on? There's no gold in those hills."

"There's stone," I offered. "Timber. Deer."

"Never heard of anyone killing over a little illegal quarrying or firewood cutting or a deer shot out of season—hell, poaching is a time-honored tradition for a whole lot of folks in those hollows. It's hardly ever reported. And if Mr. Good Citizen does call it in, Mr. Bad Citizen is usually aware of that call and gets rid of the evidence."

He rubbed his jowls, fingering a spot where a few rogue whiskers had evaded his razor and made their stand a half-centimeter from the edge of his mustache. "There are a few cases where Mr. Good Citizen knows Mr. Bad Citizen—or is related to him. Then there might be a little dustup. Usually nothing fatal."

My theory was spiraling down in flames. Like a barnstorming pilot, I clung to the controls, determined not to bail out. "Suppose this Mr. Bad Citizen is badder than usual. Suppose he's making moonshine, or meth. And suppose Mr. Bad Citizen panicked."

"Could be that Clarence stumbled on a drug lab. And somebody cooking enough meth might not balk at murder." Sheriff North pinched his nose, considering. "But he took his time killing those dogs. That's not panic."

I nodded. What I saw up there smacked of perverse pleasure. I felt an icy lump beneath my sternum and thought of Ronny, murdering Lisa, framing Willie Dean and leading him like a lamb to the slaughter, then trying to kill me. Was this killer of the same caliber? "Did anyone try to backtrack? Find out where Clarence had been?"

North glanced at a bulging folder on his desk. "Not that they mentioned."

And now rain, wind, and spring growth might have wiped out footprints, obscured broken branches.

"I'm not saying I buy it." He blew air from between his lips. "But between you and me, we got no fingerprints, no tire tracks, no motive for killing that old man and his dogs except the sick thrill of doing it."

The cold lump in my chest swelled and I fought down a shiver. Someone who got off on that would strike again as sure as winter. And strike around here, unless he was the type who moved on. I winced at the idea of wishing trouble elsewhere.

The sheriff hitched at his jeans again, returned to his swivel chair, and rocked for a moment, picking at the black electrical tape that covered the end of one armrest. "Guess it wouldn't hurt if you went up there and took another look around. You still got the key. But if you find a map—if you find anything that feels hinky—call me that instant."

"I will."

"All right then." He reached for the phone. "I'll have that logbook brought to the conference room. I expect you'll want the autopsy report too."

Dismissed, I strolled to a tiny break room that smelled of overripe bananas and burnt coffee. I considered the way my luck was running as I studied a hot-drink machine that had been kicked more often than a soccer ball at the end of the season. If you looked up "standoff" in the dictionary, there'd be a picture of this machine. The vending company refused to replace it because of a history of hard use; deputies who lost their money refused to stop abusing it until the company agreed to provide a new one.

Knowing all that, I fed in quarters, pressed the button for hot chocolate, and held it until I heard a groan from the machine's bowels. A paper cup slid down the chute and caught sideways. I raised the plastic screen and yanked the cup loose, scalding my fingers in a gush of steaming liquid. Cursing, I held onto the cup while it filled halfway with slop more gray than brown, slop smelling of mold and rust. Laughing at myself, I called it a draw, emptied the cup into the sink, and walked away.

The logbook and autopsy report were on the table when I got to the conference room. I scanned the report first and noted that, like his dogs, Clarence had been killed by a gunshot wound to the head. The bullets recovered were all from a handgun. The same gun.

I sat back and thought about what Jefferson and I saw in the house and what investigators took away. No guns. Not even an old family rifle or shotgun. Most folks around Hemlock Lake had several. Some kept them in locked cabinets or basement closets. Some displayed them on racks in the living room or den. If Clarence had a gun, it seemed he would have tried to get to it, tried to use it.

Mulling that, I went back to the report. The medical examiner found no defensive wounds or signs that Clarence struggled with his attacker. A number of scratches on his face and hands were attributed to contact with thorns or branches just prior to his death. Bruises on his knees and forearms were attributed to a fall.

Coupled with the mud on Clarence's knees and elbows, that supported my theory. A man running through the woods doesn't take time to shove branches aside and hold them when he plunges into a thicket. And a running man is more likely to fall, fall hard enough to bruise himself.

But who or what had Clarence been running from? And why?

Setting the autopsy report aside, I fingered the logbook. It had a green cloth cover and the oblong shape of old account books. As I flipped through the pages, I saw Clarence's sense of order had prevailed here too. He'd slid in two used envelopes to divide the book into three sections: one in which he entered information on specific searches he took part in; one subdivided into sections for each of the dogs and containing notations on health, weight, inoculations, and performance; and a journal in which he listed training activities and comments on weather and terrain.

To my surprise, the dogs had numbers instead of names. Had Clarence wanted to think of them more as workers than pets? Or had he lacked imagination?

Deciphering his crabbed handwriting, I learned that Dogs One and Two came from Ohio, barely more than pups at the time. Now, according to a notation, they were retired from searches. They had the letters SAR in parentheses beside their numbers. Search and rescue?

He'd adopted Three two years later and found Four wandering along the highway a few months after that. Those dogs had the letter C tacked on behind their numbers. I stared at it for a few seconds, couldn't come up with a meaning, and moved on to Five, Six, and Seven. They had belonged to a dog trainer who died. Five was listed as retired. All were tagged as SAR. Finally, Eight, my three-legged survivor, was a gift from a couple in Connecticut who watched their granddaughter star in the kindergarten pageant thanks to Clarence and the efforts of Six and Seven. The couple also donated a thousand dollars for kibble.

Kibble? I remembered the shed in the center of the kennels. Jefferson and I had been so focused on the house, and so tired of the search after we'd gone through the books, that we hadn't given it a glance.

I closed my eyes, resurrecting the emotional turmoil of Clarence's spirit that I felt when I opened the door to his house. "If you can hear me," I whispered, "help me."

Fingers spread to catch a spark, senses tuned for an electric hum, I waited. I didn't exactly feel like an idiot, but I kept my ear cocked for footsteps coming my way. It was one thing to talk to a dead man; it was another to get caught at it by someone who hadn't shared my experience.

Imagining how I must look—a man conjuring a ghost he wasn't certain he believed in—I smiled, pulled my chair up to the table, and flipped to the journal section of the logbook. A series of geometric marks caught my eye: a square, a rhombus, a circle, a triangle on its base, and one standing on its point. One of those marks followed the date at the start of each journal entry. Did they indicate zones on a map?

Brief descriptions came after the marks. I saw notations like, "Dogs moved fast. Little casting about. Confusion at stream. Reacquired trail within a minute."

I riffled to the final page of the section and found the entry for Sunday, March 31. A rhomboid shape followed the date and the numbers Three and Four. The dogs marked with a C. Next to that, Clarence had written, "7:30 a.m. Overcast. Rain forecast. 42 degrees. Humidity high. Slight breeze, NE."

Unlike other entries, which included the total time of the search, compass directions, approximate distance covered, and how the dogs performed overall, that was it.

Judging from the level of organization, Clarence struck me as a man who would have made his entries without unnecessary delay. I imagined he would have rewarded the dogs, perhaps fed them, cleaned up, maybe even eaten a meal himself, and then written in the logbook.

I sat back in my chair and studied a crack in the plaster ceiling. Did he trust himself to remember when the dogs altered course or circled to pick up the scent, or did he carry a pen and a small notebook or a stack of index cards? Maybe even a recorder. Closing my eyes, I labored to recall the items taken from his pockets, cursing myself for not bringing the list along. There had been a compass, definitely. A jackknife. Three keys on a ring. And a handkerchief. And a pen . . . no, a stubby pencil. But no recorder and no paper. I was sure.

Well, almost sure.

For a few seconds, I toyed with the idea of asking the sheriff for a look at his copy of the list, then set that aside and went back to studying the training entries in the logbook. Sessions ran a few hours. How much ground did Clarence cover? Given his age, how much *could* he cover?

I dug my cell phone from my pocket and punched in a number. It rang four times before she answered. "Hemlock Lake Post Office, Mary Lou speaking. How may I help you?" Her voice was hesitant, cautious.

"It's Dan," I said. "Are you okay? You sound—"

"I'm fine. You startled me, that's all. This phone never rings unless it's someone higher up the food chain. And with them chewing over the budget the way they are, I'm afraid the next bite is going to come out of my butt."

I chuckled.

"Laugh all you want, Dan Stone. You're a man of leisure, now."

"Sorry."

"Not your fault. I wonder how it would be if I worked for myself."

"You'd have a tougher boss than you do now."

I heard only the hiss of phone-line static for a long moment, and then Mary Lou giggled. Truce established, I got to my questions. "How old was Clarence Wolven?"

"Hmmm. He must have been pushing seventy or just on the other side of it. I remember he retired when he was fifty-five or so, but—"

"Seventy is close enough. What kind of shape was he in?" I blinked back an image of the ravaged body we'd found ten days ago.

"Darn good for his age," Mary Lou said. "He got plenty of exercise training those dogs."

"How far do you think he could walk?"

"Just as far as he wanted to. He had a little arthritis in his hands—his knuckles were kind of

93

gnarly like mine are getting—but he didn't have knee or hip problems."

I didn't ask how she knew. It stood to reason that Clarence, on his infrequent trips out of the hills, would expand a stop at the post office into a social visit. If you asked Mary Lou, she'd deny that she gossiped. She'd claim she was being polite to her customers, making conversation. But if you paid attention, you noticed those conversations covered a lot of territory and included a fair number of questions.

"One more thing. Do you know if he had any guns in the house?"

"Not in the house or anywhere else. Clarence hated guns."

That explained why he didn't make a stand. The downed wires explained why he didn't call for help. But why didn't he get in his truck and get away? "Thanks."

"I knew you couldn't leave this alone." She sounded excited, and a little smug, as if my call had won her a bet. "Especially after Priscilla threw down the gauntlet. I'll tell Jefferson."

I blinked. "Tell him what?"

"That you're going up there again."

"I—"

"Have to be Monday," she said. "Rain's coming in tonight and I expect it won't let up until an hour before Balforth cracks open his Bible."

CHAPTER 10

To fit the funeral into Reverend Balforth's Sunday schedule—three services in the morning and a wedding in the evening—we set the gathering at the cemetery for 3:30, with a potluck dinner afterward in the back room at the Shovel It Inn. As Mary Lou predicted, rain fell steadily until just after two and then, as Camille and I topped the ridge, the sun blazed out.

Raindrops glittered like chandelier crystals on the branches of trees still bare of leaves. Gravestones glowed as if lit from within and wisps of steam rose from cracks in marble and granite.

"It's a little spooky." Camille shivered and drew a gray fringed shawl tighter around her shoulders. "Like ghosts rising to take part in the service."

I eased the SUV off the gravel road and onto the grass at the edge of the Stone family plot. "Maybe they're rising to welcome Clarence to the neighborhood."

Camille unbuckled her seatbelt. "I hope this particular neighborhood doesn't have a dog ordinance."

95

"Why? We left Nelson at home."

"I had Clarence's dogs cremated and mixed their ashes with his." Camille flashed me an apologetic smile. "I was going to tell you, but you were so busy with the architect and the building permits. And I guess I thought you might tell me it was silly or a waste of money." Her voice fell away to a whisper. "I didn't want him to be alone."

I stared out at the gravestones thinking about the past and the long shadows it cast over both of us. Camille had years of keeping secrets from a brutal man to avoid beatings and punishments. And I had years of not sharing details of my life with a disapproving father to avoid caustic comments. But that was then. We could change. We *should* change.

I clicked my seatbelt loose and pulled her against me. "I might have thought both. But if it was what you wanted, I would have agreed in a heartbeat."

"I know," she sniffled. "It's hard to get used to being part of a team."

"It is for me too."

An engine whined in the distance. Another vehicle climbing the ridge. Camille fished a tissue from the pocket of her black slacks, blew her nose, and smoothed the lapel of my dark blue suit. "Is there a law against burying dogs in a human cemetery?"

"I don't know." I opened my door and stepped out onto grass slippery from the rain. "But they've been cremated, so I doubt it's an issue. Unless somebody decides to make it one."

"Somebody like Lou Marie?"

"Always a possibility." I remembered the hateful things she said when we buried my father and Lisa. "She has a knack for disrupting funerals."

Camille opened the rear hatch. "Then we'll neglect to mention it." She stroked the oblong box painted with vines and leaves. Clarence Wolven's name was spelled out in morning-glory blue letters across the top. "I don't think anyone will notice their names."

I leaned close. Saw nothing. "Where are they?"

"Here." She traced a twist of vine. I tracked her finger and spotted a six. She traced a three in the curves of two adjacent leaves. "I painted them yesterday after you told me Clarence gave the dogs numbers instead of names."

"Subtle." I kissed the top of her head. "Have I told you lately that you're a wonderful woman?"

She preened. "Just this morning when I made you those cheese and bacon waffles. But feel free to gush."

"Real men don't gush. It's a known fact." I hefted the box to my shoulder and carried it toward the hole in the ground that would be Clarence's last earthly address. Camille dashed ahead with a blue tarp and laid it beside the grave. As I settled the box on the tarp, I spotted a silver SUV topping the rise. My gut tightened and I reached for the gun that wasn't on my belt even as I told myself there was no reason, just the instincts of a boy who grew up familiar with every vehicle in an isolated town coupled with the instincts of a man who once wore a badge. "Do you recognize them?"

"No." Camille shaded her eyes. "But they have dogs in the back."

My muscles loosened. "Must be dog trainers who knew Clarence."

The SUV pulled up behind my rig and the men got out. The passenger had short legs, long arms, and gray hair in a braid down his back; the driver was lean with a shock of hair the color of autumn wheat and a brow jutting like a granite ledge. He lifted his hand to us, then opened the rear door. A pair of German shepherds leaped out, studied us with keen interest, then turned in a circle, noses lifted, dark guard hairs riffling in the breeze. The larger one whined, lowered his ears, and tucked his tail.

"Leave it," the driver said. "Sit."

The dog dropped his head, panting a little, and sat.

"I'm glad we didn't bring Nelson," Camille said in a low voice.

I nodded, remembering our discussion over breakfast, our conclusion that he had never been in a crowd of people, would have to be kept on a leash, might be confused and disoriented because he was still wearing his cone. Except for a miniature poodle in the next cage at the vet's office, he hadn't been around other dogs since the day his kennel-mates died.

Camille walked toward the newcomers, right hand extended. "Welcome. I'm Camille Chancellor. And this is Dan Stone."

The passenger gripped her fingers in a paw the size of a catcher's mitt. "Trev Rainwater." He thrust his chin toward the driver. "Virgil Stanfield."

"Pleased to meet you." Virgil gave her a little bow as he took her hand in both of his. "Thank you for letting us know about the funeral. I hope you don't mind that we brought along Prowler and Hawk."

"I'm sure Clarence would have wanted that," Camille said.

"Glad you could make it." I slid my hand into the vise of Trev's fingers and gave as good as I got, profiting with a half smile and what I took for a glint of respect in his gray-brown eyes.

Camille studied the ground in front of the dog called Prowler. "What did you tell him to leave? I don't see anything."

"That was a death alert," Trev said.

"A death alert?"

"Uh . . ." Virgil released her hand and shifted from foot to foot. "Prowler's what some call a cadaver dog."

The dog whined and Camille paled. "You mean he finds dead bodies?"

Virgil nodded. "It's a nasty job, but if it needs to be done, he's one of the best."

"Smells them right through the ground," Trev said. "Through water too."

"His nose must be in overdrive." I glanced around the cemetery thinking of two hundred years of burials, of the C marked next to dogs Three and Four in Clarence's logbook.

Camille shivered a little, hugged herself, then spoke in a voice too bright and casual. "Where are the rest of your dogs?"

"This is it," Virgil said. "All we need."

She frowned. "Clarence had eight."

His thin lips stretched into a smile that rearranged the geology of his face, creating new ledges beneath his eyes. "Most of us have only one. Clarence was . . . well, he was one of a kind."

99

"Did it his own way," Trev grunted with more than a little pride.

"He got results," Virgil said. "That's what matters."

Trev's huge fists clenched. "If I catch who killed him, we won't need a judge and jury because there won't be a trial."

"I feel the same," Camille told him. "And I'll cut him into a hundred pieces and scatter him in the woods so there won't be a funeral, either."

Trev grinned but Virgil took a step back.

"She's got imagination and she can carry a grudge." I slung an arm around her shoulders. "Fortunately, I like that in a woman."

Camille elbowed me in the ribs.

I mock groaned. "And she's feisty."

Rolling her eyes, Camille adopted a somber tone. "We'd like it if you and the dogs took places of honor at the head of the grave. And of course we want you to stay on for the potluck afterward."

"We'll be pleased to do that." Virgil glanced at a string of vehicles cresting the ridge. "Thank you."

He and Trev called the dogs to their sides and marched to the gravesite where they stood at ease, the dogs flanking them like bookends.

I got to work directing traffic and Camille hauled a huge bucket of daffodils and tulips from the back of the SUV and handed them out. At the end of the service, mourners would toss them into the grave.

Mary Lou and Lou Marie arrived and ushered people to places in a rough semicircle. Jefferson talked with Trev and Virgil and squatted to commune with Hawk and Prowler. Priscilla, driving the truck that had once belonged to my brother, came with Luke. Had she brought the handyman to make a statement about his status or to acknowledge that he was more than an employee? An employee I still knew almost nothing about.

Priscilla shook her head when Mary Lou pointed to a place near the center of the group around the grave, lifted her chin, and flounced to the end of the semicircle, the full skirt of her bright green dress brushing against others as she walked. Luke followed and took up a position two feet behind her. He kept his gaze locked on the grave, fingers pleating a voluminous black-and-red-striped shirt I suspected once belonged to Willie Dean, legs bowing out against the stiff fabric of a pair of black jeans. Priscilla continued to hold her chin aloft.

I gave up on trying to interpret the subtext between them and turned my attention to a rusty green truck with a camper shell—Colden Cornell. Telling myself this wasn't a private event and he had a right to be here if he wasn't intrusive, I waved him to an open spot and hustled to spread the word that he was a reporter. Mary Lou nodded, scurried to his side, led him to a place between Evan and Freeman, and anchored herself in front of him. When he lifted the camera slung around his neck, Evan gripped his arm and levered it down, while Freeman leaned in and spoke a few short sentences punctuated by an uplifted index finger. Colden chewed at his mustache, then nodded and lowered the camera.

Reverend Balforth, his black suit shining in the sun like a grackle's wing, was among the last to arrive. I saw his lips moving as he counted those gathered around the grave, saw him frown and pause when his gaze reached the dogs. Was he considering the propriety of their presence or reconsidering a biblical reference to canines?

Camille darted to his side, slipped a pink tulip into his lapel, and said something I couldn't hear. Balforth patted his pocket and walked to the foot of the grave. Taking her place at the end of the semicircle across from Priscilla, Camille motioned for me to join her.

I took her hand and raised it to my lips. "Write the sermon for him, did you?"

Color flared on her cheeks and I chuckled. "Busted."

"I gave him a few ideas," she murmured. "And asked him to keep it short."

"Good luck with that last part."

"Well I had to try." She shrugged her shawl off her shoulders, revealing a silky blouse the color of heavy cream. "It's getting warm out here."

"Oh no," I whispered with mock horror. "Priscilla's gelatin salad will melt."

Camille compressed her lips to stifle a laugh, Stub Wilson ducked his head like a turtle, and Marcella slapped a hand over her mouth.

Traditions come in all shapes and sizes, all colors, textures, and flavors, right down to the onion, green pepper, and celery chopped up in that yellow gelatin. Because no one ever told her the truth, Priscilla believed that everyone liked her salad and looked forward to seeing it on the table at community gatherings. And so another tradition came about—disposing of portions in creative and surreptitious ways. When we left the Shovel It Inn this evening, there would be blobs wrapped in paper napkins and tucked into purses, clumps of it on the lower branches of the maples beside the parking lot, and smears on the asphalt from servings stashed on top of tires and bumpers.

Priscilla patted at bleached and teased hair lifted in tufts by the breeze. Were we doing her a favor with false kindness and deceit? Would it be healthier for all of us, Priscilla included, if someone told her to flush her gelatin salad along with her attitude?

"Earth to Dan," Camille whispered, squeezing my hand.

I blinked, squeezed back, and focused on Balforth as he drew a few folded sheets of paper from his pocket, smoothed them, and read in his dry, singsong voice. Ordering myself to listen to the words, not the sound, I noted that he was talking about Clarence's search in the North Woods of Maine, using it as a metaphor for the journey the old dog trainer was on now. Mary Lou blotted her eyes with a tissue. Alda and Pattie followed suit.

I put my arm around Camille's shoulders and drew her close. "Nice job," I whispered. "Beautiful image."

And it had staying power.

Before I slept that night, it came back to me. And when I drifted off, it lured me into a chilling dream about Clarence's last foray and the evil that tracked the tracker.

I woke up sweating and panting, the air around me humming.

CHAPTER 11

When I pulled up beside the old schoolhouse Monday afternoon, Jefferson was splitting wood, muscles rippling beneath his gray T-shirt with each smooth stroke. He raised a hand in greeting, set the ax against the side of the building, brushed at his jeans, picked up a bottle of water, a vest, and a denim jacket, and opened the passenger door. Nelson, sporting a wide blue nylon collar with rabies and ID tags, thumped his tail against my windbreaker on the back seat. Jefferson glanced at him and cocked his head.

I shrugged. "The vet just took his stitches out, Camille's off looking at cabinets, and I'm supposed to watch him for the next few hours. If he starts chewing at the scar, the cone goes back on."

"Got a leash?"

"On the floor with the cone. But I wasn't planning to let him out up there."

"Probably best." With a grunt, Jefferson pulled himself into the seat and snapped his belt. He smelled of seasoned wood and sweat. "No telling what scents he'll pick up or how he'll react."

"Yeah." I put the SUV in gear, thinking about Prowler, the dog trained to sniff for decomposition. Clarence's yard would reek of it.

"I smelled a lifetime of death in that jungle, fresh kills and flesh rotted so bad I . . ." Jefferson rolled down his window, let out a slow breath and drew in another. "Can't even imagine how messed up I'd be now if I did my tour with a dog's nose. Might never have snapped back to my old life."

A dead body released fluids and gases. How would those smells compare to the scent of the person when he was still alive? If I let Nelson out, would he be drawn to that stain on the steps but make no connection to Clarence, or would the scent create a clear memory of the man who cared for him? Would he hunt for his master? Or would he understand that Clarence was gone?

"He's barely more than a pup," Jefferson said in a voice hollow with false hope. "Probably won't understand what he's sniffing."

"Probably not," I agreed with the same tone.

We rode in silence for a mile, Jefferson snapping and unsnapping his dark green down vest, me reaching for the radio knob twice and pulling my hand back as if it was on fire.

Jefferson cleared his throat, worked another snap closed, and shifted in his seat. "Seems like Colden Cornell collected enough information from Virgil and Trev to write a book instead of one little newspaper story. Guess that's how reporters do it." He nodded at Nelson. "Lou Marie says you'll have to read the article so you can train him."

"I don't think he'll make much of a search and rescue dog with only three legs." I peered into the rearview mirror and noted that Nelson wasn't chewing at the incision and, in fact, seemed to be asleep. "Bound to affect his speed. And endurance. Besides, I'm not thinking of becoming a dog trainer and I can't send him off alone."

"Could be interesting, though," Jefferson mused. "Being a trainer. Virgil's been to seven states and three countries."

"Well, I don't intend to go out of this county until Camille and I get our place built. And then it won't be with a dog."

But it would be with a teenager. Given Rachel's impending death—the next truckload of trauma barreling down the road toward Julie Miller— Camille and I couldn't leave her home alone. Maybe we should plan something for Christmas vacation. Hawaii or the Caribbean or London or Paris. Julie would like that. She longed to see more of the world. Her brother's travel plans were now in the hands of the military. Odds were, given the usual unrest around the globe, he'd see more of the world as well.

Jefferson fiddled with another snap on his vest. "What kind of a name is Colden, anyway?"

"Beats me."

"Could be his parents started with Holden and changed a letter. And Cornell could be like the university."

That reminded me I still had no family name for Luke. Yesterday I asked Mary Lou as we stood in the buffet line, waiting for our chance at Pattie's peach pie.

"He never offered it and neither has Priscilla. And he hasn't gotten a scrap of mail since he came." Her whisper was tinged with indignation. "They hauled his truck off for scrap and the plate went with it so you can't get his name that way. He never writes a check in the store. Or tries to cash a paycheck, either. Maybe Priscilla pays him in cash."

She paused and glanced at Priscilla who was spooning whipped cream on two slices of pie. "Or in-kind."

Her tone had been both catty and annoyed and I tamped down amusement. My curiosity had been honed by law enforcement training and encounters with a variety of lowlifes, but hers was nurtured by years at the hub of Hemlock Lake's gossip web. It was a stronger and more passionate variety.

We crested the ridge and descended into Clarence's valley, tires shimmying in the mud created by yesterday's rain. When we pulled into the yard, Nelson sat up, raised his ears, and thumped his tail against the seat. I felt a lump of sadness behind my sternum. "Sorry boy." I shut down the engine. "You're staying in the rig."

Nelson whined and lunged, getting his front feet on the console.

"No," I commanded. "Stay."

Whining once more, Nelson wagged his tail harder and panted a little.

"No. Down. Stay down."

He hesitated, but then lurched backward. His rear leg caved beneath him and he sat, then lay on the seat, nose raised, nostrils flaring.

"You training him?"

"Not yet. You can thank Clarence for what he knows." I dug two flashlights from the console, rolled the window down a few inches, and closed the door. "I've discovered about ten commands he recognizes. But he thinks obedience is optional. Camille caught him with one of her shoes last night and had to go after him with a flyswatter to get him to drop it."

"Never mess with a woman's shoes, son." Jefferson aimed a finger at Nelson. "Even I know better than that."

Nelson's tail thumped the seat and Jefferson cracked the passenger window and shut the door. "What's the plan?"

I told him about the mud on Clarence's knees and elbows and the absence of mud on the doormat and scraper. I told him I believed Clarence ran from someone in the woods and that I hoped to find evidence of where he'd been. "There might be something in the kennels, or that little shed."

"Any idea what we're looking for?"

"A notebook—one small enough that he could stick in his pocket and take along when he was training the dogs." I shrugged. "Maybe a map. I'm guessing he went north and east." I gazed out beyond the house at a swelling ridge tinged with the yellow-green of budding leaves. "The last entry in his logbook said the wind was from that direction."

"And wind carries scent," Jefferson agreed. "Let's start with the kennels. I'll take the end closest to the road."

That left me the side with Nelson's former kennel. I started there, noting that the rear panel was still off. The dog control officer who had taken him out and delivered him to the vet hadn't closed it. But why should he?

I clicked on the flashlight and surveyed the space. A simple globe light fixture was mounted in the center of the low ceiling—probably a source of heat as well as light. The switch, I expected, was in the central shed. For a moment I debated whether to walk back there, but decided the space was small enough to search with the flashlight beam. Grasping a corner of one tangled blanket, I pulled. It came loose with a ripping sound; blood had glued it to the floor. The next blanket came up the same way. I shook them both out and tossed them aside, then yanked at the sofa cushion. It came without protest and without revealing a hidden object.

The other kennels also yielded nothing except blankets, cushions, clumps of hair, and bits of rawhide chews. I found nothing in the pens, either.

"Not a damn thing," Jefferson reported when we met at the shed. With a frown, he fingered the open padlock hooked into the hasp that secured the metal door of the shed. "Been cut. Didn't Clarence have the key on him?"

"He had a ring with three keys in his pocket."

"House. Truck. Third could have been for this or his post office box or a strongbox or cabinet. Maybe his glove box."

I nodded. Perhaps investigators, in a hurry to conduct a preliminary search, had cut the lock. Or perhaps the third key on the ring hadn't fit this lock. Maybe Clarence, unable to phone for help and hoping to preserve something that would help explain what happened, stashed a clue in the shed, snapped the lock shut, and tossed the key away.

Jefferson seemed to read my mind. "Maybe he left us something."

I tucked my flashlight in my back pocket and lifted the lock free of the hasp. The metal scorched my fingers. "Hot," I yelped, letting it drop.

"He's not happy with us." Jefferson bent and, ripping up a clump of grass to shield his fingers, retrieved the padlock. "We're trying, Clarence. We're doing the best we can."

I blew on my fingers. "I understand your frustration, Clarence. I'm not what you hoped for in the next-of-kin department. But I haven't given up."

Air swirled around my head like a swarm of bees and then was still. I swung the shed door wide, felt along the wall, and found a pair of switches. I hit the first one, saw nothing, decided it must control the bulbs in the kennels, and hit the second. The light came on, revealing a room about five feet wide and ten feet deep. It was unfinished, the floor just plywood, the studs exposed. An array of round metal kitchen garbage cans—the kind with tight-fitting lids raised by stepping on a pedal at the base—hunkered along one wall. A sturdy set of steel shelves loomed on the opposite side, and two dozen hooks speckled the rear wall. Except for the switch plate, the slices of wall on either side of the door were bare.

The air hummed.

"Give us a hand, Clarence." Jefferson stuffed the padlock in the pocket of his vest and opened a trash can. "Kibble." He opened another and plunged a hand into it. "Notebook could be buried in one of these."

"Let's haul them outside and dump them."

"Want to salvage the kibble for Nelson? You might save enough to buy Camille another pair of shoes."

"Might as well." I dug in the pocket of my jeans and found the house key. "See if you can find some bags."

Jefferson hesitated for a fraction of a second, then squared his shoulders, snatched the key, and strode off. I turned my attention to the contents of the shelves—toenail clippers, a couple of cones like the one Nelson just shed, brushes and combs, a collection of rubber toys in the shape of ducks and dumbbells and footballs, nests of bowls dented and chewed around the edges, and stacks of old blankets folded into squares and smelling faintly of detergent and bleach. The hooks on the rear wall held leashes, harnesses, and a fluorescent orange vest with reflective tape strips. I ran my hands over it, feeling for a pocket or crevice. Nothing.

I felt along the length of each harness and leash. Nothing.

Back at the shelves, I checked each toy for signs it had been sliced open to hide a notebook or key. Nothing.

I picked up a stack of blankets and shook out each one. Nothing.

The second and third stacks yielded the same result.

As I was sorting through the bowls, Jefferson appeared in the doorway with a handful of black garbage bags. "Find anything?"

"Not even mouse crap."

"Notebook's got to be in the kibble."

"Or not."

Jefferson said nothing and we got to work jockeying the cans outside where we squatted and used a couple of battered metal bowls to scoop out kibble, hoping to see the flutter of notebook pages.

What we got, deep in the second can, was the key.

Jefferson gave me an okay sign with thumb and forefinger.

"Doesn't mean he put it there," I said. "It could have fallen out of his pocket."

"Yeah. But I still like our theory."

When the kibble was gone, we turned the cans over, hoping to find something taped to the underside. We tapped them in search of a hidden compartment. Nothing.

My notebook theory faded like winter twilight.

"Damn." Jefferson lurched to his feet, groaned, and massaged his knees. "At least you got provisions for Nelson."

I stood, joints warning me that forty wasn't far off, and glanced at the SUV. Nelson had commandeered the passenger seat. A circle of condensation and a trickle of drool marked the window. "Maybe Clarence didn't have a notebook. Maybe he had a cast-iron memory. Maybe he didn't have a map of the area either."

"Seems like he would have. At least at first. Until he got to know the terrain." Jefferson rubbed his brush cut. "If it was me, I'd hang it on a wall so I could see it easy."

"His walls were blank. Not a painting, not a photograph, not a nail hole or tack mark."

"He could have patched and painted," he offered in a tone that implied he didn't believe that. But then his eyes brightened. "What if he didn't pin it up? What if he taped it to a piece of cardboard or plywood and propped it on his desk?"

I scratched one eyebrow, not buying that.

Jefferson took off his glasses, pulled his shirt loose from his pants, and polished the lenses. In a moment he shoved his glasses back on, strode into the shed, and called out, "It could have been right here."

112

I found him staring at a line of three nail holes in the studs above the space where the kibble bins stood. Jefferson nodded at the hooks on the back wall. "He had a coffee can full of spare hooks in the garage, so he didn't drive nails here to hang leashes or collars." He stepped closer to the wall and peered at a hole. "He didn't take this nail out with a hammer. See how the edge of the hole is enlarged left and right."

Aware of a faint hum in the air, I examined the next hole over and saw it was the same. Someone had toggled the nails back and forth, expanding the holes until he could pull the nails free.

"He was in a hurry," Jefferson said.

"Or too tired to walk to the garage to get the hammer. Where is this thing now?" I spanned my hands, measuring between the far nails. "It's about a yard wide."

"And it's plywood, or a chunk of laminate, something tough. Not paper or light cardboard, or else he could tear it off the nails instead of yanking them out."

We turned in opposite circles, scanning the narrow room. The air sizzled like frying bacon.

"Gotta be around here," Jefferson said. "Gotta be close by."

I didn't comment, afraid of resuscitating my theory to see it shot down again.

Jefferson rubbed his brush cut, took another look around, and stepped outside. I followed and watched him circle Clarence's old truck, lift a tarp folded in the bed, then try the doors. "Locked," he muttered, and dropped to his knees in the gravel, then flopped onto his back and wiggled under the engine compartment. "Nothing here," he reported. "Or under the truck."

I let out the breath I hadn't realized I'd been holding.

Jefferson slapped a hand against a fender. "Why didn't he drive off?"

The same question I'd worried at since my visit to the sheriff's office. "Maybe he didn't realize the killer was right behind him. Or maybe he did and knew he couldn't get the dogs loaded into the truck in time. And he couldn't leave them. Wouldn't leave them."

"Why not open the pens and let them loose? Some of them might have gotten away."

"Maybe he thought if they were penned up, not a threat, the killer would spare them."

"I can see it happening that way."

But did it? Would we ever know?

We stood for a long moment staring at the empty kennels, then I admitted defeat. "Well, it was worth a shot. If he had a notebook, and if it dropped from his pocket when he fell in the woods, we could search for months and never find it, even with a map to tell us about where to search. Let's close up and get gone."

"Works for me. I'll bring the padlock."

I heard his boots crunch gravel, heard him inhale sharply. Turning, I saw him staring past me.

"There's something there." He pointed. "Under the shed."

I bent and slid my hand beneath the shed, prepared to find only a flattened cardboard box or a slice of leftover linoleum. My grasping fingers touched the rough edge of a piece of plywood. I drew it out into the light.

114

Jefferson whooped.

The air crackled.

I stared at the topographic map glued to the wood. An inked *X* indicated Clarence's house. North and east of it, on the other side of a precise rhomboid drawn in the same ink, was a rusty smear inside a penciled circle.

The person who drew that circle had pressed so hard he gouged a furrow in the paper and left the pencil point embedded in it.

CHAPTER 12

"Looks like your theory is sitting up and receiving visitors," Jefferson said.

With a grunt of acknowledgment, I peered at that rusty smear, the hair on the back of my neck prickling.

Blood? Clarence's?

Leaning closer, I spotted lines and whorls. A fingerprint?

I altered my grip on the board so I held it pressed between my palms, leaving no more prints of my own. "Let's get this in the house."

Jefferson nodded, strode ahead, slipped the key into the lock, and opened the door wide. The air whirred and purred. I propped the map on the sofa, called the sheriff from the phone in Clarence's office, and told him what we found.

"Bring it on down and I'll get it to the lab," he instructed. "Give me the coordinates and I'll get a team together to check out that spot. How far is it?"

I relayed the question to Jefferson.

"Hang on a sec," he called from the living room.

In a moment he joined me in the office. "At least three miles from this house. Depending on what they have to go over and get around. The way the contour lines are stacked up tells me some of those ridges are steeper than a ski run in hell."

I passed that on to the sheriff along with the coordinates and he asked if our map showed another way in. "Isn't there an old summer camp up around there?"

"The camp's off to the west on the other side of the Birchkill."

"Crap. That's right. See anything promising along the highway east of there?"

I passed the question to Jefferson who returned to the living room and came back shaking his head. "Nothing obvious, but the terrain out that way isn't as rough. Might be some old logging roads."

"I heard that," North said. "The day's about done and sunset's at—what?—pretty quick after 7:00. Can't get a team on it tonight." He cursed under his breath. "Might be nothing up there anyway."

"Yeah."

I felt that prickling on my neck. There was something up there. Something to kill for.

"Bring that map down quick as you can." North ordered, then lowered his voice and mumbled, "Thanks for the help."

"No problem," I told the indifferent dial tone.

"He'll send a team out in the morning, but he wants the map right away." I hustled to the living room and lifted it between my palms again.

Jefferson opened the door for me and locked it behind us. "Mind if I ride along?"

"No. But wouldn't you rather get home?"

He shifted from foot to foot and worried the snaps on his vest again. "Lou Marie wants us to have a talk the minute I get back."

117

I winced. When a woman wanted to have a talk and set a time to do it, the topic wasn't going to be sports or movies or what to have for dinner. That talk would be about her feelings, your faults, and the sorry state of the relationship you failed to contribute enough to.

"Yeah," he said with a wince of his own. "It was all so clear before I left for Vietnam. The future was laid out. I didn't have doubt one. But now . . ."

"Well, you were away a lot of years and you lived in a lot of hard places. The load of memories you're carrying would bring me to my knees. Maybe you need more time to adjust."

"That's what I told her before Christmas when she said she hoped to find an engagement ring under the tree." He gazed off up the narrow valley. "She was fine with that for a bit. But for the past month, every morning after she serves up the eggs and toast she stares at the calendar and then at her left hand. Doesn't say a word. Just stares."

Careful not to stumble and drop the map, I navigated the porch steps, imagining her harsh silence, bitter seasoning for those eggs.

"She loves me," he said in a mournful voice. "I owe her."

I didn't answer. He got ahead and gripped the latch on the cargo hatch. Nelson squeezed between the front seats and nose-dived into the back.

"She gave up her life to wait for me," Jefferson said in voice both uncertain and proud. "A lot of women wouldn't have."

But it served Lou Marie to do that just that. Donning the habit of sacrifice and taking a self-imposed vow of chastity allowed her to set herself apart from the world and craft both reason and excuse for rubbing her wound raw each day, nurturing stinging resentment, and turning her grief outward to inflict pain on others, especially her sister. Mary Lou made deep sacrifices of her own over those years, but hers sprang from the kindness and generosity that were the bedrock of her nature. If she was sugar, Lou Marie was salt.

"I thought about talking to Mary Lou. She has a way of helping me understand what . . . what I don't understand." He raised the hatch. "But I don't know if that's such a—"

With a sharp bark, Nelson hurled himself into the cargo compartment and sprawled on the carpet. "Get ahold of him," I ordered.

Jefferson released the hatch and reached for the dog's collar. Nelson scrabbled aside, flung himself to the ground, staggered upright, and headed for the house.

"Nelson," I called. "Come."

Jefferson ran after him. "I'll head him off at the porch."

I set the map in the cargo compartment. Nelson paused on the steps to sniff the dark stain and whimper. Jefferson lunged for him, but he slipped past and doubled back, scuttling along the front of the kennels, his whimper swelling to a keening, wailing yowl.

"Nelson," I roared. "Come. Now!"

"You're whistling in the wind," Jefferson panted. "You herd him and I'll sweep around behind the pens and get in front of him."

I stalked the dog as he cast back and forth in front of the kennels. "He's pretty weak still," I called. "Maybe he'll tire out. Or fall over."

119

Nelson halted at his old pen and nosed at the ground. He trembled, tail tucked beneath his legless hip, then lifted his muzzle, howled, and took off across the yard, angling away from me.

"Come," I bellowed. "Come here right now."

He kept going, crossing the dandelion-infested lawn, arrowing between two birch saplings at a hopping run, heading for the woods beyond the meadow.

Jefferson emerged from behind the kennels. "Looks like he's on a mission."

"Damn it." I slammed the cargo hatch. "It was my bright idea to save his life. I'll go after him."

"There's a proverb about being responsible for the life you save." Jefferson rested one foot on the bumper and tightened the laces on his boot. "Since I saved yours, I'll be coming along. We've got two hours of daylight left and I'd just as soon chase that dog as have a talk with Lou Marie."

He opened the passenger door and retrieved the bottle of water and his jacket. "You got a gun along?"

"No." The one I once carried burned up in the lodge along with most of the family arsenal. Only two rifles and a shotgun Ronny hauled outside in an effort to kill me survived, and those were now stashed in the rafters of the garage. After we decided Julie would be part of the family, Camille requested there be no rifle rack in the new house, no visible weapons to remind her of how her father died. "I had enough of guns last summer."

"Just thinkin' it wouldn't hurt to have one now." Jefferson closed the door and patted his pockets. "Guess a knife will have to do."

The hair on my neck prickled again and I wondered what he thought might be out there. I didn't ask, didn't want my anxiety to feed on his. Grabbing my windbreaker and Nelson's leash, I closed the doors and locked up. "I've got a knife." One that would max out slicing an apple. "You still got that flashlight?"

He nodded.

I dug out my cell phone to fill Camille in and remembered this was a dead zone. Getting into the house would eat up time better spent chasing Nelson. And we'd be back soon. How far could a three-legged dog run before he collapsed? "Let's go."

Hummocks of dead grass, like mounded graves, dotted the meadow. In the standing water between them, a few of the tiny frogs we called peepers warmed up for the evening chorus, pulsing out thin, high-pitched cries. We zigzagged, mud sucking at our boots, forcing us to lean and thrust ourselves toward the birches that marked the far boundary of the meadow like a tall picket fence. "If you see a notebook or a scrap of paper, sing out."

"Let's hope it wasn't just a scrap or it would have dissolved by now." He stumbled and cursed under his breath. "Another tablespoon of water and this would be an official swamp."

"Clarence must have come across here. Maybe there's a trail we haven't stumbled on."

"I'm betting Clarence had the good sense to go around." He pointed. "The dog did."

Off to our right, Nelson heaved himself through high grass. When he angled left, I saw our paths would intersect and slogged faster. But he slipped into the woods before I reached the far edge of the meadow.

121

"There," Jefferson said. "To the left of that blighted pine."

We passed through the line of birches, stumbled beneath drooping pine boughs, and crossed a thick mat of brown needles that stuck to the mud plastered on our boots. Jefferson skidded, cursed, caught himself against a sapling, and scraped his boots on its trunk. I kicked mine against a rock as I peered around. "I don't see him."

"Me neither. What's the plan?"

"Plan?" I panted out a fractured laugh. "Do I look like a man with a plan?" A flash of movement caught my eye. Nelson's white tail. "Wait! He's just topping that low ridge. See?" I scuffled through a welter of broken branches, scanned the hillside, and spotted the faint trace of a trail. "This way."

Keeping my eye on the jut of crumbling shale where I'd seen Nelson, I angled my way up the ridge, Jefferson close behind. Near the top I climbed almost straight up, hauling on grapevines and saplings, grunting and cursing, wondering how the hell a three-legged dog made it, how Clarence made it.

If he came this way.

I skidded on broken shale, fell to my knees, and crawled the last yards to a narrow saddle of level ground littered with suitcase-sized rocks. Beyond that the ground fell away, then rose again in a series of folds and gathers as if a giant hand had clutched at the fabric of the earth. "I don't see him."

Off to our left, stone clattered on stone.

"Could be him. Or a deer." Jefferson's fingers strayed to his pocket. "Or something else."

I heard another clatter and a yelp. "Nelson," I shouted. "Come."

Jefferson snorted and shook his head, but didn't call me a fool. A measure of our friendship. I trotted along the spine of the ridge, shouldering my way through thickets of scrub oak, stumbling over rotting tree stumps hidden by drifts of decaying leaves.

Twice more we heard Nelson yelp, always ahead of us, always climbing. We crested the last in a stack of ridges and wound through a jumble of boulders strewn in a ragged row like the broken spinal column of an enormous prehistoric lizard. I hauled myself up on one of them and, from that vantage point, spotted Nelson's pennant of a tail, only a hundred yards ahead, but gaining speed on the downslope.

Cursing, we continued the chase. The descent along the shoulder of the stunted mountain we'd climbed was gentle at first, but then Nelson plunged over the rim of a pine-studded ravine. We followed in a rush, clutching at young trees, our hands growing black and sticky with pitch. A tumble of ankle-twisting rocks clogged the banks of the narrow stream at the bottom of the ravine and we halted where water hurled itself over a lip of rock with a hiss and a splash, plummeting twenty feet into a narrow pool.

"Do you see him?" I peered into the murky depths of the deeper ravine opening below. "Hear him?"

"Can't hear a thing over this waterfall." Jefferson took a swig of water and offered me the bottle. "And there hasn't been any sunlight down there since half-past noon."

"And no light at all in about an hour." I drank, then kicked a rock over the lip of the falls. "I vote we leave him. Put water in a bowl at Clarence's place. Scatter some kibble. If he's smart enough to find his way back, he can eat, fight off coyotes, and wait around until I feel like driving up here again."

Which would be about three seconds after Camille finished chewing me out for leaving him alone in the woods.

Jefferson licked his forefinger, checked the wind, and pointed beyond the waterfall, to the end of the lower ravine and a notch shrouded with pine and hemlock. "If he's following a scent on the wind, he'll go that way."

"And if he's just out to lead us on a merry chase, he could double back and head for Virginia."

Jefferson kept his finger aimed at the notch. "That way's the direction of the bloody mark on Clarence's map."

I glanced around but saw no landmarks and only a chunk of sky easing along the spectrum from blue to indigo. "How can you tell?"

"The shadows." He pointed behind us to the top of the cut we just navigated and tapped his head. "And I've got an internal compass."

"I'd feel better if you had a real compass," I groused. "Just, you know, for the purpose of comparison."

He drew himself up. "You're speaking to a man who—"

"That's it." I snapped my fingers. "Speak," I shouted. "Nelson, speak!"

A faint bark echoed from deep within the gloom of that notch.

"Well, that's one command he obeys," Jefferson observed. "Let's go. We're close to that mark on the map. We've come more than two miles."

"How do you know?" In the maze of ridges and ravines, I'd long-since lost track of direction and distance. "You have an internal odometer?"

He didn't smile. "I've been using dead reckoning."

Dead reckoning.

The words reversed positions in my mind. A reckoning with the dead? For the dead? By the dead?

I wondered again what Jefferson imagined lay before us and picked up a hefty limb from beside the stream. Water had stripped its bark and branches and bleached it like a bone; it felt silky against my fingers, but solid in my grip. "Let's find a way down."

"Left looks easiest." Jefferson pointed at a tilting and uneven staircase of broken rock beside the waterfall. Moss grew thick in the crevices, glistening with the constant spray that nurtured it and the gnarled shrubs sprouting from fissures and on narrow ledges.

How the hell had Nelson managed that? I forced a laugh, hoping to appear cocky. "Easiest compared to what? Climbing the Matterhorn on stilts?"

"Having that talk with Lou Marie."

He turned sideways, anchored his left foot, and tested the first slab with his right. It held without a wobble and he stepped down. "It's solid. Critters use this regularly. See where the moss doesn't grow?"

Despite his confident words, he tested each step. The fourth one shifted beneath his boot with a grating sound. He grasped a knotted shrub, stomped, and sent a sliver of stone tumbling into the pool below. A ring of water rose, but the sound of the splash was swallowed by the din of the falls.

Jefferson shot me a grin and, using the edge of his boot, scraped pebbles from the step, tested his footing, then put his full weight on it.

I was starting my descent and he was halfway down when a rock tipped beneath his boot, rolling his ankle and tossing him sideways.

He clutched at a scrawny shrub.

It held for a second, then tore loose.

He teetered.

I leaned and stretched out my walking stick.

Too late.

He fell with a twist and landed on his back in a high-water litter of limbs at the edge of the pool. Eyes closed, he lay still as death.

Cursing myself, I scrambled down the remaining rocks. Could I get a cell phone signal from up on the ridge? Could I find my way to Clarence's house and then lead paramedics here?

I reached his side and knelt to search for a pulse in his neck. He groaned, elbowed himself to a sitting position and croaked out a laugh. "Watch that last step, it's a killer."

My lungs released the breath I'd been holding. "You okay?"

"Been better." He gripped my arm and hauled himself to his feet. "The thought of that pitcher of beer you're going to buy will keep me going."

"You can drink on my tab for the rest of your life and I'll still owe you."

"Walk now. Talk later." Wincing, he turned and followed the stream into the notch.

Hemlock and spruce closed in on us, branches twining to create a dim green tunnel that narrowed with every step. I tapped the flashlight in my pocket and wondered how fresh the batteries were, how

126

much light they'd produce and how long that light would last.

After a hundred yards, the stream turned to the left and Jefferson paused to study bits of violet sky framed by branches far above us. In a moment, he pointed to a ridge looming to our right. "That way's northeast."

I scanned pockets of brown needles drifted between thirsty roots along the streambed, but saw no sign of Nelson's tracks. "Speak," I shouted. "Speak!"

We heard nothing except the faint soughing of wind through the trees, the babble of the stream, and our ragged breathing.

Jefferson kept his finger leveled at the ridge. "That way."

I didn't move.

"I'm sure," he added after a few seconds. "A quarter of a mile more, then we turn back, no matter what." He shouldered aside branches, setting off up the ridge, a grunt marking each time he pushed off on his right foot.

We'd gone only a few yards when he halted and pointed at a long scar in the hillside. Something heavy had slid, plowing dead leaves and twigs ahead of it, piling debris against the thick trunk of a pine. The scar wasn't fresh—deer tracks crossed it in two places—but the raw edges weren't yet smoothed by rain and wind, and the smell of decaying leaves hung thick in the air. I probed at the spill of debris against the pine, saw something pale, probed again.

"A notebook," Jefferson said. "Clarence's?"

I bent to retrieve it and flipped through damp pages filled with penciled notations in the same handwriting I'd seen in the logbook. "Appears to be."

He nodded, lips compressed, then climbed again, grunting and huffing like an old steam locomotive gathering speed.

Sliding the notebook into my hip pocket, I leaned into the slope and followed, levering myself along with the stick, the muscles in my legs tight after our brief stop, the sweat on my spine icy with the freshening breeze. We were halfway to the top, making our way around a thicket of oak, when we heard a crackle of brush and saw a flash of movement.

"Nelson?" I dug for my jackknife. "Nelson?"

Brush crackled again and I saw that Jefferson had his knife open, saw a blade that would do far more damage than mine. He eased to one side and braced himself against a young pine. I took two steps in the other direction and raised my stick.

With a whimper, Nelson dragged himself from the thicket, head down, tail tucked against his belly. I dropped the stick and he came to me and cowered against my legs, his muzzle scratched and bloody. Tufts of hair had been ripped from his side and his legs were dark with dried mud. His eyes focused back the way he came.

"Damn you, Nelson." I whipped the leash from the pocket of my windbreaker, twisted his collar around, and snapped it on. The reek of primal fear filled my nostrils. "Where the hell have you been? What did you get into?"

"I'm thinkin' we should check that out before night closes in," Jefferson said.

"And I'm thinking we should get out of here."

"We've come this far." He whetted his knife against a sapling. "And you allowed me a quarter mile."

Good points.

But not good-sense points.

"We'll come back tomorrow. When it's light."

"Whatever's out there might be gone tomorrow."

Exactly my hope. But I'd be damned if I'd admit that.

"A quarter mile." I grasped the stick in one hand and the leash in the other. "But not one foot beyond."

"Not even an inch," he agreed.

Nelson fought me all the way to the top of the ridge, whimpering and twisting against the collar, digging in with his paws, once flopping onto his side.

"Dog's afraid to go back," Jefferson noted.

When we plunged into the hollow beyond the ridge, I found out why.

They were waiting.

CHAPTER 13

Jefferson spotted them first.

He flung out an arm, put a finger to his lips, and pointed through interlaced branches heavy with budding leaves.

There were three of them in the twilit glade.

One was stretched out on her back, head cushioned on a pink pillow fringed with silver cord. The second sat at a small folding table placed beside a trickling brook and set with a folded cloth napkin, a gold-rimmed china plate, and a crystal vase holding a withered white rose. The third leaned against a tree as if waiting for someone.

All wore high-heeled sandals, micro skirts, and plunging tops. All had brown hair that fell below their shoulders and bangs that reached their eyebrows. They might once have worn makeup, but that was gone now, weathered from ruined flesh.

"Sweet Jesus," Jefferson whispered.

Nelson whimpered, dropped to his belly, and rubbed his nose in a drift of pine needles. I gagged on the ripe stench of decay and a sour chemical odor.

Jefferson folded his knife and slid it into his pocket. "I imagined a whole lot of things out here, but this . . ."

"This is a whole 'nother kind of nightmare."

"Even over there I—"

With a menacing growl, Nelson lurched to his feet, and stared off into the woods beyond the glade, the hair on his ruff rising.

Stomach knotting, I peered past that domain of death but saw only fluttering shadows cast by wind-tossed branches.

I drew back into the shelter of the trees, pulling Nelson to my side.

"Move out," Jefferson said in a low voice. "Now. Don't stop and don't look back."

Clenching my stick in one hand, I took a few turns of Nelson's leather leash around the knuckles of the other, pivoted, and pulled. He growled once more, then spun and surged past, jerking my arm in its socket and yanking me up the slope.

Following Jefferson's instructions, I didn't glance over my shoulder, didn't try to discern his footsteps from the thudding of my own. But I couldn't stop my mind from creating images of what might hunt us.

What.

Not he or she or they.

It.

There was no humanity in the thing that killed those young women.

The same inhuman thing must have pursued Clarence, executed him, and slaughtered his dogs.

In what seemed like just a minute I reached the scar where I found Clarence's notebook, and in another flash of time made it to the base of the waterfall. It shone like a marble obelisk in the

131

gathering dusk. The splatter and splash of water and the pounding of my pulse made it impossible to hear Jefferson behind me.

If he *was* behind me.

The skin on my back itched and crawled.

Nelson hesitated and I raised my arm, lifting him by the collar. "Come on, boy."

He gathered himself, pushed off, fell short, and flopped to the ground, sides heaving, eyes rolling.

I bent and scooped him under my left arm. Forty pounds. But I was high on fear and adrenaline. He seemed to weigh no more than a paperback book.

Rocks tilted underfoot, and I stabbed with the walking stick, thrusting myself to the lip of the falls, running another dozen yards before I eased Nelson to the ground at the edge of the stream. He squirmed from my grasp, the new growth on his shaved stump prickling against my palm, something sticky coating my fingertips.

Blood?

Pine pitch?

Too dark to tell.

He stumbled, shook himself, and then lunged to the limit of the leash, propelling me to a torturous jog. The spur of fear slices deep. The stench of my terror was rank and so powerful I gagged again and again.

Had Clarence reacted the same way? Did the scent of his fear still hang on low branches and shrubs? Was that what drew Nelson to the glade. Or was it the scent of death?

Before long we faced the steep slope that Jefferson and I slid down less than an hour before. Nelson's lone hind leg gave way after a few yards, but he clawed his way upward. I dug in with the stick, got ahead of him, and kept the leash taut.

The sky visible above the trees at the summit was the color of slate. Night rose like mist from the damp ground, eddying around my knees. The weight of the flashlight pinched my hip, but to use it I'd have to release the stick or hold it along with the leash. And the narrow beam of light would be worse than useless, eroding my night vision while revealing only the terrain at my feet and acting as a beacon, a target.

Better to keep a grip on my stick and rely on the feeble flicker of the single star visible in that slab of sky at the spine of the ridge. When we reached that spine—if we reached it—I'd try for a cell phone signal.

Ears straining as hard as my lungs, I levered my way up the slope, Nelson continuing his belly crawl. We crested the ridge, boulders looming before me, that star brighter, still alone in a steely sky.

The darkness was thicker here, as if the rocks had a magnetic power that drew the night, compressing it beneath overhangs, wedging it into crevices and passageways. The broken string of boulders appeared solid, an obsidian fortress.

Stretching the stick out to my side, I dragged it along the face of the rock, found an indentation, shuffled in, and hit a wall. I retreated, tried again, found another notch, eased in. Nelson made no effort to take the lead. I held the stick before me, swaying it from side to side, tapping rock. Then it struck nothing and in a second we were through and facing the cascade of ridges dropping to that muddy meadow.

I shuffled six steps to my right, pressed my back against the rough rock, worked the leash grip down to the heel of my left hand, and used my fingers to dig the cell phone from my pocket.

No signal.

I cocked my head and held my breath until my lungs screamed.

No sound.

I released air, sucked in more, heard the whinnying cry of a screech owl and a faint but frantic rustling.

A twig snapped off to my left.

Jefferson?

Or something else?

Jamming the phone into my pocket, I hurtled down the ridge, stick swinging, thudding against trees invisible in the murky woods until they rose before me like specters. Nelson yelped, slammed against my legs, and then took the lead, pinballing right and left, setting a wicked pace.

We burst from the woods and sloshed into the mist-shrouded meadow. Too late, I remembered Nelson found an easier path on the perimeter. If the hunter took that, I might see him. If he followed my trail, the meadow would slow him, as well.

Crouching, I burrowed into the haze, zigzagging around hummocks, calf muscles shrieking and jittering. Nelson floundered and I tore him free of the sucking mud again and again. The peepers were in full cry, their calls overlapping and merging into a soup of sound that rasped on my nerves, made me want to throw myself prone and shield my head with my arms.

And then, when I thought my heart would explode or my lungs would collapse, the boundary birches stood before me like sentinels. After scanning the fringe of the meadow and seeing nothing in pursuit, I passed between them onto the lawn. In another moment my soaked shoes hit gravel and I saw a gleam of metal.

I wobbled to the SUV, fumbled for the key, flung open the door, tossed Nelson inside. Vaulting in behind him, I locked the doors.

Sprawled on the passenger seat, Nelson panted in a quick and steady rhythm. My own breaths were irregular—high-pitched wheezing rips that sounded like my lungs were tearing. I laid two fingers on the pulse point in my neck and felt a rolling tempo so rapid I couldn't count detect distinct beats. I shivered and choked on the pungent scent of sweat and fear. Yellow-green nausea swept over me like a wave.

Shoving the seat back, I tucked my head between my knees and fought an undertow of unconsciousness.

Should I start the engine, turn on the lights, illuminate the meadow?

I jammed the key into the ignition and set my foot on the clutch.

No. If Jefferson was out there, I'd light him up for whatever was behind him. And I'd give away my position.

I dug the cell phone from my pocket, remembered this was a dead zone, flipped it open anyway.

Nothing.

Make a run for the house and the phone in Clarence's office?

No. That would expose me.

Power up the SUV, leave the lights off as long as I could, and drive to the hilltop where I'd gotten a signal before?

No. If Jefferson was out there, he'd be alone, at the mercy of . . .

Of what?

By inches, I raised my head until I could peer over the dash. Stars littered the sky now and the meadow was awash with milky mist. It undulated like an inland sea, swelling and falling back, lapping toward me and retreating.

Or was my terror-riddled brain imagining that?

I rubbed my eyes to clear my vision.

A figure loomed where the lawn met the meadow, thirty feet away, just inside the picket line of birches. Tall and bulky, it stood with feet apart.

The figure raised one arm.

Gun?

Power up? Try to get away? Try to run him down?

The arm moved higher.

I gripped the key and the knob for the lights.

The hand brushed at the top of the head.

Jefferson's familiar gesture.

Weak with relief, I cranked the key, flashed the lights, and flung the passenger door wide.

Jefferson trudged across the gravel, shoved Nelson up against the console, and settled himself with a sigh that seemed to rise from the soles of his feet. "That long talk with Lou Marie has more appeal every minute."

I took off in a spray of gravel, sliding my seat forward as we went. "What was out there?"

"Maybe nothing." He snapped his seatbelt and peered into the rearview mirror. "Maybe something more at home in the dark than I ever want to be."

The fact that he hadn't seen anything and didn't know if we'd been pursued sent a fresh spike of fear into my gut. That he seemed in awe of what he hadn't seen twisted that spike.

I stomped on the gas, fishtailing in the ruts.

When we reached the top of the hill, I checked the mirrors, then braked and flipped open the cell phone.

"Where the hell are you?" Sheriff North groused. "We need that map."

"I found what got Clarence killed."

He was silent for the count of three. "I bet I'll die a happier man if you never tell me."

"You'd win that bet." In a few succinct words, I told him what we discovered.

"Christ," he moaned. "Three of them."

"Three that I saw. And . . . it's possible the killer was out there."

"Christ," the sheriff repeated. "I'll get a team together, get deputies strung out along the roads, stop anything that looks suspicious."

He paused and I clamped my jaw, waiting for what I knew would come. "I'm gonna need you to do me a favor, son."

"Someone's got to go back," Jefferson said at the same time. "They'll never find that glade in the dark without our help."

"I'll meet your team at the Shovel It Inn," I told the sheriff. "Give me about an hour to drop off Jefferson and take the dog to Camille."

Jefferson shook his head.

"Thanks," Sheriff North said. "I knew I could count on you."

I flipped the phone closed and turned to Jefferson. "I can find that place again. And I won't be alone."

"I'm coming," he said in a level voice. "But not without firepower."

CHAPTER 14

As it turned out, Jefferson didn't need his rifle.

Along the way we ran into only a couple of raccoons and, when we scanned the glade, found no sign that it had been disturbed.

Perhaps there had been no one in the woods behind us.

Or perhaps the killer had decided to let us live, to relinquish his prizes in a trade for notoriety.

It was after midnight when I grasped the knob on the side door of the garage.

Locked.

I dug for my keys and found only two—my SUV and Camille's car. The garage key, stashed in a drawer, had been lost in the fire that destroyed the lodge.

I tapped at the door panel and, after long, leaden seconds, heard hesitant footsteps and a faint whisper. "Dan?"

"Yes."

"Hang on." A short shuffle. A thump. Then the lock clicked and Camille swung the door wide, pulled me against her, and closed it again, thumbing the button in the center of the knob. I held her tight against my chest, an anodyne against the night's horror. Beyond her shoulder, the dim glow of a clock above the workbench reflected off the barrel of a shotgun.

"Is that loaded?"

"Yes."

"I never told you where I put the shells. Or even that I bought shells."

She nuzzled my neck. "You're a Hemlock Lake boy. You have guns, therefore you have ammunition."

I felt a flash of resentment about the imprint of my heritage and then she went on. "And I'm glad. Having that shotgun beside me—after I found the shells, of course—made the night a whole lot less scary. I bolted the overhead doors, but that knob lock won't hold up against even a half-hearted kick. And the door itself might as well be cardboard."

"I'll get a new one tomorrow. Did it take you long to find the shells?"

"About five minutes." She chuckled. "This place doesn't have more than a few dozen hiding places and I figured you wanted them close at hand, but out of sight and where Julie wouldn't come across them by chance. From there it was just a short intuitive leap to the shelf behind the cleaning products."

She kissed the point of my jaw. "You must be exhausted. Let's get some sleep."

I picked up the shotgun and followed her to the bed. Nelson lay on my usual side but near the foot, his chest rising and falling with deep, slow breaths. A line of butterfly bandages ranged across his stump, and antibiotic cream gleamed in the spaces between them.

"He broke open that scar and he's so tired I can't bear to move him. We'll have to snuggle together."

"Exactly what I had in mind."

Flashing me a smile, she slipped between the sheets. I spooned my body tight against her, expecting sleep to be elusive. But when exhaustion sucked me to the rim of a dark vortex, I let go and fell.

For the next three days, a procession of vehicles rolled through Hemlock Lake to a staging area along the road about a mile beyond Clarence's driveway. Marked and unmarked law enforcement cars and vans. TV satellite trucks and radio reporters in vehicles plastered with call letters. Journalists in an assortment of vehicles ranging from gleaming four-wheel-drive rentals to battered hulks in need of time on a service-bay rack.

Lou Marie did a landmark business selling snacks and pop, and the town, by virtue of being the closest population center to the dump site, was photographed from every angle. Residents who shunned the spotlight were described as tight-lipped, keeping to themselves, or too stunned to comment.

To my relief, no one turned up at my place. No one stalked Jefferson, either. When one TV reporter speculated that a hiker made the "gruesome discovery," and another credited fishermen with "stumbling across the killing ground," I knew our

141

names hadn't been released through official channels or leaked by someone currying favor with the media.

Yet.

Sheriff North called in the big guns right away: state and federal investigators, experts who'd seen this kind of thing before, who knew something about the psychology of a monster who preserved his victims' corpses and staged them. They set up a task force and clamped down on interviews.

By Friday, deprived of fresh sound bites, the media horde moved on and that evening we took our traditional places around the corner table at the Shovel It Inn. When Merle, as usual, set two pitchers of beer in front of Stub, he raised one a few inches and set it down again, sloshing a ribbon of foam from the spout. "Seems almost wrong to be sitting here," he said, "drinking beer and listening to the jukebox while the families of those poor girls . . ."

Johnny Cash sang on about walking the line, but we said nothing. Freeman glanced away from the pitcher, Alda and Pattie folded their hands at the edge of the table, and Evan hung his head.

Then Priscilla reached across Marcella for the second pitcher. "Life is for the living." She raised her chin as if daring anyone to contradict her. "They weren't from here and there's nothing we can do about what happened." She filled her glass and passed the pitcher on to Lou Marie. "So we might as well make the most of the time we have left on this green earth."

Camille laid her hand on my arm. I assumed it was half warning to hold back an attack on

Priscilla's callousness, and half plea to halt a mental review of the details of the autopsy report.

I hadn't sought information held back from the media, hadn't wanted to know about broken bones, poisons, strangulation, and amateur embalming techniques. But Sheriff North, like a man with a terminal disease confessing a lifetime of sin and seeking absolution, spilled them without preamble when he called late last night. Camille, lying next to me, overheard some of it before I threw off the blankets and moved to the far side of the garage to spare her what I couldn't spare myself.

"Tell me," she said when I returned and set the phone on the up-ended five-gallon bucket that served as a nightstand. "Don't hold it to yourself."

I knifed my legs between the sheets. "He's a monster. You don't want to know more than that."

"All right. But don't shut me out, Dan. The more I know about the nature of your wounds, the more I can help you heal." She hugged me close and I felt her tremble, a shiver that came from her core. "If it's possible to heal after an experience like you had out there."

Something I wondered about as well. By discovering that killing ground and those tortured girls, Jefferson and I had exposed ourselves to a disease, a sickness of the soul. Our flight through the shadowed woods was a metaphorical journey out of the pit of hell. But our escape didn't end the horror. We had been transformed by terror and a deepening awareness of evil—evil that might know our faces, our names.

"I'm okay." I'd kissed her hard, trying to convince both of us, then rolled from her embrace, pulling the blanket over my shoulders. "I don't have to work this case, live it every hour."

I had given statements about finding the dump site and answered a battery of questions. But investigators were done with me now and I knew enough about task forces and law enforcement hierarchies to suspect that if I had an idea or a theory I'd be looked on as a stray dog in claimed territory. "I left that job behind, remember?"

"Then why did the sheriff call you? And why this late?"

"He's an insomniac." I pounded my pillow, doubting I'd slide into sleep easily, if at all. "Some deputies speculate that he doesn't own a bed."

"But why you? There must be someone on duty he could talk to."

"He called me because I'm *not* on duty. Because I *don't* work for him."

"Oh," she said, and left me to wonder about the relationship I had with Sheriff Clement North. When he called me "son," was it merely a figure of speech, or was it symbolic of a deeper attachment?

I'd gazed up at the rafters, streaks of deeper black against the dark vault of the ceiling. Some son. I'd screwed up the arson investigation that brought me back to Hemlock Lake, and now, like a dog with its muzzle bristling with porcupine quills, I came to him with this. If he owned a bed, he might as well rent it out until the monster that killed those girls was in custody.

This morning, dazed from lack of sleep, I took Nelson to the old schoolhouse and lounged on the steps as Jefferson split firewood. For a few fleeting moments I thought of passing along what the sheriff had told me. Would that divide my fear or multiply it? Undecided, I sat in silence, stroking Nelson's back in time to the repetitive thunk of ax into heartwood. The dog's white tail flashed in the sun and I wondered if his mind played movies like mine, or whether he had been gifted with the ability to forget until sight, scent, or sound forced memory upon him. If we never returned to Clarence's house or that unholy glade, would he be spared a replay?

When Jefferson had split the last log, I stacked while he raked chips into a box for kindling. Neither of us spoke until I lifted Nelson into the back of my rig. "I was lucky to come out of that jungle," he said, his gaze fixed on the mountains at the end of the lake. "We were lucky again up in those hills. A smart man pays luck its tribute."

All afternoon I'd wondered what he meant by that.

Now, as Lou Marie lifted the pitcher of beer and steadied his glass with her left hand, light flashed from a diamond ring on her third finger and I had my answer.

Lou Marie shoved the pitcher along to her sister, then raised the glass and handed it to Jefferson. The ring flashed again, signaling a debt of honor discharged. Her gaze swept the table, checking, challenging. Camille tapped a finger on my arm and I heard Pattie suck in a breath, saw Alda lean forward and squint.

It was Priscilla who spoke. "Speaking of making the most of the time that's left, is that an engagement ring, Lou Marie? Did you finally get him cornered?"

Lou Marie gripped Jefferson's arm, claiming possession, then thrust out her left hand, fingers curved like claws. The large diamond sat high on a wide gold band loose against the skin below a knotted knuckle. I had no doubt that Lou Marie had selected it for size, showiness, and lack of subtlety. Having waited more than a quarter of a century to present proof of achievement, she damn well wanted a ring that would be noticed. But she hadn't considered all the consequences. Used to delivering sarcastic and scornful comments, she was now on the receiving end. In new territory.

Priscilla examined the diamond with a critical eye, then tossed her head. "They didn't have anything bigger?"

To my surprise, Lou Marie didn't snipe back. Instead she crimped her lips and squirreled her left hand beneath the table. It was the first time I ever saw her unsure, uncomfortable. Her awkwardness made me feel almost protective—not protective of the woman who tormented me when I returned to Hemlock Lake last year, but of the young girl who saw Jefferson off to war.

She shot a glance at him—half appeal and half demand. He squirmed and drank beer. This was fresh territory for him, too. Lou Marie narrowed her eyes and I suspected there would be another talk later.

"I'm just saying," Priscilla continued in a condescending tone, "if I waited as long as you did, I'd want a diamond the size of a headlight. When's the wedding? Are you going to wear white?"

Jefferson, eyes widening, drained his glass. Alda and Pattie gaped, Marcella moved an inch closer to Stub, Camille gripped my arm again, and Evan jammed his elbow into my ribs. I swung the pitcher over and filled his glass. He swallowed beer as if his lungs were on fire.

"She'll wear ivory silk," Mary Lou said in her unruffled way. "An A-line with bell sleeves." She refilled Jefferson's glass and then her own. "I ordered the fabric this afternoon."

Priscilla looked down her nose. "You're not going to sew it yourself!"

"Of course she is." Alda jumped in, cheeks flushed, a finger aimed at Priscilla's chest. "It will be much, much less expensive. And it will fit better than anything off the rack."

Priscilla rolled her eyes. "I'm not saying you don't have talent with a needle, Mary Lou, but . . . Well, it seems so cheap."

Lou Marie glared. "Some of us don't have big life insurance settlements."

Priscilla glared right back. "And some of us don't pinch a penny so hard it squeals. Besides, a homemade dress is old-fashioned. It's provincial."

"Like you're the empress of style and sophistication," Marcella snapped. "Like you—"

Mary Lou raised a hand. "It *is* old-fashioned. And the wedding will be the same. The last Sunday afternoon in June at the Methodist church with a reception right here." She tapped the table, smiled, and gave a broad wink. "Only with champagne instead of beer."

Priscilla wrinkled her nose, then flipped her nails against the tablecloth, pushing the argument aside. "Will you be the maid of honor?"

"Of course." Mary Lou twinkled at her sister and Jefferson and then shot Priscilla a smile just this side of spiteful. "I also ordered the fabric for *my* dress today."

Before Priscilla said another word, Alda and Marcella jumped in with questions about fabric,

147

hem length, style, and color. The men, meanwhile, got busy circulating the pitchers. Stub poured the dregs of one into his glass, waved to Merle, and signaled for refills and a platter of onion rings.

"Who'll be the best man?" Freeman asked.

"I was planning to ask Dan." Jefferson shot me an apologetic glance. "Meant to do that before, but I—"

"I'd be honored." Honored to stand by his side, pleased and grateful to have the opportunity to pay him back even this little bit of what I owed. What I didn't feel was happy that he felt compelled to choose this course.

"Are you planning a wedding trip?" Marcella asked.

"To Maine," Jefferson said. "And over to Nova Scotia."

"In Mary Lou's car?" Stub asked. "You better bring it in for an overhaul if that's what you have in mind."

"They'll rent something new and fancy. And when they come back I'll be moved into the schoolhouse." Mary Lou fixed her gaze on Freeman, Evan, and Stub. "Provided that I get a little help lifting and carrying."

"Happy to assist," Freeman said. "Just say when."

Evan and Stub nodded their agreement, and Marcella, Alda, and Pattie chimed in with promises to save boxes for the move and offers to help rearrange things in the old schoolhouse.

Priscilla, shut out of the conversation, tugged at her low-cut top, sipped beer, and cleared her throat. "A reporter from *The Mountain Missive* came to see me this morning."

"Yeah, he came by the garage too," Stub growled. "Said he was working on a piece called 'Terror in a Tiny Town' or some such shit."

"Wanted to know if we all put new locks on our doors and bought alarm systems or guard dogs," Marcella added.

"I told him to get lost." Stub poured from a fresh pitcher and passed it on. "Told him he was just stirring up crap, scaring folks, trying to get more people to buy that that fish-wrapper of a paper."

The others nodded, pretending they hadn't been hunting up keys to locks they'd never used, but Priscilla shook her head and tutted in annoyance. "You're missing out on free advertising. He took a picture of me on the dock. He's going to put it in the next edition. On the front page."

"I better order extra copies," Lou Marie said in the sharp tone I heard so often before Jefferson returned. "Two or three hundred at least."

"I see you're back to your old sarcastic self." Priscilla tutted again and glanced around the table. "Why does everyone in this town always stick their heads in the sand? Why do you all hang onto the past instead of thinking about the future?"

"Because we like Hemlock Lake the way it is," Evan said.

"Why, Evan Bonesteel." Priscilla laid a hand on her fleshy bosom, fingers spread wide. "I'm stunned. I don't think I ever heard you speak that many words in a row before."

"I talk when I have something to say." Evan aimed a scowl that was the visual equivalent of adding "unlike some people."

Priscilla tutted once more, and Evan ducked his head to his beer, but Freeman took up the gauntlet.

149

"Like you said, Priscilla, those girls weren't from around here and we didn't know them. But they died horrible deaths. It's mean-spirited to exploit that for free advertising and your own vanity."

"It's ghoulish," Alda added.

"Morbid," Pattie contributed.

"Money grubbing," Marcella chimed in, moving a little closer to Stub.

"Well." Priscilla stared at the other women, shook her head, then shoved back her chair and snatched up her purse. "I would have thought that my so-called friends would treat a poor widow better than this. At least you can't say I don't know when it's time to leave."

"You don't," Lou Marie said. "Or you would have gone five minutes ago."

Priscilla gave her a glare a Gorgon would envy, bent close, hissed something I couldn't hear, then stomped off.

Merle, coming with a tray crammed with a platter of onion rings, bowls of special sauce, and a stack of plates, did a sidestep tango and made it to the table without incident. Pattie and Alda exchanged guilty glances and Lou Marie tucked her head and slipped her hands beneath the table again. Jefferson gave me a deer-in-the-headlights glance, and then put an arm around Lou Marie's shoulder. Evan, Stub, and Freeman, however, raised their glasses to Priscilla's back.

As Merle dealt out plates, Mary Lou sighed, worked a napkin loose from the container at the center of the table and smoothed it on her lap. "Well, that wasn't pretty, but it was long overdue."

"Yes," Camille agreed. "It was good of Priscilla to open that door for us."

Mary Lou nodded. "Otherwise we might have gone right on tiptoeing around her feelings."

"With her never giving a shit about ours." Stub off-loaded a quartet of onion rings and passed the platter on. "Guess you won't be getting her autograph on those newspapers, Lou Marie."

Lou Marie flipped her hand, flashing her diamond ring. "And I guess I won't feel obligated to invite her to my wedding."

"Don't stoop to her level." Mary Lou pleated a napkin. "Of course you'll in—"

"No." Lou Marie rammed a fork into a pair of onion rings and transferred them to her plate. It's my wedding and I say who's on the list and who's off."

"Now, Lou Marie," Jefferson said in a soft and tentative voice. "Priscilla's one of us. And she's had a hard time of it."

"And I haven't? I lost the best years of my life waiting for you." Lou Marie drew herself up, color flaring in her cheeks, eyes like flint. "So don't even think that after wandering around the country forever you can waltz in here and tell me what I should and shouldn't do."

Jefferson's face remained still, unreadable. After a long moment he laid his hand over hers and nodded. But when his gaze met mine I saw his eyes were dark with dread.

How many years would he forfeit to pay his debt?

CHAPTER 15

The next day I set about hammering together a set of shelves from lengths of salvaged lumber my father stashed in the rafters of the garage. They weren't great boards—warped, full of rusty nail holes, splotched with paint in colors long out of fashion, or stained so dark the grain was barely visible—but these wouldn't be great shelves. Over the summer, they'd hold Julie's clothing and other possessions. When the house was finished they'd lurk in the garage, offering a home to odds and ends that have a way of accumulating with the years—almost-empty paint cans, broken lamps, chipped bowls—items much like those Camille hauled to the dump back in April.

Thinking about the cycle of possessing and letting go, I pounded in another dozen nails before Camille's car pulled up. "Need any help carrying stuff?" I called.

"No. I found the perfect ceiling fans, but I'll wait until they go on sale at the end of the summer."

"What about help with the groceries?"

"You're just looking for an excuse to give up on those shelves," she said with a laugh. Bottles clinked and bags rustled. "There isn't much. I stopped at Lou Marie's."

I tucked a couple of nails between my lips, set one against the wood, and pounded it home. Most folks in Hemlock Lake did their major shopping at the supermarkets in the county seat. They braved Lou Marie's moods for beer and milk, cans of beans and bags of chips, things they'd forgotten, or items they needed in order to whip up an impulse recipe or fill out a meal for unexpected company. And sometimes they stopped in because they recognized that if the general store folded, there would be a lot more borrowing sugar and flour from neighbors, and a lot more miles driven in a last-minute rush.

In a few minutes Camille wandered around the partition wall, nibbling on a chocolate-covered ice cream bar on a stick. Nelson followed, gazing at her with an expression of dumb adoration.

"That looks decadent," I mumbled around the nails.

"It is. It seduced me as I walked by the frozen food case." She licked a dribble of ice cream from the stick, her tongue curling. "If you spit out those nails, I'll share."

"It's more fun to watch you." I wiggled my eyebrows. "Lick it again."

"Pervert." She turned her back and walked to a lawn chair at the edge of the lake. Nelson trailed behind. The butterfly bandages were gone, but the scar was bright and angry.

I pounded in the last nail, then laid aside my hammer, strolled to the shore, and dropped into a chair beside her. The day was calm and bright, the lake flat and still. Far out, a fish jumped, shedding a dozen diamond drops of water and sending out a triple circle of ripples. Camille handed me the remainder of the ice cream bar and wiped her hands on her jeans. "I bought some pepper spray. But on the way home I started feeling almost silly about that. Should I be afraid?"

I took a full bite. Cold spiked into my brain. That was a question I couldn't answer.

After he dumped the grim details of the autopsies, Sheriff North talked about theories, why the killer chose specific victims, how he stalked them, took them, controlled them, tortured and degraded them, why he preserved their corpses. The youngest girl had been seventeen and the oldest twenty. All had slim builds and brown hair. The twenty-year-old may have been a prostitute. The nineteen-year-old worked as a waitress. The youngest volunteered at a library. Task force members guessed the killer would continue to hunt where he had before—in communities fifty miles and more south of Hemlock Lake.

But what if the destruction of his careful staging sent him careening off on a tangent?

"Should I?" Camille prompted, turning in her chair to study my face. "Should I be afraid?"

I ordered my imagination to shut down, bit the last piece of chocolate skin from the softening ice cream, and held the remainder toward Nelson. His tongue shot out like a frog's, nearly jerking the stick from my fingers. "He didn't hunt around here. And he went after girls. Girls with long brown hair."

She touched her short, crinkled hair. "Julie's hair is long and brown."

"She's younger than his other victims. And her hair is lighter."

Camille frowned. "And a few years and shade of color will protect her?"

"Maybe. Killers like this have distinct preferences, usually for a reason."

She chewed at her lower lip. "How many will he kill? A dozen? Two dozen?"

I'd asked the sheriff the same question. "Every case is different. Sometimes killers burn out and stop. Sometimes they evolve."

"Evolve? You mean they stop killing? They get better?"

"No, just better at what they do. They perfect their techniques." I drew the stick back before Nelson splintered the end of it. "And sometimes they become obsessed and kill to protect . . ." I searched for the right words and settled for ". . . their lifestyles."

"Lifestyles!" Camille rolled her eyes.

"Avocations?" I shrugged. "These people don't think like we do. Their sense of right and wrong is skewed."

"Or nonexistent." She chewed at her lip again, took the ice cream stick from my fingers, bent it into an arc, and straightened it again. Nelson sat back on his haunches, panting, watching. "So, he could decide that you and Jefferson disrupted his lifestyle?"

I arched my brows, pretending this hadn't occurred to me. "I suppose that's possible."

"Then let's suppose he saw you and thinks you saw him. You don't know for sure he wasn't in that glade. He could have followed you back here."

Her voice vibrated the way a taut string does when you pluck it. That set off a jittering resonance in my chest. "He wasn't. He didn't." I rubbed the knotted muscles at the base of her neck. "He's probably a thousand miles away staking out a new hunting ground."

"You don't sound convinced." She studied me for a long moment. "So the answer is that I *should* be afraid."

"No. Living in a state of constant fear could be as damaging as coming up against the thing you're afraid of. You should be cautious. We should both be cautious."

"And what does 'cautious' look like?" Her voice tightened. "An alarm system? A loaded gun beside the bed? Another on my hip?"

I'd been thinking the same things, but admitting that might make the situation worse. "It looks like whatever makes you feel safer."

Her eyes flashed. The stick snapped in her fingers. Nelson bounced off his front feet, barking the way dogs do when they anticipate a game of fetch.

"Down," I roared. "Quiet."

Nelson bounced and barked again.

"Quiet. Sit." I raised a hand to swat him.

"Don't." Camille shot an arm out to stop me, tucked the pieces of the ice cream stick into the pocket of her work shirt, and leaned to stroke Nelson's head. "Sit," she cooed.

He sat without hesitation, resting his chin on her knee. "Sure," I groused, "don't even dream of obeying the man who rescued you."

Camille smiled, a tweak of the lips gone in a second. "What about Julie? How far should we take caution with her? And do you think she'll listen?"

How much did any of us listen at that age?

She pointed at the gaping foundation hole. "This place will be crawling with strangers all summer. Construction workers, electricians, plumbers, carpet layers, delivery men." She scratched behind Nelson's ears, making him grunt with pleasure. "And what if it's not a stranger?"

Something about the way she lowered her voice to a near whisper told me she'd been asking herself that question for days. "What if it's someone who's already here? What if he picked that spot to leave them because he was there before and knew that logging road ran right to it?"

I thought about the old logging road a team stumbled across as they worked an ever-widening search area. It led to the main road—less than half a mile away. Someone had cut evergreen boughs and built a blind a few yards off the highway, a blind large enough to hide a vehicle.

"Hundreds of people might know about that old road. Hunters could have used it for years." I realized that I wanted this evil to originate far from Hemlock Lake, wanted the connection to us and this place to be tenuous and coincidental. "Maybe hikers built that blind so people driving by wouldn't notice their car and turn them in for trespassing."

"Seems like a lot of effort to go to for a hike."

"Hunters, then. Or poachers."

Camille slumped in her chair. When she spoke, it was in an offhand way, but with purpose. "What do you know about Luke?"

"Not much," I admitted. Not as much as I wanted to, as much as I should. "Why?"

"Lou Marie told me to tell you to tell the sheriff to check him out."

I snorted. "No one tells Clement North to do anything. In fact, that's the surest way to guarantee something *doesn't* get done."

"No one knows where Luke came from or what his last name is."

Defend Luke or support Lou Marie? Either choice was a bad one. I took Luke. "That's not a crime."

"No one knows where he goes on his day off."

"That's not a crime, either. In fact," I teased, "sometimes I look back fondly on the days when I lived on the other side of the county and the same could be said of me."

Camille rolled her eyes. "People saw him fishing in the Birchkill."

"Lots of people fish the Birchkill. It's one of the best trout streams in the mountains."

"It's also close to Clarence Wolven's place."

I shrugged remembering how scrawny Luke seemed standing beside Priscilla at Clarence's funeral. I thought of the dead girls and those props hauled into the staging site in the woods. Could he do that alone? "Maybe that's just a matter of geography."

"Maybe." Camille stood, picked up a stone, and skipped it along the surface of the lake. Three, four, five hops, and then a skitter before it sank. "Personally, I think Lou Marie is more interested in getting back at Priscilla than in the welfare of the community."

"Wouldn't surprise me." I went to stand beside her, kicking at the rocky margin of the lake until I excavated the perfect flat, oval stone. I rubbed the dirt from it and cocked my arm.

"Priscilla told Lou Marie she hopes she gets a bladder infection on her honeymoon from having too much sex."

The rock tumbled from my hand. "More than I needed to know."

"Me too. I don't know why Jefferson felt . . . well, it's none of my business."

"Not mine, either," I assured her. "But I know what you mean."

She skipped another rock. "I'm going to run the store while they're away."

"Really?"

"Lou Marie doesn't know." She narrowed her eyes. "And nobody's going to tell her."

I drew an imaginary zipper across my lips.

"She told Mary Lou she could do that and run the post office too and Mary Lou didn't argue. You know how she is, too sweet for her own good. But there's no way she can manage, so I volunteered."

"Lou Marie will find out."

"Maybe." Camille gave me a crafty smile. "And maybe not. After all, who wants to get their head bit off for delivering that message?"

"Good point." I retrieved my rock and bounced it on my palm. "Having somebody with a smile behind the counter will be a nice change for customers. And maybe while you're there you can manage to lose a few cans of that chili she's had on the back shelves since before the flood."

Camille punched my shoulder. "Keep joking, funny guy, because you're going to help."

I edged away as if a sinkhole had opened at my feet. Since I committed to rebuilding the lodge and staying in Hemlock Lake, I'd fought the gravitational pull of its social network. Despite my struggles, I'd become a regular at the Friday night gatherings and the go-to guy for errands to be run on my trips to the county seat. But this? No. Time to draw a line. "I'm not trimming wilting leaves off the lettuce. And I'm not ringing up overpriced potato chips."

She laughed and did her Southern belle impression. "Why I declare, Dan Stone, are you afraid of a few vegetables and a little old cash register?"

I flung the rock and crossed my arms over my chest. "No. I'm afraid of getting sucked into a situation that will eat up my time and lead to a huge explosion when Lou Marie comes back."

"Well you can stop worrying." She stepped to my side and squeezed me in a hug. "Julie will work behind the counter."

I raised a hand. "Hold it. The last time Julie spoke to Lou Marie she called her an old witch and head-butted her into a pile of dirt at the cemetery."

"Lou Marie won't know Julie's working there, either."

"We'll see if you can keep that secret until she leaves on her honeymoon. If you do, it will be a first for Hemlock Lake." I tapped my knuckles on her head. "So what's my role in this fiasco?"

"Not a big one. I might need you to move a box or two and see if you can fix that faulty fluorescent light."

"That's all?"

"That's all."

"Okay." I returned the hug. "But only because I love you." I unlocked my arms and let my hands slide to her hips. "And because I expect you to make it up to me in ways that involve a minimum of clothing."

She smiled and slid her gaze to the garage. "How about an advance payment right now?"

CHAPTER 16

Meetings with the architect and contractor ate up the next few days and Luke slipped my mind until, as I parked in front of the post office, Priscilla Denton hustled out. Without a word or a wave, she hauled herself into her truck and tore off in a spray of pebbles.

"Hair appointment," Mary Lou said before I opened my mouth. "She's late."

"About *ten years* late," Lou Marie called from doorway to the grocery store. "The best thing they could do for that over-bleached stack of straw is to shave it off and put a coat of wax on her scalp. She makes me sick. Driving around in that truck like she owns the whole town and we'd better just get out of her way." With a scowl in the direction Priscilla went, she tromped into the store and slammed the door behind her.

"She's been on the warpath since the other night," Mary Lou told me. "And Priscilla's not helping matters acting all high and might—" She clapped a hand over her mouth.

I grinned. "She really gets your goat, doesn't she?"

162

She flushed and pressed her fingers to her cheeks. "I vowed I'd be a better person after that catty comment I made about her paying Luke in-kind."

"Sometimes it's healthier to be a *real* person." I nodded toward the grocery store. "After all the years of being the anvil under that hammer, you have the right to a little flare-up now and then."

"But Priscilla's had a hard—"

"Forget it." I smacked my palm on the counter. "Priscilla didn't hear a word you said so it doesn't count anyway."

She stared at me wide-eyed, then smiled. "I didn't know there were rules about flaring up."

"Well, now you do." I glanced toward the lake, an idea working at the back of my mind. "I never notice much about women's hair except that it's there. What do they do to Priscilla's?"

"Oh, color, cut, style." Mary Lou patted her graying curls. "Sometimes she even gets a perm."

"Must take time."

"All afternoon." Mary Lou gave me a sly look. "You going to talk with Luke?"

So much for a clandestine operation.

"Yeah. But that's just between you and me."

She nodded and crossed her heart. "Do you think he's got a record? That he's wanted for some kind of crime?"

"Definitely." I grinned. "The crime of trying to have a private life in Hemlock Lake."

Mary Lou punched me, striking the same place Camille had. "Get out of here," she said with a chuckle.

Rubbing my arm, I retrieved my mail from the box and drove to the bait and boat repair operation

163

that had been Willie Dean's. Luke, wearing a ratty gray sweatshirt with the sleeves torn off, knelt on the end of the dock, screwing in nylon boat cleats to replace the splintered remnants of the wooden ones Willie Dean cobbled together years before.

I was all for progress if it meant improvement, but seeing Willie Dean's efforts tossed into a cardboard box labeled "kindling" gave me a gloomy sense of the fleeting nature of life. One day I'd be gone and someone would toss out something I built—maybe those shelves in the garage that listed to one side no matter how many crosspieces I nailed onto them.

I stepped onto the dock and aimed for casual. "Good morning, Luke."

Luke glanced up for all of a second. "Priscilla's gone to get her hair done." He turned a foot-long screwdriver with both hands.

I waited and, when he said nothing more, tried to ease him into a conversation. "Power screwdriver isn't working?"

"Don't like it." He drove the screw deeper. "Jumps out of the channels."

I squatted a few feet away and improvised on the role of helpful neighbor. "Maybe you need a new bit."

"Maybe." He sucked in a breath and sank the screw. Clad in Willie Dean's shirts, he looked weak and scrawny, but for all his stringiness, he had dense muscles, a strong grip, and stubborn determination.

"Priscilla's gone to get her hair done," he repeated as he picked up another screw and set it in place.

164

I gave up on helpful neighbor and cast myself as customer in need. "I came to see you."

He looked up again and his murky brown eyes narrowed.

"My boat had problems last summer," I said in what I hoped was an off-hand way. "I want to get the motor checked out and tuned up before I get stranded in the middle of the lake."

"What kind of problems?"

I hesitated, thinking of the severed gas line—Ronny's handiwork—that caused me to abandon the boat one night and take my SUV. If Jefferson hadn't burst from the woods to warn me, I would have driven into the line stretched across the road and triggered a shotgun blast.

"Uh, fuel line problems," I told Luke.

"Bring it over. I'll take a look." He went back to driving in the screw.

"When's a good time?"

"Any time. Any day except Monday."

I had one bit of business left in my acting repertoire—playing dumb. "That your day off?"

He grunted.

"Not much to do around here on a day off," I mused as if I just realized that. "You go to the county seat? Take in a movie? Catch up with friends?"

He gave me a flickering glance, wariness in his eyes.

I felt like I was balancing on a shrinking iceberg in a southerly current beneath a blazing sun. "I hear you like trout fishing."

He set the screwdriver on the dock and I saw a burst of fire deep in his eyes. "And I hear you used to be a cop."

165

"Sheriff's department," I corrected in a voice I hope implied ancient history hardly worth a mention.

He snorted. "Big difference."

My turn to shrug.

"What do you want from me?"

"To see about getting my boat serviced."

"We already covered that. Bring it over when you get a chance."

He sank the screw and aimed the screwdriver at me and then at the pale outline of a previous cleat inches from my feet. "Step aside."

I stepped and kept on stepping, off the dock and back to my rig, thinking I screwed up, got him riled, and therefore learned a grand total of zip. Firing up the engine, I headed home, reviewing the conversation.

By the time I passed Bobcat Hollow, I decided I came away with more than zip. I learned Luke was strong, good with his hands, suspicious, borderline belligerent, and at the edge of losing control. He could easily overpower and kill a girl and carry her body a good distance.

But if Luke was a serial killer who intended to go on killing until he was caught, wouldn't he try to keep a low profile? Why settle in a small town like Hemlock Lake? Why draw attention with taciturn silence and secrecy? Why let me see his confrontational attitude?

I braked near Silver Leaf Hollow to avoid a pair of chipmunks, stubby tails held high, racing across the rough country road as if it was a city intersection and they had the green light. Perhaps Luke was ignorant of the social weave and dynamics of a rural area. He might have grown up in a city

166

where people expected—and were allowed—a certain degree of anonymity.

The girls in that glade had lived in urban areas.

If Luke killed them, he may have come to Hemlock Lake to be near them. Perhaps that's why he was up this way when his truck died.

I sat for a few minutes, engine idling, and thought about Lou Marie's demand that I tell Sheriff North to check Luke out. With a groan, I admitted she might have a point.

When I got home, I gave North a call. "I'm busier than a one-legged man in an ass-kicking contest, son, so don't take the long way around the barn. Get to the point."

I laid out the few facts I had. A man with an unknown last name. A man who cashed no checks and never talked about his past. A man whose vehicle had been towed off for scrap so we had no plate to run and no vehicle to check for evidence.

He grunted. "That's as thin as a coat of cut-rate paint, but the task force doesn't have anyone in their sights as far as I know, so I'm willing to clutch at any straw you shove my way. I'll have someone check him out."

Three days passed. While the crew laying blocks for the foundation counted down to quitting time and the weekend, I counted the hours since I called the sheriff. The town grapevine was quiet. No one speculated about spotting a patrol car at the bait shop and Priscilla didn't vent about being badgered by officers wanting background information on her employee. If someone *had* checked Luke out, that person was a walking definition of subtle.

167

Finally, my phone rang. "Last name's Barringer," the sheriff said without a greeting. "Lived down at the south end of the county. Had a sickly mother. Worked as a short-order cook."

"Huh." A cook. Not even on my top-ten list of employment possibilities based on Luke's muscles and attitude.

"One day another cook didn't show and the owner gave him a choice—work a double shift or find another grill. He took choice number one and came home around midnight to find his mother at the bottom of the stairs with a broken neck. Went back the next morning and chased the diner owner around the place with a meat cleaver for five minutes before a waitress brought him down with a fry pan."

I gazed toward Priscilla's dock, gripping the phone and pushing it tighter against my ear. Did Luke's mother's death trigger a killing spree?

North clicked his tongue "Looked like a possibility for about five minutes. Then we did the math. He was serving the last day of his jail sentence when the second girl was taken."

"You're—"

"He's got the best alibi they make. But that aside, they don't think it fits that he'd go after his boss—a guy older and fatter than I am—and then kill young women. And they don't think it fits that he'd attack his boss in front of the breakfast crowd but hunt the girls like a phantom."

I kicked gravel. Nelson studied me from the edges of his eyes, then hopped off into the shade of a budding lilac bush.

"You gave it a shot, son."

I heard the sizzle of a match strike, heard him puff at his pipe, heard the hum of the exhaust fan behind his desk. "I told the task force it came in as an anonymous tip."

I almost thanked him for that, but held back. He'd covered his own butt too. "How'd they manage to find all that out? I never heard a whisper about anyone poking around."

"This task force guy is slick. He did it all on the phone," North said. "Never talked to Luke, focused on Priscilla Denton, let her assume he was with the state revenue department checking on the paperwork involved in the business passing to her after Willie Dean's death. He fished around about estate matters and when he got to accounting for wages and hours for employees she said she was paying someone in trade and didn't need to fill out any forms. Said any money Luke got came from boat owners, not her."

I imagined Priscilla's haughty tone. "Bad move."

"Yeah, the task force guy cited a bunch of made-up code numbers and letters and made mention of fines the size of the national debt." North chuckled. "In two minutes he got all particulars he needed to dig up everything down to the tooth Luke Barringer had filled last November."

No wonder Priscilla hadn't roared into the post office in a fuming snit. She didn't want to admit she had her tail in a crack.

"So, she doesn't know Luke has a record?"

"No way to answer that question short of asking her."

"Pass."

"She said he had a nasty divorce and wanted to fly under the financial radar because his ex and her tick of an attorney sucked his bank account dry and wanted everything he made for the rest of his life. She swore she didn't mean to break the law, she was just trying to help him save up to get his own legal tick. Fact is, Barringer's never been married."

If Priscilla knew the truth, would she go up like a Roman candle? Or would she rule the cleaver attack justified? Perhaps even find the dangerous side of Luke attractive?

"You still there, son?"

"Yeah."

"Call me if you have any other ideas. I mean that. You got good instincts."

Just not good enough.

CHAPTER 17

Sipping coffee, I sat cross-legged on the dock, tossing a stick for Nelson while I waited for the inspector to turn up and approve the finished foundation. My aim was to train the dog to come when I whistled and sit when I snapped my fingers, but we weren't making much of what even the most lenient trainer would call progress. Nelson alternated between disinterest, stubborn refusal, and casual acquiescence. I suspected he was the one training me, getting me to fork over kibble for any approximation of compliance.

Camille was off meeting with an interior designer about window treatments—a term that made me visualize white-coated doctors taking the vital signs of panes of glass suffering from corrosive diseases.

"Coverings, then," Camille said when I told her about my mental image.

That brought up another mental picture—huge foam rectangles like oversized lids with enormous handles. Explaining that earned me another punch on the arm and the observation that I was no help.

True. All I knew about treatments or coverings was that I preferred specific terms: shades, curtains,

171

drapes. The former lodge had some of each, including wine-colored velvet drapes that we drew last summer when we made love. Ronny set them ablaze when he torched the lodge.

Nelson brought the stick—so well chewed it resembled paintbrushes taped end to end—and I snapped my fingers.

Nelson didn't sit.

Knowing he'd only clamp his jaws tighter, I didn't try to take the stick, pretending instead to be intrigued by the lines in my palm. When he caved and laid it across the toe of my running shoe, I snatched it up, tossed it again, and returned to my memories of my first weeks with Camille.

The drapes my grandmother had saved so long for glowed when the setting sun slanted through the west windows. That glow burnished Camille's coppery skin. Pin-prick holes in the worn fabric allowed tiny beams of light to slip through. As the breeze made the drapes sway, those beams flitted about the room like fireflies while we made love.

Last week Camille lugged home slick-paged books filled with photographs of windows festooned with all manner of light-blocking devices. In the second minute of her discourse on the relative merits of pleated shades, mini blinds, wooden slats, and shutters, I set my hands in the time-out sign. "No drapes. Anything else is fine. You pick."

She riffled through a few more pages. "You're sure?"

"Yes." I didn't want to be reminded of what Ronny took from me. "As long as they let light in, block the worst of the sun, don't have to be dusted every week, and give us some privacy."

Privacy. Thick and dark as they were, my grandmother's drapes hadn't provided that. Lou Marie called me out at my father's funeral, asking, "You think we don't know what you did when you drew your grandmother's drapes?"

I still smarted from that. Not so much from the remark and the knowing looks, but from my muddied motives. The lodge stood alone on a spit of land. The nearest house was far across Hemlock Lake. No one could see what we did, but still I drew the drapes. Because I was ashamed of my relationship with Camille? If so, was that shame attached to who she was—an outsider with skin of a different shade?

I dug a pebble from between two boards and tossed it into the lake. No, those things that set Camille apart made her more attractive to me, made me want to flaunt our union.

Was the shame attached to feeling disloyal to my dead wife?

I smacked my hand on the dock. Now there was some major-league irony. Susanna wrote the book on disloyalty when she slept with my brother. But only Camille knew about that. Everyone else subscribed to the myth of Susanna's fidelity.

I remembered Lou Marie's virulent comments as we stood at my father's grave. Camille was a mixed-breed tramp, she said, and I was poisoning the community. I'd tamped down my anger that day, but through the months her words ate at me like acid.

"Doesn't it sting you?" I'd asked Camille this morning. "Knowing what she said about you? How can you stand to be near her?"

Camille studied me with her amazing eyes. "You said 'they don't make our rules,' remember? The first time we made love?"

I nodded.

"Well, you don't make theirs, either."

"But—"

"I've heard a lot of hateful things in my life from a lot of ignorant and fearful people and I know when to leave that be," Camille said in a resigned voice. "She'll never apologize. She can't. She doesn't have it in her."

She laughed then, the sound brittle, bitter. "And if you confront her she'll work at driving a wedge between you and Jefferson. So think of that day as just one more in a whole line of ugly encounters with the woman she was then."

"The woman she still is," I'd insisted, getting in the last word. "She's sliding back a little every day."

Nelson retrieved the stick and again refused to sit at my command. Watching him mangle the bit of branch, I thought about the on-going theme of privacy in Hemlock Lake. I sometimes longed for it, often joked about it, but recognized that I'd get little of it as long as I stayed here.

Nelson dropped the stick and barked. I snatched it up and tossed it. He spun on his lone hind leg, raced to where the stick fell on the rocky margin of the lake, and flopped in a patch of sunlight to lick his groin.

"You sure don't seem to feel a need for privacy," I called. "Or care about what folks might say."

Raising his head, he looked at me in that curious and embarrassed way some dogs have—as if they know you uttered something that's important in your culture, but they can't figure out why it should matter to them. In a moment, he returned to his task and I laughed, thinking of the old joke and its punchline, "Because he can."

That sent my thoughts cascading into darker territory. The words "because he can" could apply to the person who killed those girls. He saw an opportunity, he took it, and, so far, got away with it. And getting away with something had a way of opening the door for an attempt at getting away with something more. Every day he was free made it more likely that he would take another girl.

Nelson stopped licking, lurched to his feet and barked once. A few yards along the edge of the lake, a bullfrog leaped, spraddled out in a belly flop. Nelson barked at the rippling water and waded in to investigate.

The crunch of tires on gravel drew my gaze to the road. The building inspector?

"About time." I stood, bad leg twanging, and whistled for Nelson. He ignored the command and cast back and forth in the shallows searching for the frog, growling and plowing water with his nose. Giving up, I walked toward the foundation, primed to point out how solid it was.

But instead of a car with a township seal on the door, an old green truck rolled into view, Colden Cornell behind the wheel. He raised a hand in greeting and brought the truck to a halt beside my SUV.

I bit back a curse and halted at the corner of the garage, crossing my arms.

He seemed oblivious to my body language, smiling as he slid out of the truck with a notepad in one hand and a recorder in the other. "I could have sworn you said you were a neighbor of Clarence

Wolven." He cleared his throat, but his voice remained high, whiny. "This is a long way from his place."

When I said nothing he frowned a little, then went on in a tone that was both apologetic and pushy. "I guess the definition of 'neighbor' is different out here than where I grew up. Anyway, I'm doing a follow-up on the investigation into those murdered girls. I heard you were the one who found them."

From his tone, I inferred he thought I was well into the shade of abnormal because I hadn't called and volunteered that information. I held my stance and didn't answer or ask how he'd come across my name. Had he developed a source inside the investigation? There were always leaks; there was always someone who cozied up to the media for personal glory or to piss off a superior. I never had much respect for that and never did it. I'd seen leaks blow cases apart, and I'd seen the well of justice poisoned by reporters who released off-the-record information or got things all wrong.

"You were with Jefferson Longyear." He jutted his lower teeth forward and chewed at his wispy mustache. "The old soldier who came back from nowhere last fall."

An apt description. I wondered if he'd tried to interview Jefferson and bet he got even less than I intended to give.

He stepped closer and, with a hopeful smile, switched on his recorder. The notepad slipped from his fingers. He frowned at it, then focused on me. "What can you tell me about that experience?"

I shook my head.

The smile vanished; his mouth opened, then closed. "It must have been quite a shock, finding three dead girls out there so far from anything."

I gave him a cop's stare.

He fiddled with the recorder volume knob and his voice sharpened with frustration. "Listen, I'm just trying to do my job. My editor sent me up here because he wants a story. I have to write something, whether you speak or—"

Nelson barked.

Damn it. Why did he have to pick that command to obey?

I half turned, whistled, and snapped my fingers. Colden Cornell watched with narrowed eyes as Nelson waded from the lake, shook himself, snatched up his stick, and hopped to my side. "Is that the dog that led you to the bodies? The one that belonged to Clarence Wolven? The only one that survived?"

Nelson dropped the stick, rubbed his dripping muzzle against my leg, and whined. I patted his head and held onto my silence.

"He seems to get around fine on just three legs," the reporter said.

Nelson lowered his head, pawed at his nose, and whined again.

"Will you train him to be a search and rescue dog?" Colden's gaze skittered to the lake, and he cleared his throat again. "I mean, he led you to those bodies, right? He must have a good sense of smell."

I picked up the stick, hurled it to the far side of the garage and into the brush that had come back with a vengeance on ground I cleared last summer.

Nelson watched it fly, then went back to pawing at his nose.

"People will want to read about him." Colden fiddled with his recorder again. "What's his name? Did he have to have any special treatment or therapy after the surgery?"

I said nothing.

He turned toward his truck, stooping to pick up the notepad. "I'll get my camera."

I thought about the legality of the situation. He was on private property, so I had every right to refuse to allow him to take a photograph. But a refusal might be like a matador swirling his cape at a bull. Besides, I'd gotten into the groove of not speaking.

Hooking two fingers under Nelson's collar, I hustled him into the garage and brought down the overhead doors. Whining and snorting, Nelson watched, then headed for the side door. I darted in front of him, shoved it closed, and thumbed in the lock. Scooping a strip of rawhide from a shelf in the kitchen area, I showed it to him. "Look, a treat."

Nelson's gaze flicked toward it. I tossed it into the shadows beyond the half-built partition intended to screen off Julie's makeshift bedroom. "Get it."

Growling, Nelson pawed at the door.

"Leave it," I said. "Sit. Lie down."

He kept pawing, so I hooked his collar again and dragged him behind the partition. He fought me, snarling and making himself dead weight. I raised a hand, thought better of it, and released him. He stared at me, lips drawn up to reveal his canine teeth, then sneezed out a dense spray of muddy water.

"That's what you get for trying to track a frog," I said in a low hiss. "I'm not letting you out until he's gone. You won't be on the front page. Or any page."

I leaned against the partition, hoping Camille wouldn't come home before the reporter drove off. No matter what kind of a spin I put on it, she'd chuckle and call it "cowering in the dark" instead of "avoiding a confrontation." I thought of invoking literary and historical precedent, but doubted she'd show much patience with speculation that Thoreau might have done the same in his cabin by Walden Pond.

A full minute passed before Colden Cornell knocked on the side door and called my name. Nelson growled. I held my silence.

Fifteen seconds later he knocked louder. Nelson growled again, hackles rising, then sneezed hard enough that he lost his balance and sat, rubbing his nose against his front legs, leaving smears of mud.

More seconds crawled by and then I heard feet churning gravel, the roar of the truck's engine, and the whine of the transmission.

When those sounds faded, I raised the overhead doors. Nelson ran to the spot where Colden Cornell had parked and circled, whining.

"Sorry to keep you from your moment of glory," I told him, "but a man hangs onto the shreds of his privacy any way he can."

CHAPTER 18

Early Tuesday morning Stub and I met at the sawmill to cut pine paneling for the new house. It was impossible not to think of Ronny while we assessed the logs heaped beside the open-sided shed that housed a circular saw more than half as tall as a man. Last summer Ronny brought those logs down from the woods beyond his meadow to rebuild the portion of his house claimed by fire—a blaze no one knew he set himself until the night he confessed as he tried to kill me.

Stub was all business and seemingly unaware of the wealth of irony attached to the logs. But then, he might be hard put to define irony, might even guess it was a kind of metal. To him, the facts and logic were simple. I needed paneling. Paneling came from logs. Logs were here. They were seasoned, the ideal length, and available at a bargain price—free.

"Gotta get these cut before we lose them to pine borers. No one's gonna gripe. You have a right. They're like—what do you call 'em?—reparations."

That last sentence surprised me, made me reconsider Stub and the depth and complexity of his thoughts.

Reparations?

180

Yes.

The buttery caramel glow of the paneling and the dark knots, each like a bull's eye in a target, would give me a grim satisfaction. I was alive to enjoy the look and feel and smell of this wood. Ronny was on the other side of the grass.

So I gave Stub a thumbs-up and we checked the motor and the belts, oiled and tightened, put on goggles and heavy leather gloves, started up the big saw, and sliced a couple of scraps to knock off the winter's rust. When Stub was satisfied, we hoisted a log onto the carriage and locked it in place with the log dogs. The saw whined, eager to chew wood, and Stub fed it. Sawdust fell like golden snow and the scents of hot oil and pine swirled around me.

When it came to all things mechanical, Stub was in his element, and it was a pleasure to watch him work. He didn't waste a minute or a motion. He was almost a machine himself—rigid and yet strangely graceful.

We'd been sawing for an hour when the cell phone in my pocket vibrated against my hip. Camille knew where I was and what I was doing. If the situation was halfway urgent, she'd drive over. So I ignored the phone, catching and stacking slabs of bark and then yellow-white boards. On another day we'd bevel them and cut grooves.

The phone stopped vibrating for a moment, then started up again. That reminded me of the day Mary Lou called and asked me to check on Clarence Wolven and I felt a chill, a creepy feeling that my grandmother used to express by saying "a goose walked over my grave."

I snatched a board, tossed it on the keeper pile, and waved to get Stub's attention. "Shut it down," I yelled, drawing a finger across my neck.

Stub hit the switch and the saw mewled into silence. I shucked my gloves and goggles, dug the phone from my pocket, and flipped it open. "Yeah."

"We found another girl." Sheriff Clement North's voice rumbled in my ear.

A chill iced my spine. I stepped out into a shaft of sunlight and glanced north and east. "Up in that glade?"

"No, at the war memorial."

"That's just down the street from your office." I conjured a memory of an enormous chunk of stone topped with a bronze sword-wielding horseman with a tri-cornered hat and flowing cape. The base of the monument held bronze plaques with the names of Ashokan County soldiers and sailors dating back to the Revolutionary War and up to current conflicts. Two cannons, dragged to the knoll after the Civil War, flanked the monument, and two pyramids of cannon balls stood ready. "Only a few blocks away."

"Three," he said. "I didn't need to hear it from the experts to figure out he's taunting us."

Catch me if you can.

"You're sure it's the same guy?"

"He killed her quicker, but the poison's the same and so are the bones he broke. She could be a sister to the others." His voice grew thicker, rougher. "And he sat her up against that monument in the same kind of outfit. Troweled on the makeup too."

Streetwalker chic. Making a statement about her? About him?

182

"He didn't have her long. Parents reported her missing two days ago. Eighteen. Worked evenings at a beauty parlor over in that new strip mall."

Camille and I were at that mall last week picking out frames for two paintings the Brocktons gave us. The place was less than thirty miles from Hemlock Lake. "He changed his hunting ground. What do the experts think?"

"Son, they're riled like a nest of hornets. Arguing amongst themselves loud enough to shake the walls." He snorted and I heard the tapping of his pipe. "They *think* all kinds of things. But no one *knows* a damn thing." I heard the scratch of a match. "Anyway, thought you'd want to hear it from me instead of through the grapevine."

"Yeah," I muttered to the dial tone. "Thanks."

I tucked the phone in my pocket and turned to meet Stub's anxious eyes. "Another girl?"

"Yeah. At the war memorial."

"Shit." He kicked the heap of new sawdust.

"It gets worse. He's hunting closer. He took her from that new strip mall."

Stub studied the log on the carriage, then turned away and yanked off his gloves. "I'd best tell Marcella before she hears it from someone else." He headed for his truck. "Folks are gonna be scared."

I nodded. Everyone in Hemlock Lake knew or was related to a young woman who could be a potential victim. And who was to say when the killer might change his pattern, might hunt older women, or even men? I pulled out the phone and called Camille. "Where are you?"

"At the post office."

"Stay there. I'm five minutes away."

As I drove, I thought about Luke, about timing, anger, and possibilities.

"Riled." The sheriff used that word to describe the task force. But the killer must be in the same state. He changed his routine and took an enormous risk to dump his victim in a public place.

"Riled." I used the same word a few days ago after my attempt to extract information from Luke. Suppose, despite what the sheriff said, there was doubt about when the second girl was snatched, or when Luke was released from jail—human error was always possible. Suppose that Luke killed her. Suppose that after my visit he felt I was too interested in him. Suppose that ate at him until he needed release or decided that a quick killing and a new dump site would shift attention.

If Priscilla was still in the habit of going to bed early and wearing the earplugs she bought to cope with Willie Dean's snoring, it would be easy for Luke to slip out undetected any night of the week. Maybe he already spotted the girl and stalked her, or maybe he found her by chance. Maybe he tied her up, gagged her, and stashed her somewhere until yesterday, his day off. There were a thousand hiding places where he could torture her—the woods, storage units, vacant houses.

The road broke from the trees and I stared across the lake toward Priscilla's dock. Every bit of evidence needed to put Luke behind bars forever could be on his clothing, in his room, in Priscilla's car, or in the truck that was once my brother's. But suspicion and supposition weren't enough for a search warrant—even if I got Sheriff North to sell my theory to the task force.

184

I pounded the steering wheel. If I could cast doubt on Luke's alibi for the second murder, the rest of my theory would be solid. And perhaps I could find that doubt by using my status as a former sheriff's officer.

Camille stood in front of the post office shading her eyes against a slant of morning sun. Before I turned off the engine she had the door open, her gaze sweeping over me. "What's wrong? Did you saw off a finger?"

I slid from the seat and turned with my arms out. "All parts accounted for."

"Is Stub hurt?"

"He's fine."

Her eyes narrowed. "If you're both fine, why aren't you cutting paneling?"

I pulled her tight to my chest, felt her heart beat close against mine. "Let's go inside."

She struggled in my grip. "Tell me now."

"Inside. I don't want to have to tell it more than once."

"Sounds grim."

I kissed the top of her head. "It is."

"Rachel?"

"No."

"The murders?"

"Yes."

She shivered, drew in a long breath, and locked her elbows against her sides. I kissed her again, then turned her about and led her into the post office.

Mary Lou glanced up from shuffling through a stack of mail on a table in the rear of the room and hustled to the counter. "What's wrong?"

185

Camille slipped from my arms. "I'll get Lou Marie." She darted through the door to the general store.

Mary Lou came around from behind the counter and a second later her sister stomped through the connecting door with a frown dark enough to incite envy in a thundercloud. "I've got frozen food due in any minute, Dan Stone, so this better be important." Her words wheezed like air from an aging bellows.

Camille, trailing a few steps behind Lou Marie, rolled her eyes and Mary Lou laid a hand on my arm. "You be the judge, Lou Marie," I said. "The sheriff just called. They found another murdered girl."

Camille winced. Mary Lou gasped. "Up in the glade beyond Clarence's?"

"No. Sitting against the base of the war memorial."

Lou Marie's frown held. "Where was she from?"

"The county seat. He took her from that new strip mall."

Camille chewed at her thumbnail. Mary Lou's lips crimped. Lou Marie's frown relaxed. "That's a long way from Hemlock Lake. And I got frozen food to make room for." She spun on one heel and stalked back to the store, the untied laces of her sneakers trailing along the linoleum with a faint clicking.

"She hasn't been sleeping well," Mary Lou said with a sigh. "And her hay fever is worse than usual this year."

Camille flipped her hand and I gave her a centimeter of a nod to show I was also tired of Lou Marie's behavior and her sister's excuses.

Mary Lou straightened her plump shoulders. "I'll talk to her later, Dan."

"He's hunting closer," Camille said. "And he left her in a public place, a place where everyone could see her."

"Or see him putting her there. Does he want to get caught?" Mary Lou asked.

"He wants attention. He wants people to fear him."

"Well, if he changed his pattern, he could change it again." Camille nibbled on her thumbnail again. "I'm worried. About the girls who live around here . . . about all of us."

"We should call a community meeting," Mary Lou said. "Tonight."

"That's a good idea." Camille nodded at me. "You can tell everyone what you know."

Too damn little. "I'm not the one who should—"

"The sheriff called *you*," Mary Lou interrupted. "He trusts you and so do we. We don't need to wait until some official has time to come up here."

"Right," Camille agreed. "We need to know how to take precautions."

"All right." It couldn't hurt to have everyone on alert.

"I'll get it organized." Mary Lou swooped behind the counter and reached for her phone. "Let's say seven in the back room at the Shovel It Inn."

By five of seven, the room was packed and Camille was asking people to share the flyers she'd printed and promising to make more and leave them at the post office. Lou Marie, still with a trace of a frown, sat between Mary Lou and Jefferson in the front row. Freeman and Evan sat with their grown children and tiny grandchildren. Stub anchored the doorway, pointing out empty seats.

I paced the front of the room, checking the notes I'd written on an index card and peering out at the parking lot each time I approached the window. Priscilla, as usual, was running late. Trying to persuade Luke to come? I bet myself first that he'd have to show to find out what I knew. Then I made another bet—that he'd stay away.

At a minute before seven, Priscilla wedged the truck into a space beside a ditch and jumped out, shaking the wrinkles from her white skirt. Luke slid from the passenger seat and followed a few steps behind, an expression of long-suffering boredom on his face. When they reached the door, Stub scanned the room, then pointed to a lone chair in the second row behind Lou Marie. Priscilla scowled, but plodded to it. Luke eased to the left and leaned against the wall not far from a pair of teenage boys, residents of the new development, kids I'd seen getting off the school bus, riding skateboards down the slope from Bluestone Hollow, and fishing in the lake.

In a few sentences, I provided details that had been buzzing on the grapevine all afternoon—another victim, a new pattern, what appeared to be a taunt aimed at law enforcement. As I spoke, I kept my gaze on Luke. He glanced around the room, still with that expression of jaded disinterest, then took a penknife from his pocket and trimmed a loose thread from his shirt.

"Until they catch him, there's no way to know why he changed his hunting ground and why he left this victim in such a public place. There may have been an event that triggered the change. He could feel threatened and acted to show that he's smart and powerful, or he could be ramping up the level of risk to increase his excitement."

Gasps and murmurs swept through the audience. Luke put the penknife in his pocket, yawned, and stared into the distance as if I was talking about life insurance or describing the taste of a mashed-potato sandwich without salt.

"No one knows where he'll take his next victim or when. All we can do is be cautious. Lock your doors. Make sure someone knows where you're going and when you'll be back."

I turned my gaze to two girls—pre-teens or barely beyond—busily braiding each other's silky blond hair. "Don't walk alone, especially after dark. If someone stops to ask directions, don't get close to the vehicle, especially if it's a van. Remember what the person looks like and get a license number if you can. Call me and I'll have the sheriff's office check it out."

A man and a woman sitting behind the girls tapped them on the shoulders, pointed to me, and whispered something. The man frowned and the girls stopped braiding and sat up straight, cheeks flushing. The woman patted the man's shoulder in a way that made me suspect having to discipline their children was harder on him than on the kids.

"Carry a whistle or a personal alarm. If someone tries to grab you, run, scream, make as much noise as you can."

The girls elbowed each other. One giggled.

"If you can't run, fight back. Kick, claw, punch, bite. That could save your life."

The man sitting behind the girls raised his hand. "What about self-defense classes?" His voice was soft and hesitant, as if he didn't want to bring this up because it made the situation more real.

"Good idea." I gave him a thumbs-up.

Camille seconded me from the side of the room. "Great idea."

Luke fished a collection of coins from his pocket and sorted through them.

The woman raised a slim, tanned arm. "We have a home gym and mats. If anyone knows an instructor . . ."

"I'll check with the sheriff's office. And the teen center in the county seat."

"I'm a little out of practice, but I can teach a few basic moves," Camille offered, "until we find someone with more training."

The girls squirmed in their chairs, but the tanned woman smiled and mouthed, "Thank you." I did the same.

"I'll come by tomorrow and we can sort out the details," Camille said, "and then I'll post a notice in the store." She glanced at Lou Marie. "If that's all right with you."

Lou Marie's face scrunched up as if she was thinking it over. Jefferson leaned over and whispered something.

"I'll put one in the post office," Mary Lou volunteered.

Lou Marie leaned away from Jefferson. "Put one in the store if you want."

"I hope you never have to defend yourselves," I said, looking straight at the girls. "But it's always better to be prepared than to wish you had been."

One of the girls gave me a little pout, but the other nodded slowly.

Marcella raised her hand level with her nose. "Is there a chance he could look for his next victim in Hemlock Lake? Unless he took the long way around, he had to come through here to get to that glade. He knows how far off the beaten track we are."

Luke put the change back in his pocket and scratched his ear.

"We're isolated, yes," I said in what I hoped was a calm and rational voice. "But that might make Hemlock Lake less attractive. This is a cohesive community." I stared right at Luke. "Strangers stand out."

Evan put his arm around his daughter, drawing her against his side. Her pale hair shone against his gray shirt. "Will he stick to young girls? Single girls?"

Luke rubbed his back against the wall.

"This guy is sick. He's twisted." I locked my gaze on Luke's. "Nobody can predict what he'll do."

Evan drew his daughter tighter. The toddler in her arms whimpered and Evan patted the child's head.

"Any other questions?"

No hands went up.

"All right. Let's hope they catch him soon and the next time we get together it's for a celebration."

Luke yawned again and strolled through the open door. My fingers twitched. I wanted to lock them around his skinny neck. Camille came up beside me and then Mary Lou joined us. "You know how Lou Marie is about anything that isn't her idea. She'll come around."

Camille shot me a look that said she was miles past caring, but neither of us said a word.

Mary Lou worried her lower lip. "Why do you think he picked the war memorial?"

I shrugged. "It's a public place."

"There are plenty a lot more public."

"His mind is all screwed up," Camille said. "He could have had a hundred reasons for picking that spot. Or no reason at all."

Mary Lou worried her lip again. "I just wondered if it might be connected to Clarence." She canted her head and gazed into my eyes. "Or to you."

"To me?"

"Clarence was never in a war, but his father was. And your father and grandfather were. And your ancestors before them, back to the Civil War, the Revolutionary War. Their names are on that monument."

"Lots of names are on that monument."

"And your mother's grandfather and Clarence's grandfather helped set up that stone."

Camille's eyes clouded with concern.

"'Helped' being the operative word," I said. "It probably took twenty men to move that rock and put it in place."

"That's true." Mary Lou chewed her lower lip. "But I've been wondering if the glade where they found those girls was part of that parcel your mother deeded to the state. I could check the rec—"

"No." I batted that aside with the back of my hand. "I'd rather not know. And even if it is, it's just another coincidence."

CHAPTER 19

Coincidence, I told myself often over the next few weeks. Pure coincidence.

Lots of families in these mountains charted ancestors back to the Revolutionary War. Lots of families had relatives who fought in every war since then. And plenty of families were inter-related, cousins of some degree once or twice removed, connected through fathers or mothers or even both.

As for that glade, well, my theory was that the killer picked that spot because it was isolated, yet fairly easy to get to.

If there was a connection to me, it was coincidence.

Nothing more.

Camille got her self-defense classes going and I put out calls to a couple of guys who knew guys who worked at the jail and said they'd get back to me when they got a chance. While I waited, I made a point of letting Luke know that I had my eyes on him, taking the boat out and cruising by the bait shop, driving around the lake to check in with Freeman, and last Monday morning trailing Luke up the highway to the Birchkill and doubling back later to make sure he was fishing its waters. Otherwise, I spent my days focused on the pieces of what I'd come to think of as a three-dimensional puzzle—the house I vowed would be completed well before Thanksgiving.

At 9:00 on the morning after Memorial Day, Camille was across the lake cooking up a storm for the Brocktons in exchange for the use of their washer and dryer and a crew was framing the walls. Hammer blows and the snarl of saws echoed from the surrounding ridges. Nelson sought refuge under the table in the garage. Usually I found the noise satisfying, the sound of progress, but this morning I was at the brink of frustration, wrestling with a tape measure that wouldn't stay hooked on the garage door and kept twanging back at me. My frustration was fueled by more than the tape. Too many things, including the house, were spiraling out of my control.

A few days ago Camille mentioned that Julie would be eligible for a learner's permit in the fall. Before long, she'd want a car, a car that would need a bay in a garage so we didn't have to scrape ice from the windshield on winter mornings.

"We might want to think about a small carport at the rear of the house," Camille mused. "The garage is fine, but it's across the driveway. That's a long hike with groceries on a rainy day. Garage door openers would be nice too."

I nodded, not looking up from a biography of Patton.

"I hear they're easy to install."

"Piece of cake," I mumbled, turning a page.

The jaws of the trap closed around me. A man who admitted a task was easy had no choice but to add it to the list of things he wouldn't hire out.

Now, while I cursed the tape, I considered costs and contemplated the expanding house and the diminishing state of my finances. Julie would have money coming from Rachel's estate, but Camille and I were determined to set that aside for her college education and the travel she longed for. School and property taxes came due in the fall, and next year I suspected I might owe something more on my inheritance. Land around Hemlock Lake wasn't cheap, and the value of what had passed to me ran to seven figures. The smart thing might be to off-set that by donating my steep-sloped property above the Birchkill to a land conservancy.

The tape twanged at me again as if objecting to that plan, reminding me that my father's family held their land. I slammed the case to the floor. "Mom sold hers. Gave away some too. I can do the same. It's mine now."

Hackles raised, Nelson hopped from beneath the table, surveyed the activity outside, and retreated again. I bent to scoop up the dented tape and heard the clatter of hammers ebb and then stop.

Huh. Far too early for a water break on a cool morning with a faint but constant breeze off the lake.

I stepped out of the garage and spotted Sheriff North walking down the drive, skirting pickups and vans wedged against brush I'd need to trim soon.

Odd. What would make him drive all the way out here?

Fear knotted in my chest.

Another girl? Closer to home?

The sheriff smiled and raised a hand in greeting.

195

I relaxed. I'd worked for him long enough to know he wouldn't smile—couldn't smile—if he had a message that would cut a man off at the knees.

He hitched at his pants, the motion lifting his shoulders, making his badge glint in the sunlight.

A few of the construction workers stared at him with open curiosity, but others turned their backs and ambled to the far side of the foundation in a manner more covert than casual. There, two squatted by toolboxes, and three more sorted through a pile of two-by-fours with their heads bent. I guessed they had reasons to keep a low profile— outstanding traffic tickets or late support payments.

Once winter's back was broken and the ground thawed out enough to dig and pour foundations, men who cobbled together a living with inside projects during the dark days took up heavy-duty hammers and hired themselves out. Others came from farther afield, towing trailers or trucks jammed with gear, camping near their job sites, working from dawn to dusk through the long summer days, making money while it was there to make.

In their T-shirts, jeans, and ball caps, the men framing my house looked enough alike to be cousins. As part of a crew, individuals were anonymous, almost invisible. Any one of them could be—

The breeze chilled the back of my neck.

Was the sheriff here because the task force had zeroed in on one of these men?

In another second I shook that off. He'd send a strike team. And he'd give me a heads-up so I could be ready—or gone.

My mind, now in high gear, unleashed a flurry of questions. Did contractors, anxious to meet deadlines and stay below estimates, ask for more than identification and proof of experience? Did they check criminal records? Did they ask whether the men stalked young women and enjoyed prolonged torture? Was the killer just a few feet from me right now?

Nelson hopped from the garage and considered the near-quiet construction zone. Would he react if he caught the scent of the man who killed Clarence? Or had the shooting cauterized his memory?

"It's shaping up." Sheriff North stuck out a hand. It had the feel of sanity and I grasped it so hard he winced. "Looks like you'll have plenty of space."

"That's the plan."

"It's always good to have a plan." He moved past me, skirted a tumble of concrete blocks, and headed for the dock. Once his back was to the skeletal house, a saw started up and a pair of hammers hit their marks. "Wondered if you knew what Justin Miller's plan might be."

"Justin?" I swallowed bitter, callous guilt. I hadn't thought much about him since the day Rachel came to see us. He deserved more. No matter what he thought of me, he was just a kid who had to deal with too much grief and grow up too fast. "He enlisted."

"I'm aware of that."

I frowned, trying to recall if I'd told him.

North stepped onto the dock. It bobbled beneath him, sending a horseshoe-shaped band of ripples scudding across the lake. They collided with incoming wavelets herded by the breeze, making a waffle pattern on the water. "He went AWOL his first week."

I wasn't surprised he'd bolted. And now he was a deserter. If he turned up on law enforcement radar, he'd be arrested. "So he's in deep shit."

"That's why I'm here."

"I'm the last person Justin would ask for help." I glanced at the new boards in the dock. "And this is the last place he'd come to do that."

The sheriff's gaze fell to the dock. His face filled with recognition and he took two steps away from the spot where Ronny fell. "I figured he'd steer clear of you, but I thought he might hit the Miller place for supplies or shelter." He nodded toward the south, toward Bobcat Hollow and the house where Justin was raised, where Lisa died, where Ronny tried to cover up her murder by killing Willie Dean.

"Have you checked there?"

His shoulders tensed. "No, I . . . I thought you might take a look around, keep an eye out. You know the area."

I pondered that for a moment, inclined to refuse his request. I hadn't been near Ronny's house since a few days before he tried to kill me. At the time, I was grappling with belated recognition of my wife's adultery and I still believed Lisa's death was an accident. Helping Ronny tear out smoke-blackened walls and rebuild the room where she died had, in a strange way, helped me find a will to live he would test to the limit.

I told myself I hadn't stayed away from Bobcat Hollow intentionally, that it just wasn't on the way to anywhere. What would I feel when I returned?

Only one way to find out.

"I can do that."

Sheriff North's shoulders relaxed, then tensed again. "And . . . well, I hoped you . . ." He chewed at the edges of his mustache and made a slight sucking sound.

I let him stew for a minute before I finished his sentence. "You hoped I would talk with Rachel? Explain the situation?"

He sighed. "Yes, damn it."

I pretended surprise, riding him. "And here I've been telling people that I don't work for you anymore."

"That woman's suffered enough, son." I saw the burden of his years and his job etched in the lines around his mouth and eyes and the pallor of his skin. "She has to know he went AWOL—someone's bound to have called her—so she's already stewing. She doesn't need a visit from a deputy or from me, an old man with the social graces of a badger."

"A badger?" I barked out a laugh. "You think you're that civil?"

He stepped from the dock and stalked past, shoulders low, head bent, heels thudding on the ground. The tattoo of hammers fell away to just one pounding out a 4/4 beat. "Aw, hell," he growled. "I'll take care of it."

"No. I'll do it," I called after him. "I'll go right away."

He turned a thumb up but didn't glance back and I knew I'd been played—he never had a second of doubt. I felt a flash of resentment smothered in a tide of resignation. He'd cut me a lot of slack last summer. Like Jefferson, I had debts that cried out to be paid.

The hammers started up again and I studied the crew. Nine of them. When I got back, I'd get out my camera. This crew would be off to the next job soon, but before they went, under the guise of recording progress, I'd capture their images. If someone objected, I'd find a way around those objections. I'd get names. If someone lingered when the job was done, or returned with a later crew, I'd mount an inquisition.

In the meantime, I'd walk Nelson among them to see if he reacted. And I'd watch them the way a terrier watches a rat hole.

CHAPTER 20

I knew Camille had Rachel's phone number and address, suspected she called on a regular basis, but a quick scan of our garage digs revealed nothing resembling an address or phone book. Call it a guy thing, but no way would I call Camille at the Brocktons' house and have her say it was right in front of me. I changed into a clean pair of jeans and a fresh T-shirt, locked Nelson inside, and headed off to check with the oracle of Hemlock Lake—Mary Lou.

As I rolled past Bobcat Hollow I remembered my promise, braked, and turned up the winding road. Bobcat Creek glinted in the sunlight and the meadow below Ronny's house glowed green, lush with tall timothy grass and stalks of milkweed and Queen Anne's lace still rolled tight. Barn swallows skimmed the air and two crows lifted off from a row of pines, wings beating hard, cawing out a warning.

Watching them, I didn't notice more until I parked my rig. Then I saw that the rose bushes Lisa had been so proud of were leafless, their canes brown and broken. The lawn was patchy with weeds and spots where nothing grew. The house itself seemed to slump, as if the walls had decided the roof was too much to bear. Mud, carried by the swallows feeding above the meadow, spattered the siding and the birds had anchored half a dozen nests in the timbers beneath the eaves. Leaves and twigs plastered the front steps, drifted across the narrow porch, and lapped at the brass kick plate.

I slid out and took a closer look at the debris. The twigs were unbroken by passing feet and there was no indication of leaves kicked aside. If Justin had been here, he hadn't entered through the front.

As I walked around back, it occurred to me that I should have picked up the key from Stub. But when I tried the knob, expecting to confirm my failure to plan ahead, the door opened.

For a moment I hesitated. Had Stub left it unlocked the last time he checked on things? Or was Justin here?

I stepped into the mud room off the kitchen, listening hard, hearing nothing except a scratching scurry beneath the floor. A double laundry sink held a few dead flies. Beyond it, beneath shelves laden with dusty boxes of detergent, bleach, dryer sheets, hats, scarves, and gloves, sat a washer and dryer. The dryer was unplugged, the washer hoses unfastened from the wall faucets. Jackets I recognized as Ronny's hung from hooks on the opposite wall and below them a line of scuffed boots toed in against the baseboard. I turned a faucet handle on the sink, but no water splashed out. Stub must have drained the pipes last fall.

The kitchen smelled of old smoke and mildew. The refrigerator was unplugged and empty. I opened the cabinet doors and found that someone, perhaps Rachel, had emptied them. The shelves, covered with pale blue vinyl, held only mouse droppings and rusty circles marking where cans stood too long in one place during humid weather. The corner of the counter where the microwave had sat was vacant and the stove was uncoupled from the pipe that fed propane from a tank outside. I ran my fingers along the threads on the coupling and drew them back stained with rust.

Closing my eyes, I recalled the day, fourteen months ago, when I came here for dinner. Lisa turned from the stove and greeted me with a hug and a kiss on the point of my jaw. She served us pork chops and mashed potatoes with garlic, green beans and candied carrots with brandy. Ronny found fault with her because she hadn't made gravy, found fault with Julie because she didn't like beans, found fault with me because I had left Hemlock Lake. I acknowledged his simmering resentment, but hadn't looked into the depths of it, hadn't seen how far he might go to try to slake his thirst for vindication. If I had, Lisa might—

"Stop!"

I opened my eyes, spun, and punched a cabinet door. It slammed shut, swung open again. I punched it once more then halted, fist cocked. Was my rage, in the final analysis, so different from Ronny's?

I breathed, rubbed my knuckles. Pondering that question could ensnare me in a maze of second-guessing. "Don't think about the past. Keep moving. Forward."

Taking that advice, I checked the rest of the house. Smoke-damaged furnishings had been hauled to the dump after the blaze, and Ronny and the kids had moved in with Rachel while he rebuilt, so the rooms were bare except for a few posters on the walls, a few abandoned items. No footsteps disturbed the dust coating the stairs and the bookshelves in the upper rooms. Faded shirts and blouses hung in the depths of closets, a few shoes and T-shirts were tumbled into corners, and unmated socks lurked in the drawers of a built-in dresser.

The pull-down stairs to the attic unfolded with a squeal of rusty springs and a drift of dust. There were no traces of footprints on the treads, but I climbed and checked the space above. It was empty except for a few bed slats and a trio of cardboard boxes.

The cellar smelled of mold, rusty water, and mouse droppings. Shelves held boxes of Christmas decorations, vases, canning jars, old pots and pans. A rickety wooden table and two bowlegged chairs staked out one corner. There was no sign of Justin.

I left the door unlocked and rolled on to Stub's garage. He'd gone to get some parts and Marcella knew nothing about the lock, so I made a mental note to catch him later and headed to the post office.

Mary Lou was head-to-head with Lou Marie who leaned in from the lobby side. They were paging through a bridal magazine open on the counter.

"Sandals," Mary Lou said when I raised an eyebrow. "It's likely to be hot as the hinges of hell on the big day. And as muggy as a Louisiana swamp. We're looking for sandals that won't cost an arm and a leg and don't have heels high enough to give you a nosebleed."

Lou Marie nodded. "Or so skinny they'll snap in a stiff breeze."

"But stylish," Mary Lou said.

I kept my face neutral, wondering how Lou Marie, who usually wore threadbare black high-top sneakers or worn-down loafers, defined stylish.

"You men have it easy," she said with twist of her lip.

"If by easy you mean strapping ourselves into cummerbunds, noosing ties around our necks, and stifling in black jackets and pants, then I guess we do."

She slapped the magazine closed and went back to the grocery store walking, as always, with the jerky motions of a crow. The door slammed behind her, rattling the bulletin board on the post office wall. A thumbtack fell to the floor and rolled beneath the counter. The notice it had held level swung like a pendulum from the remaining tack.

Determined not to apologize, I retrieved the tack and pinned the notice back in alignment—a bulletin advising that last year's Fourth of July picnic and fireworks festival wouldn't be repeated this summer. What the notice didn't say was that three of the organizers were dead and the rest of us had no stomach for it.

"Lou Marie is a little touchy," Mary Lou said.

"I hadn't noticed."

Mary Lou opened her mouth, then snapped it closed. Was she growing tired of defending her twin?

I took the express route back into her good graces. "I should know better."

"Yes, you should."

"She seemed to change. Right after Jefferson came back."

Mary Lou blotted her eyes on a tissue. "She was so happy at first. But lately it seems that every day

205

she slips back into that same bitter rut. I don't know how they'll—" She sniffed and brushed something I couldn't see off her sleeve. "But that's none of my business. I made a vow to hold my tongue."

"And I'll hold mine." I glanced toward the door Lou Marie slammed moments ago. "Jefferson's a grown man but—"

"He was out of the world for a long time. And he wasn't more than a boy when he went to that war. He didn't know much about women, or anything else." She patted my arm, then closed her fingers around my wrist. "He's been up in that sandpit every day since they broke the news. Sometimes twice a day."

"I know. I heard the shots." Was he trying to kill his doubts? Or forcing himself to focus on what had to be done?

"It's natural for you to worry about him. He's your friend." Her fingers tightened, pressing skin against bone, then released. "And he's a true friend."

She didn't say, "not like Ronny," but I felt the words hang in the air. She didn't say, "and we hate to see our friends make mistakes," but those words also hung between us.

Again, I marveled at Mary Lou's forgiving personality. Her twin sister had blamed her for misfortune and treated her like a punching bag for twenty-five years, but here she was, sewing her tormentor's wedding gown, searching for the right pair of sandals. I thought back to the uneasy relationship I had with my brother long before he took my wife to his bed. I never tried to bridge the growing rift between us. Neither did Nat.

"Well." I cleared my throat, cleared my mind of the past. "I hope they'll be happy."

"So do I." Despite her smile, her eyes were bright with tears and sadness. Plucking another tissue from a shelf beneath the counter, she sniffled into it and then was all business. "What brings you in? Camille was by earlier to pick up your mail. Just a few bills and another letter from that lawyer."

"I don't know why we bother to pick it up at all," I teased. "We could just call and have you tell us about it. Pay you a fee to manage our money and we'd never have to open an envelope again."

She flushed. "Are you saying I'm nosy?"

"No. You notice things. You don't go out looking for dirt to dig through."

"I don't have to," she said with a chuckle, "it comes to me." Cocking her head, she gave me an appraising look. "Is that why you're here?"

"In an indirect way. I thought you'd have Rachel's address."

"Of course." She stooped and peered under the counter, came up with a small three-ring binder, and flipped to the tab marked with an M. Stooping again, she unearthed an index card and a pen and copied out the address and phone number. "I heard she was up to visit you a few weeks ago. And Camille mentioned that Julie would be visiting for a couple of weeks this summer."

For all her love of gossip, Mary Lou could keep a secret. Camille contended that that she enjoyed holding back a tidbit as much as she enjoyed passing one along.

I glanced at the door to the grocery store once again, checked to make sure mine was the only vehicle in the parking lot, and then leaned across the counter. "This is just between you and me."

Mary Lou crossed her heart and zipped her lips the way I imagined she might have when she was a child.

"Rachel has cancer. Ovarian. She doesn't have much time."

Mary Lou gasped and stepped back from the counter. "That's horrible. What can we—?"

"She doesn't want anyone to know."

Snatching another tissue, she blotted her eyes, and nodded slowly. "That's her way. She's a tough old bird."

"Brave, too."

"But it's a shame to shut out those who would help. And what about the children?"

"They don't know. Rachel doesn't want to put another burden on them. She made me their guardian."

"Ah. That's why you're making the house bigger." Her eyes narrowed. "You'll have your hands full with Justin."

An understatement typical of Mary Lou. "Rachel got him into the military, but he went AWOL. I'm going to tell her the sheriff's been notified."

"That poor woman. There's no end to her burdens." Mary Lou pressed a hand against her throat. "Underneath his swagger and that temper he inherited, Justin's just a mixed up kid—an orphan. Will they hunt for him?"

"I doubt it. Not actively, anyway. Unless he compounds his problems and commits a crime."

She flipped the address book closed and stowed it beneath the counter. "Was that why the sheriff was around? I saw him go past. Does he think Justin will come back here?"

"Justin has to know he'd have a better chance of staying under the radar if he doesn't."

She gazed out the window, across the parking lot and the road. This town is a fishbowl, and a tiny one at that. Are you going to let folks know what's what? If he comes around somebody's bound to notice."

"I want to talk with Rachel first." I tucked the index card in the pocket of my T-shirt. "And then maybe I'll tell a few—Stub, Freeman, Evan, Jefferson."

"The ones who won't blab it about while they keep their eyes peeled. And you'll search for him?"

"No. That's not my job."

"It's not your job to bring Rachel the news, either," she said with a coy smile. "I bet you checked the Miller place on your way here."

I hesitated, hating to admit she knew me so well. "You'd win that bet."

"You can take the man out of the job," Mary Lou chanted as I headed for the door, "but you can't take the job out of the man."

CHAPTER 21

I thought about that as I drove to Rachel's apartment. Although I didn't want to go back to the sheriff's department, I couldn't seem to step clear. Was that because Clement North called me "son"?

"Think about that later," I muttered as I pulled up in front of the eight-unit apartment complex where Rachel lived. The building had the look of a Basset Hound—long and low and sad. Gutters drooped from the edges of the roof and the railings were blotched with rust and patches of black paint slapped on to try to arrest advancing decay. I crossed a weed-choked strip between the street and the parking lot and found Rachel's unit.

Sick as she was, she'd made an effort to keep things up. The windows shone, the front step was swept, and a green mat with plastic daisies told me I was welcome. A bright blue ceramic pot overflowing with pink petunias sat beside the door and the knocker and brass 6 gleamed. I lifted the knocker half an inch and tapped, hoping I wouldn't wake her, wondering whether pain and anxiety allowed her any restful sleep.

In a few moments I heard a distant shuffling and something that sounded like a sneeze. "Who is it?" a tentative voice whispered.

"Dan Stone."

Silence. Then the scrape of a bolt. The door opened and Rachel, looking as if she'd shrunk six inches and twenty pounds in the past seven weeks, stood before me in a quilted yellow housecoat and a pair of fuzzy red slippers with matted toes. She waved me in and I sidled through the gap.

The apartment was clean and neat, but dim, lit only by sunlight filtered through thick gray drapes; it was hot and stuffy and smelled of pine cleaner and menthol cough drops. A television anchored the only wall unbroken by doorways, a staircase, or windows. Like scouts around a campfire, furniture gathered in a semicircle facing the TV screen.

Rachel pushed the door closed and looked up at me, her cheeks sunken so far I could see the outlines of her upper teeth, her eyes dull, her hair dry and brittle. "It's about Justin." Not a question.

I nodded.

She ran her hands down the sides of the housecoat. "I'm usually dressed by now. No matter how I feel, I'm always dressed when Julie gets home from school. I don't want . . ." She sighed and pointed to a navy blue sofa littered with bright throw cushions. A pair of orange flip-flops peeked from beneath it. "Sit down."

I edged to the sofa, but remained standing until she shuffled to a wooden rocker, sat by gripping the arms so hard veins stood out in her hands, and covered herself to the chin with an afghan knitted in a rainbow of colors, reds giving way to oranges, yellows, greens, and blues. Rainbows were supposed

211

to mean an end to storm and flood, but seeing Rachel wrapped in that afghan made me think only of shrouds and coffins. My perception of those bright arcs in the sky would be altered for the rest of my life.

I sat, heard something crackle, moved a lime green throw pillow, and found an empty potato chip bag beneath it.

"That's Julie's," Rachel sighed. "She's like a tornado. You'll have your work cut out picking up after her."

"Maybe she'll get the knack of picking up after herself."

Rachel gave me a bleak smile. "Don't hold your breath. When they get to be teenagers, most kids aren't eager to notice the mess they leave in their wake let alone clean it up." She clawed at the afghan, pulling it tighter across her chest. "Julie's a good girl. A sweet girl. Just a little messy."

"Messy isn't the end of the world," I assured her. "And not a deal breaker. Camille added extra closets to the floor plan. If Julie's stuff makes me crazy, I'll kick it into a closet and shut the door. And then I'll let Camille have a talk with her."

Rachel smiled again, lips stretching papery skin. "Camille's a wonderful woman, Dan. She reminds me . . ."

I nodded, but didn't fill in Lisa's name. I hadn't seen the similarity until this moment, but they were a lot alike—warm and generous, smart and social.

Rachel hung her head. "Justin didn't go back to the base, did he?"

I'd thought about sugarcoating his situation, but suspected she'd see through that. "No. And now he's listed as a deserter. Sheriff North came to tell me."

"Are they hunting him?"

"No. But if someone spots him or if he's . . ." I hesitated, then went for sugar coating and low-level offenses. ". . . caught speeding or trespassing or something like that, they'll take him into custody."

"I thought right from the start he might run," she said. "I told him he wouldn't be able to do things his way and he'd better not argue that he knew better. I told him to do what they said and keep his lips zipped."

But he's too much like his father.

Rachel raised her chin as if she read my mind. "I prayed every day that he'd come to his senses and go back and take his medicine before it got to this. I should have done better by him."

Was she was talking about Ronny as well as Justin? "You did your best."

"No, Dan, I didn't." Her voice burned with its old fire, then the flame flickered and died. "But after Buck died I was tired . . . so tired."

I leaned over and touched her hand. "No one blames you, Rachel. You did all you could for Justin." And more than I'd be able to do if I was staring at my own death in the mirror like she was. "I told Sheriff North I'd look around a little. If we find him before too much time passes, things will go easier. Do you have any idea where he might go?"

She drew in a breath. "Well, he doesn't have a yen to travel like Julie. He never wanted to go far from Hemlock Lake and those mountains." She closed her eyes for a moment and then gave me that wintry smile again. "I can't imagine him getting on a plane like you did and just heading off to a strange place where he doesn't know a single soul."

"Yeah," I said in a joking tone. "And look where I am now. Back where I started."

"You're where you are for a reason, Dan. For a lot of reasons." She flipped the afghan aside, dug a tissue from the pocket of her housecoat, raised her glasses, and wiped tears from her cheeks. "And I'm glad of it."

We sat in silence for a moment before I asked again, "If he stayed around here, what would he do? Where would he go?"

"Back to the house," she offered.

"I checked this morning. There was no sign anyone had been there for months."

"Maybe he's in the woods. He used to go out when the weather was good, build himself a shelter, and camp."

I thought of Jefferson, a ghost haunting the rills and ridges for months last spring and summer, hiding until the night he emerged to save me. But Jefferson had made his presence known by stealing food and clothing, even books. In the past few weeks no one had mentioned missing canned goods, cooking utensils, or other gear. If Justin had been careful about what he pilfered, maybe no one noticed. "Did he have any friends he might stay with? Maybe some of the guys he played football with?"

She shook her head. "I think he drove most of them away with his attitude. And after the coach benched him, he slammed the door on the few who came to say they were sorry. Then he transferred schools and never made another friend that I know of."

"What about girls?"

214

"After the one he was sweet on broke it off in the fall, he said some hateful things about her to everyone, even to Julie." A faint flush of pink flared along her cheekbones and her hands fluttered like wounded birds. "Things about what she'd want him to do to her and have her do to him. I couldn't imagine any of it being true."

Her words bored into my mind. Those girls in the woods. That had been about power and sex and sick pleasure—about things most of us couldn't imagine. And Rachel's place wasn't far from where the killer took his latest victim.

Despite the sweltering heat in the apartment, a chill seeped into my spine. Could Justin be that killer? "Do you remember that girl's name?"

"No." She shook her head. "But she wouldn't help him. Besides, she moved away."

The chill spread into my brain. Had Justin hunted her down? "Where did she move to?"

"I don't know." She lowered her head and fidgeted with the afghan, tucking a loose bit of yellow yarn back into the pattern. "Julie might. She heard all the talk from her friends at that school. But I'd rather she—"

I touched her hand. "I know."

Rachel took a long and shuddering breath. "Thank you. I . . . . thank you."

I waved that aside, wondering if Julie had talked about this with her counselor, vowing to tell Camille the sordid story later and let her decide how we should handle it.

"Julie has a yearbook from that school. The girl's picture might be in it." Rachel pointed to an arched doorway beyond which I saw a sink and counter. "Last place I saw it was on the table with her

215

homework. Forgive me, but I haven't had the strength to clean up in there today."

I assured her that didn't matter and walked to the kitchen, taking the opportunity to blot my forehead on my sleeve as I went. The room's yellow walls spoke of an effort to create a cheerful atmosphere, but the shade reminded me more of dirty snow than warm sunshine. If Camille had plans to go with lemon or saffron in our kitchen she could scrap them. Glancing at the pine table, I saw three plaid placemats shoved to one edge to make room for an open three-ring binder, a crumpled napkin, an empty glass, a pen with a gnawed top, and a book with gold lettering on its spine. I brought that to Rachel and laid it on her lap.

"She was a junior, I believe. They had their pictures taken in September. Maybe they didn't pull hers when she left." She turned the glossy pages to head-and-shoulders photo arrays of each class—a staple of every yearbook. Faces slipped past, like passengers in a fast-moving train, glimpsed then gone. Rachel's fingers traced one girl's hair, tapped another's chin, settled on the nose of a third. "This is the one. Patricia Mitchell. She went by Trish."

I bent and studied the photo. Trish had long medium-brown hair, a soft fringe of bangs, and an easy smile. She wore the layered look girls seemed to like for a reason I couldn't fathom—two tank tops that revealed her slender shoulders and the points of her collar bones. She could have been a first cousin to any of the girls in the woods or the one at the monument.

Green sickness roiled in my gut. Had her rejection been the trigger that set Justin to killing? Had he gone after others knowing that if he took her he'd be a suspect? Was he saving her, a prize to be claimed later?

Retrieving a piece of paper and Julie's chewed-up pen from the table in the kitchen, I copied down Trish's name. Folding the paper, I stowed it in my wallet, telling myself not to jump the gun and convict Justin without evidence. Trish's resemblance to the murdered girls might be pure coincidence.

Rachel closed the yearbook and reached for my hand. Her fingers were all bone, as cold and brittle as icicles. "You'll stand by him, won't you, Dan? Find a lawyer and sit with him in court if it comes to that?"

I nodded. "If he wants me to."

"He won't." Her hand gripped mine with more strength than I'd imagined she had left. "But promise me you'll do it anyway, no matter what he says. Underneath he's just a boy. And he's all alone." She blotted her eyes. "I'll pray that you find him. I'll pray that he lets you help him."

I kissed her forehead. "I promise."

For twenty miles I wrestled with the question of whether to tell Sheriff North about Trish Mitchell, about suspicions I wished I didn't have. Justin was the son of a killer, a man who murdered his own wife. Justin had objectified women. Justin knew the woods, perhaps even hunted where Jefferson and I found the three dead girls. Justin knew guns. Justin, afraid of being caught, could have killed Clarence and his dogs. Justin went AWOL a few weeks before the fourth girl was dumped at the monument.

The episode with Luke Barringer demonstrated that Sheriff North took my ideas seriously, but at what point would he consider me an alarmist, a man jousting at shadows? I had no evidence against Justin. Not a single scrap.

And, if I sold North on the idea of Justin as a killer and he presented it to the task force, someone would come knocking on Rachel's door. That might hasten her journey to the grave.

CHAPTER 22

The last construction workers were pulling away when I got back. I let Nelson out of the garage, snagged a beer, and walked down to the dock. The blast of a car horn echoed across the lake and Camille, her T-shirt like a ruby against pale green late-spring growth, jumped from her car in front of the Brocktons' house and semaphored her arms. I waved back and mimed sorting a stack of letters, letting her know I'd stopped at the post office. She mimed applause, then slid into her car and pulled away.

I passed the next fifteen minutes alternating between watching the breeze riffle the lake and checking Nelson's patrol of the construction site. When I heard wheels in the gravel of the drive, I drained the last swallow and trotted up to help her unload four baskets of clean laundry and two sacks of containers, plastic bags, and packages wrapped in foil.

"I cooked double everything." She unpacked chicken, scalloped potatoes, meatloaf, slaw, cornbread, and blueberry muffins. "It will be so nice to have a real oven again. And a real bathroom."

Stowing the last container, she patted her damp hair. "I took a long shower while I was over there."

I nuzzled her neck. "With lemon soap and vanilla shampoo." Tugging at the collar of her T-shirt, I sniffed the fragrance of her skin in the soft hollow of her neck. "Do I smell cocoa butter lotion?"

She chuckled. "You're putting Nelson's nose to shame."

I held her close, held her long, her scent and warmth calming my churning mind.

She kissed my ear, then pushed away, eyes narrowing. "What's wrong?"

"Maybe nothing." I shrugged. "Maybe a whole lot."

"With . . . ?"

"Justin." I nodded at the skeleton of our new home. "The guys working over there. The world in general."

She sucked in a long breath, then sat at the table and folded her hands. "Tell me."

I did, starting with the construction workers' reaction to the sheriff and my dark speculations about them and my intentions to check them out. Camille nodded and I took her through the sheriff's news about Justin's AWOL status and my visit to the Miller house and Rachel's comments about how Justin responded when Trish dumped him and all the things Julie heard. Camille took my hands in hers and I told about my reaction to the yearbook picture of a girl who resembled the victims and my theory that her rejection could have triggered the killings.

When I was finished she sucked at her lower lip for a few moments, then shook her head and released my hands. "I just can't see Justin killing those girls—at least not the first ones. That took cold calculation, careful planning, and the ability to keep a secret. He's a hothead."

"That's exactly why I can see him killing Clarence to save his own skin."

She worked her lower lip again. "All right. But getting back to the girls, where could he keep them while he tortured them? You just said no one's been in the Miller house."

"Right." I gave myself a mental kick. "But I didn't check the sheds." I'd been looking for signs that Justin returned for supplies, not that he sought out a torture chamber.

She brushed that aside like a mosquito. "He would have had to come and go to bring three girls up there and to . . . do what he did to them. That's taking a huge risk. Someone could have seen him. And he had to know Stub might come by to check the property."

Good points, but I felt a weird loyalty to my theory. "There are other places where he could have kept them. Hunting cabins. Storage units. Houses left vacant over the winter."

"True, but . . ." She spread her hands. "I can see him killing in a fit of anger, but I can't buy all the rest."

"Think about the timing. It was just after we found the bodies that he went into the military. Maybe he joined up to hide. And the fourth girl was killed after he went AWOL."

"The timing fits." Camille wrinkled her nose. "But I—"

"The logistics work, too." Pacing our tiny living space, I talked faster, like a salesman on the verge of closing a deal, wondering all the time why it was so important to convince her. "Justin had a car to transport the girls we found in the woods, but he sold it when he went into the military. That explains why he dumped the fourth girl so close to where he took her. If I found that car there might be some evidence inside. It's almost impossible to clean all traces of—"

Camille stood and pressed her hands against my chest. "Why are you so anxious to convict him?"

"I'm not."

"It sounds like you are."

I glared at her and spoke through gritted teeth. "I'm not."

"I hope that's true." Anger flickered in her eyes and gave way to sadness. "I hope I'm imagining that you're so proud of your theory you refuse to see any flaws. And I really hope you're not letting what Ronny did make you forget that boy is Lisa's son, too."

I sucked in my irritation and closed my eyes, admitting to the helpless rage I felt about my failure to stop Ronny before he killed Lisa. When I saw her at the Fourth of July picnic, she'd been so excited about the way things had come together, so hopeful about the future of the community.

"I'm not saying you shouldn't consider everything you told me about Justin," Camille said in a quiet voice. "I'm not saying you shouldn't try to find that girl, look for his car, and check out the sheds at the Miller place. You might be right. But at the community meeting I saw you giving Luke that cop stare and now you're focused on Justin. Promise you won't be so single-minded that you rule someone—anyone—out too soon."

Metal clattered against metal. I breathed out and opened my eyes to see Nelson, nosing his dinner bowl against the canister that held his kibble.

"There's another vote on this topic," Camille said. "The tiebreaker."

"Nelson?"

"Sure." She scooped out a cup of chunks and rattled them into the bowl. "You said you were going to walk him around among the construction workers, so why not take him up to the Miller place and see how he reacts in Justin's room? Then you can take him over to meet Luke."

Nelson cocked his head as if waiting for my decision.

"All right," I said. "First thing tomorrow."

The next morning I wrestled a stepladder to the rear of the garage, and removed a vent cover under the eaves. Then I nailed a couple of boards to the rafters above our kitchen area so I could stretch out. From my blind, I took pictures of the construction workers as they arrived. I felt foolish but I wanted to see them with their guards down and I figured that if they didn't see me, they couldn't object. Not that an objection signaled guilt—lots of people didn't want their pictures taken for all kinds of reasons, and plenty of others would raise a stink on general principles.

Half an hour later, when their hammers pounded out the overture to a raucous symphony, I snapped a leash on Nelson and dragged him out from under the table. He balked at the edge of the driveway, lying down and twisting his head in an effort to snake out of the collar.

"Come," I commanded.

He bared his teeth, the whites of his eyes gleaming in the morning sun.

"You were over here last night. What is it you don't like about the place now?"

He whined, panted harder, chewed at the leash.

Did the hammers sound like gunshots to him? Or did he smell something? Someone?

I hooked my hand in the collar. "We'll be done in a few minutes, partner. Quicker if you show me what's bothering you."

Crab-walking, I dragged Nelson to the house, hoisted him to the subflooring, and hauled myself up beside him. Two workers in billed caps, frayed denim shirts, and grimy jeans halted their hammering and gawked.

The taller man pushed back his cap and bent to peer at Nelson's stump. "What the hell happened to him?"

"Tangled with a car."

He nodded, nothing in his eyes telling me he recognized my lie. Either he hadn't, or he was too clever to give himself away.

I dragged Nelson close to the two men. His sides heaved and drops of saliva fell from his tongue. "He's been skittish ever since. I'm trying to get him used to the noise."

"Good luck with that." The shorter man turned away and resumed his work.

"Yeah," the other one observed. "Maybe he'll never be like he was before."

I studied him for a moment. Was that just an observation, or was he telling me he knew what I was up to and casting doubt on Nelson's reactions?

I forced a casual reply. "Yeah. But I thought it might help if he saw no one here was out to hurt him."

The tall worker nodded. Too eagerly? I noted the scar on his cheek and, as he braced a 2x4, made a mental note of it.

Foot by tedious foot, Nelson and I trudged through the framed-up rooms and then around the perimeter. I made sure he got close enough to each of the nine workers to get a nose full of scent. He continued to shy from the hammers and pull at his collar, but showed no particular interest in, or aversion to, the workers when they ceased pounding. That told me exactly nothing.

I let him rest under the table while I loaded the pictures into the computer and made notes about the nine men. Then I rewarded him with a dog biscuit and we drove to the Miller place.

It looked even more forlorn than it had before. Even the swallows seemed depressed, skimming the air in short and erratic arcs as if flying was just a job and the experience of being airborne was without an ounce of joy. Laughing at the presumption of putting thoughts in a bird's mind, I lifted Nelson to the scraggly lawn and let him loose. Keeping my distance, I watched him sniff around wilting shrubs and raise his muzzle to the wind at the edge of the woods.

When he completed a circuit of the house, I called him and opened the sagging door to the wooden storage shed. A riding mower hunkered in the center of the filthy cement floor. Around it were the usual rusting tools, half-used sacks of fertilizer, wooden stakes, coils of light rope, flowerpots, tomato cages, and broken lawn chairs. The dust was marred only by the prints of passing mice. There was no sign anyone had been held hostage and tortured here.

Nelson hopped alongside the riding mower, inspected the tines of a rake, and raised his upper lip at a trail of mouse droppings before making for the door. I closed it behind us and called him over to a narrow shed that had once been a smokehouse.

Back in the day, many families raised their own hogs, feeding them scraps and letting them forage for acorns and apples. Other families got a share of the meat for helping with the butchering or in trade for milk or eggs. Smoking was an art. The meat was soaked in brine before it went into the smokehouse and the fire had to smolder, not flame. Debates raged over the size of the chunks of wood that fed that fire—logs, sticks, or chips—and the amount of time that should elapse before a living tree became smokehouse fodder.

I opened the door and breathed in the damp, dense aroma of old smoke and cured pork. Nelson sniffed twice, snorted, and bounded across the doorsill. Demonstrating no fear, he stuck his nose into every dim corner and emerged a minute later, his ears festooned with spider webs. Dropping to the ground, he rolled onto his back and pawed at his eyes.

"You don't like spiders, huh?"

He gave me a look that said he'd hop through a thousand spider webs if there was a ham at the end of that, then stood and shook, collar tags jangling.

"One more stop and then I'll split an ice cream bar with you."

His ears perked up and he followed me to the house and explored every room and the cellar. He showed exactly as much interest as I'd seen him display in other spaces that were new to him—the post office and the schoolhouse where Jefferson lived—and not a single degree more. When I took him into Justin's former room a second time and plucked a crusty pair of jeans from the closet floor, he yawned. When I held the jeans to his nose, he turned aside and yawned again.

Nothing.

I kicked the jeans back into the closet.

Nelson licked himself.

I reminded myself he'd been through hell. His memory could be faulty, even wiped clean. What the hell did I know about dogs' memories anyway?

We got back into my rig and drove to the bait shop. Seven boats were tied up to the new cleats and a couple of men were loading a blue and white cooler and fishing poles into one of them. I lifted Nelson down and held him on a loose leash. He sniffed the breeze, then headed for the dock in what amounted to an amble, sniffing the tires of a late-model truck, pulling against the leash when one of the fishermen started the outboard motor.

The boat pulled away and Luke came out of the bait shop, aiming a finger at me like a gun. "Bring that dirty dog on my dock and I'll call the law."

I halted where the parking lot met the dock, pulling Nelson against my right leg. "Word is you have more than a passing acquaintance with the legal system."

Luke's lips twisted and his eyes narrowed. With long strides, he closed the gap between us, glancing toward the house, halting on the last board of the dock. "What do you mean by that?"

I nudged Nelson forward half a foot. "Just what I said."

He shot another glance toward the house. "Stay out of my personal business."

Nelson yawned and sat on my foot.

"Is it still personal if it's part of the public record?"

"You have no right to—"

A screen door slammed and Priscilla yelled, "What do you want, Dan Stone?"

"Nothing," I called. "Just passing the time with Luke." I lowered my voice. "Luke's an expert on passing time. Or should I say doing time?"

Luke's fists clamped, but he didn't say a word as I turned and pulled Nelson along to my rig. I lifted him to the passenger seat and patted his head. "We gave it a shot, boy. It's not your fault we came up with nothing."

Nelson licked my hand and settled in the seat. I started the engine, second-guessing myself about every conclusion I'd come to that morning. There were a thousand things I didn't know about dogs in general and this dog in particular. Maybe I was reading his reactions all wrong. Or maybe, like I thought earlier, his memory had been wiped clean.

Goosing the gas, I fishtailed out of the parking lot.

In the final analysis, the nothing I came up with proved . . . well, nothing.

CHAPTER 23

Over the next week, I gleaned the name of the tall construction worker, did some checking, and found he'd spent the fall and winter in California. Dead end. I walked Nelson around the site every morning, but the only result was that he fought me less as he grew accustomed to the noise. I checked on each of the other workers. More dead ends.

I went by the Miller place every few days but found no trace of Justin. After a few dozen phone calls, I found his car in a salvage yard, totaled in a rollover two weeks after he sold it. The yard's owner was scavenging parts from the engine but, for fifty dollars, agreed to cover the car with a tarp and not touch the trunk or seats until he heard from me.

Another few dozen phone calls led me to a friend of Trish Mitchell's who told me she was alive and well and spending the summer in France studying art. Another few dozen phone calls led me to a friend of Trish Mitchell's who told me she was alive and well and spending the summer in France studying art.

Heeding Camille's admonition, I kept a close eye on Luke, but he did nothing out of the ordinary. In fact, as business picked up at the dock, he gave up mornings on his day off to provision fishermen headed out on the lake. I put in more calls, but the friend of a friend at the jail didn't call back.

Frustration ate at me, sabotaging sleep, wrecking my appetite. When I snapped at Camille over a runny egg, she snapped right back. "There's a whole task force working on this, Dan. If you're so sure you've got something on Luke or Justin, then take the evidence to them. If you're not sure, admit that and deal with it before I brain you with this skillet."

Lifting my hands in surrender, I beat a retreat, Nelson close behind. We sat on the dock for a good fifteen minutes before he looked back at the garage and whined. "Yeah," I agreed, "I'm hungry. And she's got a good point."

Nelson yawned as if that was old news and I got to my feet, sucked it up, and apologized.

"It's all right." Camille kissed me long and hard, leaving no doubt that I was forgiven. "It's a sign of how much you care—about this community, about justice, about making things right—whether you want to care or not."

Another good point. Especially the last part. Somehow, I'd stopped fighting the gravitational pull of involvement. Had I taken the course of least resistance, or was I, on some level, carving out a role here?

Something else to think about later. Right now, there was more paneling to cut and then more shelves to build.

Julie's last exam was set for Wednesday the 19th. In the SUV and a truck borrowed from Freeman, Camille and I headed to Rachel's right after breakfast. Our goal was to get Julie's possessions loaded before the worst of the heat clamped down, then swim and wait for an evening breeze before we tackled the unloading. So far, this season was even hotter than last, but rain fell more frequently, doing little to cool things off and much to increase both humidity and the biting insect population.

In the three weeks since I saw her, Rachel seemed to have caved in on herself. She moved with halting steps, pausing often to draw in wheezing breaths. There was a sweet and metallic odor to her breath and skin. She apologized for everything—her inability to help, the fact that Julie hadn't finished packing, the weight of the boxes, the heat of the day.

For the first few minutes I responded to each apology, assuring her that the boxes weren't too heavy, that we hadn't anticipated military precision in Julie's level of organization, that I parked in the shade, that we didn't expect or want her to lift a finger. Finally, Camille got Rachel settled in her chair, brought her a cold drink, laid a photo album on a TV tray, and sat beside her, talking about better times.

Relieved, I disassembled Julie's bed, wrestled mattress and box spring down the stairs, and grappled with armloads of clothing. Skirts and tops slithered from hangers and, after a few attempts at replacing them, I gave up and tossed the clothing into cardboard boxes collected from behind a liquor store down the street. Camille and Julie could face the question of "to hang or not to hang" when we got home. Using a length of old pipe and some brackets, I'd built a rack, but now that I saw the welter of clothing Julie possessed, I doubted that rack was long enough or strong enough.

I flashed Camille a smile as I passed, grateful to her for taking care of Rachel, grateful that she wanted to take Julie in, grateful most of all that she simply was. And that she was with me.

When the bed of the truck was piled high and I secured a tarp over it, Camille handed me a can of cola and pointed to the chair beside Rachel. "You visit. I'll clean."

"There's no need for you to do that," Rachel protested. "I can—"

"You can sit right there," Camille said in a voice that even Lou Marie might not argue with. "You don't need to be climbing those stairs, and you'll rest better later on if you know that room is all shipshape."

"I'll have Mrs. Gallagher find someone to clean it. She'll be over this afternoon."

"Mrs. Gallagher?" I asked. "Is she a neighbor?"

"Julie thinks she's an old friend, but she's with the hospice service." Rachel flushed and dropped her gaze to the floor. "I didn't want to ask anyone for help, but I can't seem—"

Camille bent and kissed her forehead. "Sometimes it's wrong *not* to ask for help."

She shot me a meaningful glance and then, as if she'd lived there for years, retrieved the vacuum cleaner from a closet in the kitchen and armed herself with rags and cleaning products from the cabinet under the sink. "Show Dan those pictures of him at the lake," she suggested and headed upstairs.

Rachel gave me a shy smile and I caught a flash of the girl she once was as she flipped to the first few pages of the album. "There you are." She pointed to a cluster of snapshots of two boys, aged six or seven, showing off a string of trout. Ronny and I wore only cut-off shorts and gap-toothed grins. Our hair was buzzed to our scalps for the summer, our knees bore scrapes and scabs, and our feet were splotched with mud. We were alive in the moment, happy with that day's conquest, unaware of all the future would bring.

If a soothsayer had predicted the events of the last year, would we have believed it and tried to change our lives, our characters? Or would we have shrugged the prediction off as ridiculous and gone on to fulfill our fates?

Water rushed from a faucet upstairs and the sound brought the memory of the day I met Camille. I rubbed my elbow, re-experiencing that crazy pain shooting up my arm. Shackled as I was then to memories of Susanna, I would have railed against a prediction that the woman I mistook for an intruder, the woman who threw a bucket of scalding water at me, would soon share my life.

Rachel laid a hand on my arm, but said nothing. I stoked her fragile fingers and she cleared her throat. "Have you heard anything about Justin?"

I shook my head. "No. And there's no sign he's been around the house."

She glanced at the cordless phone handset on the table beside her rocker. "He hasn't called me. And he won't call Julie. They weren't speaking when he left and he's too proud to be the first to break."

Her fingers tightened on my arm. "Julie's got a lot of Lisa in her, but she's stubborn too. She hasn't asked about him, hasn't so much as flipped through the mail to see if he sent a card. I haven't told her that he's—"

"I'm home!" Julie burst through the door, shedding her backpack and flip-flops and rocketing to the kitchen.

"Where are your manners?" Rachel asked.

"Sorry." Julie popped open a can of orange soda and took a long swallow. "It's hot and the bus windows were stuck and the boys all stink like trash cans full of moldy gym socks and rotting fish. Where's Camille?"

"Upstairs," Rachel said, "cleaning your room."

Julie started to roll her eyes, then caught herself. "And I better help?"

She tacked a question mark on the end as if there was even a remote possibility Rachel might say "No," then shrugged and bolted up the stairs. In a moment we heard the roar of the vacuum cleaner and a persistent thudding.

"She rams it into the baseboard every time. You've got your work cut out with that girl."

"We'll manage," I assured her. We *had* to manage. We were committed. "Maybe we'll order rubber baseboards for the whole house."

She laughed, a dusty and distant sound. "You've got the right attitude. If you can't change it, find a way to cope with it."

I felt my throat constrict as I remembered the pills she'd stockpiled. When my time came, would I face up to it with as much determination? I leaned close and kissed her cheek. The skin was slack, dry and wrinkled like a bit of rag hanging from the ridge

234

of bone beneath her eye. This close, the sweet metallic odor stung my nostrils and I knew it for the scent of death. I wanted to jerk away, fought the impulse, kissed her cheek again. Tears welled in her eyes and her fingers closed around mine.

We were back in the depths of the album, studying a picture of Lisa when Julie came down the stairs, bumping the vacuum behind her. "Camille says she'll be done in five minutes." She jammed the vacuum into the closet, tried to close the door on the hose, made a frustrated noise like a squeaky toy, kicked the hose and slammed the door. She got two oatmeal cookies from a canister on the kitchen counter and plopped onto the carpet at Rachel's feet. "What are you going to do all summer while I'm gone?"

Rachel stretched out a trembling hand and smoothed Julie's hair back from her damp forehead. "Oh, sleep late, watch my soap operas without being interrupted, and eat all the ice cream myself."

"I'll miss you, too." Julie laughed, spraying cookie crumbs, then dropped her head and gnawed at her lower lip. "Are you sure it's okay if I go? Are you sure you'll be okay all by yourself?"

"Of course I'm sure."

"You won't get lonely?"

"I won't have time. Mrs. Gallagher drops by every day, sometimes twice a day, and there are the neighbors and old friends calling. Rachel flipped her fingers, waving aside Julie's concerns. "Besides, I have books and movies and indoor plumbing. You'll be living in a garage with an outhouse."

"But right by the lake." Julie's eyes glowed. "With Nelson."

235

"A three-legged dog is a definite selling point," I agreed.

"And Camille says you'll teach me to drive. On the back roads."

Rachel winced and I ran a mental movie of Julie behind the wheel. If she drove like she vacuumed, Hemlock Lake's residents, wildlife, trees, fences, and stone walls were in for it. And as the nominee to ride shotgun on her training runs, I'd need to stock more than a few bottles and six-packs of nerve tonic. "Camille forgot to tell me about that."

Julie dipped her chin and responded in a singsong voice. "Well, she didn't *exactly* say you would. But I told her that Justin learned to drive *way* before he was sixteen, and she didn't say that I couldn't."

Rachel shot me a sympathetic look. "Now that we know what Camille didn't say, tell us what she did."

"Um, that it would be up to Dan to decide because he knew the laws."

"That's what I thought. You need to work on separating truth from fiction, young lady."

Julie rolled her eyes and dug her toes into the carpet. The nails were painted a screaming yellow that made me grin.

"All done up there." Camille came down the stairs laden with paper towels and spray bottles. "Julie, if you get those boxes of girlie stuff from the bathroom and load them, we'll be ready to go jump in the lake."

"Yay! I'll call you every night, Grandma." Julie bounced to her feet, kissed Rachel's cheek, toed into her flip-flops, and pounded up the stairs.

"And I'll call you every morning," Camille said.

Rachel's face brightened, then tightened. "I'll be fine. You don't need to fuss over—"

"You're not *asking* us for anything" I told her. "We're offering."

"End of discussion." Camille grinned and carried the cleaning products to the kitchen.

Julie staggered down the stairs with two boxes balanced in her arms and we crammed them into my rig along with her backpack. Blinking away tears, she gave Rachel a final hug, then scurried outside without a backward glance.

"It will be a challenge, but I know you'll take good care of her." Rachel pressed her cheek against Camille's. "I know you'll come to love her."

"We already do." Camille sniffed and kissed Rachel's cheek.

Then it was my turn. I stroked her brittle hair. "You take care. Don't wear yourself down worrying about us."

"I can't help worrying, Dan. Not so much about Julie—I know you'll keep her safe and I know she'll be happy—but about Justin. I wish I knew it would all turn out for the best."

"It will," I said with as much confidence as I could muster.

"You almost make me believe that." Rachel stood and patted my head. "Run along now and let an old lady have a nap."

Just before I turned the corner, I glanced back. Rachel stood in the doorway, her hand moving back and forth as if she was erasing a chalkboard.

CHAPTER 24

Ten days later, feather duster in hand, Mary Lou fluttered from pew to pew in the sweltering Hemlock Lake Church, straightening hymnals in their racks and whisking invisible grit from the seats. Her graying curls, newly permed and set, bobbed as she worked her way toward the altar where Lou Marie and Jefferson stood talking with Reverend Balforth—or rather, listening to him talk. In a voice more pompous than solemn, he intoned his thoughts on marriage, wedding ceremonies, and the imprudence of the organist who sprained her wrist slapping a housefly thus forcing him to do double duty.

I stood off to one side, my polo shirt sticking to my back, waiting for instructions about my best-man duties and being thankful I didn't have to jam myself into the tuxedo until tomorrow. Jefferson wore a white long-sleeved shirt and a green-and-blue-striped tie, both already limp. Lou Marie's face was grim, gray, and greasy with perspiration. Her beige dress hung from her shoulders like a burlap sack but fit tight across the swell of her stomach. Her feet looked like blobs of rising bread dough, pale

238

and so swollen she'd unbuckled the straps of her canvas shoes. Even with the bottom panels of the stained glass windows cracked wide to create a cross current through the church, not a whisper of wind ruffled her hair.

Camille, wearing a short green skirt and a white scoop-neck blouse, sat on the stone steps outside the open doors, a book on her lap. Nelson sprawled on the grass in the shadow cast by the belfry, and Julie lay beside him, swinging a flip-flop from one toe as she talked on her cell phone. Even from here I could see that her body had changed since last summer. Her legs no longer looked like straight sticks and, as Camille told her last week, bras were no longer optional.

Getting her involved in self-defense training had been as simple as mentioning that every kid in town would be there. But it hadn't been easy to convince her we were serious about the safety rules we laid out—especially the ones about letting us know where she was at all times, not walking anywhere alone, and never staying home on her own. Julie clung to the image of the Hemlock Lake she'd known only a year ago.

Several times I felt my brain begin to boil with frustration—both at Julie and the killer who made caution necessary. Camille, after reminding me that I had also perceived myself as immortal when I was a teenager, took the carrot-and-stick approach. In an off-hand way, she made the observation that the road to driving lessons led through obeying the rules.

That worked until this afternoon when Julie refused to come with us to the church because of "that old witch." I couldn't blame her for hating Lou

Marie for those sniping remarks at Lisa's funeral last summer, so we compromised—she had to come along but she didn't have to enter the church until tomorrow when she could sit in a far corner and read.

Watching her sprawl in the cool shade, I wished I could make similar deals for myself.

"It's as airless as a tomb in here," Mary Lou whispered. She stashed the feather duster inside a tall vase and tugged at the belt of her yellow shirtwaist. "If Reverend Balforth wasn't watching I'd splash my face at the baptismal font."

I suppressed a smile and eyed the marble basin wondering where the water came from. How often was it changed? How many micro-organisms or mosquito eggs were floating in it?

"The forecast calls for tomorrow to be even hotter than today," Mary Lou said in a mournful voice.

I nodded. Unless a hailstorm delivered a few tons of ice pellets, we were in for a lot of misery until the ceremony ended and we moved to the cool sanctuary of the Shovel It Inn. When Shirley McDaniel hit menopause, she insisted on putting in air conditioning and Merle had valued his life enough not to argue. The cool air paid off both in terms of fewer mood swings and more summer evening business.

I glanced at Camille and decided that, even-tempered though she might be right now, I'd be wise to consider cooling her down in a similar manner. With all the other additions we'd made to the plans, what was another thousand or two for air conditioning? My frugal, progress-bucking grandfather would roll over in his grave, but it was my home now. And my money.

"At least I can still arrange the flowers tonight like I planned," Mary Lou murmured. "We cleared space in the beer cooler at the store to keep them. Otherwise the blooms would be fit only for the compost heap by tomorrow."

"Good thinking."

"There are sockets along the side walls. Would it be too tacky to bring over a couple of fans?"

I wrestled with another smile. "I'm not the right person to ask about what's tacky and what isn't. I'm a guy, remember?"

She rolled her eyes and raised a fist to punch my long-suffering arm when the reverend clapped his hands. "Let's run through it. Jefferson, after all the guests are seated, you and Dan will come in from the back and stand here." He pointed to a spot in front of the altar. "Dan, you'll have the rings."

I tapped the pocket of my khaki slacks, hoping the tuxedo Camille picked up for me this morning had pockets. She and Julie wanted me to try it on but I refused on the grounds that if we took it out of the plastic bag it would get wrinkled or stained or plastered with a layer of Nelson's hair.

"When I get to that part, you give the bride's ring to Jefferson and the groom's ring to Mary Lou to pass along when she takes the bouquet."

Balforth turned his gaze to her. "Now back to the beginning. When Dan and Jefferson are in place, I'll play the processional, and you walk down the aisle, slowly, and stand there." He pointed at another spot. "Lou Marie will follow when the traditional wedding march begins." He flicked his fingers. "Take your positions. Let's practice."

Jefferson trudged off behind the screen in back of the choir risers as if he was heading for a life sentence at a prison camp on a desert island. I followed at about the same pace. When we were out of sight of the others, I moved in front of him and locked my gaze on his. You don't have to do this, I thought. You can walk away and everyone will understand—everyone except Lou Marie.

He closed his eyes for second, shook his head, and looked down at a dog-eared book of sheet music open on a teetering music stand.

"The guests are all seated," Reverend Balforth called.

"And sweating like stevedores on a New Orleans dock in July," I said in a low voice.

Jefferson's lips twitched and faint sparks snapped in his eyes. Then he squared his shoulders and we marched to the altar.

Reverend Balforth struck up a halting rendition of a tune I'd heard somewhere before but couldn't name, and Mary Lou flashed Camille a grin and came through the double doors, hands clasped at her waist as if she was carrying a bouquet, walking with a slow stutter step. She gave me a twinkling smile and took her place on the other side of the altar.

The organ burped, Reverend Balforth struck up the "Wedding March," and Lou Marie came through the doors, eyes straight ahead. Never graceful, today she tottered, the buckles of her shoes catching on the nap of the blue runner, her right hand gripping the back of each pew as she passed.

Mary Lou mouthed, "Are you okay?"

Lou Marie scowled and pursed her lips.

Finally she was in place and Reverend Balforth brought the tune to a wheezing conclusion, scraped back the organ bench, and stalked to the altar. "This is when I'll deliver the sermon. I'll skip it this evening."

Camille, watching from the steps, turned two thumbs up.

"But tomorrow," he continued, "I'll talk about the sanctity of marriage and . . ."

I zoned out, counting the beads of sweat that broke from my armpits and trickled down my sides, watching Jefferson's jaw set like cement, imagining myself already sliding into the cool embrace of the lake at twilight.

"The rings," Mary Lou hissed.

"Sorry." I dug them from my pocket, passed the larger one to Mary Lou and held the other out to Jefferson.

He took it between his thumb and forefinger and Lou Marie held up her hand as if she was ordering someone to halt. Jefferson centered the ring on her third finger. It slid as far as the first knuckle and hung up. Frowning in concentration, he turned it like he was tightening a nut onto a bolt. The ring went no farther.

With an exasperated sigh, Lou Marie jerked her hand from his grip and pushed at the ring. The tip of her finger turned red. She grunted and shoved. The ring squeezed over the knuckle. Jefferson let out a breath. The ring hung up again on the second knuckle.

"Leave it for now," Mary Lou said in her calm and practical way. "Your hands are swollen from the heat. We'll soak them in an ice bath before the ceremony tomorrow and rub in some lotion. It will slide right on."

"It'll go on now," Lou Marie snapped.

The end of her finger was an ugly purple. I could almost see it throb. She twisted the ring and a thin circle of blood formed around it.

"You cut yourself." Jefferson pulled a fresh white handkerchief from the pocket of his slacks.

Lou Marie ignored it. The circle of blood widened.

"That cut's going to make it harder to get the ring on tomorrow," Mary Lou warned.

"It's not necessary for you to put it on today," Reverend Balforth said. "This is just the re—"

"I'll get a larger ring," Jefferson offered.

"I want this one." Lou Marie glowered at him and bore down again.

I held my breath, expecting to hear metal scrape bone. Blood welled from beneath the band as she twisted the ring. Then it slid across the knuckle. With a little cry, she jammed it against her engagement ring.

"There," she said. "It's on." Blood oozed from a torn flap of skin, seeping across her diamond, pooling in the webbing between her fingers.

Mary Lou made the sign of the cross, slipped the groom's ring onto her thumb, snatched the handkerchief from Jefferson, and wrapped it around her sister's hand. Bright blood seeped through the cloth. Reverend Balforth blanched, but Lou Marie snapped bloodied fingers at her sister. "Give me Jefferson's ring."

Mary Lou slid it from her thumb but the reverend intercepted it and handed it to me. "I think we've got the idea. Let's practice walking out now, newlyweds first."

Lou Marie scowled, but Balforth turned aside, put the altar between them, and busied himself flipping through his Bible. Jefferson, jaw clenched, took her arm and led her down the aisle. I waited a beat and stretched a hand to Mary Lou to lead her from the church, but she dropped to her knees and scrubbed with the hem of her skirt at a splatter of scarlet on the carpet.

CHAPTER 25

Camille had just filled our coffee cups the next morning when the phone rang. She snatched it up and whispered, "Hello."

I winced at this manifestation of what I called "morning stealth mode." In order not to wake Julie, we tiptoed around, opening the microwave door and unplugging the toaster oven before the timers dinged, setting things on the workbench counter without a clatter, talking in low voices.

On the opposite end of the day, however, Julie went into "evening explosion mode," talking on her phone, to us, and to Nelson in an outdoor voice, scraping boxes on the floor and hangers on the bar, and ignoring anything that looked remotely like a volume control on the television I'd caved in and gotten cable for.

Tonight, when the wedding reception was over, we'd have what my grandmother used to call a come-to-Jesus meeting about mutual respect.

"No," Camille gasped. The glass coffeepot fell from her hand and shattered on the cement floor. Coffee splashed across her bare feet and she jumped back against the workbench. "We'll be there in a few minutes."

"Don't move until I get the glass cleaned up." I bent to collect thin shards. "Where are we going?"

"Mary Lou's." She stretched out a quivering hand and set the phone down. "Lou Marie is . . . she's . . . dead."

"Dead?" Visions of the girls in the glade, Clarence, and his dogs, bloomed inside my brain like poisonous mushrooms. I straightened, turning toward the bedroom where I kept my guns in a locked chest. Glass slipped from my fingers, hit the floor, and splintered into smaller slivers. "When? How?"

"During the night." Camille snatched a paper towel from a roll on the workbench, blotted her feet and ankles, then squatted and used it to sop up coffee and plow bits of glass into a heap. "Mary Lou says it looks like she went to sleep and never woke up."

I felt my muscles relax. Natural causes. But a death nevertheless. I thought of that bright blood staining Lou Marie's hand, of Mary Lou making the sign of the cross, of John Donne's poem about the tolling bell and the ripple effect of loss.

"What's all the noise? Who never woke up?" Julie, Nelson at her side, came through the plywood door of her bedroom partition, yawning and dragging her fingers through her hair. She wore a pale blue tank top and white shorts. Her feet were bare.

"I dropped the coffeepot," Camille said. "There's glass everywhere. Go get your shoes on and keep Nelson out of here until I get it swept up."

"'kay. But who never woke up?"

247

Camille chewed at her lower lip.

"Lou Marie," I said.

Julie's eyes widened. She blanched and put her hands to her cheeks. "It's my fault. I wished on a star that she would just go away because she was so mean about my mother."

Camille and I glanced at each. I shook my head. This fly ball was hers to field. She nodded and stood. "It's not your fault, Julie. Lou Marie was sick. She's been sick for months."

I frowned. Months?

Julie rubbed her eyes with the heels of her hands. "But I—"

"You're not to blame. Now open the door and take Nelson outside, then get your shoes on and help me clean up this glass. After that we'll go into town, get a new coffeepot, and look for new bathing suits and more towels. If this heat keeps up like they say, we're going to be in the lake more than out of it."

Julie stood for a moment, her face screwed up as if she was about to cry. Then Nelson hopped to the door and she snuffled and trudged after him.

"Good job," I whispered.

"Shopping cures many ills," Camille said with a shrug. "She's young and she'll get past this in no time—especially with a little distraction."

"Hey." I spread my hands. "Whatever it takes. Get two bathing suits. Three. Four."

"I wish it could be that easy for Mary Lou." She touched my wrist. "I wasn't thinking when I told Julie we'd go shopping. If we drop her with Stub and Marcella, then I could come with you to—"

"It's okay. Julie needs you and I don't want her to feel that we're dumping her. Besides, Mary Lou and I go way back. As she's a little too fond of saying, she used to change my diapers."

Camille laughed for a second, then the laughter turned to soft sobs and she snatched another paper towel, held it to her face, and turned away.

I squeezed her arm. "This is exactly why I love you."

"You'd better go," she sniffled. "Mary Lou needs you."

I stepped behind our bedroom partition to trade my shorts for the slacks I wore to the church the day before, slipped on a pair of boat shoes, and shrugged into a brown T-shirt.

When I got to the white clapboard house where Mary Lou and her sister lived all their lives, Jefferson stood on the narrow porch gazing out at the mountains. He had the pole-axed, dead-eyed expression of a condemned man told he won't be shot at dawn but instead hanged at midnight.

"I would never have walked away," he said. "I would have married her today just like she wanted."

"No one claims you had any other intention." I gripped his shoulder and held it until he drew in a deep breath. From within the house I heard a clatter of dishes and the whistle of a kettle.

"Mary Lou's in the kitchen. Making tea." Jefferson stepped down off the porch. "I need to walk."

"Go ahead. I've got this." I opened the screen door and followed the screech of the kettle down the short, wide hallway that divided the living room from the parlor. Faded green wallpaper studded with sepia-toned family photographs in gilded oval frames lined both sides of the passage. I paused by a snapshot of Mary Lou and Lou Marie wearing long white christening gowns and caps, nestled in the arms of their parents. Lingering, I studied Lou Marie's smile, keeping my back to the staircase that led to the second floor and the room where she lay.

The screeching stopped and I heard the gurgle and splash of water and smelled a burst of orange and cinnamon. Remembering the cup of coffee I forfeited, I entered the kitchen. After Jefferson's return, when the sisters reconciled, they rearranged the furniture in the house once divided and moved Lou Marie's stove and refrigerator to the schoolhouse for him. But, uncertain about future living arrangements, they didn't fill the gaps or repaint. Lou Marie's side had the aura of a derelict building. I turned my gaze to the other half where colorful towels and potholders hung on hooks, copper-bottom pans shone, and a bouquet of roses graced the table.

Last night's heat hadn't dissipated and steam from the kettle made it worse; condensation beaded the wall above the stove. "Tea smells good."

Mary Lou set the kettle on the back burner and turned to face me. She wore a pink-and-white-checked housecoat and her hair was curled tight around knotted strips of rag. "I didn't know what else to do."

"Tea's always welcome."

Her hands fluttered and tears brimmed in her eyes. "I didn't know if . . . I didn't touch anything after I saw that . . ."

"Good. You did exactly right." I stepped to her side and wrapped her in a hug, tucking her head beneath my chin, patting her back with my fingertips. "Camille thinks Lou Marie was sick. For the past few months."

I felt her nod against my chest. "Something hasn't been right for more than a year. She was always tired. She didn't have an appetite. Her stomach swelled up. So did her feet."

And her hands, I thought, remembering her struggle to get the wedding ring on. If I hadn't glimpsed Jefferson's hesitancy about a physical relationship, hadn't been aware of Lou Marie's puritanical nature, I might have wondered if, at her late age, she was pregnant. "Was she seeing a doctor?"

"Not that I know about. She was . . . private."

Mary Lou pushed away and turned back to the business of making tea, swirling the bags she'd put in the pot, then lifting them out and setting them in a small bowl. "I remember when we were fourteen she'd get these awful cramps at that time of month. The doctor wanted to do a full exam and Mother gave him permission. Lou Marie was traumatized. She didn't speak to Mother for months. Even though the doctor gave her some pills that helped, she swore she'd never go back as long as she lived."

Mary Lou poured tea into two thick white mugs decorated with bluebirds and handed me one. I sipped, wondering if illness explained Lou Marie's backsliding after the first weeks of Jefferson's homecoming.

"I expect I'll need to call someone official." Mary Lou crimped her lips, then lifted her mug and mumbled into it. "I guess I didn't need to bother you."

"I'm glad you did. Glad I could be here." I sipped scalding tea. "Why don't I go upstairs for a minute and then I'll make the call?"

There was no reason for me to go upstairs, but something—maybe simply morbid curiosity—seemed to draw me there, and in a moment I stood in the sweltering upper hall. Four doors opened off it: three bedrooms and a bath. When they split the house—according to word that came around on the town grapevine—Lou Marie had appropriated the larger bedroom and the bath. Mary Lou, as always, hadn't complained. She accepted the two small bedrooms, used the half-bath beneath the stairway, and had a tiny shower installed in one corner of the laundry room.

I'd never been upstairs in the Van Valkenberg house, but right away I knew that the rooms to my left belonged to Mary Lou. The doors were painted white, had gleaming brass knobs, and were wide open, revealing polished floorboards and multi-colored rag rugs. I smelled sun-dried linens, roses, and talcum powder. The faint hiss of a toilet with a faulty gasket came from the room to my right. That left the dark wooden door ahead, the one with the chipped glass knob, the one closed tight.

Hauling in a breath, I stepped close and gripped the knob. It wobbled in the cylinder. The door juddered open, hinges creaking, and I peered inside.

The room was dim, yellowed shades drawn tight to the sill, blocking out both sun and air from two tall windows. A four-drawer bureau with a cracked mirror stood against the wall to my left and a nightstand and a bed claimed the wall to my right. The bed was high and narrow with a single pillow and plain white sheets. I remembered how Camille bet me Lou Marie had a fortune stuffed in her mattress. If she did, it wasn't in one-dollar bills. The mattress wasn't much thicker than my wallet and sagged in the middle.

Wearing a pair of faded blue cotton pajamas, her mouth agape, Lou Marie lay on top of the sheets, her left hand on her chest. I eased over to the bed and touched her neck. She wasn't cool to the touch because it was close to ninety in the room, but she was gone. Her body seemed shorter, thinner, more fragile, emptied of the forceful spirit that had inhabited it.

The wedding ring was still on her finger.

I stared at the gold circle and the faint crust of blood around it. She died believing she would be married today, died on the brink of having what she yearned for all those long years. She died short of facing the realities of marriage, the thousand negotiations and compromises.

Not that Lou Marie would have negotiated *or* compromised. She would have tackled marriage, like everything else, with the assumption that she was right.

I shook my head and backed away from the bed. Jefferson would have given in for a time, perhaps even for years. But there was steel at his core.

Crossing the room, I closed the door behind me and returned to the kitchen. Perhaps it was better that Lou Marie died anticipating a happily-ever-after marriage than lived to confront reality.

Jefferson's walk, according to those who spotted him along the way and filled me in later, took him down the west side of the lake, through the woods at the north end, and back up the road on the east side. By the time he returned, it was late afternoon.

In the meantime, I called the sheriff's office, drank two more cups of tea, ate several slices of cinnamon toast, phoned up Reverend Balforth to cancel the wedding, called Merle about the reception, then got hold of Alda Keefe and asked her to spread the word. Finally, I saw Lou Marie's body off. By then the small house was filled with women fussing over Mary Lou and trying to find room in the refrigerator for the traditional salads and casseroles.

I slipped out unnoticed and took my place in the circle of men beneath a spreading maple tree in the back yard, a circle formed around a cooler filled with beer. We were on our second bottles when, limping and gray with dust, his eyes still distant, Jefferson let himself in through the gate, and slid a bottle from the ice. Freeman laid a hand on his shoulder and Evan and Stub muttered that they were sorry, but that was the extent of conversation and display of emotion. We sipped, sweated, and swatted mosquitoes. Stub cleaned his nails with his jackknife. Evan occasionally imitated an owl by blowing over the mouth of his bottle.

Half a bottle after Jefferson returned, Camille came across the back porch and wrapped him in a hug, murmuring her sympathy. She handed him a damp towel and then directed the rest of us to get to work. "You all go over to the church and get some folding tables and chairs from the community room. Set them up here in the shade. A lot of food will go to waste if we don't eat it."

That galvanized the group and in a few minutes Alda and Pattie spread tablecloths across tables placed end to end. Shirley and Marcella carried out bowls of macaroni salad and platters of meat and cheese that had been intended for the reception and directed other women in the laying of silverware and plates.

Priscilla, I noticed, was not among them. I was sure that one of the women, perhaps after a meeting of minds or even a drawing of straws, had called her and passed along the news. So Priscilla was absent by choice, not due to oversight. Granted, she hadn't been invited to the wedding, but by not coming to offer her condolences, Priscilla was snubbing Mary Lou, the sister who had done her no harm. That wouldn't sit well with others. Traditions such as comforting the bereaved formed a line to be hewed to in Hemlock Lake.

Julie, subdued and speaking in a whisper only when she needed to, cut honeysuckle from along the split-rail fence at the back of the yard, put it in canning jars, then spaced the makeshift vases along the tables, filling the air with fragrance. When the tables were ready, we shuffled our feet and looked around in that vague way people do when no one wants to be first to the buffet line like a pig to a trough.

Then Mary Lou came down the porch steps and the shuffling ceased. Her curls were limp and tucked behind her ears and her eyes were red-rimmed and swollen, but she'd powdered her nose, put on pale pink lipstick, and changed into a pearl gray dress with black trim around the collar. She carried a single white rose. At the pace of the bridal processional, she walked to the center of the line of tables and laid the rose across the plate set there, then stepped to the right of that place and beckoned to Jefferson.

He came across the lawn like a sleepwalker and Mary Lou directed him to the chair on the left of the rose. "You'll sit beside him, Dan," she told me. "And Camille, you and Julie will sit beside me. And everyone else, sit with your friends and across from your neighbors and we'll have a feast that will put Thanksgiving to shame. But first we'll say a prayer for Louisa Marie."

Everyone found chairs to stand behind and we bowed our heads. Mary Lou took a lace-trimmed handkerchief from her pocket, stretched out her fingers, picked up the rose, and touched one of the thorns on its stem. "Louisa Marie, rest her soul, could be prickly. She never minced words, so today I won't either."

Alda, standing beside me, sucked in a breath, and a murmur rippled around the table.

"She wasn't easy on us," Mary Lou went on, "but she wasn't easy on herself, either. I don't know why; it was always that way. Parents don't mean to most of the time, but it's human nature to love one child more, or in a different way, than the other. Dan, you know how that is."

She paused and I felt the weight of a score of probing glances as I stared at that rose. "Right from the start, Louisa Marie made it difficult for my parents to love her. She was the one who got colic every week, howled when she was teething, refused to eat her vegetables, broke out in rashes, caught colds, and wanted everything exactly her way."

Mary Lou laid the rose back on the plate and dabbed at her eyes. "I remember once she held me down and cut off a chunk of my hair because hers wouldn't curl. I wanted to cut hers to get even, but my father gave me a lecture—not about turning the other cheek, but about the value of walking a difficult path, about the insight and depth of character I'd develop."

She chuckled and leaned to look at Julie. "Now I know that to some of you that seems like a load of hooey, but when I look back, I see that my father was right. In a strange way, Lou Marie was a gift. She was a reminder that there are a hundred little forks in our roads every day and each choice can affect the next one. If we don't think before we step, we might end up a long way from where we intended to be—from where we *wanted* to be."

Julie chewed at her lower lip, then nodded.

Mary Lou beamed at her as if she was a prize-winning student in the school of life. "And now my challenge will be to walk a path on my own without Lou Marie to help define my choices."

She took Jefferson's hand. "Even though you won't be my brother-in-law, I think of you that way. I'm glad you came back to us, and it will give me comfort if you stay on in the schoolhouse as long as you like."

Jefferson nodded and swallowed hard, but didn't speak. Mary Lou smiled up at him, dabbed her eyes, and then turned to Camille. "You came as a stranger and you stayed, even though some weren't welcoming or accepting. You won us over with your caring nature and your willingness to help. You left, but you returned at the moment you were needed."

Camille flushed and ducked her head. Mary Lou grasped her fingers. "The way of the world is that those who lend a hand get asked to lend another. You were willing to run the store while Lou Marie was on her honeymoon. Would you pitch in a little longer? Until I find someone to take over?"

"You're gonna run the store?" Julie gasped. "How come you didn't tell me?"

"Because we wanted it to be a secret. Until tomorrow. But how about it, kid? I can't do it alone. Will you help me help Mary Lou?"

"Sure." Julie flashed Mary Lou a tentative smile then frowned and whispered to Camille, a whisper that carried on the humid air. "Can we get some better kinds of potato chips and candy bars? And can we paint the walls a prettier color?"

There was a brief moment of silence and then Mary Lou chuckled and said, "Out of the mouths of babes."

She reached past Camille and ruffled Julie's hair. "Sweetheart, you can stock whatever you like. And you can make the walls any color you want. I'll buy the paint."

A wave of murmuring lapped along the tables, swelling and receding. Change was coming. And change had seldom been easy for folks in Hemlock Lake. But Mary Lou, in her oblique and gentle way, had preached a sermon more meaningful and powerful than any Reverend Balforth ever delivered.

"Let's all hold hands," she said, "and be still for a moment and look up at the mountains and wish for happiness for Louisa Marie who left us in the night but will be with us always."

"The ring," Jefferson whispered. "Do you have it?"

I slid my hand into my pocket, found it beneath my keys and a few coins, and passed it to him.

Without a word he slipped it on, then locked hands with me and Mary Lou.

CHAPTER 26

Early the next morning, Camille, Julie, Nelson, and I drove to the general store, Julie chattering all the way about the relative merits of potato chip brands and varieties, and Camille repeating, "We'll see," and reminding me we needed to check on state labor laws covering minors and make sure there was plenty of insurance.

Mary Lou stepped out of the post office to meet us. She looked pale, thinner, weighed down by the years. "I called for a replacement, but they said it would be a few days." She shot us an apologetic smile. "Guess that's what I get for never needing to be gone on personal business. They got to thinking it wouldn't happen."

She unlocked the door and stepped aside as Julie bounded into the store with Nelson on her heels. "It's pretty simple, but call me if you need help figuring things out. These are her keys." She held out a worn ring with a battered fob. Once, it had been a four-leaf clover, but green paint clung only to the center and one leaf had broken, leaving a jagged, bright-edged nub of metal.

"That snapped off when she dropped the keys just before we went over to the church." Mary Lou's face crumpled and she made the sign of the cross. "I'm not sure which key opens what."

"We'll get it figured out. Don't worry." Camille took the ring of keys. "And please tell me if there's anything we can do to help with the arrangements."

"I will." Mary Lou blotted her eyes on a tissue. "Careful you don't cut yourself on that fob."

Camille slipped the fob from the key ring and cocked her arm to toss it into the trash container at the edge of the parking lot. I caught at the sleeve of her lavender T-shirt. "Is it bad luck to toss out a lucky charm?"

"I never knew you were superstitious." She handed me the broken fob. "What do you suggest we do with it?"

"I don't know." I ran my finger along that jagged break, feeling the metal catch at my skin, then slipped it in my pocket. "I'll think about it."

"You might ask Rachel," Mary Lou suggested. "Folks used to go to her grandmother for potions and readings and charms. She had the healing touch and a bit of the gift of sight, but some said . . ." She peered into the store, and lowered her voice. "Well, some said she was a witch. Of course, that was just gossip. You know the way people go on about what they don't understand."

Or the way they go on about what they're *trying* to understand. Like the way we speculated about the monster who killed those girls and slaughtered Clarence and his dogs. Perhaps we did that to set ourselves apart from what frightened us, what we thought of as wicked, evil. And maybe we did it because we harbored a fear that we might be attracted by that evil, that we might have more darkness in us than we wanted to admit.

"It couldn't hurt to ask Rachel," Camille said. "And it might give her something to focus on besides . . ."

Her voice caught and Mary Lou hugged her and told her she knew of Rachel's illness. They stood there for a moment, comforting and drawing strength from each other and I felt a surge of pride that Camille was accepted and accepting. A pang of regret followed, regret for the years I'd shunned the comfort of this place because I couldn't see past the constrictions.

"Will you hurry up," Julie called. "I want to see what's in the back room."

"And to think that until she moved in we believed the sun was the center of the solar system," Camille said with a laugh. She broke from the hug and raised her voice. "I didn't hear that magic word."

There was a moment of silence and then Julie responded. "Puh-leeze."

"Don't be too hard on her," Mary Lou pleaded in a low voice. "She's excited, and she has a lot of pain on the way when Rachel . . ." She laid a hand on my arm. "And there's Justin. Have you heard anything?"

"No. I go by the house every few days, but there's no sign he's been around."

She pursed her lips, then turned aside. "I'll open the connecting door. Call if you need me."

Camille gave my hand a squeeze and we stepped into the store. I heard the familiar hum of the compressor in the frozen food case, and inhaled the odor of yellowed floor wax in the corners of the aging linoleum, the heavy sweet scent of apples and bananas going a little soft, and the faint sour smell of milk easing past its prime.

Camille headed for the dairy case. "I'll tackle this if you see what Julie's up to."

"What? No discussion? No negotiation? No coin flip?"

"Suck it up and get used to it. You're outnumbered by women." She opened the dairy case and blew a kiss over her shoulder.

Mock grumbling, I headed to the back of the store, found Julie waiting by a locked door, and thumbed through the keys on the ring for the one that worked. We entered a dingy room cluttered with stacks of paper products, laundry soap, kitty litter, and dog food. Nelson hopped to that stack and sat, resting his nose in the crease between two bags. To my right was a tiny restroom painted a muddy brown, straight ahead was the door to a six-by-six loading dock, and to the left was a third door. A fat padlock secured the wide strap of a scarred metal hasp.

Julie twisted the padlock in the staple. "What's in here? Why does . . . why *did* she lock it up?"

"Maybe it's where she kept the extra beer and other high-priced items." I selected a small brass key, slid it into the padlock, and twisted. It gave with a click.

"Do people try to steal those things?"

I considered that question. There was a lock on the door to the back room so shoppers couldn't slip in while she was occupied up front. And the outside door had a bolt as well as a lock—no one could come in that way unless Lou Marie opened the door. She would have done that only for deliveries.

"There isn't much profit in a little store like this,"
I told Julie. "You can't afford to have people walk off
with stuff, especially expensive stuff."

She wrinkled her nose. "But nobody around here
would steal. Nobody I know."

"But strangers come here too—hikers,
fishermen, hunters, people driving around in the fall
to see the leaves."

She considered that. "Then we'll always keep it
locked."

"Good plan."

But how long would she stick to it? A few days
ago she told us that she wasn't going to let her room
get messy or leave her things lying around in the
common space. This morning I found a wet
swimsuit on my chair and heard her promise she'd
make her bed later.

Julie swung the door wide and I saw what I
expected—beer, soda, candy, and a dull green metal
cashbox.

Julie picked it up. "It's heavy." She shook it like
a giant rattle. Coins clanked and paper shuffled.
"Money!" Her eyes shone with excitement. "It sounds
like a lot."

"Probably only a few hundred. I bet she emptied
the profits out of the cash register every evening and
stored the money here to pay for deliveries and save
up until it was worth making a trip to the bank."

"But the box is so heavy."

"Probably a lot of quarters in there." I thumbed
through the keys on the ring and found the tiniest.
"Let's see."

Julie held the box while I stabbed the key into
the lock and twisted. The second I withdrew it, she

flipped the lid open and gasped. "Lou Marie was rich."

I peered into the box. The coins we'd heard rattling were silver dimes. And the bills all had two zeroes on them.

"Wow." Julie ran her fingers through the coins and riffled the rubber-banded bills.

"Double wow," Camille said from behind us. "I wonder if Mary Lou knows about this hoard."

"Let's find out." Julie cradled the box to her chest and led our small parade to the post office where she set it on the counter. "Look what we found in the storeroom." With a flourish, she raised the lid and stepped back. "Ta da."

Mary Lou gaped at the contents for almost a full minute before she cleared her throat and spoke. "I'm not surprised she had money set aside. And I'm not surprised she didn't put it in the bank. But . . . there's so much." She stirred the dimes piled in the top trays. "I haven't seen a silver dime for years."

"Do you think there's more?" Julie bounced on her toes. "Like maybe under the floor or buried in the yard."

Camille shot me a smile. "Maybe there's a map under the frozen food with a big red X on it."

"Arrr, matey," I said in my best pirate voice. "And we'll dig up a chest full of booty. And a bottle of rum."

Julie punched my arm and Mary Lou rolled her eyes and riffled a stack of bills. "I don't think there's more. She would have wanted it all in one place."

Where she could count it every day when she locked up. I made a mental bet that Jefferson had no knowledge of this cache. I made another bet that, had she lived, Lou Marie wouldn't have told him. That wasn't in her character.

"Is it all yours now?" Julie asked Mary Lou. "Can you spend it on anything you want?"

Camille tapped her shoulder. "Is it polite to ask that?"

Julie flushed and ducked her head. "Sorry. It's just so exciting. It's like in a movie."

Mary Lou closed the lid. "Lou Marie didn't leave a will and she died before she married Jefferson." She crimped her lips and looked at me. "I'm her only living relative, but I'd like Jefferson to have half—or more. He's barely getting by on that little bit his mother set aside before she died. But right now we should get this into a safe place."

"Do you think somebody will try to steal it?" Julie hugged herself.

Mary Lou started to shake her head, then said, "Well, there's no sense tempting fate. Dan, will you take me down to the bank later on so I can put it in a safe deposit box?"

"Sure."

Julie jumped to the counter and wrapped her arms around the box. "Can I count it?"

"I don't see why not," Mary Lou said. "But take it into the back room."

"So fate isn't tempted." Julie headed through the connecting door. "Whatever that means."

Mary Lou watched her go with an indulgent smile. "From the time she was a little girl, Lou Marie always enjoyed counting the money at the end of the day. I remember her scooping up coins and letting them fall on her head like a silver shower."

Camille gave me a sidelong glance and I knew she was going over the same mental ground—the love of money and how that shapes character.

"Well." Mary Lou snatched a tissue from the pocket of her gray skirt and blotted her eyes. "I guess this proves that broken key fob isn't the bad luck charm I thought it was."

I slid my hand in my pocket and fingered the jagged metal. Camille gave me the ghost of a nod. Mary Lou could paint it any color she wanted, but that broken four-leaf clover belonged to a woman who died on her wedding day owning a box full of cash she'd never spend.

I closed my fingers around the charm, certain I wanted to toss it far away, and just as certain that I shouldn't.

CHAPTER 27

On Wednesday evening we buried Lou Marie beside her parents in the family plot. Mary Lou and Jefferson decided to have her dressed in her wedding gown and wearing her wedding ring. They also decided on a closed-casket service.

"We never talked about it," Mary Lou said, "but she'd hate people staring at her when she couldn't stare back or tell them to mind their own business."

I fingered the broken key fob I'd slid onto the ring with my keys. If anyone had the force of will to haunt us for making her a public spectacle, it was Lou Marie.

"And she wouldn't want an expensive casket, either," Mary Lou added. "Even though we could buy her the best with all that money. Almost a hundred thousand dollars."

We assured her she was doing the right thing, that no one would think less of her for that. "If there is a hereafter," Camille said, "I hope there's no such thing as social status. And I hope the quality of a box that goes into the ground doesn't determine where and how you live in the land of eternity."

"Amen to that," Jefferson said, and Mary Lou beamed at Camille and kissed her on both cheeks.

The sun hung low in the sky, but the heat was still ferocious. To my relief and surprise, Reverend Balforth delivered a blessedly brief message. That brevity, I suspected, was due in part to the black suit he sweltered in, but mainly because even a man who had conducted hundreds of services found himself taxed by the task of making lemonade out of the basket of lemons Lou Marie gathered in her contentious lifetime.

Again, Priscilla was conspicuous by her absence—an absence I knew was no accident. Camille had called her yesterday to make sure she knew about the funeral, and Alda followed up this morning, even offering to give her a lift. Priscilla dismissed her without a word of thanks. She also didn't call Mary Lou or deliver a card of condolence. Mary Lou, of course, brushed that aside but others didn't take the high road. Whether she was fuming over not getting an invitation to a wedding I bet she would have declined to attend, or whether she had other reasons, Priscilla was separating herself from the community.

Jefferson and Mary Lou gave us each a white rose and, once the coffin was lowered into the grave, we tossed the blooms onto the polished lid. They landed with the soft sounds of loneliness and loss. Julie broke into tears after she released hers and Camille plucked several spare blooms from a vase and led her to her mother's grave.

"She has a lot of healing to do," Mary Lou said as we watched them settle on the grass beside the white headstone with morning glories carved on it.

"I forget that sometimes," I said. "When she's talking with her friends or playing with Nelson she seems like any other teenager. Not like . . ."

Mary Lou patted my arm and I didn't finish that sentence. Instead I glanced toward the grave that held the mortal remains of Julie's father, the grave at the edge of the cemetery on the other side of a low rise of ground. Rachel had decided to bury him there instead of in another town.

I was in the hospital when they put him in the ground. Camille told me Priscilla screamed like a banshee about the man who killed her husband sharing the same hill. But Mary Lou understood that Rachel intended the gravesite to be a form of eternal punishment for her son. Ronny would be forever at the edge of the community, forever an outsider, his plot marked by a stone laid flat, etched with only his name and the dates of his birth and death.

Jefferson pointed at Julie, the gold band on his left hand glinting in the slanting sunlight. "Think she'll ever visit his grave?"

"She will when she's older," Mary Lou said. "When she comes to understand that not everything is black or white, bad or good."

"You ever go there?"

Mary Lou ducked her chin and spoke in a soft, apologetic tone. "I came up the day after Memorial Day and pulled the weeds. I . . . I thought someone ought to, for the good things he did before . . ."

"Did you leave flowers?" There was no trace of judgment in his voice, only curiosity.

She shook her head. "No. I . . . I didn't think that would be right."

269

I felt vaguely comforted both by what Mary Lou had done and what she hadn't, although I couldn't explain to myself why I found it soothing that her goodness had limits. I thought about Ronny moldering in his grave and decided that, before too many weeks passed, I'd come and have a talk with him.

Camille and Julie returned with a handful of wild strawberries—three for each of us, tiny bites of sweet summer. As we drove away—Julie back to her buoyant self and chattering about a song she heard that morning—I glanced into the rearview mirror and saw Mary Lou and Jefferson standing like sentinels on either side of Lou Marie's grave.

I remembered how I stood at my mother's grave long after others departed. Evening closed in and rain pattered on her coffin while I waited for a sign that it was time to walk away and leave her to the earth. It was the thought of being jeered at for being too stupid to come in out of the rain that finally sent me trudging home in soaking clothes and squishing shoes.

I don't know how long Jefferson waited for his sign that it was time to leave Lou Marie, but late that night I heard the distant echo of shots across the lake and I knew he was up in the sandpit, a night scope on his rifle, drawing a bead on some kind of peace. Despite the heat, I curved my body against Camille's, breathing in her scent. For all I had, I was grateful. And because of all I had, I felt a sharper pain for Jefferson's many losses.

The shots continued for an hour or more, each one like a punch to my heart.

The next day was the Fourth and we took Julie and two of her young cousins to a day-long festival in a town thirty miles away. The cousins, pudgy pre-teen girls with freckles, followed Julie like puppies and squealed with delight about everything from the deviled eggs to the fireworks at dusk.

"Julie needs to connect with Lisa's family," Camille said when she caught me wincing. "And the damage to your ears won't be permanent."

I acknowledged her point and rewarded myself with a double shot of whiskey when we got home. A man did what a man had to do to survive in a world filled with strong-willed women.

Friday, work resumed on the house, and I went back to sanding baseboard I'd cut the week before. When someone means you to die and you thwart their intention, even mundane and repetitive tasks take on deeper meaning. But it was hot and dusty work, so I welcomed the interruption when I spotted Jefferson easing down the driveway like a footsore man at the end of a long march.

He stood for a few minutes, watching two men fitting planks of cedar siding into place on the walls while a third anchored them with stainless steel nails. Then he came around the garage, drew up a lawn chair, and sat beside me in the shade of a clump of birches.

The thwacking of the nail gun and the hiss of the compressor were muffled here and because I was shielded by the bulk of garage, I didn't feel the need to work as hard as the siding crew. Senseless guilt. I was the boss and could do whatever I wanted, but I'd been imprinted with a family work

271

ethic passed down like a priceless heirloom and as slow to erode as granite.

"You getting any sleep?" I asked Jefferson.

"Not much. An hour here and there."

He looked it. His skin was as gray as his hair, his eyes dry and sketched with thread-like red lines, the lids puffed.

"I heard you taking target practice the other night."

He grunted. "Sorry if I disturbed your rest. I just—"

"That was a comment, not a complaint." I ran my fingers along the board, found a rough spot, and gave it a few more licks. "Whatever gets you through the dark hours is fine with me."

He nodded and we said nothing more for a while. A sorry excuse for a breeze slunk off the ridge and feathered the lake.

Jefferson rubbed at his brush cut and cleared his throat. "You heard anything about Clarence or those girls?"

"Not a word from the sheriff." I checked the rough spot, decided it met standards I'd been lowering a notch each day, and set the board aside. "And there's nothing new in the paper."

"Yeah, but that reporter we got out of the mud keeps picking at it like a scab."

He bent to one side, picked up a stick, and tossed it at Nelson who lay curled in a hole he'd excavated that morning. Given his missing hind leg, the excavation process had been slow, awkward, and amusing—at least for me. The last time he fell over I could almost hear him wondering if it was worth it, but he struggled upright and went back at it. When he determined the hole was deep enough,

272

he dropped into it with a grunt and closed his eyes. The thwump of the nail gun no longer seemed to bother him, and neither eyelid twitched when Jefferson's stick landed a few inches from his muzzle.

I considered the stack of boards left to sand and decided that if Nelson could hang it up for the day, so could I. There were hours of staining and varnishing ahead. In heat like this, a smart man paced himself. And stayed hydrated. "Want a beer?"

"You getting up anyway?"

"Got to. Nelson hasn't learned to fetch from the refrigerator yet."

Jefferson snorted out a laugh. "Don't look like he'll be doing any training toward that today."

"Or much of anything else." I levered myself out of my chair, ambled into the garage, and pawed past diet soft drinks, tubs of yogurt, and sacks of salad vegetables until I found the beer. After the house was finished, I'd keep this refrigerator in a corner of the garage to have a place where guy grub wasn't crowded out by female food.

"Guess I can't blame that reporter," Jefferson said when I handed him a bottle beading with moisture. "It's the biggest thing to happen around here since . . ."

Last year, I thought, filling in the blank. If Colden Cornell had been working for the paper back then he would have camped out at the Shovel It Inn and followed me around like a dog looking for a handout. I sipped beer, concentrated on the chill bite of the first swallows to clear that image from my mind, and watched another desultory breeze dip its fingertips in the lake.

Jefferson drank, then closed his eyes and pressed his bottle against the swollen lids. "What do you know about Luke?"

I hesitated, trying to recall if the sheriff had asked me to keep quiet about Luke's record.

"I'm all for being allowed a little privacy," Jefferson said in a rush. "And I know there aren't many secrets in this neck of the woods, but he seems to work too damn hard at keeping his close. Lou Marie had a bad feeling from the first day she laid eyes on him. She thought he was hiding something."

"Yeah, she wanted me to check him out." More like told me. Did that request have less to do with intuition than with animosity toward Priscilla?

"And did you?"

"Well—"

"None of my business." Jefferson rubbed his brush cut. "I won't be pissed if you tell me to back off."

I nodded. "Between you and me, the task force checked him out. But they did it in a way that wasn't exactly kosher. If Priscilla learns about that, I wouldn't want to be within a hundred miles of her."

"I heard that." Jefferson clinked his bottle against mine and raised it.

"The task force wrote him off for those girls. But he's not squeaky clean."

Jefferson lowered the bottle.

"He worked as a short order cook. Blamed his boss for his mother's accidental death and went for him with a cleaver. Did a short stretch in jail."

Jefferson's eyes narrowed and then he shrugged. "I might have done the same."

"Me too."

"Still, it shows he's got a well of anger."

"Yeah, but going from that to killing girls—it's a leap for the guys on the task force."

"Luke's not a big guy. Girls are easier prey. Maybe a girlfriend told him to take a hike."

"Anything's possible with a twisted mind," I agreed. "And Luke is stronger than he looks. But he was in jail when the second girl was taken."

Jefferson rolled the bottle between his hands, the glass clicking against his wedding ring, counterpoint to the sounds of saws and nail guns. Click. Click, click. Click. "Maybe he had help."

The beer I just swallowed rose in my throat, bitter, hot. A second killer. A team.

Why hadn't I thought of that?

CHAPTER 28

I remembered the scene in the glade, the furniture, the staging. The work of two sick minds?

Had the task force considered that?

They must have. Those guys were experts.

And if the killers were a team, did they always hunt and kill together? Or were the murders prompted by individual need and opportunity, and shared only when it was convenient? Was one killer in control and did the other do his bidding? Did their needs feed off of each other?

One girl was taken while Luke was in jail. But being in jail didn't prevent communication with a partner on the outside. The partner could have captured her, held her as a gift to celebrate Luke's release.

Was Justin that partner?

He and Luke might have met—somehow, somewhere—and been drawn to each other.

I gripped the bottle with both hands, bringing myself back to the sunlight. "There haven't been any more killings. Not since the girl at the war memorial."

"That we know of," Jefferson countered in a steady and undemanding tone. "He could have killed a dozen women and dumped them in these mountains and no one would find them until hunting season—and maybe not then. The woods are filled with thickets and hollows."

Justin knew these woods—knew them well. And Luke, who fished the Birchkill, might have explored the hills around that stream.

"Gotta find out more about Luke," Jefferson said. "Find out who he sees and what he does in his spare time besides fishing."

I grunted. "Won't be easy. He's as loquacious as your average rock, and I'd rather corner a skunk than ask Priscilla if she knows what he gets up to."

"We could follow him."

"With as little traffic as there is around here? He'd spot us in a minute."

Jefferson waved my objection aside. "We'll get a couple of locator devices and tag Priscilla's car and truck."

I coughed out half a laugh, then stared at Jefferson. "You've been giving this some thought."

"Had time."

I finished my beer, mulling over invading Luke's privacy and the price of getting caught at it.

"I'll put them on at night," Jefferson volunteered. "He'd never know I was there."

True. Luke and Priscilla parked the car and truck a dozen yards from the house and Jefferson made about as much noise as a falling leaf. "Let's think about it for a bit."

"Good enough." He stood, gave me the shadow of a salute, and headed up the driveway.

I watched him go, wondering why I hadn't shared my suspicions about Justin. Was I not all that certain? Was I shielding him on behalf of Julie and Rachel? Had I put Jefferson off about tracking Luke because I feared that would lead us to Justin?

I wrestled those thoughts aside and picked up a fresh board. My cell phone rang and I set the board aside and dug the phone from the front pocket of my jeans.

"I'll do it tonight." Rachel's voice, a rasping whisper. "I've got everything finished with my lawyer and I wrote out my . . . final instructions. Mrs. Gallagher has your number."

I hesitated for a few seconds—nothing in my experience had prepared me to form an appropriate sentence in response to this. "Thanks for letting me know."

"I'm sorry to have all this fall on you, Dan. But there's—"

"I'm glad to do it," I said before she could finish that sentence, remind us there was no one else, force us to relive the why of that. "It's an honor, a privilege."

"You're a sweet man, Dan Stone. You sound almost convincing." She laughed, a rusty sound giving way to a gasping cough that made my chest hurt.

"I wish it hadn't come to this."

"You must play the hand you're dealt," she said with conviction. Each word was encased in a wheeze of air I suspected was pushed from her lungs by will alone. Yet, in spite of that, I heard no regret, no yearning for another deal, better cards, a chance to draw from the deck.

"We'll take good care of Julie. And Justin."

278

"Have you—?"

"No. But I'll keep looking. I talked to a lawyer, so I know what to expect, what to do when he turns up."

She sighed, but said nothing. Despite the thwack of the nail guns, the electric song of the saws, and the voices of the construction crew, silence seemed to open before me like a pit. I gripped my chair arm with my free hand and kicked a toehold in the dirt.

"Thank you, Dan. And thank Camille. For everything."

The firm resolve with which she said the final word made me suspect she was thinking of Ronny, of Camille's bullet. I felt my throat closing up.

"I wish I'd gotten to know her better. I wish so many things."

Her last words were so faint I barely heard them. Then there was a click and the drone of the dial tone.

For a long while I gazed out over the lake, a prisoner of mortality, a hostage to the relentless passing of time. Nelson opened one eye and peered at me from his hole. "Come on," I said, "let's go for a ride."

When I pulled up in a patch of shade on the far side of the post office, Camille was filling a long wooden planter with vivid pink petunias. Figuring Nelson would make a mess of the project, I told him to mind the car. To my surprise, he thumped his tail on the seat, yawned, and curled up for a nap. I left him to it.

"Jefferson made the planter," Camille said. "Isn't it grand?"

"Grand," I agreed, watching her set the last petunia in place and tamp down the soil with her trowel, her back muscles flexing beneath a white tank top.

She dusted her hands on jeans streaked with dirt and kicked aside a litter of empty plastic containers. We stood back, admiring the box crafted from split birch logs and set on a pedestal of rocks fitted together with the skill Jefferson honed last summer building cairns. "I'm not wild about pink, but it sets off the white of the birch bark and the blue paint that Julie picked for the door. Brightens up the place."

"Bright is good."

She canted her head, studied me for half a minute, then drove the blade of the trowel into the soil and asked in a whisper, "Rachel?"

"Tonight."

She moaned, put the back of her hand against her mouth, and hung her head for a few seconds. "I thought I'd be ready."

I wrapped my arms around her. "So did I."

"When will . . .?"

"Her hospice worker comes in early tomorrow morning, so if . . ."

Camille locked her arms behind my neck, pulled my head down, and kissed me hard. "You're a good man, the best I know. I love you."

A bell jingled and the door opened wide. "How much toilet paper should we order?" Julie called out. "There's a guy on the phone who wants to know right now."

280

"Toilet paper." Camille giggled and broke away whispering, "So much for a serious, intimate moment."

I grinned. "Nothing says serious and intimate like TP."

"It's not funny." Julie planted her fists on her hips. "I don't have time to count the stock because I'm cleaning up for the interview."

"Interview?" I raised a brow.

"I'll tell you about it in a minute. Pick up those pots and the other stuff, okay?" Camille bounced to her toes and kissed the point of my chin.

"Scutwork is my middle name," I muttered, earning a light punch on the arm before she followed Julie into the store. Gathering the plastic pots, I stuffed them into an empty sack of potting soil along with four other crumpled sacks—two of soil and two of compost. Snagging the trowel as I went, I carried the sack around back to the loading dock and left it for Camille to decide whether the pots would be recycled for another purpose and whether the trowel would stay here or come home to its peg in the garage.

On my return, I passed through the post office and waited behind a woman whose manicure and makeup told me she lived in one of the homes built last year. It was a full two minutes before she finished a convoluted story about a crack in her patio and left in a luxury car. When I leaned on the counter, my intention was to tell Mary Lou about Rachel's plan, but instead I held onto that and said, "Rachel's going downhill fast. Could be any day now."

Mary Lou slid off her glasses and blotted her eyes. "Seems like every time I turn around we're at that cemetery. They say deaths come in threes. Maybe this will be the last for a time."

I leaned against the counter and slipped my hand in my pocket, fingering Lou Marie's broken good luck charm. It was all in where you counted from and the time frame you set to count within. We had six deaths last year from autumn to autumn: my wife, my brother, my father, Willie Dean, Lisa, Ronny. Two sets of threes. And now three more— Clarence, Lou Marie, and Rachel. Six if you counted the three girls in the woods. One more if the girl left at the war memorial was somehow connected to Hemlock Lake. Were we due two others?

The bell above the door jangled and Evan Bonesteel came through. "Place looks nice," he said, with a nod toward grocery store. Then he ducked his chin and, with a sidelong glance at Mary Lou, added, "Different."

She slipped her glasses back on and gave him a flicker of a smile. "This different is a good thing, Evan. I'm okay with the change."

Evan ducked his chin again, opened his mailbox, and pawed out a couple of envelopes. Before I thought of telling him we should prepare a place for Rachel in the cemetery, he scuttled off.

"I'll be glad when people stop treating me like an antique crystal vase." Mary Lou gripped the edge of the counter. "I didn't shatter all those years I lived with Lou Marie going at me hammer and tongs, and I'm not going to fall apart now that she's gone."

"That's the price of being so warm-hearted, Mary Lou. People don't realize you've got steel inside." I laid my hands over hers. "They mean well."

"I know. But sometimes I get tired of . . .being the person they expect me to be." She clicked her tongue as if chastising herself. "Does that surprise you?"

"Not in the least." I squeezed her hands. "It's the burden of living in Hemlock Lake."

"The burden of the past," she agreed. "We're like turtles. We carry that shell with us all the time."

I nodded and we stood for a moment in commiserating silence before she drew her hands from beneath mine and flicked her fingers toward the store. "You'd better get on in there, I expect those girls have a chore list half a mile long for you to tackle."

I sighed. "Another burden."

"And one you relish even if you pretend you don't. Now go on."

I did, and found Julie rearranging the candy display rack near the cash register. "Should I put the ones with mostly red wrappers on top, or the yellow ones?"

"Up to you."

She gave me the fists-on-hips stance again. "You are zero help."

Camille's laugh billowed from somewhere at the rear of the store and I ambled that way, admiring shelves with jars and cans faced in neat stacks and rows, hand-printed signs advertising special prices on pork and beans, and pyramids of cabbage, potatoes, and onions. I glanced up to see that the fly-spotted fluorescent light covers had been cleaned and noted not a trace of a flicker—the old tubes were gone and the light from the news ones reflected off a fresh coat of glossy white paint on the ceiling. Even the smell was different—a mix of bleach and lemon and vanilla.

"You've been busy."

"Gotta do something between customers." Camille barely glanced up from scraping the floor where a rack of dusty personal care items stood for as long as I could remember. She was using a razor blade and making slow progress, peeling curls of dark grime. "I'm getting blisters on top of blisters."

I squatted beside her. "Want me to scrape for a bit?"

"No. I'll get the rest of this another day when we're not facing a deadline. Right now you can slide that over." She aimed her chin at a gleaming metal cabinet with a shiny new microwave oven on top. "It's for the burritos and chili we're going to stock."

Microwavable snacks. Forget just rolling over in her grave, Lou Marie would be doing cartwheels.

"Julie wanted hot dogs, but—"

"That's Marcella's standard lunch item."

"It's her *only* lunch item. I'll bet she doesn't sell more than two in a week, but it wouldn't be neighborly to outdo her dogs." Camille grinned. "Anyway, I need to get this plugged in and working. Give me a hand?"

I muscled the cabinet closer and Camille plunged the plug into a socket and helped me arrange things to hide the dirty patch of linoleum. "I assume your deadline involves the interview. It's not with that guy from the *Mountain Missive* is it?"

Camille's cheeks turned a ruddier bronze. "Yes. He called this morning. Julie answered the phone and before I knew it . . ."

She threw up her hands, acknowledging her helplessness before the juggernaut that was a teenage girl. "I know you don't care for him, but . . . well, the article will be a distraction and I made it clear that the topic is the store. We won't talk about the murders and if he has questions about Lou Marie he'll have to go next door."

A smart man knows when something is a done deal. He also knows how to get away with his pride intact. "Sounds like you have it under control."

"I'll be right beside Julie the whole time. If he tries to make an end run, I'll shut him down."

She would. She'd give him a verbal ass-kicking. No hiding in the garage and avoiding conflict. A flush of embarrassment scorched my neck—I hadn't told Camille about that particular finest hour and didn't intend to. "If you want to get the word out about the changes you're making, an interview's the way to go."

"We're trying to avoid the word 'change.' It seems insensitive, even though Mary Lou says she's okay with it." She glanced toward the post office. "I like 'supplementing available choices' or 'enhancing the shopping experience' or 'catering to more diverse appetites.'"

"Rolling out a bunch of thousand-dollar marketing phrases won't fool anyone," I said with a grim laugh. "Folks in Hemlock Lake know change when they see it. And mostly they don't like it."

"And you and I were once poster children for the perils of change. But things have . . . well, there are some new patterns weaving into the social fabric, and I have a few ideas about how to accelerate acceptance." She laced her fingers with mine, led me to the front of the store, and pointed at a shoebox painted neon pink. "Behold. The suggestion box."

"I made it," Julie crowed as she slid a candy bar with a silver and blue wrapper into a zigzag of color on the rack.

"Impressive." I studied the neat slot sliced into the top of the box and the black question marks painted around it. "Got any suggestions yet?"

Julie's smile turned to a sour pout. "Two. From Priscilla. She suggested that I stop dressing like a streetwalker."

My jaw and fists clenched simultaneously and I glared in the direction of Priscilla's place.

"Don't go all caveman on us." Camille put a hand on my arm. "That's about what I expected from her. She also suggested we tell people that soft drinks and chips are a nickel cheaper and two weeks fresher at the bait shop." She snatched a square of paper from a stack beside the box. "After that, we refined the suggestion process."

"Now it's more like voting," Julie added.

Camille passed the paper over and I saw it was a list of possible suggestions. "What color should we paint the walls?" I read. "What would you like to see on our shelves? How could we make it easier for you to find things?"

"See," Julie said. "If a whole bunch of people say the walls should be white, that's what we'll paint them." She made the "gag me" sign. "Even though that's my least favorite color."

"You'll still get snide comments from Priscilla," I warned.

She shrugged and made the "gag me" sign again.

"If Priscilla drops in again, which I doubt," Camille said, "I'm going to turn on my syrupy Southern charm and inquire why she comes to a place that obviously offends her so deeply."

She took the paper from my hand and taped it back to back with another copy, then attached them to a broad red ribbon hanging from a pin in the

286

ceiling. "There. We're ready for an avalanche of opinion." She glanced at the clock just as I caught a flash of movement in the parking lot and turned to see Colden Cornell's truck. "And right on time."

"Oooooh." Julie did a little tiptoe dance and hugged herself. "I'm so nervous. It's my first time ever to talk to a reporter." She fluffed her hair. "Do I look okay?"

"You look terrific," I said, meaning it. She was wearing an orange sleeveless T-shirt, a short denim skirt, and her orange flip-flops. Her toenails matched her skirt.

"Are you sure? He said he's going to take pictures."

"Just of the store. And you," Camille said. "I look like I've been wrestling pigs."

Julie gave her an appraising look. "You could go home and change and he can take a picture of us together," she suggested half-heartedly.

"No, thanks. I'd have to change back so I can paint the bathroom."

"Whatever." With a tiny spark of satisfaction in her eyes, Julie skipped to the door and flung it wide for the reporter to enter. "Good morning," she burbled. "It's so neat you're going to write about the store. Can I get you a soda or something?"

"I'm good for now." With a bob of his head, Cornell stepped past her.

He wore a long-sleeved beige oxford cloth shirt with the tails out over jeans with sharp creases. I don't know why, but I was willing to bet a hundred dollars the jeans had an elastic waistband. Despite the recorder and notepad in his hands and the camera slung around his neck, he appeared unsure and uncertain, only slightly less ineffectual than the day Jefferson and I got him out of the mud.

Was it his job that made me dislike him? Or was it that, by Hemlock Lake standards set by my father's generation, he didn't seem to be the man you'd turn to in a pinch? Only two inches taller than Julie, he was more a Willie Dean than a Ronny. But was that such a bad thing?

His gaze swept the store, reached me, faltered. His cheeks turned the color of beet juice and his jaw slackened, pulling his lower lip from beneath that wispy mustache.

"Gotta run," I said to Camille. "Call me if you need any heavy lifting."

She nodded and I pushed past the reporter and strode across the lot to my rig. Nelson was sitting up in the front seat watching the store. He whined and tried to get out, but I pushed him over and got behind the wheel.

"You're not going in there," I told him. "Julie doesn't have time for you right now. She's busy with that reporter. If you get between them it won't be pretty."

Nelson whined again and I scratched behind his ears. "Let her enjoy this. She's got a lot of pain on the way tomorrow."

CHAPTER 25

I woke up long before dawn, skin burning and itching as if I'd slept on a nest of fire ants. Pulling on cutoffs and a T-shirt, I toed into a pair of moccasins, walked to the dock, and watched the last of the western stars fade and the mist on the lake glow a shimmering pearly white as dawn came on. Like melted butter, sunlight slid down the mountainsides, pooled in the hollows, and skimmed the water.

When I heard the faint buzzing of an alarm clock I returned to the garage, fed Nelson, and made coffee. Then I fired up the camp stove and fried potatoes with onions, and eggs laced with sharp cheddar cheese. Camille, after a glance that slid from my face to the cell phone I'd set on the workbench and back again, said, "Good idea. Extra carbs and protein." She slathered both butter and strawberry jam on her toast and cleaned her plate, leaving only a few shreds of potato and a smear of egg for Nelson.

Julie, usually picky in the morning, ate like she'd heard reports a great famine was due. Mouth full, she chattered about the interview, friends she hadn't called yet, whether she should have posed next to the door instead of behind the counter, whether she should have worn another top, the number of papers we'd need to buy, how jealous her friends would be, and whether they'd really have to paint the walls gray or some other lame color if that's what everyone suggested.

While her words plunked and pattered around us like marbles spilling from a jar, Camille made little sounds signifying everything would be fine or at least work out in the end. I sat with hunched shoulders, anticipating the avalanche of emotion that would follow Rachel's death.

A scrofulous pickup belonging to two guys from the construction crew—guys who had been working in Texas when Clarence died—pulled up beside the new house as I poured Camille's second cup of coffee into a to-go mug. 7:45. She hustled Julie out the door and into her car, leaving me alone with Nelson and the phone now in my pocket. It seemed to grow larger and heavier with each minute that staggered by.

What time would Mrs. Gallagher arrive? How would she find Rachel? Cold, dead for hours? Lingering in the limbo of a medication-induced coma? Weak and angry after vomiting up pills hoarded at such great cost?

In an effort to rechannel my mind, I carried the pans outside, turned on the hose, and scrubbed them in the double sink I'd set up on a couple of sawhorses. Then I wiped the table, made our bed, started a grocery list, considered getting back to my sanding project, swept the floor, and dumped potato and onion peelings on the compost heap. 8:16.

I walked over to the house and watched the crew slapping on the siding. There were no new faces, no one I needed to check on. Several nodded when they glanced my way. 8:23.

Returning to the garage, I dug through a bag of books I'd picked up at a used bookshop while Camille prowled a department store making notes about dishes and glassware, small appliances, pots, and pans. A fat volume about Lincoln's cabinet caught my eye but I put it aside for a day when I could concentrate. 8:32.

With Nelson at my heels, I walked to the end of the dock, slipped off my moccasins, and sat. The surface of the lake was still and glossy. Nelson flopped on his stomach and turned his nose to the breeze while I paddled my feet in the water, watching ripples undulating toward the far shore, and thinking of Tennyson's poem, "Crossing the Bar." If Rachel succeeded last night, had she been aware when she passed from life into—

What? Where?

I kicked hard at the water, churning up a thousand ripples. I remembered she said she was going to join her husband Buck, Lisa, and Ronny. That implied they'd all be together.

I gripped the edge of the dock until my hands ached trying to reconcile that. Lisa deserved an afterlife far from the man who bullied and then killed her. If heaven existed, she deserved a prime piece of real estate there. And if there was a hell, Ronny deserved a windowless cell in a subbasement.

I kicked the water again. If heaven and hell existed, which one would be my afterlife address? I'd

291

been prideful, stubborn, and blind to what I should have seen. I'd been jealous, angry—

The phone rang.

I dug it from the pocket of my shorts and flipped it open. 9:07. "Hello?"

"Mr. Stone? This is Bernice Gallagher." A hesitant voice. "Rachel Miller died in her sleep last night."

I raised my arm and gave the sky a high-five. Rachel had crossed the bar. But at what price?

"She went peacefully." Mrs. Gallagher's voice filled with awe. "She has the most beautiful smile."

I let out a vast sigh of relief. "Thank you for calling, for telling me that. What . . . uh, what do we do now?"

"I've got a call in to our hospice doctor to get the death certificate signed. Once he takes care of that, you can make arrangements with a funeral home right away."

"Right away? We won't have to wait on an autopsy?"

"Oh, I doubt it. There usually isn't." She sounded surprised and I worried that I'd raised suspicion, but she hurried on in a reassuring tone. "There's no reason I can see. The doctor was amazed she held on this long with the cancer as bad as it was."

I pumped my fist to the sky again. Rachel had been dealt a tough hand, but she played her final cards well. She'd go to her grave whole, her secret intact. My respect for her strength and determination swelled and I wished I'd gotten to know her as more than Ronny's mother and Julie's grandmother.

"I'll let Julie know," I told Mrs. Gallagher. "Then I'll come down and see what needs to be done."

"She planned her funeral a few days ago. I wrote down exactly what she wanted."

A plain box, I bet. And a familiar verse or two. No waste of money or sentiment.

"Sorry, but I've got another call coming in," Mrs. Gallagher said.

"Right. I'll see you soon."

Nelson trailed me to the garage, his ears lifted, his expression hopeful. "No ride today."

His ears drooped lower and lower as I changed into a pair of gray slacks and a dark blue shirt. By the time I put on socks and loafers, I had second thoughts. Julie might find it comforting to hang onto him, and Camille said he took being at the store in stride, never begging from customers, never barking, never running off, but passing the time sitting beside the front door or lying in the shade under the loading dock. I led him outside and locked up the garage. "Okay. Let's go see the girls."

I took my time, stopping to watch a doe and two fawns drinking from the lake near Bobcat Creek, reminding myself that life goes on, that Rachel knew that.

I slowed to wave to Stub at the garage, and idled the engine waiting for Alda Keefe to back out of the parking lot before I rolled in. I turned off the ignition, checked the odometer, and even worked the key off the ring and flipped it so it faced the other way.

Camille came around the side of the building carrying a dented watering can. Her gaze locked on mine and she backed up a step and set the can

293

down so hard water sloshed on her bare legs. "You got the call?"

"Yes." I got out and pulled her against me. "She went peacefully. She was smiling. It doesn't look like there will be an autopsy."

"And no one needs to know but us," Camille said. Not a question.

"Exactly." Glad that I hadn't told Mary Lou, that this secret was ours alone, I kissed the top of her head. "I brought Nelson."

"Good." She drew in a long breath and squeezed me tight enough to make my ribs ache. "Do you want me to tell Julie?"

I did. But that went against the Stone family grain. We might drag our feet, but we squared up to our responsibilities. "I'll do it."

But I didn't have to. When I opened the door, Nelson dashed through, darted to Julie, and licked her bare ankle.

"Nelson, that tickles, stop it!" She turned from yet another creative candy bar display. "Hi, Uncle Dan. What are you all dressed up for?"

I opened my mouth, but before I could find the words to ease what I had to say, a chocolate nut bar slipped from her fingers, her eyes turned dark with pain, and she slumped against the counter. "Did . . . did Grandma . . . did she die?"

I nodded. "She passed in her sleep."

"I talked to her last night. I told her all about the store and the interview and Nelson climbing in the dairy case when that carton of milk leaked even though I swatted him and told him to get out. And she laughed. She was coughing real hard, but she laughed and told me some day Nelson's pig-headedness would turn out to be a virtue."

Tears spilled from her eyes and trickled down her cheeks. "I knew she was sick. I knew she hurt all the time and could hardly eat. But when I said anything she told me she was okay, that she was just tired or getting old or too hot or too cold." Julie sucked back a sob.

"She had cancer, Julie. There was nothing the doctors could do. Nothing anyone could do."

"She wasn't very good at pretending." Julie knuckled tears from her cheeks and her voice rose to a shout. "Why didn't she tell me the truth? I'm not a kid. I know what cancer is. I know what dying is."

Camille stepped to Julie's side and hugged her close. "She knew that, sweetie. She knew you could handle it. But she didn't want you to feel like you needed to give up your friends or your school activities or your summer plans."

Panic filled Julie's eyes. "What happens when summer's over? What happens to me? Where will I go?"

"You'll stay right here with us," I said. "That's what your grandmother wanted. That's what *we* want."

"Is that what you want?" Camille asked.

Julie nodded, panic giving way to pain and guilt. "I would have stayed and helped her. I would have cooked and done the dishes and not played my music so loud. I should have stayed. I should have."

"I know," I said. "You would have taken good care of her. That's why she wanted you to come here—*because* she knew you'd want to stay."

"Your grandmother was a strong and proud woman." Camille patted Julie's back. "She didn't want you to see her getting sicker every day. She didn't want you to feel sorry for her."

Julie nodded and snuffled against Camille's shoulder, then raised her tear-streaked face. "She hated it when I complained about how much homework I had or how my hair wouldn't go right. She'd say she wasn't going out to buy balloons and pop to throw me a pity party."

I fished a couple of tissues from a box beside the cash register and pressed them into her hand. "That's the way she was."

Julie blotted her eyes, leveled a hurt and angry gaze at me, then turned to Camille. "Why didn't she pretend with you and Uncle Dan?"

Camille gave me a you-take-that-one look.

"There are legal and financial things that have to be done," I said. "She wanted us to be prepared."

Julie spun to me and her eyes flashed. "What kind of things? Why can't I do them?"

"You can when you get older," Camille said in a soothing voice. "But right now Dan will have to do it."

"But what things?" Her voice rose to a harsh cry. Nelson yipped and crowded against her legs. "What are they?"

Vague answers weren't cutting it. Julie felt she had no control, wasn't respected. "Things like collecting the rent on your grandmother's house," I said in a calm voice, "and hiring someone to patch the roof if it leaks. Things like paying the taxes and investing money for you to go to college. Making sure you have insurance for that car you'll get someday, and health coverage in case you hurt your hand swatting Nelson."

She smiled a little at that and bent to scratch the dog's head, but then her eyes darkened again. "And things like paying for the funeral?"

"That, too. I'll explain it all as we go along. Every time I get a paper that has to be signed or come up against a decision that has to be made, we'll do it as a team, okay? You'll always know exactly what's going on. As soon as you're old enough, you can take over."

"I guess. But what about Justin? Isn't he old enough to—" Her eyes widened. "Does he know that Grandma was sick, that she—?"

"Not yet," Camille said. "They don't let them communicate much when they're in training. Dan will have to, uh, call the base and see about getting a message to him."

Nice save. Smooth lie.

I groped for Camille's hand, squeezed her fingertips.

"But you'll fix it so he can come to the funeral?" Julie crumpled a tissue against her face. "Otherwise I'll be all alone."

"You're not—"

"Dan will arrange it," Camille interrupted. "You won't be alone."

I wished I felt half as confident as she sounded. For all I knew, Justin was in Alaska.

"I was so mean to him," Julie sobbed. "He was a jerk, but I didn't have to be a jerk back. He's an orphan too."

Camille stroked her hair. "You can't change how he acted or how you responded. All you can do is make it different the next time."

Julie gulped down a sob and, after a long moment, peered up at me. "Are you going down to Grandma's? Can I come?"

"If you want."

Last summer she saw her mother dead on the ground outside the house Ronny torched. She screamed and cried while I attempted to breathe life into a woman I knew was beyond all earthly help. Perhaps seeing Rachel at peace might salve those memories.

She snatched up another tissue, wiped her face, and dug behind the counter for the denim sack she used as a purse. Camille shot me an anxious glance and, when I shrugged and opened my hands, mimicked my gesture, acknowledging that this was something we had to roll with.

Julie knelt to give Nelson a squeeze, then yanked open the door, walked to my rig, and climbed in.

"Poor kid. She's had so much pain already and who knows what will happen with Justin. I know she's from tough stock and I know she'll get through this, but I still wish we could shield her." As Nelson headed for it, Camille plucked the chocolate nut bar from the floor and laid it on the counter. "Do you want me to come along? I could close the store."

"That's up to you."

"Then I'll stay here." Camille glanced toward the post office. "Mary Lou must have spotted you in those taking-care-of-serious-business clothes. She'll want to know what's going on."

I touched her cheek with the back of my hand. "I'll call and let you know how things are going. Keep Nelson out of the dairy case."

Camille rolled her eyes, rewarded me with a chuckle, and shoved me toward the door.

I trudged to my rig and found Julie slumped in the passenger seat staring at her cell phone, tears leaking from her eyes again. "I took Grandma's number out because she's gone and I can't call her anymore and now I— I'm a bad person, aren't I?"

"No." I took the phone from her hand and set it on the seat beside her. "I would have done the same. Seeing that number would make me sad."

Julie chewed her lip. "Did she love me?"

"She loved you more than anyone could measure."

Pathetic.

I tried again, using words Rachel would have called flowery, maybe even false. "She told me you were like a butterfly in her garden. Like a cardinal in an evergreen tree on a snowy day. Like a comet lighting up the summer sky."

Julie gave me a sidelong glance as if she saw right through me. "Was she scared of dying? Dying all alone?"

"Well, I don't know for sure, but Mrs. Gallagher told me she was smiling."

"Really?"

"That's what she said." I stretched my seatbelt across my chest and snapped it in place. "She said it was the most beautiful smile."

"Smiling." Julie picked up the phone and tucked it into the pocket of her shorts. "She was smiling."

"Yup." I tapped the buckle of her seatbelt. "We'd better get going."

"If . . . if I don't go, will you think I'm a bad person?"

"No. A bad person wouldn't eat my cooking or try to keep Nelson out of trouble."

"I'm not too good at that." A blush washed across her cheeks. "He got a box of cereal off the shelf the other day and ate almost the whole thing. I paid for it and didn't tell you or Camille because I didn't want you guys to be mad at him for being hungry."

"Hmm." I scowled a little and pretended to think. "Well, I doubt he was hungry, but it's apparent he's not getting the training he needs. Maybe you should stay here and work with him."

Julie flashed me a smile of relief and grabbed her phone. "I will. I'll train him today and every day. He'll be the most obedient dog ever."

She darted into the store and I drove off on my dismal mission muttering, "I'll settle for keeping him out of the dairy case."

CHAPTER 30

That afternoon and the next two days I went back and forth between Rachel's apartment, her attorney's office, and the funeral home. While Camille kept Julie busy working at the store, shopping for a dress to wear to the funeral, and writing notes to those who brought food and sent flowers, I packed up Justin's things and put them in a storage locker. Then I packed up Rachel's and did the same. This was no time to make decisions about which kitchenware, furniture, and clothing should be kept and which donated to charity. Rachel never wore jewelry except for her wedding ring, but I found a musical jewelry box filled with antique brooches and earrings and put it on a shelf in the garage for Julie to look through later.

Monday afternoon I learned we'd dodged the autopsy bullet, so I booked Reverend Balforth for a service on Wednesday. Relieved and exhausted, Camille and I sat on the dock after dinner, taking in the last of the evening light and watching reflections of the mountains stretch across the lake. In between slapping at mosquitoes a platoon of flitting bats

301

hadn't scooped up, we sipped wine and shared a huge bowl of butter pecan ice cream with chocolate sauce and whipped cream. Nelson lay between us, his gaze following the progress of our spoons. Julie floated on an air mattress, her bowl balanced on her stomach.

When the phone rang I flipped it open it warily. "Sorry to bother you, Dan," Evan Bonesteel said. "It's about Rachel's grave."

I clamped the phone to my ear so Julie wouldn't overhear, turned my back, and asked in a whisper, "What's the problem?"

"No problem. Guy's gonna dig it first thing tomorrow. Wants to mark it off tonight. Pattie left me with the grandbaby. Drove off with the kiddie seat."

"I'll meet him up there."

"Name's Dewey. I'll tell him to head that way."

I clamped the phone against my ear with my shoulder and levered myself to my feet with my free hand. "I'll be there in ten minutes."

Camille raised her eyebrows and I bent close to her ear. "Cemetery. Gravedigger needs to know where to sink his shovel."

She shuddered and set the ice cream aside. Nelson lurched to his feet and was on it like a vulture. I snatched at his collar. "Chocolate's bad for dogs."

"A little chocolate won't kill that one," Camille said. "Not after what he's been through."

Not exactly sound logic, but what the heck? I let him at the bowl. "Back soon."

Ten minutes turned into twelve when I stopped for a family of wild turkeys crossing the road at Silver Leaf Hollow, and Dewey was lounging against a dusty black pickup when I got to the hill. We shook hands and I led him to the spot, a slice of ground between Buck and Lisa. The edge of Lisa's grave was apparent—the grass was a lighter shade of green and the blades were thin and sparse—but Buck had been beneath the sod for many years and there were no clear boundaries to his final address.

Dewey got down on his knees at the center of the marker where Rachel's name, chiseled beside Buck's, waited for someone to add the date of her death. Canting his head, he peered sidelong at the ground. "I'm betting it's right along here." He raised his thumb. "Done this a hundred times. Never been wrong yet."

I hoped that string of successes wouldn't break tomorrow, raised my own thumb, and watched him walk to his truck and depart in a swirl of dust. Purple in the gathering dusk, it sifted among the dew-slicked gravestones like ground fog. As it settled, I got a clear view of the lake, lying in the crease of the valley like a slab of onyx. At its south end, the church steeple glowed like polished ivory, pointing toward the first glimmering stars in the spill of the Milky Way.

A bat swooped past, a shadow against the night, and I rotated, watching its erratic flight, thinking of all the creatures with nocturnal lives, prowling while I slept. Small creatures in search of grubs and bugs. Winged and furred predators in search of prey. And a human hunter, a creature that stalked, caught, tortured, and killed purely for pleasure.

With a jolt, the image of those girls in the glade exploded in my brain. Flickering mental pictures followed, snapshots of my retreat across the ridges, glimpses of a shadowed face that could be Luke, could be Justin, could be anyone.

I shuddered, tried to tamp down my fear, couldn't quite manage. Time to get home. Time to be behind a locked door with the lights on.

As I threaded my way among the gravestones, I heard a scrabbling sound from the direction I'd come. The hair on the back of my neck prickled and I slid my hands in my pockets, feeling for my cell phone and my jackknife.

Another scrape of sound.

A ribbon of white appeared a few yards away, floating just above the ground, coming at me.

I froze, then let out a breath.

Skunk.

If he sprayed from this distance, chances were I'd get hit with only a mist of reeking predator repellent, but that would be enough to guarantee I'd want to burn my clothes and spend half a day in the shower. By inches, I raised my right hand to shield my eyes and backed down the far side of the slope. The skunk hissed, but didn't move, a good indication he wasn't primed to unload just yet.

Saluting him, I turned to make my escape past Ronny's grave—the only one on this side of the slope—and then along the edge of the woods to the marble angel that marked the Keefe family plot. From there, I'd follow the dirt road back to where I parked.

With the rise of ground between me and town, darkness thickened. It seeped from between the trees and lapped up the hillside like brackish water, carrying the scents of damp earth and moss and rotting windthrow. A phantom breeze fingered my hair, tugged at my shirt, chilled the sweat on my back.

The dew-laden grass was slick beneath my feet. Moving sideways to the slope, I hitched along like a crab. Halfway down, my shoes scuffed loose earth and pebbles. My ankle twisted and gave way. My knee slammed into something sharp-edged and hard.

What the hell!

I pitched across it, scraping my right hand, and hit the ground tumbling, fingers scrabbling at tufts of grass.

With a rib-bruising thud I came to a stop against the trunk of a tree, pulled myself to my feet, and stared into the night, listening hard. I detected no movement and heard no sounds except the chirping of crickets and the distant muted cry of a screech owl. Rubbing my knee, I considered the barrier I came up against where none had been a week before.

For a moment I thought about leaving my questions unanswered until daylight, but then pride kicked in and I limped to my rig and dug a flashlight from the glove compartment. Making plenty of noise to persuade the skunk to steer clear, I climbed the slope and cast the beam down the other side.

It illuminated a granite grave marker. Ronny's marker.

Someone had levered it from the ground, set it upright, and braced it with a buttress of earth and stone.

Fifteen minutes later, I clamped a plastic bag filled with ice tighter against my throbbing knee and swallowed yelps of pain while Camille swabbed peroxide on the skin I'd scraped raw. "Had to be Justin," I said between clenched teeth. "Julie wouldn't go near Ronny's grave and neither would anyone else."

Camille glanced at the partition that defined Julie's bedroom. The sound of a television laugh track boomed through the makeshift wall guaranteeing we wouldn't be overheard. "When was the last time you went to the house?"

"Friday. Maybe the day before." The sizzling pain in my hand subsided and she blotted the skin with a paper towel and rubbed on antiseptic salve. "The earth was fresh and damp around that stone. He might have set it upright not long before I got there."

"How did he get here?" Camille laid gauze over the scrapes and cut off foot-long strips of adhesive tape. "He doesn't have a car. But I suppose it wouldn't take much to get another. Some of them come pretty cheap. Julie's already looking at used car ads and dreaming about the big day."

"Talk about a day that will live in infamy."

Camille rolled her eyes and put the roll of tape aside.

"And Justin knows enough about cars to know how to steal one."

"Well, either way, I haven't heard anybody mention seeing a car they didn't recognize."

And they would. "Maybe he stashed the car somewhere outside of town and walked to the cemetery. Or he took a bus. Or hitchhiked. Maybe he came just to set that stone upright and make a point. He could be gone again, miles away by now."

"Where would he go?" She smoothed a strip of tape across my palm. "I think he came back because he's out of options and resources. When you go looking for him, please be careful. He's an angry . . . boy."

A boy with the strength of a man.

"I won't go after him alone. I'll call Jefferson as soon as you finish wrapping me up like a mummy."

She cinched the last piece of tape tighter than the previous ones. "Watch how you talk to the woman binding your wounds."

"Real men let their wounds fester."

"Well, when you finally drive me off with a mammoth act of male stupidity to top all others, you can fester 24/7." She twirled the top back on the peroxide and stowed it on a shelf beside cans of soup and jars of applesauce. "You can invite Stub and Freeman and the rest of the guys and have a full-blown festering festival."

"Sounds disgusting." I kissed the back of her neck. "You won't let me drive you off, will you?"

She turned in my arms. "I don't plan on it."

I kissed her long and hard, then dialed Jefferson. When the phone in the schoolhouse rang unanswered, I tried Mary Lou. She picked up on the second ring, said Jefferson was out in the garage replacing the wiper blades on her car, and she'd call him in.

"Not much point in going right this minute," he said after I explained the situation. "It's darker than the inside of a cow out there. Moon won't be up until after midnight. Meet me at the Bobcat Hollow turnoff at four, that's always been a lucky hour for me to hunt."

307

I fingered the broken key fob in my pocket. Lucky for a sniper. Unlucky for his targets. "Four it is."

"Bring that dog. Might be a help. You can't say he gives up on a scent."

"You can't say he obeys, either."

Jefferson chuckled. "Well, he might serve a purpose, so haul him along. If I was in Justin's boots, I'd be close by the house—but not too close. He's got Bobcat Creek for water and fishing, a couple of houses not far where he can pick off a meal when someone's out, and good shelter in a jumble of rocks on a slope north of the cemetery. Slept there myself many times last summer. Moss as soft as a featherbed. Had to keep an eye out for snakes is all."

I flashed on that rattler in my rig last summer. "Justin's got his father's nerve. I doubt snakes worry him."

Jefferson grunted. "You bringing a gun?"

"I hate to." The feel of a gun in my hand might make me forget about presumption of innocence.

"I expect he'll have one." He hauled in a long breath and let it out. "Your call. I'll cover you either way."

CHAPTER 31

One minute behind schedule, I killed the engine a few yards shy of Bobcat Hollow Road, coasted to a stop on the shoulder, clicked off the dome light, and climbed out. The night was awash in stars and the road shimmered in their vague light, but darkness crouched among the trees on either side. Jefferson was here already. I had no doubt of that. And I had no doubt that I wouldn't see him until he was ready to be seen.

Snuffling, Nelson crawled across the console and I lifted him to the road. He yawned, hopped in a circle, then sat and looked up at me as if demanding an explanation for why he had to abandon his warm bed. With a shrug, I inventoried the pockets of the light jacket I wore to protect my arms from thorns and brambles, then clicked the door closed and leaned against it, listening to the burble of Bobcat Creek and the wind groping among the leaves.

"All set?"

A whisper?

Or the wind teasing my imagination?

Nelson wagged his tail. I followed the direction of his gaze, but saw nothing I hadn't a moment before. "You bet."

Starlight flashed on metal and Jefferson stepped into the road only a few yards away. He wore jeans and a dark denim shirt and held a rifle in one hand. Something pale fluttered from the other. A T-shirt. "Got this from Justin's room."

"See anything while you were up there?"

"Just a couple of mice." He offered the shirt to Nelson. "Didn't mean to horse with the chain of command and get ahead of you, Sergeant, but I've been awake since two."

"Works for me." I watched Nelson sniff the shirt and yawn. "You think he can track Justin?"

"He tracked Clarence to that glade."

But he knew Clarence. He'd inhaled the scent of the dog trainer's last minutes, the reek of fear and blood. Clarence had existed for him. Justin was a fading odor on a shirt.

"We'll start at the house," Jefferson said. "He might have been there, walking around, remembering."

"Yeah." For Justin, that house might be a malevolent magnet like the lodge where Nat killed himself after Susanna's fatal accident had been for me. I dug a retractable leash from the pocket of my jacket and snapped it to Nelson's collar.

"No lights. We'll stick to the road." Jefferson turned, glasses glinting in the starlight, tucked the shirt into his back pocket, and led the way up the road. "Maybe we'll cross his path before we get to the house."

310

I tugged at Nelson's leash and he lurched to his feet and came along, his nose high. Would he need a command to search?

I remembered paging through the logbook Clarence kept, but couldn't recall that he'd noted any commands. Odds were that we'd drag Nelson along for nothing. He might even be a detriment, barking or whining, alerting Justin.

We entered the tunnel of trees and followed the rise of the road with Bobcat Creek to our left, splashing and rushing down its channel. The road swung east, aiming for a fat crescent moon mounting the sky. My knee throbbed each time I planted my foot and Nelson lagged, extending the leash its full sixteen feet, pulling my left arm behind me until my elbow ached from the strain.

I returned pressure. He was as responsive as a stump.

As the road curved close to the creek and the trees on the right gave way to that broad meadow, Nelson whined and came to a halt, his nose to the road. I rubbed my aching elbow and watched the white pennant of his tail as he cast back and forth.

"That's right about where I crossed last summer," Jefferson whispered. "There's good cover along the bottom of the meadow, the road narrows here, and the bank overhangs the creek. Once you get under that lip at the edge of the water, you're next to invisible."

I glanced toward the stream, recalling a low waterfall cascading into a long and narrow pool with a sandy bottom. A perfect place to cool off and rinse out sweat-stained clothing. "Think he's sleeping there?"

"I wouldn't. Too many mosquitoes. And if a thunderstorm blew through that creek could rise fast." The wedding ring flashed as he raised his hand to rub his brush cut. "But I'll take a look."

He melded into the hemlocks on the bank above the stream and I waited, ears straining for the sound of voices, a shout, a shot.

Nothing.

Nelson cast toward the meadow and floundered into the ditch at the edge of the road. He thrashed, jerking the leash, and I clambered down beside him and worked the cord loose from a tangle of milkweed and thistle. Freed, he lunged up the opposite side. I clamped the leash, holding him at the brink of the ditch and away from the remnants of a barbed wire fence I knew marked the bottom of the meadow. The rusted strands of wire curled like Christmas ribbon around thick-trunked trees that, as saplings, had served as fence posts.

The woods around here were filled with such hazards and others as well—natural and manmade—most dating back decades. When I hunted Jefferson last summer I came across years worth of cans, bottles, and household waste tossed into low spots and hidden by drifts of rotting leaves and broken branches. And I stumbled over the corroded hulks of trucks and tractors abandoned when they quit for a final time and were judged more trouble than they were worth.

"There's a trace of a trail by those trees." Jefferson tapped my left shoulder. "Ease him that way."

Ease. The word choice of a man whose arm wasn't about to be pulled from the socket.

I trudged up the ditch a few yards, yanking Nelson with me until we cleared the old fence. Then, clutching at clumps of grass with my bad hand, I scrambled to the edge of the moon-washed meadow. Ronny's grandfather grew alfalfa on this meadow and his father planted it in corn, but Ronny let it lie fallow a few seasons too long and nature took it. Now it was dotted with clumps of blueberry bushes and young sumac.

As soon as I released the clamp on the leash, Nelson bolted off to the east along the tree line. Knowing Jefferson would be on my heels, I followed at a jog, the path smooth beneath my feet. We reached the far corner of the meadow and Nelson turned north toward the house. He lunged to the limit of the leash, his breath coming in sharp huffs as it had on that wild twilight chase over the ridges the night we found the girls.

We hit the lawn and I waded through knee-high grass bowed by dew. Stub had neglected it and now the blades were so long and tough they would clog a mower. With Rachel gone, I supposed I should take over this chore or find somebody who had the time.

Every day something else landed on my to-do list.

I felt the ache of annoyance, like a stone in my shoe.

Nelson bounded up the steps to the porch, then down again. I gave him his head, jogging behind. We circled the house and he shot off to the east once more.

Just before we plunged back into the woods, I peered at the sky. Charcoal gray and deep purple. The sun would be up in an hour.

Nelson bolted into the trees. A branch whipped my cheek and I raised my arm, used it as a shield, and tunneled on into the dark. It was rough going, the ground like an ocean with swells and troughs. I climbed bent over like a crone, then slid on my heels, back arched for balance.

We'd gone what I guessed to be half a mile when Jefferson tapped my shoulder. "Hold up."

I clamped the leash and hauled Nelson back. "Sit," I ordered.

He fought me for a moment, then sat, a blunt shadow among others now visible in the gauzy moonlight. Somewhere nearby a bird twittered and a small creature scrabbled among the leaves.

"Trail's heading for those rocks like I thought," Jefferson said. "Got one more ridge to get over."

Great, another climb. I took my jacket off, tied it around my waist, and wiped sweat from my forehead. Better to get stabbed by a few thorns than to swelter. "What's the plan?"

"Give me a five-minute head start and then follow Nelson. When you're below the rocks, tell him to speak. And then yell as loud as you can."

"And we'll flush Justin to you?"

"If he's there, he'll bolt right into my arms. If not, we got our exercise for the day."

Before I could say I had enough for a week, he faded into the woods. As Nelson's panting slowed, I counted to three hundred and added another twenty for insurance.

"Let's go," I whispered.

Nelson didn't move.

"Nelson, let's go."

Damn it. He hadn't needed a command to take off into the ditch and drag me around the meadow. Why did he need one now?

"Search," I said in a louder and deeper whisper.

Nelson's white plume of a tail thumped the ground, but he didn't rise.

"Get him."

Nelson yawned.

"Hunt."

He cocked his head.

"Follow."

He yawned again.

"Find."

Nelson's ears pricked up. With a grunt, he rocked himself upright, and headed off, nose to the ground, tail high. Gray light sifted through the trees. We crested the ridge and angled down the other side. Then we started up again and rocks loomed above us.

I reeled Nelson in and leaned close. "Speak!"

He barked, the sound high and sharp in the still air.

"Speak," I ordered. "Speak. Speak. Speak."

Nelson let loose with a frenzy of barking that woke the woods. Jays squawked. Squirrels chattered. Then I heard a patter of pebbles against rock. Something larger on the move.

I faced the rocks and cupped my hands around my mouth. "What's up there, boy? What are you after? Speak to me."

Nelson barked again and charged the rocks, nearly ripping the leash handle from my fist. We shot up the slope, cut left around the first boulder and right around the next, then slipped between two smaller ones leaning against each other like drunks.

315

Beyond them, on a narrow strip of level ground, a slab of rock lay against another forming a natural lean-to. Someone had spread a blanket beneath the shelter and dug a fire pit in front of it.

Nelson barked again, raced around the fire pit, hurdled a fallen tree, and attacked the slope, debris flying behind him. I flung up my free hand to protect my eyes. "What are you after, boy?"

Another patter of pebbles. A sharp cry. A thud. Another cry.

The sounds echoed among the rocks, weaving together.

I reined Nelson in, heard another thud and a clatter of metal on rock, and then nothing.

CHAPTER 32

Nerves jittering, eyes straining, I peered into the gloom. Then Jefferson called out, "I got him. Come on up."

I loosened the leash and Nelson took off. We skirted a dense stand of young hemlocks and clawed our way up a spill of broken shale. Above that, on a narrow bench of the ridge, Jefferson stood guard over his prisoner.

Justin sat against a stump, rubbing his shoulder. Even in the pearly light he looked nothing like the swaggering football player from a year ago. He was thinner, his hair curling over his ears and onto the nape of his neck, a gnarly growth of new beard on his cheeks and chin, his hands grimed with dirt and ash.

Nelson hopped up to him, sniffed at his shoes for a second, and returned to my side. Justin glanced at him, then at me, then at the rifle beneath Jefferson's right foot, and finally at the one pointed his way. "You ambushed me. You wouldn't have a chance in a fair fight."

"A man who waits for a fair fight before he gets into one isn't much of a soldier in my book."

317

Jefferson laughed, a bitter sound, high in his throat. "If you hadn't gone AWOL, you would have washed out in another week."

Justin's fists clenched. "Bullshit. What do you know about it, old man? You're the coward who shot my father in the back." He turned the glare on me. "Where's the woman you two needed to save your sorry asses?"

I took a step forward, but Jefferson raised a hand. "Stay cool."

He bent, picked up Justin's rifle and leaned it against a scrawny maple. Then he did the same with his own and turned to me. "Keep an eye on these. And keep a grip on Nelson while I give this pup the fight he wants."

I shook my head. If Justin killed those girls, he wasn't sane. A man driven by demons could have terrifying strength. The weight he'd lost balanced the weight Jefferson had gained, but Jefferson had a lot of hard years on him. Besides, I was the one who made the promise to Rachel. Justin was my problem. "Not a good idea."

"Got a better one?"

I studied the thrust of Justin's jaw and rubbed my knuckles. Setting aside my concerns about his mental state, I imagined the jolt of a punch I'd longed to throw for more than a year, knew I should be a more evolved person, but also knew an emotional growth spurt wouldn't happen today. "How about you watch the guns and hold the dog?"

"He called me old. And a coward."

"I hate you both." Justin got to his feet. "You hated my father. You didn't give him a chance."

"I hated what he *did*," I clarified. "That's a whole different thing."

318

Jefferson rolled up his left sleeve. "Your father did a lot of good for this community before he took the wrong road." He rolled the right sleeve. "But then he set himself apart and above. He played god."

"You're full of crap."

"Damn it, Justin," I raged. "He murdered your mother! He torched your home."

"Liar. Willie Dean started the fire. And Mom took too many sleeping pills by accident. She didn't hear the smoke alarm."

I shook my head, amazed at the depth of his self-deception, afraid that this ability to deny and rationalize led him to kill those girls, kill Clarence and his dogs.

"You were always jealous of him. You made it look like he did those things. He's dead and can't defend himself."

I opened my mouth, then clamped it closed. To someone locked into his beliefs, the truth sounds the same as a lie.

Jefferson shrugged, then took off his glasses and handed them to me. "I've got a cure for this nonsense."

"It's a long drive to the hospital if that cure doesn't take."

"True. See to it I'm not the only one in the ambulance, will you?"

"Count on it."

"That's not fair," Justin howled. "Two against one."

"But we're cowards." Jefferson grinned. "You said so."

"Heck, you probably won't even work up a sweat taking us geezers down." Tucking the glasses in my shirt pocket, I backed up next to a squatty oak, pulling Nelson along with me. "Sit," I ordered.

Nelson turned in a circle and rubbed his muzzle against the tree.

"All right. Scratch yourself. Do whatever you want."

Jefferson rolled his eyes, then stepped close to Justin. "Let's get the rules straight. We're not quitting until one of us can't—or won't—get up."

Justin raised his fists. "That's just how I want it."

"Good. You can throw the first punch."

Justin's eyes widened. "What?"

"Hell, you can even throw the second punch." Jefferson held his arms out to his sides and raised his chin. "Swing away. I won't punch back."

Justin grinned and sidestepped in a short arc, kicking aside twigs and small rocks, testing his footing. Jefferson turned with him, as casually as a man checking out his options on a county fair midway.

Nelson whined and rubbed his jaw against my leg. "Do what you want," I said. He whined again, then lowered his haunches, leaning against me, still panting a little.

"Whenever you're ready," Jefferson said in a lazy voice.

Justin drew back his elbow, pistoned his fist forward, and pulled the punch a foot from Jefferson's chin.

Jefferson yawned. "I didn't think much of that one, either."

Color washed up Justin's cheeks and he drew his right fist back at waist level and rotated it a quarter turn.

320

Jefferson cocked his head. "You sure?"

"Shut up," Justin roared. He took a half step and let loose.

For a split second, Jefferson stood like he was cast from bronze, then he turned sideways to the punch and blocked it with his arm. In the same instant, his foot snaked out, hooking Justin's ankle. The boy snatched at Jefferson's shirt but grasped only air. He hit with a thud.

Nelson barked and I patted his head. "Good moves for an old guy."

"Stinking liar." Justin jounced to his feet. "You said you'd let me have the first punch."

"Said I'd let you throw it." Jefferson shot me a wink. "Never said I'd let you land it."

"Bastard." Justin lowered his head and charged.

Jefferson spun, deflecting the boy's momentum, hooking his ankle again.

Justin's knee rammed the stump he'd sat against earlier. He pitched sideways down the slope and cartwheeled against a boulder with a sickening thump.

"Shouldn't have gone AWOL," Jefferson said. "Should have swallowed your pride and admitted to what you don't know—which is pretty much everything. Should have stuck around, and learned to use the speed and muscle you got."

Justin writhed in the litter of leaves at the base of the rock, clutching his injured knee with both hands. "You're not fighting fair."

"You're beating yourself, kid."

Howling and cursing, Justin clawed his way to the stump and used it to lever himself upright. Jefferson sighed and arched his eyebrows. "Really?"

Four more times Justin flung himself at Jefferson before his injured knee collapsed beneath him and he went down, arms shielding his head, face in the dirt he'd scuffed up. A spasm rippled up his back. Then another.

"You held out longer than I expected." Jefferson bent over him. "You okay?"

"What do you care? What does anyone care?" Another spasm shook him. A sob broke from his throat.

Nelson whined and rubbed his nose against my leg. I stretched my hand out and stroked one of his silky ears. "It's all right, boy."

And then, without conscious thought, I took three steps and knelt beside Justin, stroking his greasy, tangled hair and repeating the same words. Had anyone said them to him after Ronny died? Had Rachel given him the opportunity to be a boy, told him it was okay to let his guard down, assured him that he didn't have to act the way he thought a man should every minute of the day? Or had she been too bound up in grief to try to turn him before he filled the void of loss in other ways?

I patted his heaving back, then placed my hand across his spine, fingers spread, and cleared my mind. I set aside impressions about his father carried from my teen years and reinforced in the blood and smoke of last summer. I tried to see Justin as the baby Lisa gave birth to, a human being in his own right, not simply a younger version of Ronny.

Justin bucked against my hand and I pressed down, feeling the heat of his rage through cloth filthy with pitch and dirt. "It's all right. Cry it out."

He held it for a moment, then let loose, bawling like a two-year-old, sucking air, kicking his feet, pounding his fists. I glanced at Jefferson and saw him nodding.

When Justin's sobs gave way to moans, hiccups, and long gasps for breath, his muscles went slack. He seemed smaller, weaker, an angry and impulsive kid who clung to a lie because he had nothing else, who came back to a place filled with people he hated because he had no other place to go.

I rocked back on my heels, struck by the conviction that not only wasn't he a planner and a schemer, but he also wasn't filled with the kind of evil evident in that glade.

If that impression was correct, my theory that Justin worked alone or with Luke went out the window. But if—after more observation—I decided my impression was incorrect, then, while Justin was out of circulation, I could focus on finding evidence against him, finding a link to Luke.

When his sobbing subsided, I gave him something to think about besides defeat and humiliation. "Your grandmother died two days ago."

"You're—"

"You say he's lying," Jefferson threatened, "and I'll jerk you to your feet and pound the living tar out of you. You'll piss blood, you'll spit teeth, and you won't be able to walk straight for a week."

Justin rolled over and sat up. His eyes flashed with anger and then something else, perhaps respect.

"She had cancer." My injured knee throbbed and I stood, stretching out my leg. "There was nothing the doctors could do. She knew she was dying before you went into the service."

323

He dropped his chin against his chest. "Where's Julie?"

"She's been with me and Camille since school let out."

Justin raised his chin, scowled, and opened his mouth, but Jefferson spoke first. "You'd know that if you kept in touch with your grandmother. And if you ever paid attention to your sister, you'd know why she's here. Dan and Camille love her. They make her feel wanted and needed. Since Lou Marie died Julie's practically running the store."

"Lou Marie died?" Justin gaped.

Jefferson shot him a look of disgust and turned his back.

"I'll tell you about it later." I locked onto Justin's gaze. "Your grandmother's service is tomorrow afternoon. Julie doesn't want to stand by that grave without family by her side."

Justin nodded, then wiped at swollen eyes with a grimy hand.

"So you're going to come to the house and shave and shower and put on some clothes that don't smell like smoke. You're going to eat breakfast and explain to Julie that you went AWOL and what that means. Then I'll take you to talk with a lawyer about the odds of getting your tail out of this crack. Then we'll go up to your house and get that lawn mowed."

"I can do that," he said after a moment. He didn't sound eager, but he didn't sound angry. In fact, he sounded determined.

"Good. Tomorrow you stand with your sister and shake hands with everyone who turns out. You listen politely and agree when they tell you what a fine woman your grandmother was."

He nodded and knuckled his eyes.

"After that we'll go over to Mary Lou's house and have a potluck dinner like we do after every funeral. Ham and beans and potato salad and enough pie and cake to fill a dump truck."

He wiped his nose against his wrist and swallowed twice. "And after?"

"We take you to the sheriff's office," Jefferson said.

"That's not negotiable," I added. "You can walk in by yourself or with my hand on your back."

Justin thrust his chin forward with a trace of his old attitude. "I'll walk in alone." He glanced around at the clearing, then stood and met Jefferson's gaze. "Yeah, I hated basic training. I hated being yelled at and treated like dirt. But running and hiding was worse."

"Well, now you know that much." Jefferson bent, picked up the rifles, and headed down the slope. "Let's get on with the rest of your life."

CHAPTER 33

Half an hour later I pulled up beside the garage and blew the horn. Camille peered from the doorway, grinned, and said something I couldn't hear. A moment later Julie darted out, shaded her eyes with her hand, and then raced for the passenger door. "You brought him! I knew you would."

She wrenched open the door and wrapped her arms around her brother, tangling them both in the seatbelt. "I'm sorry I was such a stupid jerk. I'm sorry I didn't say goodbye. I'm sorry I didn't write."

Justin sat rigid for a moment, then patted her head with stiff fingers. "It's okay, Julie, you were only getting even. I treated you like crap for—" He glanced at me and swallowed hard. "—most of your life. I should have been the big brother you deserved. I should have told you how pretty you are, how you cheered up Grandma, how proud I am of you."

It sounded like way more than lip service, so I flashed a thumbs-up at him, unbuckled my seatbelt, and opened the door.

326

Julie raised a tear-streaked face and shoved hair away from her eyes. "You're proud of me?"

"Yeah. I hear you're running the store."

"I'm mostly just stocking shelves and making change." She wiped her tears on the sleeve of her T-shirt. "But a reporter interviewed me and took a picture and everything! It's going to be in the paper this Sunday."

"I'll make a frame for it."

"Really?"

"Sure. You pick out the wood."

"I'll set aside a paper." I opened the back door, nudged Nelson awake, and helped him down. "We're buying a dozen."

"Two dozen," Julie said. "And I can buy them myself. I get paid. Real money."

Camille laughed. "And all the potato chips you can eat."

"That's a lot of chips." Justin tugged at her hair.

Julie pouted. "At least I don't eat them for breakfast anymore."

Camille arched her eyebrows and Julie flushed. "Okay, I do. But only sometimes. The barbecue ones are really good crumbled up on scrambled eggs and cheese."

"Well, all that's left of our chip supply is a grease slick in an empty bag, but we've got plenty of eggs, bacon, bread, and coffee." Camille turned to Justin. "I'll have breakfast ready in fifteen minutes. How do you like your eggs?"

"Any way you cook them will be fine, Miz Chancellor."

"Camille. Call me Camille, please." She brushed a twist of moss from the dirt-streaked sleeve of his shirt. "I expect you'd like to get cleaned up. Dan will find something for you to wear and Julie will show you where we shower."

"It's outside, around the back. Uncle Dan built it. You have to pull a rope and sometimes the water's kinda cold." Julie took his hand and dragged him off. "How'd you get so dirty? How come you're not in your uniform?"

"I . . .uh . . . it's a long story."

"Oh. Well you can tell me after breakfast. Anyway, when the new house gets finished we'll have three bathrooms and tons of hot water."

Camille watched them go, shaking her head. "That's not the same kid who left here last fall."

"He's learning the consequences of bad choices."

She nodded. "It appears some of that learning involved falling down."

"Jefferson's teaching techniques aren't what the local school board would approve of, but I can't argue with the results."

"I'll want to hear all about it. But later." She slung an arm around my waist and drew me toward the garage. "Right now I have breakfast to cook and you need to find something that boy can wear."

The next afternoon we gathered at the cemetery and saw Rachel into the ground. Justin stood at Julie's side, shaking hands with the men and allowing the women to hug him. They shared stories about Rachel's life, commented on the service and flowers, and speculated about the weather in store for the rest of the summer. If anyone besides the few I trusted with the story knew he'd gone AWOL and had a price to pay, they kept quiet.

After the funeral, we adjourned to Mary Lou's yard and ate until our stomachs cried out for mercy. That was the tradition—to take a little of everything and to compliment the cooks—and this was a day for holding tight to tradition. The only one who hadn't done that was Priscilla. She stayed away— she didn't call, drop by a card, or send over her customary gelatin salad.

No one liked that salad, but everyone scanned the table for it and noted its absence, noted this second break with ritual. Had Priscilla intended to create this widening rift? Was she firm in her decision or did she feel she now had no choice because she hadn't acknowledged Lou Marie's death? Was she hoping someone would come to her door, beg her to let bygones be bygones, and coax her to join us? Was she waiting right now—dressed and with that gelatin salad chilling in the refrigerator—for a knock? How would she feel when no one came? How would that affect her future? And ours?

The conversations I overheard centered on Priscilla's decision to abandon community tradition, to set herself apart. But later—next week or even tonight—some might speculate about tradition itself, about purpose and relevance, about change and the doors it opens as well as those it closes.

Deep in thought, I leaned against a maple and watched Justin devour ham and potato salad, macaroni and cheese, coleslaw and tuna casserole, pie and cookies.

"The condemned man ate hearty," Jefferson observed, clinking his beer bottle against mine.

"If it was me worrying about what comes next, I couldn't hold down two sips of plain water."

"Kid's got guts. Throws a heck of a punch." Jefferson rubbed his arm. "If he had more control and better timing, I might have been in trouble."

I raised my bottle. "A toast to training. And the lack of it."

We drank and then Jefferson lowered his voice. "He thanked me for setting him straight. Asked for a few pointers when he got back."

"Make him promise not to demand a rematch."

Jefferson chuckled. "Already did."

After the sun went down, Justin and I drove to the sheriff's office. He was silent until I pulled up in front and cut the engine. Then he slid out, but gripped the door handle. "I went out west. To Denver."

I heard a trace of pride in his voice and pleading as well. He'd gone far from Hemlock Lake and wanted me to know. "When did you do that?"

"Right when I left. I took a bus that night. I took a bunch of buses."

"It's a lot of miles." The tiny part of my mind that still harbored suspicions made a note to check on exactly when he went AWOL and how that compared to the timetable for the murder of the girl found at the war memorial. "How long did you stay?"

"A few weeks. I hitched around some, went up into the Rockies with some guys I met."

"What did you think?"

"They're huge. Awesome. Wild. They make our mountains look like runty hills. But . . ."

I nodded. "But they don't feel the same?"

"Yeah."

"It would be different if that's where you grew up, where you had roots, where you fished and hunted. Or if you stayed longer and got used to feeling insignificant."

He jammed his hands in his pockets. "Maybe."

"What did you think of the sky over the prairie?"

"It was huge. Endless."

I closed my eyes for a second, recalling the enormous expanse of blue so foreign to those who live hemmed in by hills and trees.

He rocked on his heels for a moment and then said, "The sky made me feel small, insignificant, like you said. Like I was all alone. I . . . I didn't think so then, but I needed that. I went out there to hide but it was so big, so open, there wasn't any place I could."

"It has that effect."

"And I went out there to show you I'm not stuck here."

"You're not 'stuck' anywhere, Justin."

He thrust his chin toward the sheriff's office. "About ten minutes from now I'll be stuck in a cell."

"Not forever. We'll do everything we can to get you out quick."

"Why?" His eyes hardened. "Because my grandmother asked you to? For Julie?"

A day ago I would have answered those final two questions with a "yes," but Justin wasn't the only one who learned something yesterday. "I'm doing this for Hemlock Lake—for the folks who need a hand changing a tire or replacing a window or tilling a garden plot. And then there's the store. Camille took on running it because someone had to. Julie loves it, but she'll go back to school in September and she'll have homework and activities."

331

"And you'll need another pair of hands." Justin studied the bruises and cuts on his. "I don't know if I can stand behind a counter, be inside all day."

"Well, it's not glamorous work, but it's not brain surgery either," I said with a laugh. "You wouldn't have to work every day and there's a lot of downtime. Someone who was, say, getting his educational act together, could use that time to get his assignments done."

Justin's eyes brightened and he gazed past the hood of my rig as if looking into the future.

"Your father was what they call a pillar of the community. He did a lot of good for folks in Hemlock Lake and they counted on him. When you get back, the pillar position is yours if you want it."

He gave me a fraction of a smile, then shoved the door shut with his shoulder, straightened his spine, and strode up the sidewalk to the sheriff's office without looking back.

Three weeks slipped by. July made way for August.

I heard from the friend of the friend at the jail that Luke was released late on the day before the record indicated, right around the time the girl was taken. If he'd been able to get to a car within minutes, it was possible he could have done it. If he had an accomplice, it was even more possible.

I debated whether to tell Sheriff North, but decided the theory was as thin and cold as workhouse gruel. And if North asked who the accomplice was, it would get thinner, fast—unless I suggested Justin. Then it would get too thick. And too hot.

Reminding myself that the task force claimed Luke didn't fit the profile of their unknown subject, I opted instead to keep a loose watch and let him know it. I swung by the bait shop often and twice got Nelson close enough for a nose full of scent. The dog, as before, displayed no unusual reaction.

Nothing, I repeated often, still told me nothing.

Plumbing and wiring went in and walls and ceilings went up inside the house and I filed more pictures and names of electricians, carpenters, plumbers, and drywallers. Nelson got a good sniff of each of them. In every case, he was more interested in their lunch sacks or the packs of gum in their pockets.

The town vote on colors for the store tied between blue and yellow and Julie used both, adding a little hot pink trim here and there. When the decorating was done, Camille taught her about balance sheets and cash flow and they plowed through a book on marketing and promotion and discussed pricing, loss leaders, and profit margin.

Mary Lou gave Julie a blank genealogical chart and together they filled in what they knew about both sides of her family. The spaces still blank set her off on a hunt that took them to the courthouse, the library, and old cemeteries in search of names and dates going back seven generations and more. Her goal was to have it done in the fall when Justin returned. Along the way, she picked up a second form, tacked it to the wall beside hers, and penciled my name and Camille's in the spaces labeled "Father" and "Mother."

Camille put her finger on the space between. "What goes there?"

"Your baby's name," Julie said in a matter-of-fact tone.

Baby?

I glanced at Camille. She shrugged.

"You'll probably have one a year or so after you get married," Julie went on. "That's what people usually do. Except when they, um . . ." She flushed and I wondered how much she knew about the birds and the bees and where she picked up that knowledge. Lisa would have dispensed unvarnished information without flinching, but Rachel—

"Except when they don't." Camille finished the sentence. "For one reason or another. We can talk about that later—when Dan isn't looming over us."

Julie sniggered and penciled a question mark on the line. "After we get the store all fixed up and the house finished, you'll have time to plan the wedding and think about baby names."

"Oh good." I clapped my hands. "Another to-do list."

Camille gave my arm a punch, but Julie missed the sarcasm. "I'll look for wedding dresses on-line," she offered, eyes shining. "And bridesmaids' dresses. If I get to be a bridesmaid, I want something all the way to the ground and really, really pretty."

"Of course you'll be a bridesmaid. Just don't get your heart set on a date real soon, or anything *too* formal." Camille squeezed my hand. "Dan will be wearing jeans."

Julie rolled her eyes. "And Nelson will be the flower dog, right?"

"He's part of the family," I said. "Can't leave him out."

She rolled her eyes again, then wrinkled her nose. "Reverend Balforth would freak. But maybe the reporter from the paper would do a story." She hugged Camille. "Promise you'll have a flower dog."

Camille laughed. "We'll see. Nelson will have to become a lot more obedient."

"Yeah," I added. "If he lifts his stump on a pew or sniffs the reverend's crotch we'll never hear the end of it."

Julie giggled about that for hours, but redoubled her efforts to train Nelson. He seemed eager to participate, and raced outside for their sessions, but I suspected he had less hunger for learning than for the treats in her pockets. Still, while his usual response to me continued to be feigned hearing loss, he obeyed her commands to sit, wait, stay, and leave it.

Our lives settled into a lazy routine and then, just after Camille and Julie left for the store on Friday morning, the phone rang and I heard Sheriff North's voice. "Another girl's gone missing."

Greasy sickness swirled in the pit of my stomach. "When?"

"Last night."

Justin was more than a hundred miles away on a military base. "Who is she?"

"Jessica Smithers. High school junior. Lives about a mile from where I'm sitting. Told her parents she was meeting a girlfriend at the movies but she never made it to the theater. We're assuming he got her."

"Does she look like the others?"

"A little younger, but otherwise— Damn him! Damn him to hell!"

He broke the connection and I did the same.

Hooking a chair with my foot, I sat, breathing hard. What if I read Justin wrong? What if he *was* one of a team? What if this latest victim was taken in retaliation for his capture?

I flashed on a mental image of Clarence's funeral back in April, of Luke, standing behind Priscilla, the strength in his arms and shoulders hidden within the billows of that striped shirt that had once been Willie Dean's. Luke, leaning against the wall at the town meeting, trimming off a thread with a penknife. Luke, who could have lurked in the trees around Mary Lou's yard during the potluck dinner after Rachel's service, could have drawn Justin into the shadows for a conversation or slipped him a note saying he'd see that the work went on until they joined up again.

Bile churned in my stomach and rose in my throat. The chair seemed to pitch beneath me.

Where was Luke today?

I pulled my phone from my pocket and dialed Denton's Bait Shop and Boat Rental. Priscilla answered on the eighth ring. "Hold on," she said, her voice sharp with frustration. "Be with you in a minute."

I heard the thump of the phone against the counter and then Priscilla telling someone, "Keep your shorts on. Luke will fix your motor tomorrow."

The other person grumbled something I couldn't make out and Priscilla told him he was free to haul his boat somewhere else. The grumble faded to an apologetic mumble and the screen door squeaked. A riffle of papers and a few muttered curses followed, and then Priscilla squawked in my ear. "Boat dock. What do you need?"

"It's Dan. Is Luke around?"

"If he was, don't you think he'd be the one to answer the damn phone?"

Before I could respond, she went on, "He got in my truck after dinner last night without even asking. Said he was taking today off because he had business to look after. Business my foot. He has no more business than a cowbird and I'm about this close to telling him he can—"

I ended the call and punched in the number for the sheriff's private line. "Luke Barringer took off yesterday evening and hasn't come back."

"Luke Barringer?"

"The guy who works at the dock up here. The one you checked out." I took a breath. "The guy who attacked his boss with a cleaver."

The sheriff sucked at his pipe. "The cook whose mother died?"

"Right. He left here after dinner in Priscilla Denton's truck. He could have that girl."

"Didn't the task force write him off? He was in jail when one girl went missing."

"He was released earlier. A few hours, but that might have been enough."

"How do you know? How did that happen?"

"I did some digging. I don't know how it happened. Forget that for now."

He hauled in two long breaths. "All right. Any idea where this guy went?"

I glanced around at the mountains, visualizing hundreds of square miles of farm and field and forest, weekend homes tucked at the ends of winding lanes, tumble-down barns and cobbled-together, camouflaged hunting shacks on state land. "No."

His pipe tapped out a rapid rhythm. "You got a description of that truck? The license number?"

"Yeah."

After he broke the connection, I paced the length of the dock twice, then dialed the post office and asked Mary Lou if she knew where Jefferson was.

"He's at my place. He said it was time to remodel that kitchen."

"Thanks." I punched in the number and Jefferson picked up after half a dozen rings, music loud in the background. Three Dog Night. "Joy To The World." A tune from the last days of his innocence.

"Another girl's gone missing," I said. "Last night."

He grunted and turned the music off.

"Luke's gone, too. He took the truck right after dinner—"

"Bring the dog and we'll go get him."

As calm as if he suggested I bring a hammer and lend him a hand. "Go where?"

"An hour ago he was parked up by the Birchkill."

"How the hell do you know that?"

He hesitated a second, then mumbled, "I got a friend from the VA who never met an electronic device he didn't love. He gave me a couple of little bugs and a system to monitor them."

"I thought we agreed to think about that."

He was silent for a few seconds. "Lou Marie didn't trust him, Sergeant."

The mention of the rank I no longer held acknowledged questionable action. Invoking Lou Marie signaled justification. But, bottom line—none of that mattered. "I never trusted him either."

338

Jefferson grunted. "Meet me at the schoolhouse in ten minutes."

I was there in nine.

This time I brought a gun.

CHAPTER 34

"Be smart to have something of Luke's." Jefferson wedged his rifle beside the seat and set a water bottle on the floor by his feet. He wore a dark green ball cap, a gray T-shirt, jeans, and a khaki vest loaded with zippered pockets. "For Nelson."

"How do you propose we get that something? Tell Priscilla you admired one of his shirts so much you want to buy it?"

"Not hardly. I was thinking I'd keep on bending the law and appropriate something while you distract her. Drive on over there, cruise past, and we'll scope the terrain."

I drove, slowing to a crawl as we approached the bait shop. Priscilla squatted on the dock, her back to us, bent over what looked like a coil of rope. Her hands made jerky motions that set the loose skin on her underarms flapping.

"Perfect." Jefferson unbuckled his seatbelt and opened the door. "I'll meet you a hundred yards back up the road."

Priscilla stood, gave the rope a vicious kick, and squatted again. I shuddered. "How about you distract her and I'll do the pilfering?"

"Because I'm already halfway there." He slipped out, tossed his cap and vest on the seat, pushed the door closed, and waved me on.

By the time I turned into the parking lot, he'd faded into the trees that screened Priscilla's house, making no more noise than a whisper. In the name of distraction, I revved the engine, then killed it, told Nelson to stay, slammed the door, kicked my way through the gravel, and stomped along the dock. Diversion overkill.

"Some fool got a knot in there that won't come loose?" I called.

"I tell them just wrap it around the cleat a few times but they never listen." Priscilla's voice sizzled with frustration. Her bleached hair was spiky with sweat and streaks of perspiration, edged white with salt, marred her pink tank top.

"Want some help?"

"If I did, I'd call somebody who knew his butt from a hole in the ground."

Insult noted. "Thought I'd make the offer."

"Well, now you have."

Meaning, get off my dock. I'd do that in a New York minute if I knew Jefferson had what he needed and was on his way to the road. "Luke hasn't come back, has he?"

"You see him?"

"No."

"You see the truck?"

"No."

"Then why ask?"

"Truck could have broken down. He could have gotten a lift back."

She shot me a glare that could scorch paper.

"You sure you don't need a hand. You might break a fingernail on that."

"Already have. I'm taking the cost of a manicure out of Luke's pay. Unless you want to kick in for it."

"Seems like it's his debt." I glanced toward the house. No flicker of movement. "Uh, how's business been this summer?"

"You doing a survey? Starting up a chamber of commerce?"

"Just wondering."

"Must be nice to have nothing better to do than stand around wondering while other people sweat themselves sick in this heat. Must be nice to have money, to live a life of leisure."

Counting to ten to tamp down my anger, I tipped my head back and sucked down a gallon of air. "You sure I can't help with that rope?"

"You want to help?" She leaped to her feet, kicked the knotted rope once more, and then spun on me, her face blotched red and purple, shiny with perspiration. "Get the hell off my frickin' dock."

"Be glad to." I raised my hands in surrender and backed up, toe to heel, watching the house from the edges of my eyes.

"Now, Dan Stone. Get off my dock right now!"

Something fluttered at the corner of the house, Jefferson waving a shirt. I groaned and took one more for the team, tangling my feet and dropping to the dock in a pratfall worthy of a third-rate summer-stock theatre production. Clutching my knee, I flopped about while Jefferson shot across a narrow strip of open ground and vanished among the trees.

"Oh for the love of last night's leftovers," Pricilla raged. "Stop whining and act like a man."

342

Struggling to ignore her needling, I stuck to my act, lurching to my feet, feigning a limp, and emitting a series of gasps and groans designed to keep her focused on me. I milked the performance until I reached my rig, then made a miraculous recovery, leaped in, and burned rubber.

Jefferson was waiting around the bend, a smile stretching his lips, eyes twinkling. "You missed your calling."

I shot him a sour look. "I hope that's Luke's shirt and not a dust rag because that's one tough audience and I'm not planning an encore."

"Got it from a heap in the laundry room. It's nasty." He tossed it into the back seat beside Nelson.

Nelson sniffed it, then wrinkled his lips and backed away.

"If he pukes, you're mopping it up."

Jefferson raised his hands. "Not my fault Luke smells like summer in the swamp. Priscilla should hose him off now and then."

With that image in my mind, we rolled past the post office and store and then climbed out of the valley that cradled Hemlock Lake. Heat and above-average rainfall had set brush and vines on a rampage of growth that gave us only glimpses of the Birchkill as we topped the ridges defining the west boundary of its valley. We started down the slope toward the bridge and Jefferson pointed ahead and to the left. "Truck's somewhere up there."

"That's the road to the old summer camp." I swung the SUV onto the rutted remains of the road. "I haven't been up here since I was a teenager, and it was falling apart then. The owners went broke,

343

stopped paying the taxes, and then walked off and left it."

Stones clattered against the undercarriage and brush raked at the doors. "Seems like every year or so someone floated a plan to fix it up for a retreat or a nature center or even make it a camp again, but they never did."

"Might still be a building standing to give him some privacy for his . . . pursuits." Jefferson leaned forward, one hand on his seatbelt buckle, the other braced against the dashboard.

Pursuits.

I shuddered, remembering how the victims had suffered, imagining the horror and hopelessness of a girl taken, trapped, tortured.

"Or he might have used the road to get the truck off the highway and then struck off into the woods in another direction. He could be anywhere." Jefferson glanced over his shoulder. "The dog will find him."

I checked the rearview mirror. Nelson was as far from Luke's shirt as he could get, hanging his head out the open window. "It appears the last thing he wants is a fresher whiff of Luke Barringer."

Jefferson laughed, then pointed ahead, to the truck that had once been my brother's, gray as an aging ghost among the trees.

Crimping the wheel, I set my rig crosswise between two thick oaks about ten yards back. Jefferson nodded in approval. If Luke tried to run, he'd have to do it on foot.

We climbed out and I lifted Nelson to the ground, snapped a short leather leash on his collar, and snatched Luke's shirt from the seat. "There's a shotgun in the back. Mind carrying it for me?"

344

Jefferson hooked the water bottle to his belt and slid the rifle sling across his shoulder, then opened the hatch and gripped the shotgun. "Is this the gun that went into the lake when Camille shot Ronny?"

"Yeah."

"I thought they took it as evidence."

"I got it back when they closed the file."

He hefted the gun, lowered the hatch, and arched his brows. "Huh."

"What?"

Jefferson stroked the polished stock. "Trying to figure out if keeping the gun that almost killed you is a sign of sentimentality or insanity."

I'd wondered about that more than once since I signed for the double-barreled shotgun and had a gunsmith recondition it. "It's a good gun." I fingered the spare shells and the broken clover medallion in my pocket. "It was my grandmother's. She used to take it when she picked blueberries or hunted butternuts and black walnuts in the fall. Emptied both barrels at a charging bear once. Cut him to ribbons."

Jefferson grinned. "Bearskin rugs are overrated anyway. But she was lucky to bring him down. I'll stick with my rifle." He thrust his chin toward Nelson. "Let's get him up by the truck and give him the scent."

He walked ahead and stooped beside the rear bumper of Priscilla's truck. In a moment he straightened and slipped two gadgets not much larger than cell phones into one of the pockets of his vest. "We don't need to tell the sheriff about this."

"Tell him about what?" I winked, led Nelson to the driver's side of the truck, and held the shirt to his muzzle. "Find him. Find Luke."

Nelson jerked his head, backed to the limit of the leash, and lifted his lip.

"Find him." I wrapped the leash around my hand and pressed the shirt to his muzzle again.

He shook, drool flying from his canines, then lowered his head and charged up the road. We passed between a pair of rotting posts and stepped over a heavy chain sagging to within an inch of the ground. Its links were furred with rust and the letters on a thin rectangle of metal at the center were no longer legible. I guessed they once spelled out *NO TRESPASSING.*

"Like that does a lot of good," Jefferson said in a low voice.

I didn't waste breath agreeing. For families that went back generations in these mountains, signs weren't a deterrent—in fact they often had just the opposite effect. Men like Freeman and Evan who hunted these hills read such warnings as *I DARE YOU.* Most of the people who posted their land up here were newcomers, those who had a beef with their neighbors, or folks worried about liability and big insurance pay-outs.

"How far is the camp?"

"Maybe a quarter of a mile, maybe half." I gestured at the encroaching woods. "Lots of growth since I was here last. There used to be an open glade with archery targets and a meadow filled with wildflowers. And birdhouses in the trees. Kids used to make them. Wind chimes, too."

"Never went to camp," Jefferson said. "Used to say it was for city kids who couldn't build a fire without a pack of matches and the full Sunday edition of the paper and couldn't find their butts

346

without a compass. Then I went to a different kind of camp. Now I sometimes wish . . ."

The road forked and Nelson took the left-hand branch, climbing slantwise up the ridge along a track that grew fainter with every yard.

"Where does the low road go?" Jefferson asked.

I thought of the song, almost said "Scotland," recalled the dark story behind the words, and told him, "Down to the Birchkill. They dug out a pool of sorts and diverted water from the stream so kids could swim."

"Probably couldn't do that now without filing paperwork with at least six state agencies and ending up in court even if you managed to get a permit—which I'm betting you wouldn't."

"Yeah, times were simpler then. And ignorance was bliss."

I boosted Nelson across the barrier of a fallen maple and clambered after him, my breath coming in sharp huffs. When the house was finished, I'd set up an exercise program. Jogging. Weights.

"I'm not saying that regulations are all bad. Can't have everyone with a bulldozer and a whim rearranging the watershed, but . . ." He plucked at my sleeve. "Hold up."

I pulled back on the leash. For moment Nelson continued to dig at the slope with his front paws, then turned his head and gave me the kind of look dogs do when they know you're crazy but are forced to acknowledge you're also in control.

Jefferson moved to the base of the fallen tree and kicked at a heap of leaves. "Someone dropped this not long ago." He ran his hand across the jagged stump. "Cut it close to the ground. Covered the cut to try to make it look natural."

347

I felt a frisson of anticipation and vindication. Why would Luke do that unless he had Jessica Smithers? Unless he wanted to slow down anyone who came after him, force pursuers to move the tree or come on foot?

"I'll scout ahead," Jefferson whispered. "Before we stumble on him and be damn sorry we did."

I felt a flutter of fear beneath my sternum and peered around. The leaves were so thick and full I couldn't see more than a few dozen yards into the woods. Luke wouldn't be able to, either. But if he'd heard us coming, he could be behind a rock or log even now, squinting at us along the barrel of a rifle. I tried to recall the guns in Willie Dean's arsenal, remembered at least one rifle and a double-barreled shotgun handed down from his father. If Luke took the truck, why not take a gun?

I held Nelson back and nodded to Jefferson. He leaned my shotgun against a birch and faded up the track. The dog whined and tugged at the leash but then flopped in a rut, front legs stretched out, rear folded beneath him. I sat, my rump on the raised center of the old road. Around us, the woods hummed with sounds—the chitter of birds, the skitter of a tiny creature, the chatter of a squirrel, the staccato tapping of a woodpecker, the whine of a mosquito beside my left ear.

I slapped at it, heard it again near my right, slapped once more knowing odds were I'd miss. A scatter of gnats performed a dizzying aerial dance in a shaft of sunlight. My tongue felt rough and my neck itched with drying sweat. Nelson rubbed his nose against the side of the rut as if trying to rid himself of Luke's scent.

I thought some more about Willie Dean and his guns, especially that rifle. He hadn't been noted as much of a shot by Hemlock Lake standards, but his father had talent, so the rifle would be a good one.

A twig snapped somewhere below me. I turned my head, saw nothing, but hunched over, making myself a smaller target.

The squirrel chattered again. A warning?

I glanced over my shoulder at the shotgun. Six feet away. Maybe seven. If Luke was watching, making a lunge for it would guarantee he'd fire.

I patted Nelson's head and hunched deeper into the rut. If Luke had been watching us, he'd faced a choice. Follow Jefferson up to the camp, shoot him and then come back for me. Or take me out and then go after Jefferson.

Another twig snapped, this one above me. I hunkered as low as I could. Luke knew us—from first-hand experience and community gossip—knew that in a situation involving guns, I was the weaker link. It would be easier to take me out, but shooting me would put Jefferson on alert. The hunted would then become the hunter.

So—if he thought it through like I had—Luke would take out Jefferson first, then come for me.

I laid the leash in the rut. In a race for our lives, it would be every man and dog for himself. Jefferson would expect me to run, not linger and give Luke the opportunity to eliminate both of us.

Inch by inch, I shifted about until I was facing downslope, then I tightened the muscles in my calves and lifted my heels, anticipating a shot like a runner in the starting blocks.

"He's at the old camp," a voice whispered

My heart thudded against my windpipe and my breathing halted with a strangled gasp.

Nelson didn't flick a single whisker. Maybe he'd smelled Jefferson. Maybe he'd heard him. Maybe he didn't care.

"He's digging a hole," Jefferson said. "A grave-sized hole."

CHAPTER 35

Calf muscles shrieking, I lurched to my feet and snatched up the leash. Jefferson stood beside the birch. "He's got something in a blanket."

I dug for my cell phone. "The missing girl?"

"About the right size."

"Alive?"

He tapped the scope on his rifle. "Didn't see any movement."

Too late. We came too late.

"Could be unconscious," he muttered. "Or drugged."

"Let's hope. I'll call the sheriff."

"I'll go down for a closer look."

"And then?"

"That depends on Luke." He gave me a twitch of a smile. "If I see that bundle move or if he dumps it in the hole, I'll persuade him to put his hands up."

"Persuade?"

He stroked the stock of his rifle. "Non-verbal communication."

Telling myself to let go of legal process and focus on results, I flipped open the phone. "No signal here. I'll have to get up on the ridge."

351

"Might be best to leave the dog. Don't want him barking at the wrong time."

"I'll tie him up and be right behind you."

He grasped my shotgun. "There's a pile of stones at the crest of the ridge as the camp comes into view—maybe the remains of a signpost support. Good place to get a phone signal. I'll leave your gun there."

Without waiting for my acknowledgement, he strode off, making no more noise than fog. I walked Nelson to the birch, unsnapped his leash, wrapped it once around the trunk, threaded the clasp through the loop of the handle, and hooked him up again. "Stay," I ordered. "Sit. Quiet."

True to form, he jerked at the leash and whined as I walked away.

For the first few yards I concentrated on my feet, trying not to turn an ankle when the ruts deepened and wondering how Jefferson moved as if he was weightless. In a minute I abandoned that in favor of speculation about the bundle. If we unrolled that blanket and found the missing girl still alive, we'd be heroes. If she was dead, the guys on the task force might call us vigilantes and claim we screwed up their crime scene. But if there was nothing more than a dead dog in that blanket and Luke got a lawyer and claimed I'd been harassing him . . .

Maybe Jefferson and I should check it out before I called the sheriff.

No, phone the sheriff now.

Let him take heat if there was any to take.

I abandoned attempts to muffle my footsteps, made time to the top of the ridge, and made the call.

"Jefferson Longyear and I tracked Luke Barringer to an old summer camp up the Birchkill,"

352

I panted. "He's digging a grave and he's got something wrapped in a blanket. About the size of a girl."

Chair springs creaked and the sheriff's pipe cracked against the desk. "How do we get there?"

"There's a road before the bridge on the north side of the highway. My rig's up there blocking his truck. When the road forks beyond that, take the upper one."

"Got it. Watch him." He paused for a second. "Just watch him. That's all. Unless . . ."

"Yeah," I said. "Unless." A word with a lot of elasticity.

I tucked the phone in my pocket and went for the shotgun. Just as I gripped it I heard a grunt and turned to see Nelson, tongue lolling, eyes bulging, heave himself up the final few yards of the ascent.

"How the hell did you get loose? Come. Nelson, come here."

He didn't veer from his course.

"Stop."

Releasing the shotgun, I lunged for him. His tail slid through my grasping fingers. I snatched at the gnawed end of the trailing leash. It burned across my palm. Then he was past.

"Damn it!"

Seizing the gun, I gave chase. The road plunged into a hollow and I leaned, digging in my heels, fighting to remain upright. Nose to the ground, lone back leg working like a piston, Nelson widened the gap.

Abandoning caution and balance, I hurled myself down the hill, burst through a screen of saplings and followed the faint trail that skirted the angle of two warped and sagging walls. A window

353

long devoid of glass gave me a view of the rusted frames of four bunk beds staggering beneath the collapsed roof. The remains of another cabin lay to my left and ahead, beyond the skeletons of swing sets and a climbing frame overgrown with wild roses, stood a massive octagonal pavilion, its roof fallen away to reveal a geometric design of timbers and struts. They cast a web of shadows across shattered plywood and torn shingles jumbled on the stone floor below.

Nelson scrambled up three shallow steps, turned a tight circle, then reversed himself, and leaped to the ground as I closed to within a few yards. Jefferson hadn't said where Luke was, but I knew this pavilion, the place where kids had danced and put on plays, was the center of the camp. The kitchen and dining hall lay off to my left. Beyond the pavilion were more cabins and a baseball field. Earth scraped off to level that field formed a knoll out past center field.

"Come," I ordered Nelson in a hoarse whisper. "Sit. Stay."

Without lifting his eyes, Nelson cast right, then left, then right again. I dove for him. Too late. I plowed weeds with my chin and he took off along the arc of the pavilion. Cursing, I stumbled after him, slogging through thick, tangled grass, skirting the second of what I knew were four sets of steps to the pavilion—one for each cardinal compass point.

Metal clanged on rock. Nelson barked.

"Get out of here," a rough voice shouted.

Nelson barked again.

"Get away."

I cleared the edge of the pavilion and spotted Nelson just beyond it, in an open space where campfires once had burned and ghost stories been recounted in tense whispers.

"Get away from that."

Luke's voice.

He was visible only from the waist up, a shovel held out like a bayonet.

Nelson tugged on the satin edging of a pale blue blanket secured with silver tape around what I'd bet my entire inheritance was a body.

Luke jabbed the shovel at the growling dog. "Get back."

The blade fell short, hit rock with a rasping scrape. Luke yanked it back and glared at me. "Get him away from her or I'll beat him to death."

Her?

I studied the blanket-wrapped object. Not a trace of movement. If she was alive, she was unconscious or drugged into a stupor.

Nelson growled and pawed at the blanket.

"I mean it." Luke howled and raised the shovel. "I'll kill him." Rage flamed in his eyes and his gaze skittered from the dog to me. "I'll kill you, too."

"Maybe." I raised the shotgun and pulled back the hammers. "And maybe not."

He howled an unintelligible curse and lowered the shovel.

"Leave it," I ordered Nelson. "Leave it. Sit."

Given Nelson's track record, I was stunned when he gave the blanket one more tug and then sat, his sides swelling and compressing like a bellows, his tongue drooping from the corner of mouth.

"Good boy," I praised, scanning the terrain for Jefferson's hiding place. In the trees beyond the ball field? Behind the remnants of one of the cabins?

Luke let go of the shovel, set his grimy hands at the edge of the grave, and levered himself out. His jeans were crusted with red clay. His shirt, the same one he wore to Clarence's funeral, was streaked with sweat and dirt. "What the hell are you doing here?"

I almost laughed. "What I'm *not* doing is digging a grave."

His face tightened to a knot of anger. "You got no business up here. This land is posted against trespassers."

"I didn't realize you owned it."

"I don't." He puffed out his chest. "But you don't either."

"I guess that makes us even."

"You followed me. You're invading my privacy." He clamped his lips, his breathing quick and loud.

"What's in the blanket?" I prodded it with my toe. It gave a little, about the way skin and muscle might.

He squatted beside it, smoothing the blanket, tucking in the edge Nelson pulled loose. "None of your business."

"The sheriff's on the way. We'll see if he thinks it's *his* business."

Luke unleashed a banshee's wail and came up under the shotgun, ramming his head into my groin. I fell, drawing my knees to my chest, cramping pain exploding through my gut. My finger jerked, pulling both triggers. Shot blasted the sky.

Nelson barked and lunged at Luke.

Luke scrambled to the shovel, seized it, and used it as a mallet, slamming the flat of it against the dog's back.

Nelson yelped and tumbled to the edge of the hole.

Luke came at me, raising the shovel high and bringing it down in a powerful arc.

I parried with the shotgun.

Metal rang on metal. My hands stung from the impact. My arms vibrated and my fingers grew numb.

Luke stepped back and raised the shovel again, rotating it so the blade pointed down. He chopped at my legs. I kicked at him, worming my way backwards.

Where the hell was Jefferson?

Nelson growled and scrabbled from the lip of the grave, coming at Luke on his belly, his back leg dragging behind him.

The shovel blade struck the steel toe of my right boot. Pain seared along the arch of my foot and up my leg.

Luke raised the shovel again. I kicked with my left foot, connected with the side of his knee. He lurched sideways, jammed the shovel down like a crutch, straightened, raised it, and came at me again.

Snarling, Nelson thrust himself the last few feet and clamped his jaws around Luke's leg.

With a yelp, Luke torqued about and raised the shovel.

Still and silent, Nelson gazed at me, the whites of his eyes gleaming. Like the blade of a guillotine, the shovel blade sliced toward his neck.

A shot rang out.

The shovel handle splintered and jumped from Luke's hands. The blade fell a yard from Nelson.

Luke roared, dropped to a crouch, fingers digging into Nelson's ruff, twisting his collar, choking him.

Nelson remained still and silent, not blinking, his gaze locked on me.

Wood scraped and Jefferson emerged from the ruins of the closest cabin, rifle aimed at Luke. "Kill that dog and the next shot goes into your head."

Luke hesitated for the time it took me to get to my feet, then released Nelson and lifted his hands. "He's tearing up my leg." He whined like a little boy. "It hurts. It hurts bad."

Jefferson halted a few yards away. "What's in the blanket?"

Luke gritted his teeth and his eyes narrowed to slits. "None of your damn business."

"Dan?"

"Looks like a body. It's not moving." I fumbled two shells from my pocket and into the shotgun. "I can't see any sign of breathing."

Jefferson bent for a closer look, stretched out a hand.

"Get away," Luke screamed. "Leave her alone. She's mine."

Spoken like a jealous lover.

"We'll see about that in a minute." Jefferson straightened and his gaze swept from the blanket to Nelson, jaws still locked on Luke's leg. "Think you can do something about that dog?"

"I might if I gave a damn about Luke. But since it looks like he killed a girl and snapped Nelson's back, I don't."

"I didn't kill anyone." Luke was back to whining. "And that dog came after me."

"Because you came after me." I pulled back the hammers. Nelson lay like a stone.

"I enjoy a good standoff as much as the next man," Jefferson said, "but it will be tough to take

358

Nelson to a vet with Luke attached. Not to mention tough to book Luke with a dog attached."

"Book me for what?" Luke raged. "You threatened me. Shot at me. It's your fault your dog's hurt."

"I think he's beyond hurt," Jefferson observed. "When rigor sets in, we might need a pry bar to get his jaws apart."

Luke moaned. "I can't feel my foot. Do something."

I knelt beside Nelson, the gun resting across my thighs, and put my hand on his muzzle.

Nelson growled deep in his throat, vibration more than sound.

"He's still alive." I ran my hand along his back and touched a lump the size of my fist. Nelson didn't flinch, didn't whimper. "I think he's paralyzed."

"He's tearing my leg off," Luke sobbed.

"You're a good dog." I stroked Nelson's head. "You did a good job. You got him. Clarence would be proud. Now you can leave it. Drop it."

"Make him let go," Luke moaned. "Shoot him."

"If I shoot anybody it will be you," Jefferson said.

"You're a good dog. The best I could ever ask for." I scratched a spot behind Nelson's ear, then touched the lump again. He didn't move.

"We'll all miss you. Especially Julie."

Nelson's tail thumped the ground.

I blinked. "Julie."

His tail thumped again.

"Want to go see Julie? If you do, you have to drop it."

Nelson tucked his rear leg under his belly and stood. Then he opened his jaws, hopped back a step, and shook himself.

"The damn dog's fine," Luke raged. "Get him away from me."

I stood. "Good boy, Nelson. Good boy. Come."

Nelson wagged his tail, tipped his torso, and let loose a stream of urine that spattered Luke's shoes.

Cursing, Luke leaped aside, then sat on the pile of earth he excavated from the grave and pulled up his jeans to reveal deep tooth marks but no broken skin or blood.

Jefferson nodded to the blanket-wrapped object. "Got your knife, Dan?"

I pulled it from my pocket.

"No." Sobbing, Luke threw himself across the bundle. "Leave her alone. Leave her in peace."

As if he'd done the same. "Is she dead?"

"Yes. Yes, she's dead."

"Did you kill her?"

"No. No." He wrapped his arms around the bundle and pressed his face to the blanket, rubbing his lips against it, leaving a smear of dirt on the baby-blue fleece. "I loved her. I would never hurt her. It was an accident."

Jefferson snorted in disgust. "I suppose all the other killings were accidents too."

Luke gaped at us, his cheeks streaked, his nose dripping, his mouth open. "What killings?"

"The girls," I told him. "The three in the glade. The one at the war memorial."

Anger drained from his eyes, leaving clouded confusion. "I didn't . . . I would never . . . not a girl . . . I would never hurt a girl."

"What about this one?" Jefferson asked.

"This isn't a girl." Luke buried his face in the blanket again. "This is my mother."

CHAPTER 36

"His mother." Sheriff Clement North lowered himself to the floor of the pavilion, scratched one eyebrow, and watched his team photograph the scene.

Luke was in handcuffs, secured to the rusted base of an old pump. He alternated between screaming at them to get away and sobbing that he tried to do what she wanted and they had no right to hold him.

"His mother," the sheriff repeated, a mixture of amazement, disgust, and horror in his tone.

I felt the same when I cut away the tape, sliced a hole in the black plastic beneath the blanket, and revealed the face of a gray-haired woman many months dead. "They were close."

"Maybe a little too close," Jefferson added.

"And he says he dreamed that she wasn't happy?" The sheriff scratched the other brow. "That she told him the others in the cemetery didn't like her?"

I nodded. "Pretty much."

"She went to camp here when she was a girl. He claims he dreamed about her singing camp songs. That's how he knew where she wanted to be." Jefferson glared at me. "He sang a bunch of them—off-key—while Dan was taking his sweet time strolling to the top of the ridge to call you."

I snorted. "Sweet time, my—"

"If I hear the one about the ears hanging low again I'll—"

"Enough." The sheriff held up a hand, palm out. "Save the lyrics for the official interview. Save the argument for the drive home. I've already got my quota of headaches."

He pinched the skin at the bridge of his nose. "What the heck do I charge him with? Desecrating a grave? Being a nut job in possession of a shovel? Failure to carry a tune?"

I coughed out a chuckle. Not because his remarks were that humorous, but because I was glad to see him making an effort to relieve the stress he'd been under since April. "Maybe he kidnapped the latest girl. Before he dug up his mother."

I tried to sound more convincing than desperate, but heard myself falling short. "He left Hemlock Lake right after dinner last night. How long does it take to dig up a grave if it's only a year or so old?"

"Less time than it takes to dig a fresh one, I expect." The sheriff drew a handkerchief from his pocket and blotted the back of his neck.

"Especially in the spot he picked." Jefferson poured more cold water on my theory. "Clay, roots, rocks the size of my head. And he was down a good three feet when we stopped him. He must have been at it since dawn." He shook his head. "Logistically I don't see it. He couldn't dig up Mom until after dark.

362

It's a fifty-mile drive and then he's got to drive back and carry her in here."

"Okay, I'll admit it's a tight timetable, but let's say he's on his way to dig up his mother and he spots Jessica Smithers. She's alone. She looks like his other victims. He seizes the opportunity and grabs her. It wouldn't take more than a few minutes to tie her up or drug her and stash her somewhere."

Interest flickered in North's eyes. "Where?"

"I don't know." My mind churned over a hundred possibilities, then I glanced at the body in the blanket. "But the way he feels about his mother could be the leverage you need to make him tell."

"Good idea, son." North swatted a mosquito on his forearm, leaving a smear of blood between two brown age spots. "No point in you two sticking around. Someone will catch up and interview you later." He cocked his head and shot me a broad wink. "And ask how you just happened to find him after telling me you had no idea where he might be."

I wanted to stay and watch them sweat Luke, but the middle sentences sounded a lot like orders and the final one was a homework assignment. "There's nothing I'd like more than to get home and shower, but there are at least four vehicles between my rig and the road and it's a hell of a long hike back to Hemlock Lake."

"So we might as well make ourselves at home." Jefferson took a long swig from his water bottle and passed it to me. "Maybe we can pick some berries for lunch, gather nuts, dig roots."

"Too late on that. They logged the shovel as evidence." I drank, then cupped my hand and offered water to Nelson. He slurped it up, his eyes bright, his tail wagging as if the lump on his back didn't hurt a bit. "I've got emergency rations in my glove compartment."

"Dehydrated potatoes. Canned meat?"

"No. Nuts, candy bars, chips, cookies, and whatever else Julie stuffed in there. She gets hungry on the drive to and from the store."

Jefferson's eyes widened. "It's not much more than five miles."

"She's a teenager. She's hungry all the time." I capped the water bottle and handed it back. "And at the moment that's working in your favor."

He shot me a sheepish grin and clipped the bottle to his belt. "Point taken. Let's go check those provisions."

We were halfway to the top of the ridge when a red-faced deputy broke out of the trees. "They found the missing girl," he blurted. "She's alive."

Without a word, we turned and trotted in his wake.

". . . flagged down a car." Breathing hard, the deputy reported to Sheriff North and the others. "About ten miles from here. She says he tied her up, gagged her, put a sack over her head, and stuffed her in the back of a van or a covered truck. She felt a metal floor and walls. He drove for about half an hour, shot her up with something, and left her in a shed. When she woke up she got lucky. Came across a piece of an old saw blade. She's on her way to the hospital."

North nodded and pointed to three of the team. "Get on this. Get to that shed and see what you can find. The rest of you finish up here." He glanced at me and then at Luke Barringer. "Looks like your theory might be solid enough to hold a little water."

Jefferson grunted and clapped me on the back, and for a few seconds I let myself feel like a hero. "Except for the truck part. The truck Luke drove last night isn't covered. And it has a bed liner."

North waved that aside. "The girl was scared out of her mind. She's not the most reliable witness."

"Well, if she was in that truck, we'll know by the end of the day," one of the crime scene investigators said.

North crossed his fingers, but my gut told me they'd find no evidence she'd been Luke's prisoner.

Half an hour later I jockeyed my SUV out from between the trees and followed the patrol car bearing Luke down the trace. Behind us, two deputies stood guard over the truck that had once been Nat's.

"Priscilla's going to be as mad as a hooked pike," Jefferson said. "They're taking her handyman *and* her truck."

"Bet we'll catch the brunt of it. We should make ourselves scarce."

"Hard to do short of leaving town."

I toed the brake and lagged farther behind the patrol car. "Then we better get that just-passing-by story straight."

"Yeah. Can't have it look like we had it in for poor little Luke." Jefferson sighed, opened the glove compartment, and excavated a squashed peanut butter cup from beneath a four-pack of flashlight batteries. "We need a story that explains why we happened to have guns with us. And Nelson."

The dog sat up and leaned between the seats, concentrating on Jefferson's efforts to peel the wrapper from heat-softened chocolate. "This stuff's bad for dogs."

Nelson cocked his head and whined.

"Would I BS you?"

Nelson whined again and Jefferson sighed, gnawed chocolate from around the filling, and offered that on the palm of his hand. Nelson unfurled his tongue and reeled it in.

"This is the part Julie likes best." I braked to a stop and turned in my seat to get a better look. "When the peanut butter sticks to the roof of his mouth."

Nelson pushed his tongue against his upper teeth and drew it back again, making a thwupping sound.

"That's entertainment," Jefferson agreed. "What did we do for amusement before Julie moved in?"

His question echoed one I'd asked myself for the past few weeks. Despite my trepidation at taking in a teenage girl, my concerns about the impact on my relationship with Camille, and my anxiety over Justin's situation, I wondered how I considered my life full before she hurtled into it. "She's a keeper, isn't she?"

"She is, but I'm glad you're the one in charge of the keeping." Jefferson wadded the wrapper and stuffed it into the glove compartment. "Back to our cover story."

"How about this? I got the tax bill for that parcel of land my father left me and had the urge to walk the boundaries. You, being our resident expert on the hinterland, volunteered to come along. I brought

Nelson because I didn't want to leave him cooped up in the garage."

"I'll buy that." He pulled out an open package of peanuts and sniffed. "Stale." He emptied the package onto the back seat for Nelson who inhaled them in less than a minute and, when no more food came his way, flopped down and closed his eyes.

"Wish I could fall asleep like that." Jefferson stroked the stock of my shotgun. "Okay, we brought the guns because you never know what you'll run into—rabid skunks, angry bears, poisonous snakes."

"And we didn't see the truck until after Nelson got loose and took off. He led us to Luke the same way he led us to those dead girls."

"Works for me."

"Then that's what we go with." I pulled back into ruts churned to sticky mud by official vehicles and fishtailed around a turn and down the final slope.

"Whoa." Jefferson pointed to a truck coming toward us. "Isn't that the reporter we ran into up by Clarence's?"

"Yeah. Colden Cornell."

"How did he get wind of this so fast?"

"Maybe he picked up some chatter on a scanner. Or he's got a source in the sheriff's department."

"Looks like he's about to get himself stuck."

"*Déjà vu* all over again."

"Yeah." Jefferson grinned. "Want to run him off for old time's sake?"

"So bad I can taste it. But he must have seen the sheriff's team leave so he knows something's going on."

I slewed to a halt a dozen yards above the truck. Cornell's wheels stopped spinning. He peered through the windshield at us, glanced over his shoulder, and looked at us again, gnawing at his lower lip.

"I'd give ten dollars to see him parallel park that truck. He probably needs grease and a shoehorn." Jefferson leaned out the window. "Back it up," he yelled. "We have the right of way."

"No we don't," I said. "He—"

"Doesn't know that," Jefferson said.

Cornell frowned, then turned sideways in his seat. The truck wobbled downhill a hundred yards and halted at the main road, leaving space a foot shy of what we needed to get past. The reporter climbed out with his notebook, recorder, and camera.

"Smile pretty." Jefferson pulled the bill of his cap low over his eyes.

Peering into the back seat, I spotted the edge of a paint-spattered red visor protruding from beneath Nelson's haunch. I yanked it free.

"Dog's out for the count," Jefferson said. "That didn't even break the rhythm of his snoring."

Cornell took three steps toward my side of the rig then, reversed course for the passenger door and Jefferson. "I talked with the sheriff. He said he had a man in custody but he wouldn't give me a name." Cornell halted three yards away and thrust out the recorder. "I saw someone in the back of that last car but he ducked down. What can you tell me?"

"Not a damn thing the sheriff didn't," Jefferson said.

"But you were up there. You must have seen who they had in custody."

"We were chasin' Dan's dog. It's a full-time occupation."

368

Cornell frowned. "So you didn't see—?"

"Saw plenty. Squirrels, crows, deer, a Pileated Woodpecker."

The frown deepened to a scowl and he spun about, slipped, and went down on one knee. Flapping his arms, he got to his feet again and stalked to his truck, yelling over his shoulder, "Dump the mountain hick act. It's pathetic."

"Mountain hick," I repeated. "That's harsh."

"Mountain hick *act*," Jefferson corrected. "Appears I'll get a bad review in the next theater column."

Cornell backed his truck out onto the highway, wheels slinging clumps of muddy leaves. Jefferson tipped his cap as we drove past. Cornell shot him the finger.

We stopped at the store to fill Camille, Mary Lou, and Julie in on events of the day. Julie was less interested in the kidnapped girl than she was fascinated by Luke's activities, pronouncing him "freaky, icky, and gross" and in the next breath asking if I thought he dug up other people, and if he'd be out of jail and back in Hemlock Lake soon.

"Not if I can help it," Camille said under her breath. Then she pointed at a roll of paper towels and a spray bottle of cleaner. "We'll talk about it as much as you want and Dan will answer all your questions when we get home. But right now we need to clean that lower shelf before the delivery truck gets here with the canned goods."

"In a minute." Julie snatched a bag of beef jerky from the snack rack and headed for my rig. "Nelson was so brave. He needs a reward."

"What about me?" Jefferson pleaded his case to the closing door. "What about Dan?"

"I guess we're on the reward-yourself plan," I said with a chuckle.

"Take a six-pack of beer," Camille told him. "On the house."

"No, on me." Mary Lou slipped a hand into the pocket of her denim skirt and pulled out a ten. "And Lou Marie. She didn't like that man from day one."

"I didn't either," Camille said. "But . . . well, I feel sorry for Priscilla."

"I do too." Mary Lou touched Camille's hand. "She lost Willie Dean and now she's lost Luke and she's all alone running that business. After I close up I'll go over and see how she's doing."

Jefferson blew out a sigh of exasperation. "Priscilla wouldn't waste a minute feeling sorry for Camille if Luke killed Dan."

"Still . . ." Mary Lou put her hand on his arm and locked her gaze on his. They stood in silence for a moment and I guessed they were thinking of another lonely and bitter woman.

When Julie blew back through the door, Jefferson dropped his chin. "I'm not going with you."

"I never expected you would." Mary Lou fixed her gaze on me. "I still don't understand why you were up at the old camp. The best way in to that property your father left you is from the other side of the Birchkill, from the top of the road to Clarence's place. If you so much as glanced at a map you'd know that."

Jefferson gave me an I-told-you-so look, slunk away, and got busy pawing through the beer cooler, clinking bottles. I offered Mary Lou an apologetic grin. "Hemlock Lake men don't need maps."

370

Mary Lou raised a finger, but Julie rescued me. "If you followed the map, you wouldn't have found Luke."

Jefferson returned swinging a six-pack. "I don't know about you, but I need a shower."

Mary Lou shot him another puzzled frown.

He dodged it and hustled out the door.

I was right on his heels.

CHAPTER 37

I got home, gave Nelson a bowl of fresh water to wash down the peanuts and jerky, drank about a quart of iced tea, showered, and made a roast beef and cheese sandwich. Wrapping it in a paper towel, I carried it out to a lawn chair on the dock along with another glass of tea. The drywallers were finished at the new house, so Nelson and I were alone. I was chewing my second bite when Priscilla's wreck of a car barreled down the driveway.

I swallowed a lump of half-chewed bread. "Uh oh."

Priscilla heaved herself out from behind the wheel like a breaching whale and came at me screaming. "Thanks to you, Luke's in jail."

Nowhere to hide.

Nelson whined, got his hind leg under him, and belly-flopped into the lake.

"Come back here you coward," I called. "Don't make me face this alone."

He swam on, his lone hind leg like a broken rudder, taking him in a wide arc toward the shore beyond the new house.

I set the sandwich at the edge of the dock beside the tea, stood, and got behind the lawn chair.

"You never gave Luke a chance. You had it in for him right from the start." Priscilla came at me, clawing air. "You're not the law around here anymore and you did a piss poor job of it when you were. Where do you get off spying on him?"

Halting, she leaned across the chair, her face less than a foot from mine. Her eyes were wild, her nostrils flared, and she breathed through her mouth, releasing the acrid scent of stale coffee. Retreat was impossible, so I launched a counterattack. "The man's not right in the head. He dug up his mother! He said she told him to do it."

Her eyes never flickered. "So what? Nobody would have known—or cared—if you didn't butt in."

Did she believe that made it okay? Was she blindly defending him? Or, choice three, was she as crazy as Luke? "Maybe a judge will agree that—"

"Listen to you." Priscilla put her hands on her ample hips and mimicked me in a falsetto. "Maybe a judge will agree . . ." She stamped her foot, making the dock bounce and sway. The glass tipped over, spilling tea and ice cubes.

"Plenty of people around here break the law and no one does a damn thing about it, especially you, Dan Stone. They trespass and hunt out of season, they drive and drink before they come of age, and they don't turn a deserter over for two days."

I bit my lip so I wouldn't toss back something about people who tried to cheat on their taxes and not declare their employees. Keeping my face still, I listened to tea drip between the boards of the dock and gazed past her at Nelson shaking himself in the shallows.

"Well, I'm telling you and you can tell Mary Lou and all the rest that I'm done taking crap. I'm done with Hemlock Lake. And I'm done with all of you."

She shoved the chair, knocking my sandwich into the lake, and stormed off.

Never a dog to miss an opportunity, Nelson came on the run, leaped into the lake, and salvaged my lunch.

I made a second sandwich, traded tea for something with more punch, and was staining what seemed like a quarter mile of baseboard when Camille pulled up, flung open her car door, and bounded out. "You're not going to believe what happened."

"Make him guess," Julie yelled. She hurled herself from the passenger side and danced toward me. "Make him guess before you tell him what Priscilla is doing."

Barking, Nelson ran to her and bounced off his lone hind leg. Julie grasped his front paws and held them aloft. Together they executed a series of steps and hops that bore a vague resemblance to a tango. Nelson appeared to be both delighted and embarrassed. Despite the lump on his back, he showed not a trace of pain. "Guess, guess, guess, guess. Guess what she's doing."

"Burning me in effigy?"

Grinning, Camille hauled a bulging sack of groceries from the back seat. Her motions were slow and she grunted as she lifted the sack. Tired, I thought. Working at the store and riding herd on a teenager were taking their toll.

"Wrong," Julie said.

"Going door-to-door collecting for Luke's bail?"

"Wrong. And that's a stupid guess because nobody likes him so nobody would give her any money anyway."

Camille chuckled and handed me the sack. "But being Priscilla, it would be in character for her to try."

"But no one would give her even a penny," Julie said in a voice filled with scorn. "Guess again, Uncle Dan."

"She's going on a diet?"

"No."

"Taking cooking lessons."

"No."

"Selling minnow sandwiches in the bait shop?"

"Wrong, wrong, wrong." Julie released Nelson's paws. He sat, squirmed about, and licked himself. "Yuck. Nelson, you're disgusting." She turned her back on him. "And you're the worst guesser in the world, Uncle Dan."

I set the sack on the picnic table outside the garage and raised my hands in surrender. "Then my last guess is that I guess you'll have to tell me."

Julie rolled her eyes. "That doesn't count as a guess."

"Let's put him out of his misery." Camille lowered herself to the bench attached to the picnic table. "Priscilla is selling her house and the bait shop. There's already a sign on the road."

Julie dug into the grocery sack and came up with a handful of potato chips. Nelson ceased licking his groin, ran to her side, and sat at attention. "I wonder who will buy it. I hope it's somebody nice. Maybe somebody with a handsome son."

She tossed a chip. Nelson tracked it with his eyes, twisted his neck, and caught it with a snap of his jaws.

"I'm going swimming." Julie stuffed the rest of the chips into her mouth and mumbled through them. "When's dinner?"

"Whenever you get it ready. It's your turn, remember?" Camille nodded to the grocery sack. "Everything you need is in the bag."

Julie's lower lip slid out and then back. Pout cancelled. "Right after I swim?"

"Okay, but put the cold stuff away now."

Sweeping the bag into her arms, Julie darted into the garage. In a second I heard the clink of jars and the muffled slam of the refrigerator door.

"Hot dogs again?"

"And Julie says you're not a good guesser." Camille stood and stretched out a hand. "Let's walk through the house. We need to talk."

I rocked back a step and put a hand to my chest. "Talk?"

"Relax. It's not a relationship talk."

I blew out a sigh and slung an arm around her shoulder.

"And it's not about why you were up at that old camp. Mary Lou's been worrying on that all afternoon but all that matters to me is that Luke's gone."

I held in a second sigh. No point in making myself any more transparent. We crossed the driveway and mounted the steps to the porch. Shade stretched out to meet us. The porch roof had enough of an overhang to keep off the worst of sun and rain and there was room for a double swing at either end with plenty of space left for chairs and small tables.

Camille stopped before the door, took my hand, and ran it across wood silky from sanding and around the pattern in the stained glass—a blue lake, green mountains, sky shot with the fiery colors of sunset. The winter sun would blaze through the glass as it set, throwing color across the living room. "I love this door."

"You better. You designed it."

"My talents know no bounds." She grasped the brass handle and swung the door open, revealing a room much like the one claimed by fire last fall. A huge stone fireplace rose along the exterior wall and the knotty pine paneling Stub and I had milled covered the others. By trial and error, I'd mixed a stain that approximated the caramel color of the original walls.

Camille hugged me close and tipped her head to peer up at me. "Are you glad you did it this way?"

It was a question I wrestled with every day. Recreating the sense of the room would forever conjure memories of a past I once tried to break with, yet I found it comforting, a symbol of my survival. "Maybe not glad, but definitely satisfied."

She kissed the tip of my chin, then led me into the kitchen, a room twice the size of the previous one, with an island, a greenhouse window, and spreading counters. It had space for an enormous refrigerator, a double oven, a six-burner stove, and an informal dining area where Camille planned to put an oak table she said would seat ten or twelve. When I questioned the size, she countered that Julie would bring friends home and that, knowing us, "mail and stuff would pile up on one end." We

377

circled the island, and Camille hugged herself. "I love this room."

"When do you think you'll use it for more than grilling hot dogs and hamburgers? The store sucks up all your time."

"It does. But I have ideas about that. And about other things."

She stepped through the frame for a sliding glass door and out onto an expanse of graded earth. Stacks of flat stone waited for the stonemason to lay a patio and build stone benches and planter boxes for herbs and flowers. To the left, outside what would be the master bedroom, pipes and wires jutted and boards marked the perimeter of what would be a concrete pad to support a hot tub—a recent addition to plans I'd given up trying to rein in.

Perching on a pile of stone, she plucked a pebble from the ground, and tossed it. It arced across the rose garden that my mother—and then Camille—had nurtured and dropped among the branches of the lilac bush I fell beneath the night Ronny shot me.

The past was close here. Palpable.

"Pattie Bonesteel's daughter is in a bad marriage. She's depressed. She needs to come home, but she needs to feel she's not crawling back in disgrace."

A familiar theme. "You want her to run the store?"

"Well, I'd run it." She scavenged another pebble and bounced it on her palm. "I enjoy organizing and ordering and handling the financial part of the business and it's making enough now to support a paid employee."

"What about Julie?"

"With school and activities, she'll be too busy except for summer and holidays." Camille tossed the pebble high, caught it, and clenched her fist around it. "I know you mentioned the store to Justin," she said in a rush. "But I'm worried that Julie will feel pushed out. And it seemed like he wasn't crazy about the idea."

"He wasn't." I remembered Justin's words—he'd never pictured himself standing behind a counter, being inside all day. "I bet you have a better idea."

She flushed and her fist clenched around the pebble. I recognized my blunders and backtracked. "I meant that as a compliment. I never considered that Julie might feel shoved aside, but I should have thought of that. I don't want her to feel she's in second place."

"Neither do I. She deserves better, and she's done a terrific job of dressing the place up and making it more fun than work." Camille's fingers relaxed and she tossed the pebble from hand to hand.

"So what's the better idea about Justin?"

"Well, maybe it's more a different idea than a better one. It will be expensive, and the return might be slow. But I think it's a good investment—for Justin and the whole community." She chewed at her lower lip before she spoke in another rush. "I'll throw in everything I've got left. It's not much, only about ten thousand."

I hesitated, pacing, thinking hard before I blundered again. Camille was offering a whole lot more than ten thousand dollars. She was offering to sacrifice her financial independence, her way out of Hemlock Lake and our relationship. I needed to acknowledge her willingness to cross a new threshold. "If you're that confident, then it must be a good investment. But why don't we pencil out the numbers first and see whether you need to go all-in on this gamble or whether we could swing it if you bet only part of your pot? Every woman needs a walking-away fund. Even if the guy she's with hopes to hell he'll never be such a jerk that she'll use it."

She smiled, tears bright in her eyes. "I feel guilty. You've spent so much more than you planned for."

"Yeah, but I'm good for now. I don't have to go to the sheriff and beg for my job back." I sat beside her on the stone pile and drew her against my chest. "If that's what you're worried about."

"I'm worried that you'll think I don't pull my weight. I'm not asking you to show me your bank statements," she mumbled against my shirt.

"You pull more than your weight." I stroked her bare arm. "As for the bank statements, you can do more than see them, you can balance them."

She laughed and I tipped her chin so I could look into her eyes, those wonderful reddish brown eyes. The shade of a fox's fur at sunset. "How about after dinner? I'll lay out everything and show you what's invested where and what it adds up to."

She squeezed her eyelids closed. Tears seeped through the lashes and she rubbed her face against my shirt. "I don't care what it adds up to. I'd stick with you if you were down to your last dime."

I kissed her, long and deep. "What about the day I spend that dime? What if I have nothing left in the world except Nelson?"

She chuckled. "Then I'm outta here."

"As long as I know where I stand." I kissed her again, longer, deeper. "Now tell me about this idea."

She nodded and took a deep breath. "The idea is that we find a way to buy Priscilla's house and the bait shop. When he gets out, Justin could live there and run the shop and do caretaking chores for people in the new development like Priscilla and Luke have been doing."

I blinked. I hadn't seen that coming.

Camille rushed on. "Priscilla's going to ask the moon, but she won't get it. The house needs a new roof and a lot of upgrades. Justin could do some of that and I think living on his own would be . . . good for him."

Better for us too. And for Julie.

"It will take weeks to close a deal, maybe months," Camille said.

"True."

"But if the deal went through quicker, I'm sure Freeman and Evan will help with the bait shop and caretaking until Justin gets back." She gazed up at me, eyes pleading. "Maybe you could too."

I felt a flash of resentment, the way I always did when someone made plans for me, when I felt cornered by expectations. I tried to shake it off, but it came through in my voice. "Not until this house is finished."

Her eyes clouded. "It was just an idea."

I told myself she hadn't made a commitment for me, only a suggestion. "I know. I just—"

"I'm sorry. I didn't think. I'm getting to be like everyone else in Hemlock Lake, making plans for Dan."

"It's okay."

"You have all that baseboard to finish. And the other projects."

"And they'll get done, or get put off. There's no law that every last detail has to be perfect before we move in."

"But—"

I slipped my hand across her lips. "Let's put that aside. Let's put your money aside. If Julie and Justin agree, we might be able to finance part of the deal by selling Rachel's house. Or the other one."

Camille shivered. "I can't imagine either of them wanting to live there."

I flashed on an image of flames and smoke, saw Ronny carry Lisa down the stairs and lay her on the ground, heard Julie's screams. "No, but they might not be able to let it go just yet."

She nodded. "Rachel's house isn't that old and it's in good shape, so it might sell fast. Justin could mill lumber to rehab Priscilla's place."

The plan was alive, growing. Then I swung the executioner's axe. "But Priscilla won't sell to me or to you, no matter how much we offer."

"You're right." Camille sagged against me. For a long moment we were still and then she tipped her face to look at me and wrinkled her nose. "But what if we use a little sleight of hand?"

CHAPTER 38

It took us five minutes to come up with a strategy, and about an hour the next morning to hammer out details with the attorney handling Clarence's estate. He was a far younger man than the Stone family lawyer, healthier, heartier, and quicker on the up-take. He hadn't minded making an appointment for Saturday morning, and he didn't so much as blink when we explained what we wanted. Even as he snatched a yellow legal pad from a desk drawer, he let loose with a string of initials referencing corporate law and tax codes.

When the pieces were in place, I prepared for my role as Judas goat by reminding myself that we'd bent over backwards for Priscilla after Willie Dean's death. Her wish was to leave Hemlock Lake and, ultimately, this plan would make that financially possible.

I drove to the bait shop and found her hanging laundry on a line stretched between two trees beside the house. "Get off my property," she said by way of greeting. "You're a worthless excuse for a man. There's a serial killer out there on the hunt, but you don't give a damn about that. No, you're too busy harassing a poor, hardworking man, setting your dog on him, and getting him arrested just for looking out for the only family he has."

Denying that we'd harassed Luke or set Nelson on him was pointless. And I suspected mentioning the only family Luke had was a dead woman would kick the conversation over the line from heated to incendiary. I raised my hands in surrender and waited her out.

"Go over to the Shovel It Inn, fill yourself with beer, and celebrate with your friend Jefferson." She yanked a pink pillowcase from the laundry basket and shook it out with a sharp snap. "Thanks to you, Luke says he's never coming back, even if you get down on your knees and apologize."

I wondered what made her think that was even a remote possibility but, tempting as it was to learn about the workings of her mind, I didn't ask. Nor did I mention the lab work being done on her truck that might put Luke away forever.

She flung the pillowcase over the sagging line and jammed a clothes pin into the center. My mother taught me to hang sheets and pillowcases by the corners and edges so they dried faster and with fewer wrinkles, so my fingers itched to pull the pin out and do it the "right way." I stuck my hands in my back pockets as Priscilla snatched a pair of jeans and tossed them across the line. "Well, I finally saw the light," she snarled. "I'll be out of here just as soon as someone makes me an offer I can live with."

"That's why I'm here."

She passed on pinning the jeans and dug out a mottled green towel before she did a slow double take. "You? You want to make an offer?"

"Yes." I swept my gaze across the house. "But your asking price is too high. The roof is in bad shape, the deck is sagging, those windows should have been upgraded twenty years ago, and the insulation . . .

I took a step toward the house and waved a verbal red cape. "Would you mind if I took a close look at the carpet and linoleum?"

"Damn right I mind! Don't you dare go near my house!" She wadded the towel and slammed it into the laundry basket. "You can't waltz over here and give me a pathetic lowball offer and expect I'll be grateful."

"I would never try to lowball you, Priscilla." I put a hand over my heart. "You'd see through me in a minute. But you have to admit the house needs work. A lot of work. How does fifty-five thousand less than your asking price sound?"

"Fifty-five thousand!" Her eyes glinted and her cheeks turned purple with rage. "That's highway robbery. And even if it wasn't, even if you offered full price, I wouldn't sell to you if you were the last person on earth. Not after what you did to Luke."

I couldn't have scripted a better response. Frowning, I glanced at the house and then the sky. "Can you do that? Can you refuse to sell to someone who offers full price?"

Priscilla's eyes narrowed. I scratched my head, playing the puzzled but concerned citizen. "Isn't that discrimination?"

"I don't give a damn." She kicked the laundry basket. A T-shirt bounced out and sprawled in the dirt beneath the line. "I'll burn that house before I sell to you. I'll take a chainsaw to the dock and sink the bait shop."

Exactly what I hoped for. "You must have amazing insurance coverage."

"I don't care if I have no coverage. I'd rather die broke than sell my property to you."

She kicked the laundry basket again. Her flip-flop folded back and her toes slid between the plastic slats and lodged there. As she bent to pry them loose, I strolled away, firing my parting shot in a quiet voice. "I'll check with my lawyer and see what he says about that discrimination thing."

"If some chickenshit lawyer tells me I have to sell my house to you then I won't sell it at all," she screamed. "I'll stay here in Hemlock Lake and make your life a living hell."

An hour later my lawyer made a call to Priscilla's real estate agent. Just before sunset, he phoned to say they struck a deal for forty-three thousand less than her asking price.

Camille was out at the end of the dock reading while Julie floated on an air mattress, painting her toenails purple and talking on her cell. "We got it," I crowed in a low voice.

Camille grinned, then chewed at her lower lip. "She can't back out? I mean, if she finds out we're the C&S Corporation?"

"Unless she does some digging, and only if she wants to get tangled in an expensive legal snarl. The key word being 'expensive'."

"What if the paperwork for the corporation isn't finished before the sale?"

"Then we'll stall the sale. But let's not worry until it happens."

Camille sighed and shook her head, her hair like dark flame in the slanting beams of the sun. "I thought I'd feel good about this, but . . . Did we do the right thing?"

I chewed on that for a moment. The right thing could be questionable, open to debate, morally ambiguous. In the grip of a bent mind, the wrong thing could appear to be the right thing. Ronny believed he did the right thing when he burned and killed. I sat beside Camille and rubbed her back. "We did a good thing. For the community."

"I know." She leaned against me, her hair warm against my neck. "But the way we did it was so underhanded."

An easy wind fanned my face. I breathed it in, held it, then concentrated on breathing out my feelings about Priscilla, putting aside the question of right or wrong. "I guess we'll have to judge the means by the end. It's not like we stole the property. Her real estate agent admitted the offer was above anything they expected."

Camille nodded, her hair tickling my jaw. "But if she finds out, she'll be furious."

"Furious is where Priscilla starts from most of the time."

Camille reached up and stroked my cheek. "True. And sometimes I don't blame her. Maybe, in a warped kind of way, we've given her a gift by going behind her back."

"A gift?"

"Well, she needs to get away and start over. But if she ever has doubts about leaving Hemlock Lake, she can remember this and tell herself we're a pack of cheating scoundrels and the smartest thing she ever did was leave us behind."

"Cheating Scoundrels. Same initials as Chancellor and Stone."

Camille winced. "If she figures that out she'll be twice as mad."

"Let's hope she's long gone when she does."

The cabinet crew was at work in the kitchen and I was setting my baseboard puzzle pieces in place to make sure they fit when Sheriff North called on Monday morning. "You want an update on your boy Luke?"

Laying the board aside, I got to my feet and walked out to the porch. "I thought you'd never ask."

"Well, there's not much to tell. They're grilling him like a burger at a barbecue, but he' sticking to his story—never kidnapped or killed any girls, dug up his mother because she told him to, and doesn't understand why he's behind bars. Either he's telling the truth, he's so twisted he's convinced himself that *is* the truth, or he's the best liar I ever came across."

"I'll take doors two and three."

"I would too, if we had any proof." A match scratched and he puffed at his pipe. "They searched that old camp and took that truck apart, but so far they found zip—not a hair, not a fiber, not a print from Jessica Smithers or any of the other girls. It's possible he used another vehicle in the past—maybe that truck of his that went for scrap. But if he got another one, he didn't register it."

"Maybe it's in someone else's name. Maybe Luke doesn't hunt and kill alone."

And Justin was miles away and locked down.

For the first time since the worm of the idea that he was part of a killing team burrowed into my brain, I felt the muscles in the back of my neck unkink.

"The task force is sticking to the one-man theory."

"But that theory's based on what they encountered in the past."

North sucked at his pipe. "Point me at a likely killing partner and I'll go to the mat to change their minds."

A twisted idea bloomed in my mind. Could Luke have persuaded Priscilla to help him dig up the grave or transport his mother's body to Hemlock Lake while he went out to hunt and kidnapped Jessica Smithers? Priscilla seemed committed to overlooking, rationalizing, and defending his behavior. Had she taken that to a deadly extreme?

I shook that off. Priscilla had been boiling mad that Luke left her to deal with the bait shop on a day he should have been working. That felt real to me Friday morning. It still did. And much as she hated sweaty work and broken fingernails, I couldn't see her shoveling cemetery soil at midnight—not for love nor money.

But if Priscilla wasn't Luke's companion in crime, then who was? "What did they find in the shed? And on Jessica Smithers?"

"Not a whole hell of a lot. A few dark fibers—I'm betting he wore a ski mask—a single hair without the root, and flecks of base paint."

"Paint?"

389

"Black. Thick. Oil based. They speculate he painted the bed and sides of the vehicle to seal scrapes and rust, make it easier to wash down and remove evidence."

My stomach churned. Did the killer have a torture chamber on wheels?

The pipe tapped against his desk. "Anyway, we're going to hang onto Luke as long as we can on whatever charges the prosecutor comes up with. We'll see if we can't connect him to another truck or van. If no other girls go missing while he's our guest that might tell us something. On the other hand . . ."

He didn't finish that sentence but I knew what he left unsaid and brooded on it for the rest of the day. If a girl disappeared while Luke was out of circulation, we'd know he hadn't committed that particular crime. But that wouldn't clear him of the earlier ones.

No matter the evidence or lack of it, he was still my strongest candidate.

When I heard the distant echoes of gunshots that evening, a shard of memory broke loose in my brain and I drove up to the sandpit beyond Freeman's house at the end of Bluestone Hollow.

Jefferson lay on the lip of the pit, aiming at a row of cans wedged into the sand of the far bank. "Just mounted a new scope," he said without looking up. "We're seeing how we like each other."

As if they were dating.

I grunted and sat with my back against an oak. Jefferson squeezed off a shot. A can at the left of the row jumped. He fired twice more, dislodging the cans next in line, then made a tiny adjustment, rolled over, and sat up.

I nodded at the scope. "Think she's worthy of dinner and a movie?"

"She's playing hard to get, so right now I'm not committing to more than the movie—maybe with a tub of popcorn." He grinned and stroked the scope. "What brings you up here?"

"Something I need to check out so I can put my brain in sleep mode tonight. Remember when you told me about your friend, the electronics guy? You said he loaned you a couple of bugs. Did—?"

"Priscilla's car? Yep."

"I was hoping you'd say that."

"If you don't see that you need to cover all the bases, you shouldn't be in the game. Want me to leave it there?"

"Probably easier than going back to get it." I picked up a twig and broke it into finger-sized lengths. "Tell me about the monitor for that tracking device. Does it store information?"

"Sure. It feeds it to a computer."

"So you'd know if Priscilla took her car out the night before we caught Luke."

"She didn't. Only the truck went out that night, down to that cemetery and back up here to that old camp."

"Any side trips?"

"Not a one."

Damn it. That not only cleared Priscilla of the kidnapping, but it cleared Luke as well. I tossed the bits of twig aside.

Jefferson took off his glasses and cleaned them on his sleeve. "I didn't mention that because I'm not in the business of helping out a man I'd rather not have living back among us."

"Plus, making use of those devices put us on the far side of legal."

"That, too." He slid his glasses back on and rubbed his chin. "You were thinking Priscilla helped Luke kidnap that girl."

"Yeah." I stood. "I knew it was a long shot."

He nodded and stroked the scope. "Well, sometimes a long shot hits the mark."

The next morning I drove up to Clarence's place to check on it as I promised his attorney—now also my attorney. The real estate agent who listed the property had hired someone to toss gravel into the ruts to improve traction so potential buyers could get over the ridge and check out the place. To no one's surprise, despite a huge sign out on the highway and a number of ads, there hadn't been a lot of viewings.

I had mixed feelings about the house being on the market. In a way, I wanted it sold, the deal sealed, the book closed. But I also wanted it to remain empty long enough for Clarence's spirit to come to terms with his final moments. If that ever happened.

"Place gives me the willies," the agent told me the one time I ran into him at the post office. "Had a client up there on the hottest day of July and he told me he felt a chill on the front steps. Claimed the place is haunted."

Jefferson and I had never mentioned what we experienced, and I wasn't about to then. I forced a laugh and made mundane comments about how the wind funneled between the ridges. Before he could say more, I claimed a meeting with my contractor and took off.

"Wish I'd never taken the listing," he called after me. "Not a chance in hell I'll renew when six months are up."

When I pulled up out front, I relived the electric air, the sparks that shot from the key, the searing padlock. "It's just me, Clarence," I called, feeling the false bravery of a boy whistling past a cemetery at midnight.

Circling the house, I checked for indications of vandalism or burglary, but saw only signs of low-level neglect—grass three inches too long, a scatter of leaves on the porch, dust on the railing.

"I'm sorry, Clarence." I lowered myself to the steps where he fell, hesitated for a second, then placed my right hand on the spot where his blood spilled. "I thought we had him but I couldn't make the pieces fit."

I groped for a word to describe how I felt—heartsick, bereft, dispirited—but no combination of syllables conveyed the depth of my rage or the weight of my sadness.

A chill stream of air blew across the porch. I turned my face into it and spoke to the ghost. "The good news is that he's starting to make mistakes. The last girl got away."

The wind veered left then right. "They'll nail him before too long. I know they will. I'd give everything I've got left in the bank to be there when they do."

The wind warmed, dropped to a faint breeze. I got to my feet and faced the kennels. "I'm pretty sure that young dog's not training up to your expectations, but he's got a good nose and a lot of heart. Julie loves him and he loves her. I wouldn't trade him for any amount of money."

The breeze warmed more, swirled around me, then raised an eddy of dust that sparkled in a slant of sunlight before it slipped between the birches at the edge of the lawn and drifted across the meadow toward the forest.

CHAPTER 35

The weeks slipped by without a call from Sheriff North, without another girl going missing.

No evidence turned up to link Luke to Jessica Smithers or the other girls, but he remained in jail, refusing to consider bail, refusing an attorney, insisting that he would defend himself. Meanwhile, Priscilla bragged about how she sold her property out from under the man who persecuted her and her handyman, and I played at being disappointed the sale hadn't gone my way and concerned that the property would go to some corporation from outside Hemlock Lake.

Folks went on locking their doors and keeping an eye out for strangers, but I sensed wariness eroding with each day that passed. They might not believe Luke was the killer, but they wanted to believe the killing was over or at least that the killer had moved on. They wanted to get back to life the way it had been—or at least life the way they wanted it to be.

Even Jefferson relaxed. He spent less time up at the sandpit shooting and channeled his energy into remodeling Mary Lou's kitchen, borrowing tools and talent when he couldn't manage tasks alone.

Julie worked at her genealogy charts, winnowing through birth and death certificates, baptism records and marriage licenses. She crowed with delight when she discovered a link in a chain of ancestry, moaned in frustration when she couldn't graft branches to her spreading trees, dug through crumbling cardboard boxes of photos stored in the attic of the old schoolhouse, squinted at words written in faded ink, and mourned photo albums and baby books lost to me when the lodge burned.

At first the names of the dead conjured stark memories. But after a time Camille and I agreed it felt like standing at the rail of a boat as it leaves the dock and sets off across an ocean. We imagined a spreading wake and widening distance and knew we were never going back to that country called the past and were eager to get to the far shore.

Camille and Julie and I spent almost every evening in the new house, painting ceilings, walls, and the insides of closets. The windows went in, the carpet and linoleum went down, light fixtures went up, and sinks, tubs, and toilets got connected to plumbing. On the last day of August, while Julie sorted through boxes of clothing in search of the perfect outfit for the first day of school, I nailed the final pieces of baseboard into place in our bedroom and wiped my hands on my jeans. "Want to move the mattresses over and sleep here tonight?" I asked Camille.

"The furnace isn't hooked up yet." She sprayed vinegar on a cluster of greasy smudges marring the glass door.

"We won't need a furnace until this heat breaks." I made a show of wiping sweat from my forehead. "Besides, there's no furnace in the garage."

"Well, the cabinets aren't all up in the kitchen." She scrubbed at the fingerprints with a wad of newspaper. "And the table and chairs won't arrive for two weeks."

I chased that around my brain for a minute, but didn't see the logic. "We'll use the ones from the garage."

"No."

"But we—"

She dropped the newspaper to the floor and looked at me with red-rimmed eyes. "I want everything in place before we move in. Please."

"But we'll have more space if—"

"I never had a home as nice as this." She swallowed and rubbed at her eyes with the backs of her wrists. "We've spent so long planning and shopping and I just want . . ."

Crossing the room, I pulled her against me and kissed the top of her head. Between the store and this house and carting Julie around to buy school clothes, she'd been working too many long hours. And the heat made us all snappish, as my mother used to say. "We won't move in until the last picture is hung, the last potholder is on its hook, and the last scented bar of guest soap is centered on some pretty little dish. You let me know when it's exactly the way you want it."

She laughed and kissed the underside of my chin. "Thank you. I know it's silly, but I want to wake up here on October first, not before. It's—"

"It's what you want. So let's do it. I won't even lounge on the porch railing until the grand opening."

"See that you don't," she said in a lighter voice. "And see that your dog stays outside—especially if he's covered with dirt from digging up moles."

"*Trying* to dig up moles. And, in case you haven't noticed, he's ceased even pretending that he's my dog."

She tilted her head and looked up at me, her eyes twinkling. "Do I detect a shade of jealousy and disappointment?"

Pleased that I could make her smile, I mock-griped. "I saved his life. I paid his vet bills. I buy his kibble."

"And Julie takes him out in the canoe and feeds him potato chips and marshmallows." She shuddered. "I'm amazed his teeth haven't rotted out."

"I'm amazed he hasn't hurled on every square inch of the garage."

"He's tough. Like you." She put one hand over my heart. "Except for what's right in here. That's as tender as—"

"Your pot roast?"

"I was going to say young grass, but pot roast sounds wonderful." She wiggled from my arms and snatched up the newspaper. "We'll make that our first meal. Pot roast with potatoes and carrots and onions."

"And a gallon of gravy? And homemade biscuits? And apple pie?"

"All of the above. But only if I don't find Nelson's paw prints on the new carpet before then."

Raising my right hand, I swore allegiance to the roast, promising to police a dog that took as little notice of my commands as he did of the fireflies flitting among the trees at twilight.

Julie went back to school after Labor Day, catching the bus outside the post office with a group of kids wearing shirts in layers, ripped jeans, and thin-at-the-heel flip-flops. Most carried new backpacks and all wore expressions of blasé indifference. Nelson tried to follow her onto the bus, but couldn't make the leap to the first step and sprawled on the edge of it before tumbling to the parking lot. Julie jumped out, dusted him off, kissed his nose, and assured him she'd be back in no time. He didn't seem convinced and, when the bus disappeared around a bend in the road, howled like someone had cut off his ears. He kept it up until Camille distracted him with a bag of peanuts.

That evening Julie praised his loyalty and consoled him with half of her ice cream cone. Later, they sprawled on the dock and she drew him his own family tree on a sheet of paper from her three-ring binder. It was a lopsided affair, with "Unknown" written in the space reserved for his mother, and Clarence listed as his father. Camille, glancing at it as she sat to paddle her feet in the water, pointed out that Clarence was related to my mother.

"Then you're related to Nelson," Julie told me. "You're like an uncle or something."

"Or something," Camille said with a chuckle.

The next morning, before she left for school, Julie knelt beside Nelson, told him he couldn't come to the bus stop, and promised she would fill in more blanks over the weekend when Mary Lou took her to a meeting of her genealogical group.

Three more weeks slid into the past. Blinds went up in the new house and furniture trucks pulled up carrying an enormous refrigerator and the colossal stove, beds and sofas, the dining room table and chairs, nightstands and dressers. Camille carted home ceiling fans, lamps, sheets, towels, dishes, and glassware.

I spent my days assembling racks and shelves to fit inside closets and my evenings alternately hiding my amusement or holding my temper while I moved furniture an inch this way or that. I drove nails for pictures and then spackled the holes, touched up the paint, and drove new nails. By telling myself it was important to Camille and counting down the days to the first of October, I even managed to feign interest in a debate over the merits of stowing the silverware in a drawer near the dishwasher or one closer to the table.

"Nesting," Evan told me one evening when, with six full days remaining before the move-in date, I checked my patience level, found it down a quart, and retreated to the bar at the Shovel It Inn.

Stub rolled his eyes. "It's a female thing."

Merle glanced toward the kitchen where Shirley was scraping the grill, then contributed in a low voice. "In the spring it's cleaning and organizing and throwing out all your favorite clothes."

Freeman crossed his arms as if protecting his green plaid flannel shirt with the fraying collar. "In the fall it's kind of like getting ready to hibernate. Winter's coming on and you'll be spending a whole hell of a lot of time inside those walls. No matter how much room you have in a house, comes a time when it feels like a pretty tight cave, so it better be a cave you can live in without clawing each other to shreds before the snow melts."

We sipped our beer and nodded the way men do when they discover common ground or a common enemy. No one said a word for a good five minutes, then the door creaked open and Jefferson came in with a blast of autumn air that smelled of dry leaves and distant smoke.

He slid onto the stool next to mine. "You look like owls on a branch."

"We've been trading wisdom about women," I said.

"Bet that didn't take long."

Merle chuckled and drew a beer. "About twenty-five seconds."

"Well, I doubt I could have extended the conversation." Jefferson drank away half the glass and wiped his mouth. "I just got orders to haul everything out of the old schoolhouse. By Monday morning."

"Monday?" Stub leaned forward and swiveled his head to get a better look at Jefferson. "Mary Lou get a bee up her butt to make the schoolhouse into a museum before the snow flies?"

"Nope. That plan's dead and buried."

Like the owls he'd compared us to, we widened our eyes and leaned toward Jefferson. He drained the rest of the beer and set the glass down with a snap. "All the stuff she's been saving is going to the county historical society—except what's being boxed up for the genealogy folks."

"Whoooo," Evan said, drawing the word out the way an owl does.

He and Freeman and Merle laughed like hyenas. Stub looked disgusted for a moment, then joined in. Jefferson rolled his eyes, reached across the bar, and refilled his glass at the tap.

"So what's the new plan for the schoolhouse?" I asked when the last guffaw faded.

Jefferson blew foam from the top of the glass. "Kids' club."

"Whooooat?" Evan said, and we all leaned again.

"She says Julie and the others need a place to hang out after school and on weekends—a place where they can't get into all that much trouble. They can help each other with their homework and listen to their music and everybody can keep an eye on them so . . ."

He let that sentence trail off, but the grim looks on the others' faces told me we'd all filled in the blank—so if the killer wasn't gone, so if he tried to pick off a girl from Hemlock Lake, someone might be close by to stop him.

How long would that shadow hang over this valley? How much time had to pass before we could feel he was gone, this was over? Would we ever? Was it like cancer where people shied away from using the word "cured."

"A kids' club is a good idea," Freeman said.

Evan nodded. "Damn good."

"Wait a minute, Jefferson." Merle tossed a bar rag on a drip of foam. "You're living in the schoolhouse. Does Mary Lou's plan include you being den mother to a pack of teenagers?"

"Her plan calls for me moving out."

Every head swiveled Jefferson's way. "Out of Hemlock Lake?" Stub asked.

"You can't," Freeman and Evan said together, echoing the words in my mind. Since the day we discovered Clarence's body, Jefferson and I had a bond—a bond defined more by things unsaid than those put into words.

"I'm not," he answered. "At least not unless Mary Lou changes the part of the plan that calls for me to rent a room in her house."

Heads swiveled and nodded through a stretch of silence and I guessed they were making comparisons to other living arrangements in Hemlock Lake—mine and Camille's, Priscilla's and Luke's. And I guessed they were considering what this arrangement entailed. If Jefferson was aware of our churning thoughts, he gave no sign.

After a time, Stub cleared his throat. "Makes sense. No use wasting that space. And Mary Lou must be lonely by herself."

Silence expanded again. If I spent the days at the center of the Hemlock Lake web as Mary Lou did, I'd relish time alone. But she was a more gregarious soul and, even after all those years of silent hostility before Jefferson returned, the house must seem hollow with Lou Marie gone.

"And cooking just for yourself takes the edge off your appetite," Freeman said. "When Alda goes off to visit her sister I—"

"Come in here every night," Merle observed.

"And eat breakfast at my place," Stub added.

"And make baloney sandwiches for lunch," Evan said half under his breath.

Freeman raised his hands in surrender. "The point is, eating's better with at least two at the table and Mary Lou's a darn good cook."

Jefferson raised his beer in salute and patted his stomach. "Amen to that. And I'll need every spare calorie to get that schoolhouse emptied on the schedule she set and round up some old sofas and lamps and a table or two."

"I'll help," I said. "What time do you want me there?"

Eagerness I couldn't disguise set off a round of guffaws. "If you told him, 'Right now,' Dan wouldn't argue," Stub said. "Anything to get out of the way of a nesting woman."

Jefferson shot me a questioning look and I offered a shrug in exchange. "Well, I'm happy for his help no matter what the reason," he said. "And while Mary Lou's at work that schoolhouse is a woman-free zone."

"Woman-free?" Freeman tapped his glass on the bar. "Count me in."

"I'll bring my truck," Evan said.

"Marcella's been wanting a new sofa." Stub smiled and rubbed his chin. "I could make her a happy woman if I donated our old one to the cause."

Merle glanced toward the kitchen where Shirley was still scraping the grill. "I wouldn't mind a little more happiness around this place. We got some chairs in the living room Shirl's been threatening to set on fire."

"I'll donate the microwave and the TV from the garage," I offered. "After we move into the new house on the thirtieth."

Freeman thumped my back "We'll hold a place for them but, hell, Dan, the thirtieth's a lifetime away. I bet if we all pitch in we'll have the rest in place before that."

Jefferson slapped a ten-dollar bill on the bar. "You're on."

We started at eight the next morning with two trucks and my old trailer, but word spread as people went to the post office to collect their mail, and by noon there were a dozen of us shuffling boxes and furniture into three more vehicles. By the time kids got back from school and came by to gawk, everything destined for historians and genealogists had been hauled to its proper destination. By half-past dinner time, Jefferson's gear was stowed in his new quarters, Lou Marie's old stove had gone to charity and the twenty-by-twenty room was empty except for the aging refrigerator wheezing in a corner.

Exhausted, we leaned against the walls, munching on chips and cookies left over from lunch, firming up plans for the next day, and watching Evan shove a push broom along floorboards stained almost black and ridged where softer wood wore away leaving raised lines of grain.

"Kids will have to keep their shoes on or they'll be picking splinters every day," Freeman observed. "Better put up a warning sign."

"They're teenagers," I reminded him. "Putting up a sign is a sure way to see they go barefoot right through the winter."

"And a few splinters never killed anyone," Stub said.

Freeman scowled. "Well, better put up a sign anyway. And Mary Lou better look into getting extra insurance. If a splinter festers and a parent gets all worked up and says we were negligent . . ." He shook his head in apparent disgust and amazement at the legal state of the world.

"I'll tell her," Jefferson said. "I don't know if she's thought of that. But better safe than sorry."

"Even when you try to do a good deed," Merle said in a mournful voice, "there are those who'll find a way to stick it to you."

My phone chirped.

"Incoming," Jefferson said with a chuckle.

Evan grinned and covered his head with his arms. "Duck and cover."

"Camille wants the towel bars raised half an inch," Freeman said.

"Or lowered," Stub suggested.

I groaned, dug the phone from my pocket, and flipped it open.

"It looks like he got another one," Sheriff North said.

CHAPTER 40

I braced myself against the wall. "Who? When? Where?"

"Amanda Dearborn. This morning. Just down the road from this damn office."

Jefferson stepped to my side. "Another girl?"

I nodded. His trigger finger curled. The others moved closer, faces grim.

"Parents run a diner," the sheriff said. "They left before five. She's a high school senior. Gets to school on her own." He paused, swallowed, cursed softly. "They didn't know she was missing until her friends started calling the diner because she didn't answer her cell phone."

"What can I do?" I surveyed the men clustered around me. "What can *we* do?"

I held the phone away from my ear so everyone could hear North's reply. "I wish to hell I knew. We figured it was a waste of time, but we checked the shed where he stashed Jessica Smithers and we combed that whole area. We're getting bulletins on every TV and radio station." He cleared his throat. "This guy's been like smoke and there are lots of rocks he can crawl under. But the more people looking, the better. Get the word out, keep your eyes open for vehicles you haven't seen before, check empty buildings."

"We'll do that."

"Be careful. Anything doesn't look right—anything at all—call it in." His voice grew steely. "Don't go testing some theory or chasing this guy on your own. We don't need dead heroes."

"Got it." Dead was the last thing I wanted to be. And I was all out of theories.

As I ended the call, Stub dug his keys from his pocket. "I'll check Ronny's old place and Rachel's and everything between here and there."

"I'll take care of Silver Leaf Hollow on the way home." I nodded at a trio of elderly men who lived in the core of the community. "Can you take the main part of town?"

They nodded back and huddled together to make plans.

Freeman tapped Evan's shoulder. "We'll check everything on the west side of the lake. Up Bluestone Hollow, around the new development, and down to the Brockton place."

Jefferson headed for the door. "There's an hour of daylight left. I'm going to that glade. I'll check the old camp and Clarence's place on the way."

The image of those girls filled my mind with cold horror. "I'll go with you."

"No need."

I tucked the phone in my pocket and repeated, "I'll go with you."

He spoke without turning to face me. "I appreciate the offer, Sergeant, but you're needed here to coordinate things. I can handle this mission on my own. And he won't be in that glade yet, not until . . ."

Until he tortured her, killed her, and dressed her for that stage.

"Thought I'd go up and leave some signs that I'd been. Make it clear we're increasing the level of risk."

"All right. But if I don't hear from you in two hours we're all coming after you."

He strode off and, like fallen leaves caught in a gust of wind, we scattered in his wake. I called Camille, then drove up into Silver Leaf Hollow and walked their property with the four owners I found at home. I checked outbuildings around the other two places and hunted for fresh tire tracks but found none. By the time I got home, the sun had settled behind the mountains and the sky glowed with lavender light.

Camille and Julie came out to greet me and I gathered them against my chest while Nelson hopped around us.

"Will this girl get away like the other one did?" Julie asked. "Will they catch him soon?"

"I hope so," I said, answering both questions.

"Maybe we should move into the new house tonight," Camille said. "It would be safer."

I didn't say what came into my mind—that he would be too busy torturing this girl to hunt for another right away. "Let's stick to your timetable. We're closer together in the garage. You'll feel safer."

"But we have to go outside to use the bathroom," Julie said.

"We'll make it a group activity."

Neither of them laughed. Julie slid a cold hand into mine. "Will you show me how to use the shotgun?"

"I don't think that's—"

"He will," Camille said. "Right after he has a decent dinner." She cocked her head to look into my eyes. "Every girl should know how to lock and load."

I wasn't sure how safe I'd feel when Julie had a gun in her hands, but I wasn't about to argue with the woman whose knowledge of firearms saved my life. I went along into the garage and dedicated myself to a hot roast beef sandwich.

Jefferson called as I was finishing. "Nothing. Not a footprint, not a broken twig, just a creepy graveyard feeling."

"What you expected."

"Yeah. Clarence's place is buttoned up. Nobody's been there since the rain on Monday. Nobody's been to that old camp, either."

"Thanks for scouting it out. I'll let the sheriff know. See you tomorrow."

The next morning, every child in Hemlock Lake, even the boys, waited for the school bus with a resolute parent or relative hovering close by. That afternoon adults returned in an angry swarm to collect them. Thankful I no longer wore a badge to serve as a target for impotent rage, I watched from the schoolhouse until Julie entered the store and passed into Camille's care.

For the next two days, with a radio tuned for updates that provided no new information, we patched the old schoolhouse walls and painted them with leftover paint from half a dozen different

410

renovation projects. We hauled old sofas and chairs and tables, dragged in a huge square of carpet, and brought over lamps, and shelves. I kicked in for king-size packages of paper towels and toilet paper, pencils, and notebook paper.

Every hour or so someone stopped working, stood as if struck by lightning, and shouted out a possible hiding place—a hunting cabin not used since an uncle died, a tumble-down barn, a rusted truck up on blocks at the edge of a field, the tiny storage shed at the cemetery. Like a panther, Jefferson stalked off. The rest of us waited, nerves humming, until he returned and shook his head.

And every hour or so someone threw down a paintbrush and said, "Damn it, we ought to be out there hunting for that bastard."

"Hunting where?" someone else would ask. "He could be anywhere. In another county, another state."

"There are a hundred places he could hide her," Sheriff North said when he called Thursday afternoon. "A thousand. He could be the guy living down the street, that nice young man who helps his neighbors scrape snow off their cars. As long as he keeps her quiet and out of sight, keeps pretending to be normal, he's under the radar." North sucked hard at his pipe. "All we can do is hope she gets loose or he screws up."

On Thursday evening we handed out fliers with pictures of Amanda Dearborn and went over the ground we'd covered before. None of us found a thing.

Early Friday afternoon we made another sweep, just ahead of a cold front that swept down from Canada pushing chill rain ahead of it. It thrummed on the roof and gurgled in the downspouts. Camille borrowed a space heater from Freeman and set it up in the garage, but it fought a losing battle against an insidious wind that threaded its way in at the edges of the overhead doors, moaning and sighing, making the hair on the back of my neck prickle. I stuffed rags around the doors, tried to read, but thought about that glade instead.

Camille and Julie packed clothing into boxes for me to haul to the new house, had me escort them out to the portable toilet, and headed to bed, Julie dragging Nelson beneath the comforter beside her. I checked the locks once again and tossed an extra blanket on our bed. Camille snuggled against me, a heating pad at the small of her back.

Saturday morning dawned clear but the wind stung like a hornet. I was drinking my second cup of coffee when the lawyer called and asked me to check on Clarence's house. "The real estate agent's out of town and the forecast's calling for frost."

I promised to turn on the heat, cover the outside faucets, and take care of anything else that needed to be done. But first there were chores—carrying more clothes and books over to the new place and clearing away the rubble left from breakfast. When Nelson licked the last plate clean, I tossed him a chew stick, locked him in the garage, and headed out with my shotgun on board.

Rain had washed the sky and settled the dust and the September sun glittered off yellow leaves fluttering on stands of birches. Along the ridge tops, sunlight burnished maple and oak leaves where green had already given way to deep gold, bronze, and streaks of scarlet. Where the highway crested the ridge, I braked and pulled to the shoulder, drinking in the autumn show, feeling both privileged and pensive. Winter would come soon, too soon.

Feeling the wind of time on my shoulders, I jerked my rig back onto the road and goosed the gas. I hit the turn into Clarence's road faster than I should have, skidded and fishtailed. My rear bumper scraped a sapling and the edge of the front caught another before I straightened out and churned up the hill.

That's when I spotted the tire tracks.

I slowed, peering through the windshield at the muddy slope. Two sets of tracks, left by the same vehicle. Someone had come and gone after the rain.

Jefferson?

I dug out my cell phone.

No signal.

I studied the tracks, decided they were too wide for the tires on Mary Lou's compact car. These looked like they'd been left by a truck.

Maybe a hunter scouting territory. Maybe Freeman or Evan or Stub. Or Jefferson driving a borrowed truck. Finding nothing wrong. Otherwise I would have heard.

I set the phone on the passenger seat, eased out the clutch until I had traction, and chugged to the top of the ridge, then rolled down the other side, past the spring, and out into the narrow sunlit valley. Two rabbits, alerted by the crunch of wheels on gravel, made a broken-field run across the lawn and dove through the line of birches into knee-high golden brown grass. An obliging breeze rippled the meadow, obscuring the trails to their burrows. A pair of swallows patrolled the sky and a jay lodged a complaint from the top of a pine.

413

As I reached the kennels, a sense of furious helplessness, faint, but swelling, swirled in my brain. I braked, shut down the engine, and heard the jay, the swish of wind in grass, and the creaking of boughs rubbing against each other. Beneath that was an electrical buzz like the droning of bees in a teeming hive.

I grasped my cell phone, then remembered the dead zone. Glancing behind me, I considered returning to the top of the ridge and calling the sheriff. "And telling him what?" a voice in my mind jeered. "You have a creepy feeling?"

"Good point." I slipped the phone into my pocket, got the shotgun from the back seat and stuffed spare shells in my pockets. "No one's here," I told myself. "The lockbox is closed. No one's inside. Clarence is just riled up because someone was in and out and maybe walked around."

That dampened my anxiety, but didn't put out the fire. I took the keys but left the driver's door open and then, instead of approaching the house head-on, bent low and trotted around the side, staying beneath the level of the windowsills. Crouching at the far corner, I studied the ratty lawn and the back steps. The grass was fine and sparse, broken by patches of moss, clover, and damp, bare earth. In one of those patches, footprints overlapped. The pattern said hiking boots, the length said male, and the depth said he was no lightweight. Freeman?

Clumps of dried mud, dead grass, and a broken twig littered the steps. That the bulk of the debris was on the mat on the top step told me he'd stomped his feet like most of us do before we enter a house.

Enter?

The buzzing ballooned behind my sternum.

Clarence hadn't liked this man. Not one bit. He hadn't wanted him inside.

I duck-walked to the steps and from that angle spotted the splintered doorjamb.

The buzzing billowed like a thunderhead.

The air smelled of ozone.

My thoughts collided and clashed.

Was the intruder gone as the tire tracks and footprints seemed to indicate? Or had there been two in the vehicle? Had one stayed behind? What kind of a man broke into a house with a pry bar, but cleaned the mud off his boots?

That last question knocked the others down like dominoes and cleared my head of all but a commanding feeling that Clarence wanted me on the other side of that door. Wanted me there now.

I mounted the steps in a crouch, flattened myself against the wall, and tapped the door with the toe of my boot.

It opened half an inch.

I waited a moment and tapped again.

Two inches more.

I counted to ten, then kicked the door wide and went through in a dive, finger across the triggers, gaze strafing the kitchen and the living room beyond.

No one there.

I heard an electrical click from the hallway. Air eddied around me.

The person who broke in had turned the furnace on.

Staying low, I crossed to the archway. Not a floorboard squeaked to betray me. With my back against the solid wall of the hall, I sidestepped to the open door of Clarence's office.

No one there.

No sign that anyone had been except for the empty cradle and the cordless phone lying beside it.

Had someone tried to make a call and tossed the phone aside when they discovered service was disconnected? Or had someone lifted the phone to confirm the line was dead?

The bathroom door was also open, the shower curtain pulled back.

No one there.

The bedroom door was closed. I pressed myself to the wall beside it, listening, feeling.

The buzzing ceased and the pressure in my chest abated as if Clarence had backed off to give me space, allow me to focus.

But on what?

I crept to the office, rolled the chair from behind the desk, and pushed it along the hall, grateful for the carpet that muffled the wheels. I positioned the chair with the back half an inch from the door and stood to one side, bracing my foot against the seat. On a mental count of three, I turned the knob, shoved the chair against the door, and dropped to the floor behind it.

The door crashed off the wall, bounced, slammed against the chair.

I swung the shotgun left and right.

The battered girl on the bed struggled against the ropes that bound her and stared at me with anguished eyes.

CHAPTER 41

"I won't hurt you."

I sprang to my feet, checked the closet, peered under the bed, then dug my jackknife from my pocket.

Her eyes widened and she struggled harder, her moans muffled by the silver tape covering her mouth. The layered flounces on the hot pink mini skirt rustled like dry grass against the bedspread. The strapless black tank top revealed chains of bruises on her arms and around her neck. Others bloomed along her jaw and beneath her eyes. The skin above one cheekbone had split and dried blood crusted her ear and clotted in the tangles of her long brown hair.

With the blood and bruising, it was hard to tell how closely she resembled the previous victims. She looked younger, not much beyond Julie's age and just about her size.

"I won't hurt you. The knife's to cut the ropes." Keeping the shotgun leveled at the doorway, I crouched by the far side of the bed and sawed left-handed at the yellow nylon rope. Her hands were blue from lack of circulation, her knuckles swollen and bloody, her nails torn. She'd fought him, fought hard. Without whatever he put in the syringe on the nightstand, she might have had a chance.

As soon as one hand was free, she pawed at the tape, getting no purchase on the edges of it.

"Hang on. Stay calm. I'll get to that as soon as I cut the ropes on your ankles."

She nodded, shaking her hand, rubbing it against the bed, moaning.

The ropes looped around her ankles weren't as tight, and her feet, encased in glittery stockings and shiny black high-heeled sandals, had only a faint blue tinge. I glanced out the window at my SUV. Ten yards from the house. She might be able to walk. But I doubted she could run.

With that in mind, I unbuckled the sandals and slid them from her feet before I sawed through the ropes around her ankles and freed her other hand.

As soon as she was loose, she scrambled from the bed and dropped to her knees. The back of her skirt was dark with sweat and urine and the acrid odor of her fear was like a punch to my stomach.

"Give it a minute."

She sat with her back against the bed, stamped her feet on the carpet, and worked the tape from her mouth.

I glanced out the window again. The rabbits were back on the lawn, nibbling at a patch of clover about twenty feet in from the meadow. Their ears twitched and one sat up on its haunches.

My early-warning system.

"Are you Amanda Dearborn?"

She nodded.

"I'm Dan Stone. I can't call for help because the phone's disconnected and we're in a dead zone."

Her gaze darted to the window, then settled on the shotgun.

"If he comes back, I'll shoot him if I have to."

A lie.

If he came within range, I'd shoot him whether I had to or not. "Did you see his face?"

She ran a hand across her face from brow to chin, then shuddered and hugged herself. "Mask. A clown face."

I stretched out a hand. "Can you stand now?"

Her fingers latched onto mine, gripped hard. I pulled her to her feet and relaxed my hand, letting her know she was in control. "You'll have to walk. I know you're hurting, but I can't carry you and manage the shotgun. Lean against me if you need . . . if you want to."

She hesitated, her eyes dark with doubt, then clamped her hands around my arm.

I glanced one more time at the rabbits and then, step by wobbling step, we eased along the hallway. She hesitated in the archway to the living room, looking around with a puzzled frown.

"This isn't his house. It belonged to a man he killed."

Was that the reason he brought her here? Because he knew the house was empty? Or because it fit a pattern only he understood?

She shivered and clutched my arm tighter. I halted beside the door and peered through the peephole at the 180-degree fish-eye view. My SUV hulked straight ahead, grill glinting in the sunlight. To my left, the dog pens. To my right, the lawn, the rabbits, the row of birches, and the meadow. But from here, from the slight elevation of Clarence's living room, I could see only a few feet into the meadow. Birch branches, thick with gold leaves, obscured the rest.

If someone was out there he was still—so still the rabbits weren't frightened.

I touched the broken charm in my pocket.

If someone was out there, why had he let me get this far? Was he playing with me? Was he using the hope of rescue to torture the girl?

Watching the rabbits, I turned the knob to pull back the bolt, and reached for the doorknob.

The rabbits twitched their ears, raised their heads, and bounded for cover, cottontails flashing.

"Get down."

She obeyed without pause, sliding to the carpet and flattening herself against the wall beneath the picture window.

I held my breath, pressed my ear against the door, and heard nothing.

I peered through the peephole again. A shadow crossed the lawn, tilted, slid toward the meadow. A hawk.

I breathed once more, watching through the peephole.

A rabbit poked its nose from behind a birch, then hopped a few feet onto the lawn.

I put my hand on the doorknob again and motioned for the girl to stand. "How are your feet? Can you feel them?"

"Yes," she whispered.

"Do you think you can run?"

She shifted her weight and grimaced. "I can try."

"Good. I don't think he's out there, but . . ." I gave her what I hoped was an encouraging smile.

"When I open the door, run for the driver's side of my rig, get across to the passenger seat as fast as you can, then get down in the footwell. Don't run in a straight line. Zigzag. Stay low."

Her eyes widened, but she sucked in a breath and nodded.

I didn't give her a count of three to think about it, just turned the knob and yanked the door wide.

The rabbit bolted for the meadow and she brushed by me, that fluffy skirt rustling like October leaves. Right hand thrust out, she tottered down the steps.

I scanned left and right. Amanda wobbled like a slowing top, glittery stockings flashing. Above the meadow, a hawk wheeled against the wind and sailed in our direction.

In slow motion, Amanda stumbled and sprawled on the scraggly grass.

High on the hillside, rock clattered on rock. I swung the shotgun that way and fired.

Amanda screamed and crawled to my rig. I leaped down the steps and ran. With a rending rip of fabric, she clawed her way onto the seat, scrabbled across the console, and crammed herself into the footwell.

I fired a second shot, dug the key from my pocket, crammed myself in the seat, and cranked the engine. Crimping the wheel, I popped the clutch, and arced across the lawn, rocks and twigs rattling against the undercarriage.

No time to worry about preserving tire tracks I hadn't obliterated on the way in. I aimed for the ruts, felt my wheels settle in, and stayed with them to the top of the ridge.

At the spot where I called the sheriff after Jefferson and I discovered Clarence's body, I let off the gas.

"Don't stop," Amanda moaned. "Please. Don't stop."

Exactly my instinct. But help was a long way off. If I didn't call now, if someone was lying in wait on the downslope . . .

I ripped the cell phone from my pocket and flipped it to the passenger seat. "See if you can get a signal."

She stretched out a trembling hand and pinched the phone between her thumb and forefinger.

"Who do I call?" Her voice was soft and as uncertain as a small child's.

"9-1-1 should do it," I said, keeping my tone serious.

"What do I say?"

We hit the downslope, tires rocking in the ruts, gravel peppering the hubs. The steering wheel juddered in my hands and the vibration distorted my voice. "A dispatcher will answer. Say your name. Say you're okay and you're with Dan Stone. Say we need an ambulance and investigators from the task force to meet us at the Hemlock Lake store right away."

She grasped the phone, index finger hovering. "Do I really need an ambulance? I'm not hurt too much and Mom and Dad worry about money."

I muscled the SUV around a tight turn, tires bouncing from the ruts, branches clawing at the windshield. "I'll pay. Just call."

She hesitated again.

With a jarring thud, the SUV lurched back into the ruts and hit the steepest part of the descent. "Call."

"Okay." Her finger punched the numbers. "Can I ask them to bring me something else to wear? I hate this outfit."

When I opened the door and ushered Amanda into the store, Julie's eyes widened. "Oh my god, you're Amanda Dearborn. What—?"

I raised a hand. "Where's Camille?"

Julie blinked. "In the back. The sink plugged up. And it's so not my fault." She turned her head and yelled. "Camille."

"Just a minute," Camille called back.

"Amanda, this is Julie."

"Hi," Julie said. "Do you want a soda?"

"Yes, please." Amanda twisted her fluffy skirt in her fingers. "Sorry I look like—"

"Don't," I told her, my voice raw with rage. "You're not to blame for what happened or how you look."

Amanda sucked in a breath.

"Dan's right. It's totally not your fault." Julie stepped from behind the counter. "What kind of soda do you like? Cola, orange, lemony, limey, grapefruity, diet or regular?"

"Cola," Amanda whispered. "Regular. But I can get it." She took a step toward the cooler, her hands quivering, her cheeks flushed. "I don't want to be any trouble."

"Julie will get it." I snatched a chocolate bar from the rack, stripped down the wrapper, and held it close to her mouth. "You're shaking. Take a big bite of this."

She did. Chewed, swallowed, and took another.

As I held out the candy bar, I felt my arms tremble. "I'll take a cola too," I called to Julie.

The phone on the wall behind the counter rang once. Julie dashed back from the cooler, but no second ring followed. "Camille must have picked it up." She handed me a can and thrust the other at Amanda. "Here."

I raised my palm. "Open it, please. Hold it for her so we don't contaminate the evidence any more than we already have."

Both girls shot me puzzled frowns. "What evidence?" Amanda asked.

"You fought him. You may have bits of his skin under your nails. Someone will scrape it out so they can send it to the lab."

She gazed at her broken nails. "Will it hurt?"

"No."

Julie popped the top on the can and held it to Amanda's lips. "It's probably like getting a manicure."

Amanda nodded and sucked at the cola.

"I'll bet they take your clothes," Julie said. "That's what they do on all those police shows."

"They can have them." Amanda's voice rose. "They're trashy. Skanky."

I opened my cola, took a long swallow, and decided I wouldn't tell her that they'd take every scrap of clothing, photograph her bruises, examine—

"He didn't rape me."

Julie gripped the counter. "That's . . . good."

"I don't know what he did after he stuck that needle in my arm besides putting me into these slut clothes, but I know he didn't do that." Amanda's face crumpled and she sobbed. "I want my mother. I want to go home."

I grappled for words, got nothing. Tears brimmed in Julie's eyes.

Mary Lou appeared in the doorway to the post office lugging a brown metal folding chair. She snapped it open beside Amanda and shot me a look that said I didn't have the brains I was born with when it came to taking care of women. Amanda sat with a thump and a rustle of fabric.

A door closed at the back of the store and Camille appeared with a bottle of drain opener. She set it on the counter and bent so she could look into Amanda's eyes. "I'm Camille. That was the sheriff on the phone. He sent a deputy to get your mother and bring her to meet the ambulance."

Amanda gulped and sniffed back tears.

Julie slipped her cell phone from the pocket of her shorts. "Does your mom have a cell phone?"

Amanda nodded and raised her hands to wipe her eyes.

"Don't." I snatched a tissue from the box by the cash register.

She nodded and folded her hands in her lap. I blotted her tears.

"What's your mom's number?" Julie asked.

Amanda reeled it off and Julie punched it in, then held the phone by Amanda's ear.

Camille took my arm and led me into the post office with Mary Lou right behind. "Where did you find her?"

"At Clarence's place. Tied to his bed."

Mary Lou put her hand over her mouth.

Camille's eyes narrowed. "That's bold. He couldn't miss the real estate sign on the highway. He had to know someone might come to look the place over."

"There are hundreds of other places in these mountains," Mary Lou said. "Is he stupid? Or crazy?"

"Crazy's a given." Camille ran her fingers through her hair. "Does he want to get caught?"

"I've heard that, subconsciously, some killers do." I shrugged. "They're proud of their work, and proud of getting away with it for so long. They want their names in the headlines."

"Headlines!" Mary Lou made a noise of disgust. "We'll have that pack of reporters back here before the sun sets. Why did he have to pick Hemlock Lake?"

Camille nodded in agreement. "Why take that girl to Clarence's place?"

"He knows where it is. He knows it's empty."

"He also knows it's dangerous to go back there."

"But he gets off on that. Taking a risk might give him as much of a thrill as the torture and killing."

Camille worried her lower lip with her teeth. "When he put that girl by the war memorial, it seemed like he was taunting the sheriff and the task force. But now it seems like he's taunting you."

I shook my head.

"You found Clarence."

Mary Lou nodded. "And you found those girls."

"You're reaching too far. Jefferson was with me when I found the girls. Maybe the killer's taunting him." I forced a laugh. "Or Nelson."

426

Camille waved that aside. "Now you messed with his plans for this girl."

"It's coincidence." I fingered the broken charm in my pocket. "That's all."

Mary Lou frowned and shook her head.

A siren throbbed, close and getting closer.

"That will bring the whole town," Camille said. "We'd better get in there and hold them at bay."

"Lock the door," Mary Lou advised. "I'll guard this one and keep out anyone who doesn't need to be inside."

There were plenty of ruffled feathers, and plenty of finger and nose prints on the windows, but Mary Lou did her job and in thirty minutes Amanda Dearborn was in an ambulance with her mother and I was in the schoolhouse providing a more elaborate version of my story for the benefit of Sheriff North and every investigator who wasn't headed for Clarence's house.

"It was pure chance," I told them. "If the attorney hadn't called, I wouldn't have gone up there. We split up territory on Wednesday. Jefferson checked that place then and again on Thursday and Friday."

"What time Friday?" North asked.

"Not long after lunch. Maybe around one." I shrugged. "He's over at the post office helping Mary Lou with crowd control. Ask him. He'll know to the minute."

The sheriff jerked a thumb toward the schoolhouse door. "Tall guy with a gray brush cut and a back like a ramrod."

A scrappy investigator with thick brows and a thin mustache hustled out.

I went on, scavenging my mind for a hundred tiny details, editing out only those that concerned Clarence's agitated ghost. An hour later I slipped through the back door to the store and found Camille leaning against the counter and looking out at a mob of milling people, a small herd of reporters, and a fleet of TV satellite trucks.

"I got interviewed." Julie turned from the doorway and shook a bag of corn crunch snacks like a rattle. "I'm gonna be on TV."

"I tried to head that off," Camille said in a low voice.

"But it was like keeping a moth away from a flame?"

"A moth determined that all her friends would be green with envy."

"I told the reporters you found her, Uncle Dan. They want to interview you."

I groaned and Camille chuckled. "Jefferson's got your back. He moved my car behind Mary Lou's house so you can escape."

"Do you mind?"

"No."

"We could close the store and all sneak off."

She shook her head and dropped her voice to a whisper. "Getting Julie to leave in the midst of this would be harder than scraping that old wax by the dairy case with my fingernails. Besides, I've got a guy coming in to pitch me on a new brand of ice cream—if he can get through the mob. And I have to admit I have a morbid fascination with the way some people act in front of a camera."

"Look, it's the guy from the paper," Julie crowed. "Colden Cornell. The one who did the story about me and the store." She darted into the crowd, waving the bag of snacks.

"Go home," Camille told me. "I'll have Mary Lou tell reporters the sheriff sent you off somewhere to help with the investigation. She's got the best poker face in town."

When they got home Julie dashed into the garage, grabbed the TV remote, and announced that she'd let us know when her interview came on. Camille rubbed the small of her back and sat at the kitchen table. "I hope you weren't expecting a real dinner tonight."

"Not tonight or any other night." I put my hands on her shoulders and massaged taut muscles. "Besides, this is my day to wait on you."

She tilted her head and shot me a smile. "Keep talking like that and I might fall in love."

I leaned down and whispered in her ear. "What if I said pasta salad with shrimp, apple crisp, chilled white wine?"

"Perfect. But I'll take iced tea instead of—"

"There I am," Julie shrieked. "Come see."

We obliged, catching glimpses of her video interview on two broadcasts as she flipped through the channels.

"Maybe there will be more later," she said when news anchors moved on to other stories. "Did I look okay?"

"You looked terrific," I assured her.

She smiled and fluffed her bangs. "Was my hair okay? Should I cut it?"

"I like it the way it is." Camille patted her own springy curls. "When it's short there isn't as much you can do with it, but when it's long you can wear it a hundred different ways."

Julie twisted her hair into a knot on top of her head and struck a pose.

"Ah," Camille said. "The silly sophisticated look."

Julie giggled and let her hair loose.

My smile froze. She looked like Amanda Dearborn, like the other girls the killer picked.

CHAPTER 42

Sunday morning we tackled the last bit of sprucing up around the new house, trimming bushes, sweeping the patio, and hanging hooks for towels by the hot tub. That afternoon Julie and Mary Lou went off on a genealogy field trip to cemeteries and churches and Camille and I made the beds and put books on shelves while Nelson pursued a bullfrog along the rim of the lake. When his muzzle got so crusted with mud he could barely breathe, I tossed him off the dock to clean him up.

The lawyer called, concerned about the state of Clarence's house, and I told him it was still a crime scene, but I'd get up there the minute Sheriff North gave me the okay. He said he'd hire a locksmith and a cleaning service and have them check with me.

Monday morning brought a gray drizzle. Heads bent against it, two dozen parents waited with their kids for the school bus. Reporters and photographers recorded the event and another dozen on-lookers milled around drinking coffee, shoulders hunched against a north wind.

"I feel like we're under siege." Mary Lou gazed at the hills surrounding the town. "Like any minute that beast will come out of the woods and carry someone off."

"That's your imagination," Stub said. "He's gone."

"Has to be," Freeman agreed. "All this hoopla must have sent him running for the border."

Evan nodded, but Jefferson clenched his jaw and shook his head. I remembered last summer when the men gathered here led search teams across the hills and hollows around Hemlock Lake. They found no trace of Jefferson and speculated that their search drove him off.

They were wrong then. Were they wrong now?

When the bus was out of sight, I went back to the garage and tackled the task of moving the few things that were going with us to the new house—the coffeepot and our favorite mugs, the few cans of soup remaining in the cabinets, a couple of pots, a frying pan, and the ever-growing pile of Julie's combs, curling irons, and hair clips. Nelson followed me back and forth, whining now and then as if worried about where his place would be.

The plan was for me to collect Camille and Julie at the store when they closed and for Jefferson and Mary Lou to join us for a feast at the Shovel It Inn. For our early lunch, Nelson and I batted clean-up on what was left in the garage kitchen—tortilla chips, the last dabs of hummus and salsa, a tomato, three slices of Swiss cheese, and a handful of cookie crumbs. After that, I loaded the table and chairs into the trailer, covered them with a tarp, and delivered them to the schoolhouse along with a lamp, two TV trays, the TV, the DVD player, and the microwave.

The schoolhouse smelled of fresh paint and anticipation, and I lingered for a few minutes, imagining Julie and the other kids kicking back on the sofas, teaching each other dance steps, or watching a movie.

I shook myself, went back to the garage, stripped the beds, loaded frames, mattresses, pillows, lamps, blankets, and old cookware into the trailer and hauled it all to a thrift store in the county seat with Nelson riding shotgun. As I passed the post office, the last of the TV trucks pulled in behind and trailed me to the intersection with a road heading south. Hemlock Lake was no longer news.

Back again, I unhitched the trailer, stuffed sheets and pillowcases into plastic sacks and carried them to the new laundry room. After second thoughts, I carried the sacks back to the garage for Camille to decide their destiny. For all I knew, these might be the rags of the future.

Stripped of our possessions, the garage became itself again. Familiar odors seeped from walls and floor—the scents of old motor oil, sawdust, mildew, rust, and dry rot. The space felt smaller, meaner. While Nelson watched and whined, I attacked the makeshift partition with a hammer, dismantling the walls and stacking plywood and 2x4's for later projects. I was sweeping up nails and chips, my stomach rumbling at the thought of a cheeseburger and fries, when my phone rang.

"Julie's gone," Mary Lou shrieked. "He clubbed Camille and took Julie."

A steely spike of fear drove into my heart. "Who? Who took Julie?"

"I don't know. I don't know."

I ran for my rig, shouting into the phone. "Call an ambulance. Call Jefferson. Call the sheriff."

I tore open the door. Nelson lunged past me and leaped, pawing at the seat. "No." I grabbed for his collar. "Stay home."

But he pulled himself in, lips drawn back in a snarl.

I shoved him across the console, threw myself behind the wheel, started the engine, and tore out of the driveway. Nelson bounced off the door and slid into the footwell.

We thundered through the turns and slid into the parking lot on locked wheels. Jefferson stood at the door, holding it open. "Camille's coming around," he shouted. "The ambulance is on the way. North's scrambling a team."

I hurtled past him and found Camille stretched on the floor in front of the counter, her head in Mary Lou's lap, a wad of tissue pressed to a spot behind her left ear. Nelson shot past me and raced to the rear of the store. I fell to my knees and put my hand against Camille's cheek. "I'm here. It's okay."

Her eyelids fluttered and she moaned.

"I was getting ready to close up. I heard a crash," Mary Lou said. "I yelled out, asked if they needed help. Nobody answered. Then I heard a car start up."

"Gunned the engine and burned rubber," Jefferson added. "Heard that from Mary Lou's kitchen. Thought it was a kid showing off. I didn't look out until I heard Mary Lou scream."

"You couldn't know," I told him.

He shook his head, accepting blame that wasn't his.

434

Camille moaned again and raised a hand. Mary Lou intercepted it, guided it to mine. "Open your eyes," she said. "Come back to us. We need you."

I squeezed Camille's fingers, leaned close and kissed her. "Who took Julie?"

"Sorry," she whispered. "Sorry."

"It isn't your fault."

"We'll get her back," Mary Lou added. "Dan and Jefferson will get her back."

Nelson barked and raced past, scrabbling at the linoleum. Nose to the floor, he cast back and forth by the cold-drink case, growling, the hair on his ruff bristling.

Camille twisted her long fingers from my grip and closed them around my wrist, her nails stabbing my skin. "Cornell," she whispered. "Colden Cornell."

"That reporter?"

Colden Cornell dropped things, got his truck stuck in the mud, was soft, and incompetent.

Or was that exactly what he wanted us to think?

Jefferson's eyes narrowed and glinted like ice and I knew he'd come to the same conclusion. "The truck," he said. "The camper shell."

A mobile torture lab.

And Julie was in it.

Camille's voice grew stronger. "He said he stopped in to get a soda and went around to the cooler. Julie was in the bathroom. I . . . I had a piece of cardboard folded up. That potato chip rack wasn't level."

I glanced at the toppled rack and spotted a dented family-size can of pork and beans among scattered bags of chips. He hit her when it she bent to jam the cardboard beneath the rack.

435

"If only I looked out the window," Mary Lou mourned. "I'd know which way he went."

Ignoring the scattered chip bags, Nelson charged for the door. Whining, he dug at the edge of it.

"He went east," Jefferson said.

"No other choice," I agreed.

The road west led to the county seat. Help would come from that direction—already I heard the throb of a siren—and Colden Cornell would multiply his risk by picking that road.

"I'll get my rifle," Jefferson said. "Pick me up at the house."

Despite a snap and snarl, I gripped Nelson's collar and Jefferson opened the door. A murmuring group of people stepped back to give him room; their eyes were wide, their lips pinched with anger.

I kissed Camille hard on the lips. "We'll bring her back. We'll all wake up tomorrow in that new house. Just the way you want."

Tears welled in her eyes and she shoved my shoulder. "Go. Go now."

Nelson broke from my grip and I dashed behind him to my rig. The door was open and he leaped, higher this time. For a second he sprawled across the seat, then clawed his way into the back, nails clicking on the shotgun.

I blasted out of the lot, picked up Jefferson on the fly, and roared out of town, up the ridge, and down to the Birchkill, tires shushing on the drizzle-slicked road. "You think he's going to the glade?"

"Yes. No. He might—" Jefferson pointed at the road to Clarence's house. "Stop. Pull over."

I braked, lost traction, steered with the skid, heard Nelson thud against a door and Jefferson curse. We rocked to a stop, slantwise to the drive.

Jefferson bolted out and ran ahead, scanning the ground. "Fresh tire tracks."

I jockeyed my rig around and caught up. He jumped in. "Gotta be him."

"What if it's not?"

"It's him. He's getting back at you. You took his prize. Now he took yours."

An electrical storm of scarlet rage swirled through my brain. "Julie?"

Nelson barked and thrust his front feet onto the console.

"She matches his victim profile. You're her guardian." Jefferson patted his vest pockets and I heard the clack of loose bullets. "He wants to hurt you. Probably had a smile on his face when he clubbed Camille."

I clenched my hands on the wheel, knowing that last sentence was intended to make me put doubt aside, psyche me up for the hunt.

It wasn't necessary.

I was in the zone.

We reached the high point of the road and I dug for my cell phone. "Call the sheriff and tell him where we're headed."

Jefferson made no move to take the phone. "And when he tells you to hold back until he gets a team up here?"

I hesitated for just a second. "We can't."

"We won't. But there's no harm in taking out a little insurance." He flipped open the phone and punched in a number. In a moment he spoke, "Mary Lou, he's taking her to Clarence's. We're on his tail. I need you to remind the sheriff there's no phone service in that hollow."

He was silent for a few seconds, then added in a soft voice, "I always come back. You know that."

He closed the phone and stuck it in the glove compartment, then wrapped an arm around Nelson's neck, holding him as we shot down the hillside.

Cornell's truck was beside the dog pens, the doors open. If he was barricaded inside the house, it made good cover for us.

I swung in behind it and cut the engine. Nelson whined and wiggled onto the console. Jefferson and I hunkered low in our seats and peered over the dash.

A crow swayed on the topmost branch of a birch and a swallow sieved the air over the meadow. Yellow tape stretched across Clarence's front door. If Cornell went in the front, he hadn't disturbed it.

I reached around Nelson, and got my hand on the shotgun and the box of shells I'd bought for Julie's next lesson. Breaking the gun, I rammed in two shells and crammed a few more into my shirt pocket. "I'll go in the back and drive him out."

"He might not drive that easy. And he'll use Julie as a shield." Jefferson seemed to settle back into himself, pressing his lips together, gripping Nelson so hard the dog whimpered. "I'll go."

"No. There's open ground between here and the house. I can run faster."

"And I have less to live for."

Jefferson swung his door wide, but before he could vault out, Nelson bounded across him and tumbled to the ground.

"Damn it," I shouted. "Come back."

Nelson lurched to his feet and thrust his nose into the wind.

"Plan B." Jefferson gripped my arm and jerked me lower in the seat. "Stay put and see if the mutt draws fire."

CHAPTER 43

Nelson snorted, tossed his head, then streaked toward the house. At the base of the steps he halted, raised his muzzle, and let loose with a howl that felt like a cold knife on my neck.

The air smelled the way it does when a thunderstorm is about to break and in another second Clarence was with us. His anger sizzled and popped like a downed wire. I held my breath, staring at the house.

Nothing.

Only the frenzied electrical crackling of a ghost.

Nelson turned in a tight circle.

"He's not in the house," Jefferson said.

"Or he went in the back."

Nelson cast a wide circle on the lawn, nose to the ground.

I recalled the day Colden Cornell came to see me, how Nelson whined, snorted, and pawed at his muddy muzzle. If I hadn't hauled him into the garage—

Jefferson pointed to the ridge we climbed the day we found the girls in the glade. "If he's in the woods, we'll be like ducks in a shooting gallery crossing that meadow."

"Just one duck. And one sniper hanging back here." I nodded at the house. "Up on the roof."

He glanced at his rifle and I knew he was thinking about that new scope. "No."

"Yes." I tugged the keys from the ignition, worked the broken charm from the ring, and, hoping to raise another ghost for the battle, tucked it into a small pocket near the shoulder of Jefferson's vest. "That was Lou Marie's charm. She kept it even after it broke. She must have believed it had some luck left in it."

He touched the pocket, shook his head.

"That line of birches screens the meadow. He probably saw me come down the hill, but he might think I'm alone. It's our only advantage." I seized on the habit I'd once tried to break him of. "That's an order. Get a position on the roof."

Jefferson gave me a tight nod. "Yes, sir."

"You said he's taunting me. If that's true, he'll put Julie where I can see her. He'll let me get close enough to watch her die."

He let out a long breath. Through the lenses of his glasses, his eyes seemed larger, focused on something in the far distance. "Close enough so he can take you down when he's done with her."

"Except he won't get a chance to hurt her. You'll get him first."

He fingered the pocket that held the broken charm. "It's not much of a plan, Sergeant, but your dog's already on it."

Turning my head, I spotted Nelson streaking between two birches into the tall grass of the meadow. I gripped the shotgun and raced after him.

"Don't try to reason with him," Jefferson called after me. "Rattle him."

I raised a thumb and ran on. The hummocks were mounded with new growth and the channels between them filled by recent rain and overgrown with creeping vines and brambles. Nelson hadn't gone around, and within a few yards I overtook him. His chest and belly were slathered with viscous mud and he grunted each time he tore a foot loose from its grip.

"Stay," I ordered, knowing it was in vain. "He'll shoot you."

To torture Julie. To enrage me. To entertain himself.

Nelson drew his lips back and thrust himself onward.

I hurtled a mass of brambles and picked up the trail on the other side, spotting a shred of pale blue denim caught on a thorn. Fabric from the frayed jeans Julie wore to school. I snatched it up, tucked it in my pocket, and plunged on, Nelson howling and thrashing in my wake.

A dozen yards from the forest the ground sloped up and dried out. I halted, breathing hard, heart thudding. The trunks of the boundary birches glowed and sunlight spangled across leaves bright as new gold coins. Beyond stood the blighted pine that marked the trail we followed in pursuit of Nelson on the night we found the girls in the glade.

"All the cops in the region are coming," I shouted. "Let Julie go."

For a moment I heard nothing except a sizzle in the air, then Cornell called back, "She's mine. For what you took from me."

His tone was surprisingly relaxed, almost as if we were old friends working out who would buy the beer or spring for movie tickets. That chilled me more than his words.

"I didn't *take* anything. I found Amanda Dearborn. And the others."

An awkward shadow moved beyond the paling of birches and I caught a flash of turquoise—Julie's pullover.

"It's not just about them."

"Okay. Then come out and tell me what else. Why me? Why Julie? Come out. Be a man about it."

The shadow moved again. I strained to see Julie's face, but couldn't make it out in the gloom.

"You be a man. Put your gun down," Cornell called.

"While you keep yours? Is that fair?"

"Fair," he screamed. "Why should I be fair? Nobody was ever fair to me."

"So you tortured and killed four—"

"Shut up. Throw that shotgun down," he screamed. "Throw it down or I'll kill her right now."

I bent and set the shotgun on the ground, then stepped back and raised my hands to show him I was no threat.

It all came down to Jefferson.

The shadow staggered closer, Julie and Colden Cornell in lockstep. Silver tape held her hands against her sides and another strip covered her mouth and wrapped around her head. Her eyes brimmed with tears, the lid of the right one pulled to one side where the barrel of his gun pressed into her skin.

Come on. Come on. Just a little closer.

443

They stepped between two birches and a streak of sunlight fell on her face. All I could see of him was his left ear, one corner of his mouth, and the left arm he held tight across her neck.

Even if Jefferson saw as much as I did, I doubted it was enough to risk a shot.

The voltage in the air shot up, scorching my skin. Had Clarence summoned others—Lou Marie, Rachel, Lisa, perhaps even Ronny?

"It's gonna be fine, Julie," I said. "Camille's okay. We'll have supper together just like we planned. And we'll wake up in the new house tomorrow."

"The perfect family in the perfect home," Cornell mocked. "You got it all handed to you. Just like Clarence. You don't give a damn who got shoved aside so you could profit."

I didn't rise to that bait but my mind churned. Shoved aside? Was he talking about the disruption of his gruesome agenda? Or something else?

"Which would hurt more," Cornell mused, "for her to watch you die? Or for you to watch her?"

Julie jerked forward and for a heartbeat I glimpsed the top of his face, his eyes wide and wild. Parallel scratches, red and raw, gouged his forehead and cheeks. Julie had gone for him before he got her under control.

Good girl.

He yanked her upright again.

No chance of a shot.

I rubbed my chin, pretending to think. "It depends on which one of us you enjoy torturing the most. If that's Julie, you'll kill me first—maybe blow holes in my legs and arms, make me suffer before you finish me off."

I flinched as I planted the idea in his mind. If I had to trade my pain to draw him out and set up a shot for Jefferson, I'd do it. "If it's me, you'll kill her. But you'd better make your choice quick. You'll hear sirens any time now. Maybe a helicopter."

The air whirred as if the sky was filled with locust. The voltage spiked again. Sweat broke out on my forehead.

"You don't have to go down this road," I told him. "Stop now and you might live."

"In a cell?"

Nelson barked, close behind me.

The corner of Cornell's mouth tightened. "That damned dog," he screamed, his voice rising, fracturing. "I should have made sure he was dead."

I played to his rage. "But you screwed up. You screwed up then and you screwed up again with Jessica Smithers and again with Amanda Dearborn."

I raised my voice to a shout. "You. You screwed up. It's your fault. Nobody else's. Not me. Not the dog. You're a screwup. You. You."

The barrel of his gun jerked toward me.

I braced.

He fired.

Missed.

Seething rage swirled in the air.

Nelson growled and lunged past, ears shredded by brambles, ropes of saliva hanging from his jowls, legs and chest dark with mud.

Cornell swung the gun across his body.

Julie moaned and closed her eyes.

Cornell fired again.

Nelson yipped, twisted, rolled.

445

He nipped at a ribbon of fresh blood on his legless hip.

"You screwed up again," I jeered. "You missed me. You didn't kill that dog. You can't do anything right, can you?"

"Shut up." Cornell pointed the gun at my chest, his arm visible clear to the shoulder.

Jefferson! Take the shot!

"You're a failure," I taunted. "You're worthless."

The air seethed, steamed.

Cornell's hand shook. Sunlight glinted on the gun.

Nelson struggled to his feet and charged, baying like a hound from hell.

Julie's eyes pleaded.

"It's okay, Julie," I shouted. "He can't hit Nelson. He's a screwup. We can take him down. You're not a victim."

"Shut up. Shut up." Cornell's finger tightened on the trigger.

Nelson leaped.

Julie drove her heel into Cornell's ankle and threw her weight against the restraining arm.

Cornell fired.

An explosion of bright blood filled the boiling air.

CHAPTER 44

While Justin and I sat at the long oak table jamming chunks of meat and vegetables onto metal skewers, Camille and Julie scurried back and forth in the steamy kitchen, chopping and stirring. Now and then they peered out at the October sky and speculated about whether the forecast was correct, whether the sun would burn off the mist as predicted, and whether the feast would be ready on time.

Julie's hair, clipped short to cover the mess I made when I sliced off the tape wrapped around her head, stood up in pixie spikes. Camille's forehead shone with perspiration and she stopped often to knead her lower back.

"Slow down," I told her. "Pace yourself. That baby's only going to get heavier."

That baby.

Our baby.

I felt a surge of panic mixed with pride and wonder.

Camille flashed me a smile like Christmas morning and I thought how blind I'd been to the signs—the same signs every woman in town picked up on. They'd held Camille's secret close, shielded it from their men, understanding her fears about jinxing the pregnancy, losing the baby if she spoke too soon.

"April Fool's Day." Julie scattered basil leaves across thick tomato slices spiraling on a white platter. "That's when he's coming."

"He or she," Camille said. "We're going to be surprised, remember? And this baby *will not* be born on April First. I'll tie my knees together and stand on my head to keep that from happening. Kids have enough problems in this world without throwing a weird birth date into the mix."

Julie giggled and drizzled olive oil on the tomatoes.

Justin nodded, but said nothing. In the few days he'd been back, his words had been, to quote my grandmother, as scarce as hen's teeth. Each morning he asked Camille for a list of chores and by nightfall checked them all off. Together we split and stacked wood, raked leaves, and gathered the last vegetables from the garden without sharing more than a dozen sentences.

Even Julie gave him space and let him wear his silence like armor except when she pestered him about the next driving lesson. We'd bought him an old clunker and those lessons—and bonding time with his sister—were part of the repayment plan.

The lawyer handling the deal swore he'd have it sewn up by Thanksgiving, but Priscilla was negotiating every last hook, line, and sinker, so we hadn't revealed the bait shop plan to anyone.

A thick bubbling sound sent Camille dashing to the stove yelping, "The barbecue sauce." She thrust a wooden spoon into a pot and stirred viciously. "I hope it didn't scorch."

"It's going to scorch anyway when we paint it on the meat," Julie said.

Justin nodded again.

"Throw in a little beer to hide the scorch and it will get by," I suggested.

"I want it to do more than 'get by.' This is our housewarming. And Justin's welcome home party."

I shrugged. "I can't recall a cookout in Hemlock Lake where something wasn't burnt to a crisp or somebody didn't have to run out at the last minute to get a sack of chips or some whipped cream."

"Whipped cream!" Julie squawked. "We forgot the whipped cream." She abandoned the tomatoes, rushed to Justin and put a hand on his shoulder. "You love whipped cream on apple pie."

"Marcella's pie, yeah. It needs a ton of cream. But you made this pie from Mom's recipe."

Julie chewed her lower lip. "But what if—"

"Mary Lou's bringing cream for the chocolate mousse," Camille said. "She'll bring plenty."

"But if there isn't enough to make you happy," Justin said, "I'll let you drive to the store and we'll get more."

"Yay." Julie grinned and hugged herself.

Justin turned to me and we rolled our eyes at each other, two guys at the mercy of women and not-so-secretly enjoying the spot we were in.

Wheels crunched on gravel, halted for a minute or two, then started up again and rolled to a stop beside the house. A door slammed and Mary Lou scurried across the patio carrying a casserole dish large enough to float a rowboat. Jefferson followed, loaded down with bulging cloth sacks.

Julie opened the door for them, letting in an eddy of autumn air seasoned with the scents of smoke, rotting leaves, and wet wood.

I stood to help Jefferson unload, but Mary Lou and Camille both raised their hands like frustrated traffic cops.

"Raw meat," Justin said. "You might contaminate the chips."

"Ah." I sat and contented myself with needling Jefferson while Julie transferred his burdens to the far end of the table. "Is there anything you didn't bring?"

"Just that worthless dog of yours. He's at the head of the drive acting like he drew sentry duty. Wouldn't budge until Mary Lou tossed out a handful of chips."

"He obeys about as well as the average rock," Camille said, "and he's so stubborn he makes a mule look accommodating."

I speared a chunk of zucchini. "And those are his best qualities."

"I'd better go get him." Julie snatched a cube of cheese from a tray. "Before somebody runs him over."

"Probably tear out their transmission before they do any damage to Nelson." Jefferson got a beer from the refrigerator and toasted me with it. "He's run through three lives since April. You sure he's not part cat?"

"I'm not sure of a damn thing."

Mary Lou slid the door closed behind Julie and turned to face me. "How's she doing?"

"Pretty good. Camille had a brilliant idea about counseling."

"More dirty trick than brilliant idea," Camille said. "I told her I thought Nelson needed help coming to grips with getting shot again and since she was the only one he'd listen to, she had to be the one to see the therapist with him."

"So she talks to the counselor about Nelson's experiences and the counselor asks her if Nelson worries about how she's coping and they get around to talking about what she went through."

What she went through, nice words for being kidnapped by a killer and showered with bone, blood, and brain when Jefferson's bullet tore into his head.

"I'm pretty sure she knows what we're up to," Camille said. "But she didn't argue and she hasn't had a nightmare for a week."

"She hasn't had time," Justin said. "Between homework, learning to drive, rehearsing for the school play, and coming up with names for the baby, she doesn't have time to sleep."

"You forgot to mention planning the wedding," I added.

Mary Lou spun to face me, her eyes glowing. "You set a date?"

"No, but we're homing in on one. Probably in February."

"Good choice." Jefferson rubbed his brush cut and ambled over beside Mary Lou. "Give folks something to look forward to during January storms."

Mary Lou's gaze shifted to Camille's waistline.

"I'll be waddling like a duck that swallowed a watermelon." Camille laughed. "But that should stop folks from asking if I'll wear white."

451

"It will be a denim wedding," I said. "Casual clothes for everyone."

"And no rings," Camille patted her bump. "I'd rather put the money into this kid's college fund."

"Have you talked with Reverend Balforth?" Mary Lou asked.

"Nope." I skewered a chunk of chicken. "I'd rather take out my own tonsils than listen to him drone through another service. We plan to ask Sheriff North if he's legal to pronounce."

Mary Lou turned to Jefferson, cocked her head, and raised her eyebrows. In a moment he turned a thumb up and she raised her hand and laid it against his cheek. Jefferson flushed, cleared his throat, and choked out, "Think he could marry us while he's at it?"

Camille squealed and ran to hug Mary Lou and Justin and I rushed for the sink to wash up so we could shake Jefferson's hand and pound him on the back. I looked deep into his eyes as I congratulated him and saw not a trace of obligation or resignation, only peace and purpose.

"For all we've been through and all we lost along the way, we're the most fortunate guys in the world," I told him.

He reached into his pocket and pulled out the broken clover charm. "And we had help when we needed it most," he said in a low voice.

That was something we decided to keep between ourselves—the feeling that Clarence had summoned others to the meadow that afternoon.

And now they were gone.

I'd been up to Clarence's house several times and heard only the autumn wind in the pines and the complaints of that raucous jay. The electrical buzz of anger was gone. The house felt empty.

Julie slid the door open and charged in, Nelson at her heels, the newest scar on his hip a wine-dark slash. "Freeman and Alda are here. And the sun's coming out."

"It's going to be a perfect day," Mary Lou said.

And it was.

We ate and drank, threw horseshoes and darts, and ate some more. We talked about baby and bridal showers, weddings, how right it seemed that Mary Lou and Jefferson were together, and how they deserved every minute of happiness that came.

Julie and Justin were cleaning up the kitchen, the other guests were gone, and stars glimmered over the lake when Mary Lou settled into the porch swing beside me. With a deep sigh, she drew a folded piece of notebook paper from the pocket of her skirt. "I've debated on this for more than a week and I still don't know whether it would be best to let it lie. But Jefferson says you'll want to know."

I felt a cold and greasy knot in my gut. "Know what?"

"Why Colden Cornell had Clarence in his sights," Jefferson growled from the other swing. "And you."

Mary Lou unfolded the paper and tipped it so light fell on it from the citronella candle on the porch railing. I recognized it as the family tree Julie drew for Nelson. Names and lines filled in the upper half of the paper, most in Mary Lou's neat writing. "I thought I'd finish this for Julie. But now I'm sorry I did, sorry I'm so good at tracking down names and relationships better left lost and forgotten."

453

She put her finger on the paper beneath a woman's name. "This is Colden Cornell's grandmother. She's also Clarence's younger half sister by his father, born on the wrong side of the blanket as they say and never given the family name."

I sucked in a breath. "Did Clarence . . . ?"

"Know Colden Cornell? I doubt Clarence ever even knew he had a sister. I never heard so much as a whisper about it. She was born in 1950, back when most people still hushed up things like that if they could. Clarence was grown by then and his parents lived apart—his father drank and couldn't hold a job." She tapped the paper. "Anyway, this half sister had a daughter when she was fifteen, also out of wedlock, and that girl gave birth to Colden when she was about the same age, again without marrying."

And Colden Cornell's mother died of an overdose when he was ten. The task force dug that up along with details of her arrests for prostitution. Someone leaked it all to the media and everyone who could read a newspaper or work a TV remote had heard theories about his killings being connected to his childhood and feeling about his mother.

"His grandmother was alive up until a few years ago," Jefferson said. "Maybe she found out Clarence was her half-brother. Maybe she told Colden that Clarence got an inheritance that should have been divided between them."

"Though if he bothered to check he'd know Clarence made every dime he had on his own." Mary Lou rattled the genealogy chart. "And paid for his father's funeral because the old man died in debt up to his eyebrows."

"So when he put the girls up in those woods," Camille mused from the lounge chair, "was he hoping Clarence would be blamed for killing them?"

"We'll never know," I said. "He didn't write anything down."

"Kind of surprising," Jefferson said. "Him making his living with words."

"Well I'm glad he didn't," Mary Lou said. "There are some things we don't need to hear about on the news or from our neighbors." She touched my hand. "That's the other reason we decided to tell you about this. Forewarned is forearmed. In case someone else works this out."

She tipped the sheet of paper to the light again and put her finger beside a name on the side opposite Colden Cornell's. My mother's name.

I remembered then that Clarence was her second cousin. The knot in my gut tightened. Colden Cornell, in a roundabout way, was related to me. Had he believed I was Clarence's heir? Was that why he said I had it all handed to me?

"In case someone else works what out?" Camille asked.

No one said anything for a few seconds, then Mary Lou whispered, "Works out that Colden Cornell was related to Dan."

"No." The chaise overturned with a metallic clatter as Camille hurled herself from it, one hand across her belly as if to shield our child from its lineage. "That can't be true."

I stood and pulled her tight against me.

"What's the matter?" Julie stood in the doorway, Justin behind her. "What can't be true?"

"That Dan is. . ." Camille let out a long shuddering sigh. "I can't even say it."

455

"Are you sick like Grandma was?" Julie wrapped her arms around both of us. "Don't be sick. Please don't be sick."

"I'm not sick." I freed an arm and stroked her hair. "Mary Lou found out I'm related to—"

"That monster," Camille hissed.

Julie pushed away from me, snatched the chart from Mary Lou, and held it to the light. Justin stepped onto the porch and peered over her shoulder.

"It's just by marriage." Mary Lou patted the air. "Dan's grandmother was Clarence's mother's first cousin. Dan's related by blood only to Clarence's mother. Colden Cornell was related by blood only to Clarence's father."

"No blood connection," Jefferson said.

"No blood connection." Camille breathed the words like a prayer.

"Odds are no one else will ever work this out," Jefferson said. "Mary Lou had to dig for it."

"Promise me you won't tell a soul." Mary Lou fixed her gaze on Julie and Justin. "No one. Promise?"

"Promise." Julie shoved the chart at Justin. "Anyway, I'm done with genealogy. I mean, it's neat to know where I came from and stuff, but I have too many other things to think about—the baby and the wedding and learning to drive."

Mary Lou gave Julie one of her sweet and patient smiles.

"And *I* already spent way too much time on a dead-end road into the past." Justin snapped off a salute to Jefferson and got one in return. "You have to take the fork that goes to the future if you want to get on with your life."

456

"Words to live by," Camille said.

She turned from my arms, took the chart of Clarence's family tree from his hand, and held it to the candle flame.

Also by Carolyn J. Rose
Hemlock Lake
An Uncertain Refuge
A Place of Forgetting
No Substitute for Murder
By the Sea of Regret (Fall, 2012)

By Carolyn J. Rose and Mike Nettleton
The Big Grabowski
Sometimes a Great Commotion
Drum Warrior

For more information:
www.deadlyduomysteries.com